LECHE

Leche

A NOVEL

R. Zamora Linmark

COFFEE HOUSE PRESS
MINNEAPOLIS 2011

COPYRIGHT © 2011 by R. Zamora Linmark
COVER AND BOOK DESIGN by Linda Koutsky
AUTHOR PHOTO © Lisa Asagi
COVER PHOTO © Lesley Magno, Getty Images

Coffee House Press books are available to the trade through our
primary distributor, Consortium Book Sales & Distribution,
www.cbsd.com or (800) 283-3572. For personal orders, catalogs, or
other information, write to: info@coffeehousepress.org.

Coffee House Press is a nonprofit literary publishing house.
Support from private foundations, corporate giving programs,
government programs, and generous individuals helps make the
publication of our books possible. We gratefully acknowledge their
support in detail in the back of this book.

To you and our many readers around the world,
we send our thanks for your continuing support.

LIBRARY OF CONGRESS CIP INFORMATION
Linmark, R. Zamora.
Leche : a novel / by R. Zamora Linmark.
p. cm.
Sequel to: Rolling the R's.
ISBN 978-1-56689-254-4 (alk. paper)
1. Gays—Fiction. 2. Filipino Americans—Fiction.
3. Americans—Philippines—Fiction. 4. Philippines—Fiction. I. Title.
PS3576.A475L43 2011
813'.54—DC22
2010039304

PRINTED IN CANADA
1 3 5 7 9 8 6 4 2
FIRST EDITION | FIRST PRINTING

for Frank Villalon Linmark (1916–2008), my Virgil

BOOK I

1   The Sea They Carried

12 Tourist Tips

13 Headrush

16 Sleeping with One Eye Open

23 Tourist Tips

BOOK II

27 Shame Dubbed

42 Tourist Tips

44 Ambushed

52 Ode to Fellini

59 Postcards

63 Son of Brando

BOOK III

69 Postcard

70 Tourist Tips

71 CCP, or Complexion-Conscious Pinoys

85 Tourist Tips

86 And Introducing Vince De Los Reyes

BOOK IV

111 Who's Afraid of Cat Stevens?

116 Postcards

120 Tourist Tips

122 Paste & Cut

131 Tourist Tips

132 Postcards

135 AnthrApology

BOOK V

139 Are You There God? It's Me, Margaret Mead.

149 Tourist Tips

150 Ride Me, Baby

BOOK VI

163 Islands in the Stream
173 Tourist Tips
175 Vince on the Verge
180 Postcards
183 Tao of Cartography
186 Postcards

BOOK VII

191 Sexxxy
203 Postcards
207 Filipinese
212 Postcards

BOOK VIII

217 PM Talking with Yours Truly
235 Postcards
242 Blow-Up
251 Tourist Tips
253 My Dinner with Jonas
267 Signs of the Times
268 Postcard
269 Carte Blank
297 Postcards
299 Coda

BOOK IX

305 Fuseli Revisited
316 Tourist Tips
317 Full Strings Attached
327 We Won't Go Back to Subic Anymore
331 The Eleventh Commandment
343 Scavenged

Resist—a plot is brought home—The tour.
—JONATHAN SWIFT, *Gulliver's Travels*

But to draw the lessons of the good that came my way,
I will describe the other things I saw.
—DANTE, *Inferno*

BOOK I

The Sea They Carried

TURBAN LEGEND

By the time Vince arrives at the Philippine Airlines departures terminal,
it is already bustling with restless souls who, with their balikbayan boxes,
have transformed the terminal into a warehouse, as if they're returning
to the motherland on a cargo ship rather than Asia's first airline carrier.
Comedians use these durable cardboard boxes as materials for their
Filipino-flavored jokes. "How is the balikbayan box like American
Express to Filipinos? Because they never leave home without it."

Everywhere Vince turns are boxes, boxes, and more boxes. Boxes
secured by electrical tape and ropes. Boxes with drawstring covers made
from canvas or tarp. Boxes lined up like a fortified wall behind check-in
counters or convoying on squeaky conveyor belts of x-ray machines.

Boxes blocking the Mabuhay Express lane for first- and business-class passengers. Boxes stacked up on carts right beside coach passengers standing in queues that are straight only at their starting points before branching out to form more—or converge with other—lines, bottlenecking as they near the ticket counter.

Boxes that ought to be the Philippines' exhibit at the next World's Fair, Vince tells himself, as he navigates his cartload of Louis Vuitton bags in and out of the maze. An exhibit that should take place none other than here, at the Honolulu International Airport, he laughs, as he imagines the entire terminal buried in the Filipinos' most popular—and preferred—piece of luggage.

With a balikbayan box, Filipinos can pack cans of Hormel corned beef, Libby's Vienna sausage, Folgers, and SPAM; perfume samples; new or hand-me-down designer jeans; travel-sized bottles of shampoo, conditioner, and body lotion gleaned from Las Vegas hotels; and appliances marked with first-world labels that, as anyone who's been to the Philippines knows, can easily be purchased at Duty Free right outside the airport, or from any of the crypt-like malls that are so gargantuan they're a metropolis unto themselves.

Filipinos will even throw themselves into these boxes, as was the case of an overseas contract worker in Dubai. The man, an engineer, was so homesick that, unable to afford the ticket—most of his earnings went to cover his living expenses and the rest to his wife and children—he talked his roommate, who was homebound for the holidays, into checking him in. He paid for the excess baggage fee, which still came out cheaper than a round-trip airfare. En route to Manila, he died from hypothermia.

Vince, who had heard the story from his older sister Jing, didn't buy it. There were too many loopholes, too many unanswered questions, like wouldn't an x-ray machine in the Middle East detect a Filipino man curled up inside a box? He simply dismissed it as a "turban legend."

"You're missing the point, brother," Jing said. "It's not the mechanics that matter. It's about drama. The extremes a Filipino will go to just to be back home for Christmas with his family."

SAME YELLOW SMELL

When Vince, Jing, and their younger brother Alvin left the Philippines to begin a new life in Hawaii, they arrived with such a box. This was in 1978, when President Ferdinand Marcos and his spotlight-driven sidekick, Imelda, were at the height of their conjugal power, looting the national treasury and depositing their ill-gotten gains in the Alps, or using it to buy prime real estate properties in the U.S. under their cronies' names.

Back then Manila International Airport went by its acronym—MIA. There were no boarding gates for families to huddle at and lengthen their farewells. That ritual took place at the fountain right outside the terminal, where vendors sold soft drinks in plastic bags and photographers offered to capture Polaroid moments for seven pesos, the equivalent of one U.S. dollar back then. Ten-year-old Vince was captured on film wearing a denim suit with a matching cap. Jing, age eleven, had on a faux-fur coat concealing a spaghetti-strap dress. Alvin, who had just turned nine, stood between them, wearing a two-toned polyester suit. And behind them, their grandfather Don Alfonso and their maid Yaya Let, who told them that before Filipinos could touch America, they must first pass through heaven.

No one wanted to be in the picture.

"We didn't come to America," Jing told Vince and Alvin years later, during one of their get-togethers at the Waikiki condo the two brothers rented. "We were sent to a costume ball on Gilligan's Island," she continued. "I was Sissy Spacek in *Carrie,* Alvin was John Travolta in *Saturday Night Fever,* and you, Vince, who were you?"

"Denny Terrio from *Dance Fever,*" Vince said.

"Remember those plastic backpacks we carried around?" Alvin said. "What were we thinking?"

"It was a status-symbol thing," Vince said, remembering the see-through backpacks that every kid who belonged to (or wanted to be part of) the upper class had.

"Do you remember the nice mestiza Pan Am stewardess?" Jing asked.

"The one you had a huge crush on?" Vince asked. "The one Alvin wished was his mother?"

"Yeah, her," Jing said, overlapping with Alvin's "No, Vince. That was *your* wish."

"Mimi," Vince said, recalling that it was Mimi who had given them previews of what to expect in Hawaii: Coke came in cans; boys, as well as girls, danced the hula; "aloha," which is "hello" and "I love you," also meant "goodbye."

"She was so sophisticated," Jing said, "from Forbes Park, Makati, I think."

"And the way she spoke English, just like the six o'clock weather girl," Vince said. "China-doll bob haircut, fire-engine-red lips, a mole above her left eyebrow."

"God, Vince, the things you hold on to," Alvin said. "No wonder you have separation anxiety."

"And periodic nightmares," Jing added.

"I wouldn't talk," Vince said. "You're the one who keeps giving George a second and third and fourth chance."

"Because a great fuck only comes once in a lifetime," Alvin said. "And when you find it, you put out until it wears you out."

"I second that motion," Jing said, gesturing her brothers to toast. "To the one great fuck of our lives," she said.

Vince took a sip of merlot. A series of snapshot memories of that afternoon at the airport thirteen years ago rushed back to him: of him clinging to his grandfather, not letting go until he promised to visit him in Hawaii; of Mimi escorting them away from Don Alfonso and Yaya Let, guiding them through automatic sliding doors while a porter trailed behind them, pushing a cart stacked with suitcases and a balik-bayan box with "VICENTE DE LOS REYES" and "HAWAII" written on it; of he, Alvin, and Jing melting in their clothes in the terminal because the air-conditioning was broken; of passengers fanning themselves with mustard-colored passports or rolled-up calendars of the Virgin Mary or manila folders fat with immigration papers and other documents proving their legal alien status; of him praying for his grandfather to appear at the last minute and take him back to San Vicente.

"Remember the piped-in music that kept playing?" Vince said.

"*Times of Your Life,*" Alvin answered

"By Paul 'King of Airport Music' Anka," Jing laughed.

"Talk about melodrama!" Alvin said.

"What a sad-assed soundtrack!" Jing said.

"Oh, my god," Vince said, breaking the silence of nostalgia that had settled between them like dust. "Remember the old woman who carried a life-size statue of Christ on the cross?"

Jing burst into laughter. "Who could forget?" she said. "She was as old as Gethsemane."

"What about those brooms that practically everyone brought with them to the plane?" Alvin said.

Vince smiled as he imagined Filipinos walking toward a jumbo jet with their wispy brooms held high in the air, as if they were en route to fight a war. "No wonder we always get stereotyped as maids," he said. "It started back home."

"Wrong, Vince," Jing said. "Filipinos came to America to clean it up."

"And Park Marlene. Remember her and her goddamn leis?" Alvin cut in.

Park Marlene, as typed on her Honolulu International Airport ID badge, was a middle-aged Asian woman assigned to look after Vince, Alvin, and Jing. She was also their introduction to English in Hawaii as a language with missing verbs. "So adorable, you three," she told them when Mimi passed them on to her. "My name Mrs. Park, but you kids call me 'Auntie Marlene,' O.K.? O.K. Oh, you guys wen' puke? So sorry. But no worry, you guys almost home." She tried to place one of the three leis she'd been holding over Alvin's head, but he recoiled.

"How come you no like?" Park Marlene asked Alvin. "This only plumeria."

"That's kalachuchi," Alvin said.

"No, this plumeria."

But Alvin insisted it was kalachuchi and he wasn't having any. Vince also refused.

"How come you guys no like my flower?" Park Marlene said. "You guys allergic?"

"In the Philippines, those flowers are for the dead," Jing explained.

Minutes later, inside Customs: "What get inside your da kind?" Nishimura Blaine asked, staring down at Vince.

Vince raised his eyes to the Customs officer, whispering to Park Marlene, "What is he asking me?"

"You know," Park Marlene pointed to the box. "What get inside your da kind?"

"Da kind?" Vince asked. "What's 'da kind?'"

Three years of learning English at a Catholic private school run by Dominican priests and nuns, where he'd won blue ribbons and gold medals and was chosen from his class as San Vicente Elementary

School's "Most Likely to Succeed in the English Language," and he couldn't answer a very simple question: "What get inside your da kind?"

"Never mind," Nishimura Blaine said as he razor-bladed the box open. "Ho, da hauna," he said, stepping back and scrunching his face. "Smell like one dead shark. What you wen' pack in there, boy?"

Tongue-tied, Vince held onto the plastic strap of his backpack stuffed with snacks, Tagalog komiks, a Henry Huggins book, and official documents, one of which was an 8 ½" x 11" x-ray film that showed he had clear lungs, and watched as Nishimura Blaine dug his hands into the box. "What's dis?" he said, holding and sniffing a powder-sprinkled package wrapped with torn komiks pages. "My goodness," he said, unwrapping the smell of dried fish, "you wen' carry one dead sea all the way here, kid?"

Vince's eyes started to water. Jing squeezed his hand. "Huwag," she told him. *Don't.*

Nishimura Blaine continued to inspect the box Don Alfonso had packed with Vince's favorite foods: dried fish of all sorts—bangus (milkfish), tuyo (herring), and dulong, tiny fish that, when dunked in vinegar, soy sauce, or patis (fish sauce), and served on a bed of rice, are called a farmer's delight.

"I can't believe you stopped eating dried fish because of that asshole, Vince," Alvin said.

"I know," Jing said.

"Well, they do stink," Vince said.

"When you became an American," Alvin said.

"Ay, naku, we all better snap out of 1978 before it ruins Vince's sleep again," Jing said, laughing and winking at Alvin.

Outside Customs, anxious greeters in t-shirts, shorts, and rubber slippers held up placards, shouting, "Here! Here!" as if wanting to be rescued.

Scared and overwhelmed by the loud noise of reunion, Vince and Alvin clung to their sister while they searched the crowd for a familiar face. Each on the verge of tears. Each wanting to run back onto the plane. Each praying to be deported.

From the invasive looks of strangers, mostly brown-skinned with even darker faces, Vince received another lei of culture shock: he had left the Philippines, puked twice during the nonstop flight across the Pacific, been shamed about his favorite diet of assorted dried fish, and endured jetlag for a week, only to arrive on a foreign soil populated by Filipinos and more Filipinos. It was as if he hadn't left his small provincial town of San Vicente at all, or if he had, it was only to take a bus ride up north to Ilocos.

Park Marlene stood behind them, doing everything she could with her medium-built frame to shield them from getting hit or knocked down by people rushing out the sliding doors with their cartloads of boxes.

"Eh, kids, you guys got picture of them?" Park Marlene asked.

Jing fished out a studio portrait of her, her two brothers, and their parents taken a month before their parents migrated to Hawaii in 1972, right before Marcos declared martial law. At the center was their mother, Carmen, in a sleeveless dress that showed off her svelte figure. On her lap was Alvin, only three at the time, in shorts, a sport coat, vest, and a bow tie. Vince, four, sat to her right, wearing knee-high shorts and a white shirt with a sailor collar. Jing, age five, wearing kung fu attire, was to her left. Standing behind them, looking slick in a dark suit and pomaded hair, was their father; his lips slightly parted to form a half-smile. Jing handed the photograph to Park Marlene and, tightening her grasp on her brothers, continued staring at the sea of strangers around her, as if she knew whom she was looking for, as if geography and time hadn't broken her memory of her parents.

MEMORY INTERRUPTED, HONOLULU INTERNATIONAL AIRPORT, MAY 1991

At the Mabuhay Express lane, Vince is trying hard to ignore the group of women gossiping about him literally behind his back, which is not uncommon. Filipinos talking loudly behind your back is their indirect way of showing you that you are important enough to kill time with. If they don't do it behind your back, they'll do it beside you or in your face. And if you're not within sight or hearing distance because you're in Serengeti National Park, or glacier-sighting in Patagonia, they'll make certain their words reach you.

"Mom, das da kind, yeah?" a teen, wearing all black in the ninety-degree heat, says in a thick Hawaiian Pidgin-English accent.

"What da kind da kind you talking about? Speak English, Jennifer," her mother says, impatient because the line for coach travelers hasn't moved an inch, held up by passengers who, despite repeated pleas that they've weighed the boxes at home using their bathroom scale, refuse to either pay the exorbitant excess baggage fee or sacrifice a dozen canned goods or that transistor radio or VCR or those rolls of toilet paper, paper towels, bath mats, face towels, or back issues of *Time* and *Life,* until the digital scale reads "70."

"Not so loud, Mom," the girl says, "he can hear you." Using her mouth, she points a yard away to Vince.

Her mother digs into her Fendi purse for her Carolina Herrera glasses. As she puts them on, she nudges the woman beside her.

"Que quieres, Mare?" she says, addressing her companion as "Mare" to denote the depth of their friendship.

"He is here, Mare."

"Who, Mare?"

"The 'Let America Be America Again' guy, Mare."

"Ay, really? Where?"

The woman stretches her pursed lips to Vince.

"He looks so much better live than on my Sony Trinitron," her friend says, eyeing Vince up and down through her rhinestone-studded glasses.

"And so much more guwapo than that Negro who won."

"He's a gay, you know, Mare," she whispers loud enough for the natives on Easter Island to hear.

"Talaga? A gay? Cannot be."

"Yes. Since high-school days. He went to school with Nelson before Nelson transferred to Punahou," she says, her words drowned out by the matriarch in front of them, yelling, "I told you I weighed the damn box myself" at the supervisor, a gray-haired Filipino man, who tries to appease her with, "I understand, ma'am, but your balikbayan box exceeds the maximum weight limit by thirty pounds."

Vince shifts his attention to the supervisor—the veins on his forehead are bulging, ready to pop.

"So what are you telling me? My bathroom scale is a liar?" the matriarch says.

"No, ma'am," the supervisor says, unfazed. "I'm only informing you of PAL's baggage policy, which is stated on your ticket."

Silence leads to a deadly five-minute staring contest. The matriarch finally concedes. She hands him a hundred-dollar bill but not without muttering the cuss word that she throws at him like a thousand machetes. "Leche," she spits, as if the word tasted sour.

Vince understands what she means, and though it's been ages since he's heard the word used in that context, hearing it again brings a smile, small as it is, to an otherwise stressful day. The word conjures up childhood memories of melodrama movies, when deceived lovers, during a confrontation scene, threw it in the face of their cheating partners before walking away, as if to tell them no one could ever break their heart again. The word has a definitive weight about it. It is fierce and final—an amulet to guard them from future heartbreak.

His grandfather used to say it all the time. "Leche," he'd say, the word leaving his body like a switchblade—small, beautiful, deadly. His voice deceptively dulce so that one never knew what he was thinking or feeling, if he were angry or sad or remembering, just like the word that has come to mean different things to different people. Leche. "Milk" in Spanish. But to Filipinos, "Shit!"

Tourist Tips

- "Philippines" is derived from "Felipinas," after King Philip II of Spain. The name was coined by Spanish explorer Ruy Lopez de Villalobos during his 1542 expedition to the Visayan islands of Leyte and Samar.

- Filipinos are also Spanish cookies covered in dark, white, or milk chocolate.

- "Filipinos" to Westerners; "Pilipinos" to nationalists.

- "Pili" is the verb for "to choose."

- "Pino" means refined, well-bred, or finely crushed.

- Filipinos have many names. First name, middle name, last name, plus a million colorful nicknames—Pochay, Bebot, Pinky, Baby, Buboy, Bobot, Chichay, Dimpy.

- Some names have an echoing effect: Dongdong, Bongbong, Kringkring, Dingdong, Jingjing, Kay-Kay.

- Other names conjoin the names of parents. For examples JoBert from Joanne and Albert, or Ordette from Orlando and Bernadette.

- Filipinos are OCDs (Obsessive-Compulsive Decorators), constantly decorating everything from altars to jeepneys to rearview mirrors to the English language by inserting an *h* into their names: Ehlvis Tatlonghari, Mhadonna Whigley, Ahlain Dhelon.

Headrush

Window seat. First class. To Vince's right, a window revealing the clouds of cliché—fields of sheep, floating marshmallows, feast of cellulite. Below them the blue of the Pacific, glinting like car windows hit by light.

Turbulence interrupts audio programming. Seat belt signs go on. Passengers scramble to their seats, banging their knees and hips against armrests, bumping their heads on overhead bins.

Vince, being knocked around in his seat, forgets that he's an atheist and quickly makes the Sign of the Cross three times. Prayers to the Virgin Mary, Fatima, Mediatrix of All Grace, Medjugorje, Guadalupe, Manaoag, ululate from every mouth.

Overhead compartments pop open, spit out canned goods, portable CD players, toasters, macadamia nuts, plumeria leis.

The tail of the plane rips apart. Vince shuts his eyes to the sky sucking out lavatories, meal carts, passengers, flight attendants, cans of Hormel corned beef.

The plane

p

l

u

n

g

e

s

in

slow

   mo

      tion.

Vince opens his eyes as heaven slowly drops him from an empty sky. The plane and everyone in it have vanished except him. He is still strapped in his seat, still praying to the Marys.

A procession of canned goods, led by a can of Libby's Vienna sausage, floats past him.

His best friend Edgar sweeps across the sky as if he owns it, disrupting cloud patterns. He folds his giant wings and hangs onto the armrest of Vince's seat. "You coming or not?"

"Where?" Vince asks.

"To Hula's. It's make-a-date night. Hurry, before you end up with the leftovers again," Edgar says.

Vince unbuckles the seat belt. Hands hold him back, massage his back, his shoulder blades. Tongues bathe his ears, his neck, inside his thighs.

Queen's Beach, Waikiki.

A bluer-than-blue sky.

A jetty separating sunblock-nosed tourists from gym-conscious fags in butt-floss swimwear.

Vince, in black thong and Ray-Bans, is savoring the sweet taste of a clove cigarette when a balikbayan box falling from the sky thuds on Dave Manchester, a local celebrity and model for the J.Crew and International Male catalogs.

Coppertone-oiled fags, hags, and Japanese tourists huddle around Dave, trying to pull his head out of his viscera.

Vince looks at the sky—"Thank you, God"—then takes a long drag of his sweet cigarette.

Kapiolani Park.

Dusk is cool, so cool desire is a song of freedom that George Michael sings in Vince's ears.

A flying blue can with huge yellow letters smacks Vince on his forehead.

"Oh, shit!" Vince exclaims. "It's SPAM, the ultimate Filipino hors d'oeuvre."

A second can of SPAM whacks him in his face.

Vince runs for cover across the street, inside Honolulu Zoo, in the children's playground that used to be an avian cage for the world's oldest toucan in captivity. Adrenaline-filled, he turns his head and sees the swarm of SPAM gaining on him. He slams into a body, blacks out.

"You're ruining my movie!" It's Tippi Hedren, her face beak-sliced; on her forehead, a hematoma the size of a mango.

"Who are you? Where are my birds?" she shouts at him, as a voice in the background yells, "Cut!" followed by "Vicente."

Vince opens his eyes, startled not just by the bizarre unfolding of scenes dreams often assume, for he's had many. It was the voice of his grandfather, a voice gone raspy from decades of smoking, that made him sit up and search the cabin for signs of his presence. A voice too distinct and too much of the present to be part of a dream.

The flight attendant, noticing the perturbed look on Vince's face, stops to ask if everything is all right. "Would you like a glass of water, Mr. De Los Reyes?"

Vince sits up. "Yes, please," he says, seemingly calm, "and a cup of coffee. Black. No sugar."

He looks at his watch. Maybe it was something I ate, he tells himself. He pulls out the menu from the seat pouch to see if the source is spelled out in bold italics. It isn't the dried milkfish; he'd stopped eating dried fish a long time ago, gave it up, in fact, just hours after he arrived in Hawaii. Under Selection B, he put the issue to rest, attributing his nightmares to: fried chicken dunked in fermented fish sauce; two servings of laing (pre-boiled taro leaves cooked in coconut milk and spiked with red chili peppers); leche flan; and a glass of Cabernet Sauvignon.

Sleeping with One Eye Open

> **From** *Decolonization for Beginners: A Filipino Glossary*
>
> **bangungut,** *noun.* a contraction of *bangun* (to rise) and *ungul* (to moan). See also *batibat, hupa, Sudden Unexpected Death Syndrome.*

GLUTTONY

It is common for Filipino men to die mysteriously in their sleep, as was the case with eighty-four Filipino plantation workers in Hawaii between 1937 and 1948. Vince had read about it in Bonifacio Dumpit's essay "The Contagion of Folk Beliefs: Bangungut and Racial Profiling in Hawaii's Plantation Camps." The course was "Ethnic Literature in Hawaii" and was taught by none other than the author himself, a cultural anthropologist who had gone to Hawaii during the early seventies on a Fulbright Senior Scholar fellowship.

According to Dumpit, the deaths of these men, whose ages ranged from twenty-five to forty-four, had baffled Honolulu's forensic doctors, including Dr. Alvin V. Majoska, who would go on to become the state's chief medical examiner and one of the leading researchers of bangungut. In 1948, Dr. Majoska caused panic and mass hysteria among islanders when he published his "Nightmare-Related Deaths" report, noting only Filipino men as victims. All were migrant plantation laborers. Many were young and all were healthy. Autopsy findings showed no signs of foul play, food poisoning, or intestinal parasites. Each of the victims had a swollen heart, massive fluid in their lungs, a pancreas that wouldn't stop bleeding, and abdominal cavities that contained semi-digested meals. After ten years and with no other explanations possible, Majoska attributed the deaths to acute hemorrhagic pancreatitis. The culprit: a heavy Filipino meal high in sodium, cholesterol, and uric acid right before shut-eye.

However, to Filipinos raised on Catholicism and folk superstition, like Vince, the killer nightmare had a name. To the Tagalog-speakers in and outside Manila, it's "bangungut"; among the Ilocanos of Northern Luzon, it's "batibat"; and to the Southern Visayan islanders, it's "hupa."

Dumpit's essay went on to discuss how the sleeping sickness had further divided the already racially stratified camps. When it became apparent that only Filipino men were the chief targets, the Korean, Portuguese, Puerto Rican, and other field laborers resorted to the double armor of paranoia and scapegoating. The Japanese and Chinese, who had already left the camps to set up their own businesses in downtown Honolulu, were also drawn into the hysteria.

Hatred, fear, and ignorance spread from one plantation to another, from one island to another. Folks went to sleep without eating or ate without sleeping because they were fed too many superstitions and believed them all. Don't eat before going to bed or you'll be digesting in hell. Sleep with Filipinos and you'll never dream in this world again.

Suspicious glares, racial epithets, and rumbles in the fields under the blue heated sky only solidified Hawaii's racial divisiveness, perpetuating negative stereotypes of Filipinos as strikebreakers, flat-nosed sexual predators, carriers of TB, hepatitis-B virus, and a mysterious ailment that had yet to find a name in Western medicine.

What's even more terrifying about the killer nightmare is that the victim returns momentarily to the world of the living, only to witness, in his limbo state, the final scene of his life—moaning and kicking helplessly. He wants to get up but he can't. He opens his mouth to scream but he can't. Because sitting on his face, which is how survivors of the nightmare described their near-death experiences, is the bangungut, shoving his fat cigar down the victim's throat, determined to drag his young and healthy prey to the underworld.

CRUSH

When Vince was growing up in San Vicente, a small provincial town four hours north of Manila by car, he read about the bangungut from the Tagalog komiks Don Alfonso bought him.

From kindergarten to third grade, his grandfather, who was already in his fifties when Vince had begun his studies, fetched him from school and took him straight to the magazine stand right across the plaza. The kiosk was owned and managed by his grandfather's kumpadre, Don Noli de Guzman, who, like Don Alfonso, was a World War II veteran and a member of the Knights of Columbus.

From the kiosk they proceeded to the panaderia owned by Doña Teresing Campos y Viuda de Lopez—Our Daily Bread Bakery. At a small table in the back corner Doña Teresing reserved especially for them, grandfather and grandson spent the remains of the afternoon reading. As the blades of the single electric fan whirred, Don Alfonso sipped coffee and caught up with world events via *Life* and *Time*. Vince, seated beside him with a towel on his back to soak up perspiration and thereby prevent him from catching a cold (Yaya Let's folk remedy), drank Coca-Cola, ate a roll thickly coated with sugar and butter called ensemada, and fueled his imagination with Tagalog komiks.

Side by side they read in silence, breaking it only when necessary, only briefly. Reading was a serious matter to Don Alfonso, an attitude Vince had inherited from him. It was like praying, which allowed the individual access to a higher plain of reality and to connect with a supreme being or other beings. It was like dreaming, which opened the door to other worlds familiar or strange where the reader played the part of a sympathetic observer, an objective bystander, an accomplice, a protagonist, a villain, or all of the above.

"Reading is like dreaming with eyes open," his grandfather said. The fewer interruptions, the better. "Read with silence, hijo," he said. "Let your imagination make all the noise." This from the man who had taught him at age three how to read, out loud at first, and then only with the eyes.

When their parents left San Vicente for Honolulu, it was reading books and Tagalog komiks that helped lessen Vince's sadness, suppress his desire to ask why a mother would leave her three-year-old son in the hands of a maid, or a father remove himself away from his only daughter. Reading deterred him from wanting to know if his parents were ever coming back, or why they left in the first place, nagging questions that eventually lost their urgency with time and more important matters.

It was reading that bonded Vince to his grandfather and imagination that solidified that bond. So when the afternoon arrived, it meant another reading session of komiks, the Philippine version of serialized comics. Of the five komiks his grandfather had bought him—one komik for each working day—his favorite was "Stories of the Unexpected," which hit the newsstands every Friday. Published by King Komiks, it had stories about the bangungut, which disguised itself as a nomad by day, wandering around Metropolitan Manila for potential victims, then transformed into a cigar-puffing hairy beast that terrorized them in their sleep.

The stories came with illustrations bordering on the grotesque and the absurd. A doctor watching flesh-eating bacteria slowly eat him up. A politician being pursued by an army of barbed-wire lips. A bank manager running into a clothesline that has his kidneys hanging from it.

In each issue, the bangungut preyed on a new victim, usually crooks and greedy men like Mr. Smith, an American businessman who ran an illegal logging business on the island of Leyte, where much of the virgin forest had been destroyed.

Vince could not keep his mind off Mr. Smith. He bore a striking physical resemblance to his grandfather, who was also very debonair. But unlike Mr. Smith, who was a womanizer, Don Alfonso, who could've re-married any woman he chose, had sworn to his dying wife that he would remain a widower until he died, because a love once lost could never be replaced. Back then, both Mr. Smith and Don Alfonso pomaded their hair back, had pronounced widow's peaks, wore khaki trousers and vintage Hawaiian shirts, and had slanted, blue eyes.

"He was my first crush," Vince confided to Alvin and Jing years later. "It was so obvious," Jing said. "Your hot lips were all over the pages."

"And you were so stingy with your komiks," Alvin said. "You held on to them the way Yaya Let hung on to her rosary when she prayed the Sorrowful Mysteries."

"You should've just eaten the damn story," Jing said, "shoved Mr. Smith and his bangungut nightmare down your throat."

Jing was right. For months after reading about Mr. Smith, Vince went to bed thinking of him, kissing him good night, telling him, "Sweet dreams, Mr. Smith," "I love you, Mr. Smith," "Do you love me, too?" Walking to school, sitting at his desk, during recess, or down with the flu, he daydreamed of Mr. Smith asking him to join him for a ride on the Ferris wheel, of Mr. Smith letting him lick his yam-flavored ice cream, of Mr. Smith taking his siesta nap with him in his arms, of Mr. Smith holding his hand as they walked along the promenade of Manila Bay, chitchatting about full moons, wedding bells, and the houses, love-nest resorts, and nurseries he would build for them and their babies. Other times, Vince wished he were Cassandra, the young, dark beauty from Siquijor, a Visayan island known for its witchcraft. Mr. Smith had fallen for her the morning they'd crossed paths in the lobby of the Manila Hotel. He'd introduced himself to her. In a matter of days, they were engaged, had chosen the date, time, and place to exchange their vows—in the Philippines and in Wisconsin, USA, where Mr. Smith was from. On the night of their honeymoon, she ("That bruja!") transformed back into her true identity as the cigar-smoking beast, straddling him and stuffing his mouth with her cigar until he choked to death.

"You were so obsessed with him it almost killed you," Jing said, referring to one of Vince's childhood nightmares. It began with him and Mr. Smith having their usual sunset stroll along Manila Bay. They had just shared a hot dog and a bottle of Coca-Cola when Mr. Smith stopped Vince and, under the memorial statue of Dr. Jose Rizal, proposed to him. "Yes," Vince said right away and threw his arms around Mr. Smith's waist. Mr. Smith knelt down to kiss Vince, who had already closed his eyes. As he rolled his tongue inside Vince's mouth, Vince began imagining a sprawling mansion, a beachfront honeymoon resort, babies with slanted blue eyes and black hair. But the longer they kissed, the weirder the images got: Vince pushing a stroller that had a blonde infant with the body of a zebra in it, then nursing a baby with the snout of a giant anteater, then craving air as a tongue fat as a python slithered from Mr. Smith's mouth and down into his throat.

Had it not been for Alvin and Jing, who heard his moaning, kicking, and gasping through the thin walls that separated their bedrooms, the bangungut would've sucked out Vince's last breath, smelling of Mr. Smith's kisses.

A decade later, when he had already succeeded in surrendering one nationality for another, swapping Philippine customs for American ways, replacing Tagalog with English, getting used to his adopted culture and newly-forged persona, Vince sat down one afternoon in Dumpit's class and found himself reading a handout that reunited him once more with memories of the bangungut and a childhood favorite pastime—komiks. Memories that ushered him back to those afternoon sessions with his grandfather in Doña Teresing's Our Daily Bread Bakery. And though the country that once housed his first dreams was now an ocean and a day away, Vince's discovery that the bangungut had found its way into the plantation camps of Hawaii as early as the 1920s only reinforced the cliché that you can take the Filipino out of the Philippines but you can't take the nightmares out of the Filipino. And regardless of time and geography, Filipinos, whether they like it or not, wherever they end up, will bring or drag with them their balikbayan boxes, stuffed with superstitions and plaster saints, hopes and homesickness, dreams and disappointments, laughter and libido, dust and drama, wardrobe and music, to go with the memories. And, last but not least, desires and nightmares.

Tourist Tips

- The Philippines is a very loud country: bring earplugs.

- "Pinoys," a nickname for Filipinos, is also spelled "P-Noise!"

- Filipinos cannot live without making noise, hearing noise, or being noise.

- Their motto is: Je fais du bruit, ergo sum (trans: Noise—c'est moi!)

- Filipinos can meditate to heavy metal music.

- Filipinos fight for noise; cacophony is worth dying for.

- Filipinos don't pray in silence; they ululate in tribes.

- At wakes, they don't weep. Rather, they wail, screech, tear the roots of their hair, hold vigil-long monologues to the dead, complete with a live brass band on the patio.

- According to the World Health Organization, one out of ten Filipinos is born with a hearing problem. Six will go legally deaf by age thirty.

- Filipinos are marathon talkers—on the phone; in movie houses; with food in their mouths; during a church sermon, senate hearing, or academic lecture; when committing acts of crime or passion; and while sleeping.

- "Por awhile" in telephone lingua is "to place someone on hold."

- "Who's this?" is often pronounced "hos-tess."

- Their hi-fi mating calls can be heard as far north as Taiwan and Borneo in the south.

- The Philippines has the highest population growth rate in Southeast Asia.

- There are approximately seventy million Filipinos in the Philippines. Ninety percent of them reside in Manila.

BOOK II

Shame Dubbed

In the Name of Shame is the in-flight film dubbed in English on channel 2. Directed by Bino Boca, it is set in present-day Manila with flashbacks to a provincial town, circa wartime 1942, and stars the inimitable Kris Aquino, youngest daughter of President Corazon Aquino and the late Senator Benigno "Ninoy" Aquino, whose assassination in 1983 precipitated the downfall of the Marcos dynasty. In this historical melodrama—a departure from the slasher-massacre-horror flicks, like the *Shake, Rattle, Then Die* series, that made her a bankable star—Kris takes on the demanding and dual roles of Lola Maria, a seventy-year-old grandmother haunted by an evil secret, and her granddaughter Mia, who works in Tokyo as a cultural dancer/bar hostess.

For Vince, the meat of the movie is wrapped up in the first half hour. Lola Maria is watching daybreak through an open capiz-shell window, her face at a three-quarter angle to the camera. Soft focus. A faint smile crosses her lips as she hears the opening sounds of dawn: crowing roosters, the piercing wails of vendors selling fresh-baked rolls or balut—duck egg with an almost-developed embryo.

Mia embraces her grandmother from behind, kisses her on the cheek. "Morning, Lola."

"Morning, hija."

Together, they peer out into the street with its electric cables crisscrossing the air and rows of tin-sheets-and-plywood dwellings standing on what is supposed to be a sidewalk; their rusty roofs are held in place by tires and hollow blocks. Behind the shanties is the imposing wall of a subdivision. Camera closes in on Mia's lips reading the sign on the wall. BAWAL UMIHI DITO, (Do Not Piss Here), then, in English: PISSERS WILL BE PROSECUTED.

"Mia." Lola Maria turns, brushes a strand of hair off her granddaughter's cheek. "I have something to tell you."

"What is it, Lola?"

"Hija, I . . . killed . . . your mother."

Mia shifts her gaze to her grandmother.

"Did you hear me, hija?"

Close-up of Mia's face in dream-mode. "What, Lola?"

"I killed her. I didn't want to, but I had to."

"Kill? Kill who, Lola?"

"Your mother."

"What are you talking about?" Mia slides the window shut.

"It's the truth," Lola Maria says, clasping her hands. "It's best I tell you now because I might die anytime, and I don't want to bring any secrets with me to hell."

Mia takes Lola Maria's hand and leads her to the couch.

"Hija, please. You've got to believe me."

Mia shakes her head. "What's wrong with you? Is it because I didn't take you shopping at the Duty Free? Is that why you're acting like this?"

"No, hija," Lola Maria says, on the verge of tears. "I'm telling you the truth."

"Lola." Pause. "Did you take your Valium?"

"No," Lola Maria answers, "and I'm not going to. Why do you always force me to take those pills? Do you want to kill me? Do you want me to die right now? Is that what you want? So you can finally have my kayamanan and this house to yourself?"

"I don't care about this house or your mango farm, Lola. I don't care if I inherit zilch from you."

Mia stands up, walks to the bathroom.

"Don't turn your back on me," Lola Maria says. "Where are you going? Don't leave me."

"I'm not going anywhere, Lola," Mia says. "I'm just going to get your medicine."

Mia returns to the living room holding a vial in her hand and a bottle of mineral water. "My mother died in her sleep," she says. "It's public knowledge. You said so yourself, Lola."

"That's only half-true," Lola Maria says.

Mia twists the cap. Tiny pills fall into her cupped palm. She hands her a tablet. "Here, take these."

"Punyeta!" Lola Maria cusses.

"It's not Valium," Mia says. "It's Norvasc. For your high blood pressure."

"Oh." Pause. Lola Maria pops the pill into her mouth, swallows it with water.

"You know why I did it, hija? You want to know why I killed her?" Lola Maria continues. "I did it to stop her from going ahead with her plans."

"Plans?"

"To sell you," Lola Maria answers. "Oh, Mia, you were such a beautiful baby. Everybody wanted to adopt you."

Mia's back stiffens.

"She was going to sell you so she could go to America with her G.I. Joe lover," Lola Maria says.

Silence. Close-up of Mia's pale face, her eyes welling with tears. She opens her mouth, can only say, "My father was an American?"

"No," Lola Maria pauses. "Muslim."

"Muslim? No, I don't believe you, Lola. Why are you doing this to me?"

"Hija, listen to me."

"No. I don't think I can take one more revelation."

"I'm sorry, hija, but it's best I bring everything out in the open. For who knows if the Lord will grant me another tomorrow." Pause. "Where was I?"

"You were talking about my father," Mia says.

"Ah, yes. Dead before you were born. Killed instantly when the motorcycle he was on collided with a bus. Your mother never loved him. Not once did I see her shed a tear during his wake or funeral. She never loved anybody. She didn't know love if it snuck up on her from behind and hugged and kissed her. Love, hate, hate, love: both were the same to her. She only thought of her selfish, greedy self. It wasn't her fault. I'm all to blame. Me and mea culpa. I was the one who taught her to look out for herself, to think only of herself, not as a daughter or a mother or a wife but as a woman. I told her just because this was a man's world didn't mean a woman had no place in it. I told her only she could make herself happy, only she could make herself miserable. I did it. I created her—that bitch, my monster."

"Lola!"

"Truth hurts," Lola Maria says. "But it's all we've got now. And if your mother had her way, she would've sold you. Black-market baby—that was how she saw you. Or worse."

Close-up of Mia, tears coursing down her cheeks. "But how did you find out about her plans?"

"God works in mysterious ways, hija." Pause. "I found it out from her best friend. She was going to sell you for a million pesos to an American couple stationed at Clarke Air Force Base in Angeles City."

"I could've been an American citizen?" Mia asks.

"Or a drug addict," Lola Maria says. "But I stopped her." She crosses herself. "Oh Lord, forgive me for what I'm about to say."

"What did you do, Lola? Did you poison my mother? Is that why she died in her sleep?"

"No, hija. I took strands of her hair, wrapped it in her dirty under-wear, and I went to that mangkukulam, Manolita."

Cut to the first of a series of flashbacks. A dim room. A woman, gagged, is dragged across a floor by bad special effects. She's flung against a wall, held down on a mattress, her ankles and wrists bound. Her skirt is slowly pushed up her thigh.

Vince, more bored than amused, mistakes Manolita, the witch doctor, for a badly lit Imelda Marcos.

BLIND DATES & BINDHIS

The rape scene brings back memories of the Barbara Hershey B-movie Vince once saw on a blind date masterminded by Edgar.

"His name Winston," Edgar, speaking in Pidgin English, told Vince over the phone.

"Winston? As in cigarettes?" Vince said.

"As in Churchill, Nobel Prize for Literature and author of one book," Edgar said. "I met him at Hula's last night. Winston Chin. McKinley High grad. Class of '84, Chinese-Japanese."

"Lethal combo, Edgar," Vince said. "How tall is he?"

"Not very. Five five max," Edgar said. "But he's lean."

"Edgar, you just described ninety-nine percent of the Asian faggots in Hawaii."

"If he were a bottom, yes," Edgar corrected him. "But he isn't."

"He's a top?"

"No. Versatile."

"Then forget it."

"Why not?"

"'Versatile' is the euphemism for a big bottom. We all know that, Edgar."

"Vince, it's only a one-night stand. You not gonna interracial marry him."

"Edgar, remember the last time you arranged a one-night stand for me? It turned out to be a sad-assed ABC miniseries."

"I know and I'm sorry. But Winston ain't the fatal-attraction type, Vince."

"How do you know?"

"I just do. Besides, he lives in Massachusetts now. He goes to school there—MIT. Engineering."

"So?"

"Do I have to spell it out? He a Chang. He not gonna waste his money on long-distance calls, unless you borrow money and no pay him back."

"He can always call collect."

"Trust me, Vince. You'll like Winston. Very nice looking. Very Fred Perry preppy type."

"Really?"

"Plus he get moles on his face."

"When's he going back to Massachusetts?"

"Next Saturday."

"Tell him I'm free all day Monday, Tuesday, Wednesday, and after six on Thursday and Friday."

"Perfect."

MOLECULAR

Vince has a weakness for moles. Not the motherfucking witch's tit or elephant-skin-looking ones sprouting hairs. Not the bindhis that Indian-from-India women wear to signify they're married to the Salman Rushdies of the world. Not melanoma moles. But those small dots of desire. And Winston had three on his face: one peeking from the left eyebrow, another below the right eye, and the third above the upper lip, which means money, money, money to superstitious Filipinos.

On the day of their date, Winston phoned Vince and asked him if they could alter their original plans of dining at the Old Spaghetti Factory then catching the last showing of the new Tom Cruise movie, *Rain Man,* at the Varsity Twin Theaters.

"What do you have in mind?" Vince asked.

"I was thinking of something more laid back, more domestic," Winston answered.

"Oh?" Vince's ears stood up at the word "domestic."

"Why don't you come over for dinner at my Auntie Janine's apartment on Pensacola Street? She lives right across from McKinley High. We can have dinner, then take it from there, O.K.?"

"What about your aunt?" Vince asked.

"She's in Vegas," Winston replied. "She goes there twice a month."

"Need me to bring anything?"

"Just dessert."

"Guava chiffon cake sound O.K. to you?"

"I meant you, Vince," Winston said, which, to Vince, was a better selection than Dee-Lite Bakery's most popular cake.

Winston's idea of something-laid-back-something-domestic turned out to be a bottle of Carlo Rossi Chablis and a dinner that consisted of mashed potatoes, buttered corn, Salisbury steak, apple pie, and a two-hour couch date with *The Entity,* the ABC Sunday Night Movie. That's what they ended up doing after their Sara Lee meal. In the movie, Barbara Hershey, pre-collagen-lips days, played a single mother who moved her family into a haunted house, where an evil spirit raped her every night. Ten minutes before the movie ended, she finally found the courage to flee. Go figure.

"That's what you getting all worked up for?" Edgar said, when Vince phoned him later that night. "He lacked fine-dining etiquette. Big deal. The main thing is you got laid, right? Isn't that the goal of a one-night stand?"

"But you didn't tell me you'd already slept with him," Vince said.

"I never. We only made out at three thirty in the morning, in the parking lot of Blowhole Lookout."

"I don't want your leftovers, Edgar. I already told you that."

"He wasn't a leftover, Vince. You was his main course. I was only his hors d'oeuvre."

"And by the way, he wasn't versatile."

"That's what he told me. How should I know? I told you we only made out. Look, Vince, it was a one-night stand. The guy gave you good head. You said so yourself. So move on, Vince. Move on."

"Next time, give your leftovers to someone else."

"Vince, wake up. We live on one island. We all leftovers here."

BACK TO THE IN-FLIGHT MOVIE

Cut to: Present-day Manila.

"I don't believe you, Lola! Please tell me you're lying!" Mia shouts, her eyes puffy from crying, her lips trembling, her shoulders shaking.

"Believe me, hija," Lola Maria cries. "I had no choice. I begged her not to sell you, but all she could think of was America. She said she'd tell the world about me and the Japanese if I tried to stop her."

Mia gasps. "Oh, my god, Lola. You? The Japanese?"

"I was twenty when the war broke out—already too old for the soldiers," Lola Maria says. "They wanted young girls, like your Lola Ligaya, who was thirteen then, and your Lola Pilita, who was only eleven. I tried to protect my sisters. I offered them my body instead. But the Japanese just laughed at me, said my breasts were older than the sun. They made fun of me, hija, those racist slanty-eyed pigs. They said I could keep my sisters' virginity if I told them where the mayor hid his daughters. Oh, Lord—" Lola Maria clutches the crucifix around her neck, kisses it. "I betrayed them, hija, and told the soldiers. That night, the mayor's daughters, along with fifty other young girls, were pulled out of the cellar of Nana's bakery and taken to the elementary school they had turned into their headquarters."

Lola Maria drops to her knees. "Lord, take me now. Throw me in hell. Burn every part of my being. I deserve it, Lord. I conspired with Satan. I betrayed my people. I betrayed my country. I betrayed you, Lord. Because of me, teenage girls lost their innocence. Because of me, they are scarred for life. Please Lord, Our Savior, take me. Kill me. What I did was shameless, unforgivable."

Mia kneels beside her. "Stop it. Stop it, Lola. The war made you do that. War brings out the evil in all of us."

"How do you know? The only war you've witnessed is on the news. You don't know what it was like. You never had to sell your soul to the devil. You never had to ration your food. You know what we lived on, Mia? Do you? One slice of bread a week to feed five people."

Lola Maria collapses on the floor. "Lola!" Mia scoops her up into her arms. "Don't die on me! Please, Lola," Mia cries.

They have a Pietà moment, cut short by Lola Maria scrambling for air.

"Lola, please don't die on me. Lola, please don't . . ."

From the pocket of her housedress, Lola Maria takes an old piece of paper folded into squares, then releases her last words on earth. "You will know some of these names, but most of them are dead now. Find those who are still alive, hija. Tell them they must tell the world what the Japanese did. Promise me they will break their silence. You have to promise me. It's the only way they can remove their shame. And mine," Lola Maria concludes, then dies peacefully in Mia's arms.

Vince, taking his headphones off, gets up to use the lavatory. He is about to be assaulted by a clogged toilet when the sign on the door stops him, apologizing for the inconvenience and instructing first- and business-class passengers to use the lavatories in the coach section. While waiting, he wonders if all the passengers are hard of hearing, because it seems they've got the volume on their headsets turned up to max, making it possible for him to watch and listen to Mia speaking to a lifeless Lola Maria. She tells her grandmother she will find the comfort women, no matter what it takes. She will track them down and get them to end their silence. Then she will join them in their battle to get the Japanese government to admit, apologize, and atone for their war crimes.

Caption: ONE WEEK LATER.

Mia meets with Sister Marie and Manila Mayor Alfredo Lim (playing themselves), who help her track down the eight surviving comfort women, collectively known as "Lolas." Already in their late seventies, the Lolas narrate their horrifying stories, eliciting a chorus of "dios mio"s from the passengers.

Following the fifteen-minute confession, shot in talking-heads-style, is a cameo appearance of President Corazon Aquino in her trademark outfit—a yellow housedress. She is in her office in Malacañang Palace signing a piece of paper on a large mahogany desk as Mia, Sister Marie, and the Lolas look over her shoulder. Scene shifts to Mia, Sister Marie, and the Lolas on a flight to Japan, where they plan to demand retribution from the Japanese government and apologies from Emperor Hirohito.

A woman gets up from her seat and stands behind Vince. "It's so smoky here," she says, taking a red handkerchief from her purse and holding it over her nose. "Have you been waiting long?"

"Forever," Vince answers.

"It's the coconut milk," she explains. "Parang spoiled."

They turn their attention to the screen, where a showdown between Sister Marie and Emperor Hirohito is happening. "What about the textbooks?" the vigilant nun asks Emperor Hirohito as his advisors escort him out of the room. Sister Marie removes her sandals and sprints after him. Bodyguards resembling Samoan sumo wrestlers block her. "Your people have the right to know about their past, Emperor," she shouts. "You can no longer exclude us from your history. Stop lying to yourself, Emperor."

"She's a real nun, you know," the woman says. "Big star siya sa Philippines. By the way, ako si Esther." Catching herself speaking in Tagalog, she apologizes, and in English says, "I'm Esther."

"Vince."

"As in Vincent?"

"No, Vicente," he says, his eyes fixed on the screen as Sister Marie loses it in a ramen restaurant, pounding her fist on the counter, making more noise than a sober Japanese person could ever produce in a lifetime. "What's wrong with you quiet people? How is it that you remember Hiroshima but not Bataan? Nagasaki but not Pearl Harbor? Mickey Mouse but not your Korean and Chinese neighbors?" she yells to the customers. "You think you were the only victims of the war? No! You were not the only victims!"

The Lolas plead with Sister Marie. "Tama na, Sister, tama na," which the subtitles translate into "Stop na, Sister, enough na." Mia, grasping the nun's elbow, apologizes in Japanese to the offended patrons. "Sumimasen, sumimasen," she says. Sorry, sorry.

"You know who she is, right?" Esther asks.

"President Aquino's daughter?" Vince asks.

Nodding, she says, "And the highest-paid actress in the Philippines. She was paid five million pesos to play Lola Maria and Mia." Then,

"Your first time to the Philippines?"

"First time back," Vince says. "I was born there."

"So nakakaintindi ka pa rin nang Tagalog?" Esther asks.

"I understand it but don't speak it."

"Bakit? When did you leave the Philippines?"

"Thirteen years ago," he answers.

"You grew up in Hawaii?"

"Over half my life."

"How come you don't have that Pidgin-English accent?"

"I don't speak Pidgin," Vince says, "but I understand it."

"Like Tagalog."

"Yes."

"You remind me of my friend in Hong Kong," she says. "I used to live there."

"Doing what?"

"Housekeeper."

"So when did you move to Hawaii?" he asks.

"Seven years ago."

"You fly back to the Philippines often?"

"No," she says. "This is my first time back since I left. And you? Are you going for business or pleasure? How old are you, anyway?"

"Some work, more play," Vince answers. "Twenty-three."

"You go to college?"

"Just graduated. Two weeks ago, in fact."

"What did you take up?"

"Film," he says, omitting his second major, lit.

"You going to make movies?"

"No. Film studies," he says. "More on the theory stuff."

"Oh," she says, sounding disappointed. "But you should be in the movies. Or model, at least. You have the looks."

Vince laughs.

"I'm not kidding," she says. "You'll have no problem getting into showbiz over there."

A DIGRESSION ON FILIPINO SERVITUDE DATING BACK TO THE SIXTEENTH CENTURY

My name is Esther. I have two children, two boys. Ben is in sixth grade; the other one, Jasper, he is in third. Very smart boys, just like their father. I work in Hawaii now, in Lahaina, Maui, as a caregiver to Mr. Strand. I call him Sir. Before that, I was in Hong Kong as a D.H. Domestic Helper. Fancy word for maid, no? Sir is already seventy years old, still strong, no sign of slowing down. He is very kind to me. A widower. Like myself. His wife was Pinay. Ilocana. From Vigan, Ilocos Sur. Cancer of the liver. She was young too. Only thirty-five. Sayang nga lang they had no children. My cousin Efren was the one who helped me get the job. He is a nurse. Maui General. He took care of Sir's wife. That's how he and Sir became good friends. I owe a lot to Sir. Very, very nice. He paid for my ticket home. Birthday gift he said. Plus ten days off with pay. I cried. I could not help it. I have not seen my boys since I left P.I. for Hawaii. But who's going to watch you, Sir? He can manage he said. No sign of slowing down talaga. Still, he is all alone in the house. Sir said if I want he will marry me so I can petition for Ben and Jasper. Ben is already graduating from elementary school and Jasper, he is going to be a fourth grader come June. Sir said if I like, he will hire a lawyer right now to work on our papers. The sooner the better he said. He said my boys and I, we have no future in the Philippines. True. You have to buy future in the Philippines he said, and future there is very, very expensive. My name is Esther. I am a widow. I have two boys. Ben is in sixth grade. And the other one, Jasper, he is in third.

POST-BREAKDOWN

By the time Vince returns to his seat and resumes his attention to the screen, Sister Marie has already been discharged from the Tokyo hospital where she was admitted for a week for psychiatric evaluation, and Mia has already fallen in love with Rick, an American ex-marine teaching English in Tokyo; they met in the bar she used to work in, in Shinjuku.

"You sure this is what you want, Mia?" Sister Marie asks. She and Mia are at the boarding gate of Narita International Airport, along with the Lolas and Rick.

"We're in love, Sister," Mia says.

"But hija, you've only known each other for three days," Sister Marie says.

"Love is not measured in days, Sister," Mia says.

"Sabagay," the nun says, which the subtitles translate to "I guess so."

Mia kisses and hugs the Lolas, apologizes to them once more for what Lola Maria did to them. All is forgiven but not forgotten, the Lolas tell her, then thank her for helping them remove their shame, and say that there is hope left in this evil world.

THE END

As the plane begins its descent from thirty-five thousand feet, the flight attendants collect headphones and pass out baggage and currency declaration forms. Vince, peering out the window, catches glimpses of the diverse landscape of the Philippine archipelago: verdant mountains, winding rivers, fisheries, crab farms partitioned into squares, endless rice fields, then—nothing. As if the islands are suddenly erased. The ocean, too, has disappeared.

Pressing his forehead against the window, he gazes down below for traces of land, water, life. Nothing. Except air the color of ash. For a moment, he is convinced that the engines have shut down because he can no longer hear them droning. Pinching his nose, he tries to pop his ears, which feel like they've been stuffed with cotton. He pushes the call button, then cancels it when bits and pieces of the city appear—a metropolis without uniformity, without a semblance of a grid. From above it looks cluttered, compressed, sprawling. A formless beast extending its limbs into the sea.

Soon as the plane touches down on the tarmac, whistles and applause break out in the coach section as the pilot announces the current weather conditions in Manila. "Very sunny with a temperature of ninety-seven degrees Fahrenheit and humidity of ninety-seven percent."

Some of the passengers are so excited to be back in the motherland that they unwittingly forget about FAA rules and regulations. To Vince's surprise, three are from first class, one of them an older white man married to a Filipina (or is she his daughter?). Vince watches the couple bolt out of their seats, retrieve their bags from the overhead bin, and head for the front exit door, only to be escorted back to their seats by a screaming flight attendant, who just finished reminding passengers to remain in their seats with seat belts fastened until the captain has turned off all illuminated signs.

Once a semblance of order is restored and the lead flight attendant has regained her composure, she turns the PA system back on and finishes her monologue. "If this is your final destination, we welcome you home," she says. "For those continuing on, we wish you a pleasant and a safe journey. Once again, thank you for choosing Philippines Airlines. Mabuhay."

The last word, equivalent to the Spanish "viva," prompts passengers to shout it back. Explosively. Energetically. Passionately. As if the word contained seventy million heartbeats.

Tourist Tips

- The Philippines has four seasons: hot, wet, melting, flooding.

- Annual average temperature is eighty degrees Fahrenheit. Annual average humidity is ninety percent.

- Ratio of temperature to humidity: 1:1.

- Invest in a metric conversion calculator and a dual wattage adapter; voltage in the Philippines is 220.

- Manila flees to the malls to breathe, rehydrate, take siestas.

- Bring tons of shirts and shorts.

- Do not bring a raincoat unless you're traveling during the typhoon months, from June to November. If that's the case, bring a life vest and an inflatable kayak.

- Slippers and sandals are not recommended: Manila is the capital city of 7,107 puddles and potholes.

- Manila is very rich in air pollution.

- According to the World Bank and the Stockholm Development Institute, more than ninety thousand Filipinos suffer from severe chronic bronchitis. Four thousand Filipinos die annually from it.

- Filipinos are obsessive compulsive when it comes to personal hygiene. They shower twice, sometimes three, four, five times a day.

- Invest in particle masks or protect your lungs with nicotine.

- There are loads of laundry and dry-cleaning services, like Washing Well and Let's Talk Dirty.

- Malls do not discriminate; there is a mall tailored for every class. A is elite, B is wannabe-upper, C is upper-middle, D is middle-middle, E is poor-but-not-so-poor, F is poor-enough, G is floating-on-air.

- Shanties and billboards are part of the skyline.

- Dress down for less attention; dress up for better service.

- It's not unusual for a salesperson to ask you about your marital status.

- It's not unusual for a massage therapist to ask if you prefer happy over sad endings.

- Do not be tempted: go with God, not with guys, goons, or guns.

- Blending in will not work because the locals are trying to blend in with you.

- You are a tourist and will be seen and treated as one.

- Show some class: reject with a smile.

Ambushed

"Excuse me, Mr. De Los Reyes, but you're in the wrong line. This is for returning Filipinos only," says the immigration officer, a young black Amerasian named Whitney Latishamorena Concepcion.

"But I am a Filipino. I was born here," Vince says. "It says so right there on my passport."

"You *were* a Filipino," Whitney says. "You're *now* a balikbayan with a U.S. passport. You need to stand over there with the other *forenjers.*"

Vince, confused, looks to where her finger points. There are several lines for OFWs (Overseas Filipino Workers), a VIP line for Filipino politicians, another special line for foreign diplomats, ambassadors, embassy and consulate employees. There's a rapidly thinning line for Filipino military personnel. And then there is the single and very long line marked BALIKBAYANS AND OTHER VISITORS.

"But your sign says 'Returning Filipinos.' And I'm a returning Filipino," Vince insists.

"No, you're not. You're a blue-book holder. A U.S. of A. citizen."

"In Hawaii, Filipinos don't see themselves as Americans."

"I know," she exclaims. "You're a Hawayano."

"No, I'm not."

"Then what are you?"

"I just told you. Filipino."

"Then why do you have a blue passport instead of brown?"

"What's the difference between a returning Filipino and a babalikyan, anyway?"

Whitney snickers, corrects him. "It's ba-LIK-bayan," she says. "Ba-ba-lik-yan is 'I shall return . . . eventually.' You know, as in Dugout Douglas MacArthur."

"Where on the sign does it say this line's for returning Filipino nationals only? I don't see the word 'national' on it," Vince argues.

"The sampaguita flower, sir," Whitney answers, pointing to the jasmine lei circling the word "balikbayan."

"How the hell was I supposed to know that?" Vince asks, ignoring the Greek chorus behind him ("Hurry up!" "What's taking him so long?" "Dumb American, trying to pass for a Flip.")

"If you're a true Filipino, Mr. Vicente De Los Reyes," Whitney tells him, "you'd know that the sampaguita is our national flower."

NARRATIVE DIGRESSION TO BRING YOU THIS IMPORTANT TOURIST TIP

To avoid a customs officer cutting open your balikbayan boxes and giving you the third degree for every item you bring into the country, place a five-dollar bill in your passport before handing it to him. Put a tenner, and you'll receive a "thank you" with a smile.

Vince, navigating a wobbly cartload of Louis Vuitton bags, passes through the automatic sliding doors and, for the first time in thirteen years, is assaulted by unbearable heat and humidity. He thinks he's going to faint or die from heatstroke. *Clean air,* as he writes to Edgar on one of his postcards later that evening, *is the first thing you give up in Manila. Whatever oxygen was left in my body was sucked out the minute I stepped out of the Arctic Zone–cold terminal and into the Ozone.* To Alvin: *It feels like slamming into an invisible wall and getting stuck there.* To Jing: *You need a third lung to get to the kitchen from the living room, a fourth to answer the front door, and an oxygen tank to cross the street.* And to his mother Carmen: *P.S. I am learning how to breathe with a paper bag over my head.*

It is so relentlessly hot and humid that, in a matter of minutes, the Armani sport coat is tossed carelessly across the cart's handlebar. The long-sleeved Armani shirt he wore buttoned to the neck with its tail and front ends tucked in is now unbuttoned, untucked, and so sweat-soaked that he wants to take it off and wring it out.

Is this the same airport he left thirteen years ago? The question nags at him. He scans the area for something familiar, a tangible sign from the past—a fountain, soft-drink vendors, photographers soliciting for farewell and reunion snapshots, Paul Anka airport music. Nada.

Then, suddenly, he is seized by the frightening thought that he cannot breathe, or has stopped breathing. He clutches his chest and, finding comfort in a heart beating hard and fast, he moves his cart quickly away from the sliding doors. While waiting for his heart to slow down, he watches the horde of passengers exiting the main terminal, blindly steering their cartloads of balikbayan boxes down the winding tunnel that leads to the arrivals and waiting areas.

At the arrivals area, hawkers approach Vince with warm welcomes to the Land of Smiles. They ask him if he needs his dollars changed or a car service to his destination. One even guaranteed his safety—"One hundred percent, sir"—by assuring him that their drivers carried guns for additional protection.

"No, thank you," Vince says, gesturing that he has a ride by pointing to the procession of cars, vans, cabs, and jeepneys perpetually honking their horns as porters scramble to load boxes and suitcases at a record-breaking pace.

Parking his cart in the R-S-T section, he looks out at the sea of anxious faces pressed against a fence manned by an armed guard chewing a toothpick. This is the designated waiting area, where groups of friends and family members, sometimes the size of a town, wait and scan the arrivals area for a familiar face.

Unable to find "Reyes" on any of the placards, Vince squeezes between people, briefly disrupting reunions as he proceeds to the D-E-F section, where he hopes to see a chauffeur holding up a placard with "De Los Reyes" on it. None. So he turns the cart around, about to head for the J-K-L section, when he's almost knocked down from behind by a woman. "Dingdong-*Anak,* you're back!" she cries, her arms wrapped around his waist, moisture from her breath on his arm. "I thought I lost you forever."

Vince almost passes out from the dizzying smell of gardenia perfume and old clothes. He searches around for a guard as he struggles to free himself from her clutches.

"Please, Anak," she says. "You're hurting me."

"Let me go," Vince says.

"You're hurting me, Anak!"

"I am not your son."

They stumble around, bump into people and boxes. Finally breaking free from her grasp, he pushes her away. She loses her balance and, despite hitting herself against a cart, begins crawling toward him.

Vince rushes to her. "I'm sorry," he says, aiding her back onto her feet.

"No need for sorry, Anak," she says. "I know you did not mean to."

"Oh my god," Vince says, noticing the swelling on her forehead.

"Ate Lynn!" A guard, addressing her as "Ate," or "older sister," shoves through the small crowd that has gathered to watch.

"She's your sister?" Vince asks. "Better take her to the hospital. She fell and hit her head." He is about to explain what has just transpired between them, how she had him locked in a Heimlich embrace and wouldn't let go, when she screams, "No hospital, Anak. Please. I'm all right. I am."

"There must be a clinic here in the airport," Vince says, his eyes on the hematoma that has swollen to the size of a baby's fist.

"It's O.K., sir. She's—" the guard pauses, twirls a finger by his ear.

"What?" Vince looks at her. She doesn't appear crazy, unless mistaking a person for someone else; sporting do-it-yourself hair dye, a shoulder-padded blouse, and a skirt smelling of musty cabinet drawers; and dousing oneself with a bottle of gardenia perfume are now signs of madness. "Then why is she here?" he asks, "and not at home or *in* a home?"

"No money, sir," the guard says.

"Get her out of here," Vince says, "before she gets you into trouble."

"Dingdong-Anak, why are you sending me away?" she asks.

"Ate, stop it. He's not Dingdong," the guard says. "Wala na si Dingdong."

"Dead?" she laughs. "Bulag ka ba? Can you not see him? He's right here, in front of our eyes."

"Why does she insist I'm her son?" Vince asks, horrified at the realization that he's being mistaken for somebody dead.

"Because you have his face," the guard says.

"Let's go home, Anak," she says.

"Ate, he's not Dingdong," the guard says, pulling his sister back as she reaches her hand out to Vince, who nearly backs into a stack of balikbayan boxes.

"He's taller than Dingdong," the guard says, unconvincingly. "His hair's too brown. And his nose is too straight."

She eyes Vince up and down. "Don't lie to me. I know he is my son," she says.

"But I'm—" Vince says, distracted momentarily by the sight of Esther, the caregiver from Maui, scanning the crowd in the waiting area.

"Smile, sir," the guard says.

"What?" Vince says, not sure if he's heard him correctly.

"Please smile, sir."

Vince complies.

"See, Ate," the guard says, "he's only got a dimple on one side."

"You're right," she says, then, to Vince: "Impostor!"

"You better get her out of here," Vince says.

A guard brandishing a firearm and acting as if he belongs in a combat zone approaches them. "Is she causing trouble again?"

"No trouble. Slight misunderstanding, that's all, officer." Vince's words seem to have gone in one ear and gotten lost there, because the guard just grabs the woman by the elbow and yanks her out of the scene, while her brother pleads with his coworker for mercy.

With the crowd thinning and no signs of the chauffeur anywhere, Vince turns his attention back to Esther, who is waving frantically and shouting "Rina, Rina" to a woman standing beside two boys. They must be Benjamin and Jasper, he thinks.

Rina hisses to the guard and points Esther out to him. The guard tells them they've got five minutes before letting them past the gate. But the two boys refuse to budge, they cling to her skirt. Rina scolds them, points her finger at Esther, reminds them who she is, hurry, it's getting late.

"Benjamin! Jasper!" Esther opens her arms to her sons, who are being forced by their aunt to hug their mother who, through all these years, appeared only in their memory as a name mentioned in passing, a face in photographs surrounded by familiar faces. Vince watches the two boys clinging to their aunt, the way Vince had once wrapped his arms around the leg of his grandfather's pants, not letting go until Don Alfonso promised to visit him in Hawaii.

It is not because of shyness that Esther's sons are not rushing to meet her embrace, Vince tells himself. It is fear and doubt and disbelief and, above all, disappointment. Disappointment because the mother who is awaiting her much-deserved recognition from them is not the same mother they have created and re-created in their dreams, the mother they came to know as Mother of Matriculation Fees, Mother of Christmas and Birthday Gifts, Mother of Drums and Toy Guns, Mother of Leather Buckled Shoes and Skateboards, Mother of Domestic Helpers and Caregivers, Mother of Departures Terminal, Mother of Homecoming. No. The woman they are being forced to approach is only a stand-in, an apparition of the mother of their imagination. She is merely a messenger who, after seven years, has finally shown up to validate her absence in their lives. And it is this absence, which they have grown accustomed to, that, at that moment, is making them rebel against what they can no longer deny: Esther is their mother, she is of their flesh and blood, and she has exchanged them in the name of sacrifice, in the name of survival, in the name of a semblance of a promising future, another kind of hope. Who are they going to trust? Vince asks. Their imagination that has remained loyal to them all these years, that has stuck beside them and helped them give life and voice to gifts and photographs? Or this flesh-of-their-flesh, blood-of-their-blood woman who is asking them for a mere embrace?

Vince tightens his grip on the cart. He turns his face in the opposite direction, only to be assaulted by his own memory, back to Honolulu International Airport, 1978, when he, Alvin, and Jing nearly spent their first night in Hawaii at the airport, waiting for their parents to show up and claim them inside an office crammed with lost and found items. Park Marlene explained their situation to the woman manning the desk. The woman had stopped typing to look at the three De Los Reyes children. "You kids stay here with Auntie Ida," Park Marlene told them. "No make any kind trouble now. I give you Coke when I come back, o.k.? o.k." The woman pointed to the balikbayan boxes stashed in the corner. "Wait over there," she said, and resumed her typing. Overhead, Vince heard his parents being paged: "Carmen and Ronaldo De Los Reyes, please approach any of the Philippine Airlines counters." An hour later, their mother showed up, by herself. "Those are mine," she said, pointing at her children. "I can't release them," the woman said, standing up from her desk. "I need to see proper identification first."

Ode to Fellini

Twilight. The worst time to be traveling in Manila. Vince is in the back-seat of a blue Toyota that has come to a standstill in the fifth lane of a two-lane road marked "Expressway."

"Can you blast the air conditioning?" Vince asks, fanning himself with his complimentary copy of the in-flight magazine and ignoring the procession of pushy vendors rapping on his window, enticing him with everything from pickled mangoes and Coke sold in plastic bags to hand and facial towels to bottled water to cigarettes sold by the stick to candies to dustrags made from leftover fabric.

The driver, who showed up at the airport an hour late, apologizes, says this is as strong as the air conditioning can get.

A peanut vendor parks his pushcart beside Vince's window and lifts the lids of three plastic buckets containing garlic-roasted, boiled, and salted nuts. Again, Vince shakes his head.

Unable to bear the heat inside the cab, Vince rolls down his window only to raise it back up when three children—all naked and covered in dirt and sores—refuse to take his no for an answer. With their sad and sleep-deprived faces—one of them is cradling an infant in her arms—they plead with him to buy the strands of jasmine wilting in their hands. *Sampaguita, sir, five pesos lang.*

"Could you please tell them to go away?" he asks, scooting to the center of the cab's seat.

The driver leans over to roll down his window and, in Tagalog, sends them away with coins in their palms.

In the rearview mirror, Vince sees the flashing red light of an ambulance with the paramedic's head stuck out its window. The thought of fighting for his life inside an ambulance stuck in gridlock makes him want to climb out of the cab, stretch his arms and legs out, birdlike, and fly away from the aggressive vendors, the amputee beggars, the wilting flowers, the soot and sadness.

Fly away. Soar straight for eternity. As in the opening of *8 ½,* his favorite Fellini film starring Marcello Mastroianni as Guido Anselmo, the philandering director afflicted with creative block and mid-life crisis. Vince's version, however, differs from Guido's because Guido actually escapes by climbing out of the car window and flying above the congestion until he's roaming with the clouds.

For Vince, escape is impossible. He is stuck in the backseat of a four-door blue Toyota, perspiring, suffocating, conjuring up another movie in his head to keep his anxieties at bay.

"Can I smoke?" Vince asks.

The driver turns off the air conditioning and rolls his window down.

Vince does the same but only halfway down. As he smokes, he gazes out the window at a food stand on the sidewalk. A girl dunks bananas in a wok of hot oil while another swats flies above a pan of skewered, sugar-coated bananas.

"Sir." A boy is trying to push Vince's window down. Startled, Vince pulls himself away and is about to roll it up when a blind man motions the child to move on.

"Where are we?" Vince asks.

"Parañaque, sir," the driver answers.

"Still?"

"Welcome to Manila, sir."

The cab moves, then stops after five seconds, affording Vince another frame of a day in the life of Gloria's Eat & Run: a two-star eatery that consists of vinyl-covered tables, plastic chairs, and a long bench facing the counter on which a row of covered, heated pots containing today's dishes is guarded by a ponytailed woman holding an industrial-sized flyswatter. A bare-chested man finishes a bottle of San Miguel beer and gets up from the bench he shared with three boys in school uniforms.

Another frame: a teenager, sporting a tattoo of Christ with a crown of thorns on his bare back, rubs into his armpits Tawas, a white powder used either as a deodorant substitute or for relieving cold sores.

Squeezing its way around a bus that has stalled in the middle of the highway, the cab goes through a series of potholes and makes a sudden left turn. Vince nearly bites his tongue off, shouting, "Look out!" to the driver, who swerves just in time to avoid hitting a girl shampooing her hair on the curb.

At a gate marked UNITED MULTI-NATIONAL VILLAGE, a guard signals their vehicle to slow down.

"This is Sir Vince De Los Reyes," the driver says to the guard, then adds that Vince will be staying at so-and-so's townhouse for the next ten days.

"Good afternoon, sir," the guard smiles.

The iron gates open and the cab coasts along tree-lined streets named after revolutionary heroes, horoscope signs, and positive attributes, like Mabait (Well-behaved) and Magalang (Respectful). Vince rolls his window down and is surprised to be greeted by fresh air, as if the subdivision were another country, in another time. The cab passes row after row of mansions with grassy lawns and iron-grille gates, mansions hidden behind walls that, like the walls that circle the enclave, are crowned with broken glass and barbed wire.

BLACKOUTS

Hanging above the couch in the living room is a tapestry of a Chinese-looking naked man and woman, emerging from two giant bamboo trees. Beside them, a fowl with colorful wings.

"Is that Elvis and Priscilla?" Vince asks.

"No, the owners of this townhouse," the driver says, as he drops his bags on the tiled floor. "They are in Yugoslavia, praying to Our Lady of Medjugorje."

"They look very familiar," Vince says.

"The man is the first cousin of President Aquino but is a Marcos loyalist," the driver says. "They own the Joji's Kamayan Restaurant chain here and in the States."

Vince nods. Joji's Kamayan Restaurant. Frequent sponsor of Filipino American social events in Hawaii, including U.S.–Philippine Friendship Day, scholarship pageants, and beauty contests, like Mister Pogi.

"Aning! Aning! Sir Vince is here," the driver calls out.

Aning doesn't answer, so the driver slides open the shoji screen doors of the bedroom. "Hoy, Aning, wake up na!"

Stretched out across the futon in the dark is Aning, her feet dangling from the off-white mattress.

"Oh, excuse me, sir," she says, climbing out of bed, the top of her head grazing the ceiling. "How was your trip? Turbulence-free ba? Are you hungry? You want to eat? There's fried chicken with banana sauce. I can heat it up in the micro if you want. You want?"

"Are you the cook?" Vince asks.

"No," Aning says. "I'm your maid. But I only work part-time. Twelve to four lang. Today is an exception, of course. Follow me." She pushes a door open and motions Vince to enter the bathroom. "Everything is in good working condition, except for the shower." She points to the showerhead covered with plastic and fastened with rubber bands. "It's broken.

But that's all right because the giant bin is filled with water. I just changed it this morning. If you want to take a hot shower, you have to boil water pa. So never mind na lang. Besides, it's so hot outside and another besides: cold showers are good for you. They wake you up faster than instant Nescafé. Let's see. What else? Oh yes, blackouts."

"Blackouts?"

"Yes, blackouts," Aning repeats. "There's no electricity from ten in the morning to three p.m., and again from two a.m. to five a.m. So, if I were you, best na lang to spend your days at the mall. Too hot in here. You might get heatstroke. For running water, the times are different."

"Are you serious?"

Aning laughs. "It's 1991, Sir Vince. We're still in the heart of the Dark Ages. In this country, water shortage goes hand in hand with power outage, revolution with Midnight Madness sales. Don't worry, there are lots of candles with matching candelabras here. The matches are in one of the kitchen drawers. I think there's also a flashlight somewhere in the house. You might need to replace the batteries, though."

She closes the door, looks at herself in the mirror on the wall by the dresser. Vince looks at the unmade futon. It's been almost a day and a half since the last time he laid down, including the eighteen-hour time difference.

"If you have any questions, Easy-Page or call me. The fax machine only accepts faxes but you can make local calls from it." Aning pauses to paint her lips. "My number is on the pad, right on top of the aparador, next to the stack of postcards. You can have them if you want. Our last guests forgot them. German real estate investors from Düsseldorf. They own five or six resorts in Boracay. And oh, I almost forgot. There's a fax for you from Hawaii. It came this morning. From a Mr. Edgar Ramirez, I think. Anyway, I better get going. Don't want to spend the next ten years in traffic. I'll be back tomorrow."

"What about the driver?" Vince asks.

"What about him?"

"Is he going to drive me around Manila?"

"He's not your chauffeur; he's only my husband."

"Then who's driving me to the event tomorrow?"

"Taxi," she says.

"Can I call for one?"

"You can try, but it's faster if you walk to the gate and hail one your-self. Don't worry, Sir Vince, if there are two things this country never runs out of, they're entertainers in the government and taxicabs. Oh, we'll go na. You look like you're ready to pass out. Sleep tight and dream many dreams, Sir Vince. You're in the Philippines now."

KALEIDOSCOPE

Despite two electric fans whirring overtime to produce false comfort, Vince is unable to sleep. He walks into the kitchen and opens the refrig-erator door, his body almost pressing against the wire shelves. From the pink pitcher labeled POTABLE, he pours a glass of iced water and sits at the table, leaving the refrigerator open. Curious at the three-ringed design superimposed on the table's checkered cloth, he rubs his forefinger on it. He sniffs it, is reminded of Silver Swan soy sauce, patis, bagoong (fermented shrimp), and Customs Officer Nishimura Blaine's upper lip curling over his mustache as he sliced open Vince's dead-shark-smelling balikbayan box at the Honolulu International Airport thirteen years ago. But it is while spotting Judas Iscariot and Jesus Christ inside the 3-D portrait of the Last Supper that hangs between a giant wooden spoon and a fork that he is reminded he is not having a nightmare: he is definitely inside a Philippine kitchen, where the kalei-doscopic, complex, dialectical, incongruous, and illogical-but-very-logical Filipino psyche thrives.

So to bide time, he inspects the cupboards, filled with everything his internist, Dr. Lawler, has forbidden him to eat: pyramid stacks of Reno's liver spread, Libby's corned beef hash, SPAM, Mami instant noodles, Pure Foods corned beef, Silver Swan soy sauce, and Knorr's chicken noodle soup (fortified with vitamins, minerals, and MSG).

Vince crosses the living room, passing the couch cocooned in plastic, the fourteen-inch Phillips television with its manufacturer's label still on the monitor, and the hole-in-the-wall makeshift altar, crammed with plaster saints and a tiny reproduction of Michelangelo's *Pietà* beside it. He stops in front of the authentic Yamaha baby grand, pecks a key on it, and knows right away that it was last tuned during the Commonwealth period, circa 1935. He returns to the bedroom, opens the envelope containing Edgar's fax to him. *Vince, wet dreams come true at Leche. Check it out. It's in Pasay City. Always, Edgar from the grapevine.*

MANILA

Edgar,

10 p.m. Practically writing this inside the fridge because it's hell in the living room with its tapestries and Persian rugs. Everything there is wrapped in plastic, wall clock included. Even hotter in the bedroom, which feels like a mausoleum. I've forgotten how sticky this place gets. Already had three showers in the past two hours. But can't complain really; it's a change from purgatorial Honolulu.

In the heat of the wrong kind,
Vince
P.S. They call me "Sir" here.

Edgar Ramirez
1586 Murphy St.
Honolulu, HI 96819

DR. JOSE RIZAL, MARTYR AND PHILIPPINE
NATIONAL HERO.

*10:45 p.m. Remember La Saraghina in Fellini's
8½? Big-boned, bushy-haired whore who lives
in a shack on the beach and dances the
rhumba for Catholic schoolboys? Anyway,
refresh your memory and you'll get a sense of
what my maid looks like. She's sort of a maid.
Caught her napping on my bed when I got
home from the airport. Her husband's a
chauffeur but not mine. Btw, they drive f-ing
crazy here. No regards for pedestrians. None
whatsoever.*

Praying for sleep,
V

Edgar Ramirez
1586 Murphy St.
Honolulu, HI 96819

MOUNT APO, DAVAO

*1:30 a.m. Still can't sleep. Guess whose
townhouse I'm staying at? Owners of Joji's
Kamayan Restaurant. As in "Name 'Em, We
Cook 'Em, You Dig 'Em." Proud sponsor of my
greatest embarrassment. Thanks to you. I guess
this is where they accommodate the titleholders.
It's near the airport, inside a subdivision that
makes you think you're not in Manila at all,
until you smell the burning trash and hear the
karaoke stereo blasting next door. Thirty more
minutes, then electricity goes out.*

*Vince,
in Barrio Insomnia*

Edgar Ramirez
1586 Murphy St.
Honolulu, HI 96819

THE PHILIPPINE EAGLE

*3 a.m. Fell asleep until the dogs started
howling because the electricity came back an
hour before it was supposed to. Good sign, no?
Or maybe there's a schedule but nobody follows
it, like the traffic signs. And judging from
my first joyride this afternoon, sidewalks
and crosswalks exist, but definitely not
for me. Shit. Just what I need right now:
an orgy of cats on my corrugated tin roof.*

Vince
*P.S. Like this eagle in captivity is exactly how I
feel right now.*

Edgar Ramirez
1586 Murphy St.
Honolulu, HI 96819

Son of Brando

Pagsanjan Falls, Laguna. South of Manila.

Asians, Americans, and Europeans dangle naked from the branches of balete trees.

In the shallow part of the river—more brown and white people impaled on bamboo stakes.

Strewn along a moss-covered pathway that leads to the mock temple are decapitated heads sheltered from the sky by cutout cardboard boxes. One of them is Vince's mother. Beside her are Alvin and Jing, fanning her vigorously with folded newspapers and, when nobody is looking, stuffing her mouth with water, rice, and shrimp paste.

Daylight disappears inside a cave lit by a kerosene lamp. Vince, Alvin, and Jing as children, laughing while they smear each other's faces and bodies with blood and toothpaste. Out of nowhere, Don Alfonso appears and begins talking more to himself than to them about forms and shadows.

In the dark, the three siblings hold their breath as they listen to him recite the first lines of a T. S. Eliot poem. He is the shadow they pray to. They are his children. His jungle bastards.

Steps along a river's edge. Children, women, and men wearing tribal costumes stop whatever they're doing and bow to Vince when he passes them. Vince is all grown up now, an owner of a five-star resort where Brando's kingdom once stood.

Sunburnt tourists pose beside giant stones carved into Cambodian faces. They're here to see the remains of a Hollywood war epic.

A hippie-looking photographer with ten cameras around his neck takes a snapshot of Vince. Vince walks up to him, grabs him by his Banana Republic collar. "Take my picture again," Vince says, "and I will throw you to the tigers. Intiendes?"

A boatman in a dugout canoe waves to him, motions him to wait, and points to the bare-chested man he is ferrying across the river. The man is wearing green cargo shorts; a dog tag hangs from a silver chain around his neck.

"I'm Martin Sheen," he tells Vince.

"I know who you are," Vince cuts him off. "I was there when you split my old man open with a machete." Noonday sun beats down on them. Sweat washes the dirt down Sheen's face.

"I was only following orders," Sheen says.

"You're not a soldier. You're a robot who wanted to play hero for a day. Assassin to an assassin." Vince looks into Sheen's eyes—sometimes green, sometimes blue. "But it was you," he says. "Of all his savages, it was you he chose to finish him off."

"He was going mad."

"You think so? No, man, he was a poet."

"Poet?"

"My old man had Eliot coming out of his ass. You knew that. Poetry was his third lung. He couldn't live without it. But he expected his savages to do the same. You actually did us a favor."

Vince lights a Marlboro, offers Sheen one. Sheen takes it, smokes it like a joint. "So what brings you back?" Vince asks. "Another monkey-see-monkey-do mission?"

Sheen shakes his head no. "It's this fucking place," he says. "I can't get it out of my blood."

"What about Hollywood?"

"Sucks. I'm thinking of going to prime time."

"You plan on staying long?"

"Maybe. I'm thinking of putting everything down, you know, in a book."

"Then stay as long as you want. I'll upgrade your room to the Napalm Suite."

Sheen yawns.

"Better get some rest."

Sheen bows to him before turning away to climb the steps up to the hotel. Vince calls the boatman. "I want his head as a bookend by twilight."

A dusty road. Bataan. 1945.

Vince is a nine-year-old informant for the U.S. Army. Under a burning sun, he and the barrio kids watch American and Filipino soldiers drag their war-ravaged bodies in two columns along a dusty road. One column is for the American soldiers and is headed by John Wayne, the other, led by Anthony Quinn, is for Filipino guerrillas.

A Filipino carrying his entrails drops to the ground.

Children start counting to see how long it'll take a Japanese soldier to rush over to the prisoner of war and end his misery. Four.

Next, an American wobbling on crutches decides to give up. A buck-toothed soldier orders him to rise. By the count of seven, he pulps his head with the butt of his rifle.

A tank approaches and temporarily breaks up the procession, flattening those too weak to move to the side.

A soldier in tattered fatigues and a bowler hat catches Vince's attention. He is waddling to and fro between the G.I.s and guerrillas.

Vince recognizes the matching paste-on mustache and brows, the cane in lieu of a rifle. "Lolo Al," Vince calls out. "Get in line. Quick."

"But which one?" his grandfather asks. "Filipino or American?"

"Doesn't matter."

"Of course it does."

"Hurry, Lolo Al, hurry," Vince says, his eye on the Japanese soldier running toward them, the blade of his bayonet glinting under the sun.

BOOK III

THE BLACK NAZARENE, QUIAPO CHURCH

Jing,
Can I blame it on Black Jesus? Or that
genius, F. F. Coppola? Can I blame it on
Holly-fucking-wood? The hot-and-cold war?
The jungles of Mindoro and Isabela?
Postcard-perfect river of Pagsanjan? The
Philippines as the prime location for a
silver-screen war zone. Stand-in for
Cambodia; Xerox of Vietnam. No. I blame
it on our grandfather for taking us to the
movies, and the movies for lying so well.

See you soon,
Vince of the Jungle

Jing De Los Reyes
513 North Kuakini
#6
Honolulu, HI 96817

Tourist Tips

- The best way to get around Manila is by taxi.

- Fares are so cheap, taxi drivers have a name for it: highway robbery.

- When riding the cab, make sure the meter is on.

- An alternative mode of transportation is the jeepney. There are gazillions of them, which is why traffic is so bad. Stick to cabs.

- Tip the driver generously and he will be indebted to you.

- Filipinos practice the concept of utang na loob, or debt of gratitude. "Utang" is "to owe"; "loob" is "the interior" or "from inside."

- It is the act of generosity and not the monetary value that can never be fully repaid, regardless of whether the gesture is genuine or not.

- Servitude, kinship bondage, emotional blackmail—all have their roots in utang na loob.

- Feudalism still exists in the provinces and in the enclaves of Metro Manila.

- Filipinos are governed by values, like "amor proprio" ("love of self") and its antithesis "hiya" ("shame").

- "Walang hiya!"—or "having no shame"—is one of the worst insults you can give to a Filipino. It can lead to ostracism or murder-suicide.

- Another phrase to avoid is "Putang ina mo!" ("Your mother's a whore!"), which should not be confused with Lutong Ina Mo ("Your mother's a great cook!"), a popular bar and grill.

CCP, or Complexion-Conscious Pinoys

Far is a long, long way to run. Sew, a needle pulling thread. La follows. Then ti with jam and brake and toot toot and putang ina and putang ina mo rin and leche and leche ka rin and puck you and puck you too and madapaka sana motherpucker.

Traffic—or trapik!—is one of Manila's worst nightmares, right behind dengue mosquitoes, cronyism left from the Marcos era, and shabu (crystal meth). A recent study conducted by the Ministry of Transportation and Public Roadworks shows that an alarming number of Filipinos die each year from highway fatalities. Researchers predict that by the year 2001, highway fatalities caused by speeding, panic attacks, passive-aggressive driving, and road rage (known to the locals as "drive-amok") will become the leading cause of death in the capital, overtaking cardiac arrest, hypertension, respiratory diseases, and dengue fever.

Motorists, however, argue that the main reason why so many are crushed, pinned, and accordioned to death is because the roads are full of holes, the lines dividing the lanes need to be repainted, and those damn traffic lights are mere decorations that get turned on only twice a year: in December and in July for the Christmas in July Midnight Madness sale.

To combat the problem, the Ministry of Transportation and Public Roadworks produced a series of government-paid TV ads promoting highway safety and tolerance. All featured the movers and shakers of Philippine society—basketball players and showbiz personalities from the film, TV, and recording industries, a third of whom are seeking political seats in the upcoming '92 election.

What happens, though, when the gauge of patience points to E and no one has moved an inch?

SPUR

It is the tattoo of a cockfight on the cabdriver's right arm that takes Vince's mind away from the traffic and the unbearable heat inside the Nissan compact. The tattoo is that of a golden rooster puncturing his opponent's throat with the razor-sharp spurs attached to his legs. Vince is fascinated by the look of triumph caught in midair, amazed at how beautifully the largest organ of the body can become a canvas for blood and champions, for such brutal and smooth killing.

From the driver's earlobe, Vince's gaze travels down to his nape, his brawny shoulders, his hairless arms, and lingers at his finger circling the can of Coke in the console. He picks it up and shakes it. Empty.

The driver clears his throat, asks Vince in Tagalog if he can smoke. But Vince is too preoccupied with glancing at the laminated ID of Dante Vasquez that's clipped onto the visor. His voice is a knot beneath his sternum.

Voyeurism, like meditation, requires great concentration. And Vince has mastered it. Nothing distracts him from drinking the man in with his eyes. Not the cardiac-arrest-inducing horns of hand-me-down buses from Japan and Korea. Not the screaming lungs of vendors and malnourished children waltzing through the traffic. Not the radio's latest techno-sampled version of Anne Murray's *You Needed Me*, recorded by a Filipino band working in a hotel lounge in Seoul.

Dante asks again if he can smoke.

Vince raises his face to one of the seven rearview mirrors and looks into Dante's eyes. "Go ahead," he says.

Rolling down his window, Vince pitches his embarrassment out. It lands on the sidewalk, where a scrawny man in boxer shorts is soaping himself. Behind him—more squatters residing on a construction site that, according to a huge sign, will soon be joining the many condominiums lined up along Roxas Boulevard. Some are living in tents, others inside drainage pipes.

Dante's "pssst-pssst" sparks a race among the vendors, shirts wrapped over their heads as protection against the heat and soot.

"Three sticks nga," Dante tells a vendor. Then, "You want Hope cigarette, sir?"

"No, thanks." Vince prefers to smoke his own brand.

A Paula Abdul song comes on the radio and gives Vince instant spine shivers. "Promise of a New Day" reels him back to what is now the most humiliating moment of his life. Performing with four other twenty-something Filipinos to a medley of Paula Abdul dance tracks in the opening song-and-dance number of the Mister Pogi pageant. As choreographed by none other than his best friend Edgar.

"Can you please change the station?" Vince asks.

Dante switches the dial to 1050 DZZM, Manila's only Pinoy radio station.

"What are those over there?" Vince points an unlit cigarette at a series of Zen-like buildings.

Dante takes a deep drag, blows a menthol-flavored response. "That, sir, is the CCP complex."

THE QUEEN & I

The idea of building a cultural center on reclaimed land from Manila Bay was first conceived by the Philippine–American Cultural Foundation. Imelda Marcos, who was then-Governor of Metro Manila and Minister of Human Settlements, took the idea and made it her own. "Imelda was familiar with the pain of abortive talent," wrote Kerima Polotan, her biographer. "She knew that many a Filipino artist died unheard because he had none to hear him, and nowhere to be heard."

Imelda needed only a few months to demonstrate to the world that a Filipina could raise thirty-five million pesos for art's sake. From her office in Malacañang Palace, she and her team of speechwriters wrote letters to world leaders, *Forbes's* top one hundred wealthiest people, the Sultan of Brunei; her impeccable penmanship soliciting donations ASAP. *P.S. Nothing is more tragic than art without a home.*

She organized benefit dinners, film screenings, ballet and opera performances, and Broadway musicals like *Flower Drum Song,* with the country's best directors and actors, who gave their services for free.

Her VIP list was composed of stockholders of San Miguel, Caltex, Jollibee, and Philippine Airlines; foreign investors such as Westinghouse; tobacco heirs; Chinese businessmen. She persuaded her friends to donate their heirloom jewelry, Amorsolo paintings, silver and chinawares, and antiques for an auction. She charmed her dear friend, fashion czar Caloy Romero, to design butterfly-sleeve gowns for a fashion show. In return, she thanked her donors and volunteers by throwing them 'til-break-of-dawn soirees at Manila Hotel, entertaining her guests with her singing and dancing.

JOHN & MARSHA LAW

"That's the CCP?" Vince asks, recalling the numerous pictures he'd seen of the cultural center with its towering glass doors, red-and-gold carpeted lobby with three hanging chandeliers, and an orchestra pit that Imelda wanted to equal or surpass Lincoln Center's.

"Where's the Film Center?" Vince asks.

"At the back, sir," Dante says, "next to the Philippine Plaza hotel."

Vince had read about the infamous Film Center in a cross-discipline course called "Filming Literature" at the University of Hawaii. The Film Center was mentioned in a footnote in chapter seven of Bonifacio Dumpit's *Mr. & Mrs. John and Marsha Law,* a pastiche novel that tackled race, gender, homelessness, pop Americana, the cruelty of memory, and the contagion of myth.

Chapter seven (there were fourteen chapters altogether) opens with John Law, an American cultural attaché officer, debating whether he and his Filipino wife, Marsha, should accept the invitation from Imelda to attend the premiere of her dear friend George Hamilton's flick *Love at First Bite.* The narrator, however, gets so engrossed in discussing the controversy over the Film Center that the footnote ends up invading the chapter. (Mr. and Mrs. Law don't resolve their dilemma until the end of chapter eleven.)

If Vince remembers it correctly, Imelda herself had chosen the waterfront on Roxas Boulevard as the site for her latest complex. Her point being: with dirt and rocks, a woman can turn a body of water into the Parthenon of the Orient.

Even before construction began, she had already sent out invitations to Hollywood, Cinecittà, Bollywood, et al, for the first Manila International Film Festival (MIFF), with the set date of January 18, 1982. Eight days a week, workers labored round the clock—"That's how hardworking we Filipinos are" (Imelda)—to make one woman's delusion come true. They were given exactly seventy-seven days to build Imelda's edifice. Double-seven—favorite number of her very superstitious husband, El Presidente.

In the midst of the frenzied haste, one of the scaffoldings collapsed at about three in the morning on November 17, 1981. Over 170 workers fell into the pit amidst debris and fast-drying cement. Steel bars, ropes, shovels, and poles were thrown to them. One was miraculously pulled out of the rubble. Most were left to their entombment.

No one was allowed to enter the site until a formal statement was released, per the order of Malacañang Palace. Only Bino Boca, who rushed to the scene soon after he learned of the accident, was given access after he promised the guards walk-in parts in his next movie.

On film, Boca shot close-ups of victims crying out for help, moaning in pain, pleading for an instant death; of nuns, priests, and bystanders holding a vigil outside the construction site; of Sister Marie leading a prayer. Also included was a ten-minute clip of the anti-Marcos filmmaker interviewing a young man buried up to his torso in cement. Boca's harrowing document on the Film Center instantly became an underground hit in the Philippines, resurfacing in international film festivals as a sixty-minute documentary. Banned by the Marcos regime, the documentary, now considered a cult classic, became the most popular bootleg tape in the country, second only to the Dovie Beams sex scandal tapes.

Nine hours into the disaster, rescue teams and paramedics entered the site, with men being lowered down by ropes to crack open the cement with pickaxes. Desperate and exhausted, they resorted to electric drills, aborting that plan after blood spurted from the concrete. Noon arrived with no survivors in sight. Construction resumed later that afternoon when the foreman received a call from Malañacang Palace to remind him of the double-seven deadline.

The Film Center was completed on January 18, 1982, fifteen minutes before the seven thirty p.m. ribbon-cutting ceremony with Brooke Shields, George Hamilton, Franco Nero and other international celebrities and film representatives from thirty-five nations.

Because the Marcos regime had complete control of the press, the accident sank into the quicksand dailies of martial law. What was emphasized instead was the First Lady's vision in her welcoming speech that night. She said: "Let us inaugurate a new era in human culture . . . welcome them to the celebration of that human spirit in all of us—the spirit of creation."

The Manila International Film Festival folded after two years, presumably due to lack of funding.

"You know what else, sir?" Dante says, breaking Vince's memory of the Film Center tragedy.

"What's that?"

"I don't think the spirits want to rest, sir. Halos lahat nang mga religions in the country—the Catholics, Muslims, Iglesia ni Kristos, Born-Agains, El Shaddais—already blessed the Film Center. Last week, an Igorot priest slit the throat of a rooster and sprayed its blood against the walls. I saw it on TV. Pero wala pa rin. The place is still haunted. The spirits, sir, they don't believe in peace."

A DRAMATIC PAUSE SHATTERED BY:

"You married, sir?" Dante asks.

Vince holds up his ring finger. "Nope. And you?"

Dante flashes a gold band.

"Any children?"

"Two boys and one girl, sir."

"You look pretty young to be a father."

"I'm old na, sir. Almost thirty-eight."

"You don't look it."

"How about you, sir?"

"Twenty-three," Vince says. "I'm Vince, by the way."

"Hi, Sir Vince. I'm Dante."

"I know; I saw your badge."

"Is Vince short for Vicente, sir?"

"Yes. And Dante, please cross out the sir."

"O.K., sir. You have a nice name."

"What?"

"Vicente, sir."

"So is Dante. You named after the poet?"

"Poet? No, sir. My mother named me after Dante Rivero, the movie star she had a crush on."

"Actor or poet, Dante's still a nice name."

"So is Vicente, sir. After the Patron Saint of Judgment Day, right?"

"I guess."

NOM DE GUERRA

In the Philippines everyone had their unique way of pronouncing Vince's name:

"Bicente, do you know that Captain & Tenille love song, 'Muskrat Love'?"

"Hoy, Bicente, don't porget me when you're in the United Estates na, O.K.?"

"Ay, susmaryosep, Santo Bicente de Perrer, you're going to give me a heart attack."

Problems arose when he crossed the International Date Line:

"Aloha, Mr. Vincentay De Los Reyes, welcome to Ha-Y."

"No, not Vincentay. Vicente. Only one *n*."

"Vincent, what's the capital of North Dakota?"

"It's not Vincent, that's Van Gogh. I'm De Los Reyes."

"Venice Rays, please go to counter five."

"Venice Rays?"

"And who might you be, pretty boy?"

"Vicente?"

"Vincente?"

"No, *V. V. V.* cen, te."

"Vincente."

"Screw it. Call me Vince."

Vince: Perfect for imperatives:

"Go do the dishes, Vince."

"Vince, Anak, go to confession."

"Can I conVince you to sleep with me?"

"Hurry up and come, Vince."

"Vince."

"Nice name, Vince."

"Comes from 'Vincere.'"

"Which means?"

"Conqueror."

"But of course."

Vince: short for InVincible.

SOLILOQUY

"Sir Vince." Dante looks in one of the rearview mirrors. "What are you going to do in Malate?"

"I'm going to attend the Santacruzan," Vince answers.

"Wow. The Santacruzan? Are you in showbiz?"

"No," Vince says. "Why?"

"Because, sir, only celebrities, politicians, and socialites attend the Santacruzan in Malate."

The thought of elbowing with the rich, the famous, and the corrupt amuses Vince for a moment.

"Do you need a ride home tonight, sir?"

Vince is speechless: to say or not to say yes—that is the question. Whether 'tis nobler to say, yes, Vince. Accept the invitation and cruise.

No, Vince. Say thank you, Dante, but no.

But we're talking about the cockfight of the century here.

What do I know about this guy? He's a taxi driver by day, but he might be a shabu addict at night.

Who cares? Drughead or pusher, the guy's hot.

So? What about the consequences? Think about the consequences. Think long and hard.

That's right. Think long and hard. And thick.

That's not what I meant.

Then what am I babbling about? O.K., say he drives me home, and then what?

Then we fuck the night away. He goes home. Finis. Kaput. Tapos.

What if he returns for an encore?

Even better.

What if he starts seeing me on the side, and then one day he drives me to his home to introduce me to his wife, three children, neighbors, extended families? And then the next thing I know the entire Squatterville wants to marry me.

Stop. How do I know he's from the squatters?

I don't.

Then shut up and just sleep with him.

But what if . . . what if I fall?

Fall where?

Fall flat on my face. Thud-thud. Splat. Next thing I know, I'm paying for his children's tuition fees, going to the market with his wife, treating his mother to Duty Free, becoming godfather to his first grand-child born out of wedlock. And, after my savings are depleted, I move in with them and wake up at five in the morning to stand in line at the water pump with three plastic buckets.

For fuck's sake! It's a one-night stand. In one hole, out the other. An itch in dire need of a scratch. Think temporary.

Which leads to permanence.

Wrong! Temporary leads to repetition.

I'm gonna want *him* again and again and again.

Wrong again. I'm gonna want *it* again and again and again. It's the act, not the person.

It's the person, not the act.

It's the now, not the consequences.

When was the last time I had sex?

Six, seven months ago.

That long ago?

Rub it in.

Who was the lucky guy?

Dave Manchester.

My condolences.

And this was when?

I know, I know. I'm drier than the Sahara. Might as well get me to a convent.

More reason to take the risk. So what if Dante turns out to be an extortionist, or worse, a serial killer? At least I got laid before getting chopped.

"Sir Vince?"

"Huh?"

"How will you go home tonight, sir?"

"Cab, I guess."

"Let me take you home."

"I appreciate the offer, Dante, but I don't know what time the party will end."

"That's o.k., sir."

"But I don't want to keep you waiting all night."

"I don't mind, sir. You're new to Manila, and I don't want anything bad to happen to you. Manila is a different world at night. Best if I take you home."

"Are you sure?"

"I'm sure, sir."

"Dante?"

"Yes, sir?"

"How much are you going to charge me?"

"That depends, sir."

"On what?"

"On the meter, sir."

MALATE

Pulse of Manila. Crammed with bars, restaurants, hostels, motels, cafés, and potholes. A small fishing village during the Spanish colonial period, the name was derived from the Tagalog "maalat"—salty— because of the seawater from the nearby Manila Bay that seeped into the drinking wells.

In the 1900s, the district became a popular residential area for American families. Hence the streets were named after states that had participated in the Philippine-American War. They were changed in the sixties and seventies to Filipino revolutionary and anti-imperialist figures, like Apolinario Mabini, M. H. Del Pilar, and Julio Nakpil.

One only has to read the names of the establishments to get a feel for the place. Along Adriatico Street: the wetmarket-like Mister Piggy's, where every Friday barely-of-age boys cavort with the Robinson Crusoes of Australia, Europe, and U.S. of A. Next door to Mister Piggy's is the Library, a karaoke bar where emcees tripling up as transgenders, singers, and stand-up comics get their punchlines by ganging up on patrons in need of a makeover, a face-lift, liposuction, or skin bleaching.

Parallel to Adriatico is Mabini Street, dubbed "the Second, Third, and Fourth Coming of the Japanese" in the seventies because of the Japanese businessmen and tourists that frequented the seedy bars and eateries. Lined with Muslim-run moneychanger kiosks, pubs, and restaurants, its main attraction is the Hobbit House, a restaurant with a live band that's owned and staffed by dwarves, midgets, and people short enough to pass for either. It is also one of the few remaining red-light districts in the world that still depends on kerosene lamps because of the periodic blackouts and raids by the Morality Crusade, headed by Manila Mayor Alfredo Lim.

Along Nakpil Street and Maria Orosa Street are bars and clubs for the alternative, ergo bohemian, ergo easily persuadable groups—Rush, Vertigo, Insomnia, Sigh, Rimbaud, and Blue Café, where patrons sit on James Dean, Monty Clift, Cary Grant, and other faces of Hollywood's golden era.

And at the center of it all, where six streets intersect, is Remedios Circle, a plaza bereft of botanical landscape; its only green are the weeds that have sprung up from cracks in the pavement. It is teeming with homeless people, cigarette and chewing gum vendors, and self-proclaimed parking attendants watching parked vehicles in exchange for tips. After liberation from the Japanese, the Circle was a popular rendezvous spot for American G.I.s and Filipino male cross-dressers.

Dante makes the sign of the cross as they pass Malate Church, where women having difficulty getting pregnant go and say a novena to Our Lady of Remedios. "I'll wait for you here," he says, stopping the car beside Aristocrat's, a restaurant famous for its tripe stew.

"Thank you," Vince says, handing him several hundred-peso bills. "Keep the change," he says, praying a tip twice as much as the fare will be enough to bring Dante back to him.

Tourist Tips

- Staring is a favorite Filipino pastime. Don't take it personally. A Filipino stare can also be a compliment. Or viewed as curiosity. Or the start of a love affair.

- Staring can't kill you; otherwise, Philippine colonial history would have lasted in a blink rather than four hundred years.

- *Oops & Psst*, a lunchtime TV game show, once held a contest with twenty Filipinos trying to outstare each other. No one lost.

- Filipinos have a tendency to meddle in your personal affairs; don't take offense. It's just their Pinoy way of showing you they care.

- Try not to overreact.

- Filipinos can enter the state of juramentado—physical and emotional violent outbursts, usually leading to a homicide.

- Nothing is personal or private in the Philippines. Everything is shared, like food and secrets.

And Introducing Vince De Los Reyes

Remedios Circle is bursting with Santacruzan spirit. Café Adriatico, Tia Maria, and other restaurants have set up food and beverage stands for the occasion. Fluttering in the air are banderitas—flags and banners touting the products of the event sponsors: Block & White soap ("Blocks the sun and whitens the skin!"), Palmolive shampoo ("Special care for Asian hair!"), and Super Wheel laundry detergent ("I'd rather be beaten by a snake!"). And posted everywhere are the ubiquitous signs reminding everyone that, if caught, pickpockets will be prosecuted.

In preparation for this much-anticipated religious event, Mayor Lim evicted the vendors, squatters, and self-employed parking attendants and had the plaza barricaded to provide extra security and privacy for Manila's who's who, composed of celebrities, politicians, elites, social climbers, and anyone who could afford to pay for glamour or buy a spot in heaven. When it was ready, Remedios Circle looked as spic, span, and squatter-free as it did in 1966 when U.S. President Lyndon B. Johnson visited the capital to get President Ferdinand Marcos to send Philippine troops to Vietnam.

Vince jostles his way through the crowd, squashing toes here and muttering apologies there. He is about to step onto the red carpet when a guard seizes him by the arm.

"Red carpet is only for VIP, Boss," the guard says.

"I *am* a VIP," Vince retorts.

"Your pass, Boss."

"What pass?"

The guard draws a rectangle in the air.

"How about this?" Vince says, pulling a sash from his coat pocket with "Mister Pogi" on it.

"No can do, Boss," the guard says.

"But I'm here to participate in the Santacruzan," Vince explains. "I'm supposed to escort the queen, Reyna Elena."

"Are we speaking the same language, Boss?" the guard asks. "I make it easy for you. Three hundred pesos."

"That's blackmail!" Vince says and tries to walk past him.

"Freeze." The guard pulls a gun from his holster and points it at Vince, who quickly throws his arms up. The crowd gasps as Vince tries to motion to the guard to hold fire while he digs into his pocket for his wallet.

The guard, taking the money from him, tucks it into his pants pocket.

Are you going to give me a pass, stamp my wrist, anything? Vince is about to ask when the guard orders him to move out of the way. Vince takes cover behind a fat woman holding a huge soft-focus poster of Kris Aquino and Sister Marie. "Hoy," the guard yells at two street kids leaning against the barricade, one of them on the shoulders of the other, trying to get a glimpse of what's happening inside the Circle.

What an asshole! Vince thinks. The power a blue polyester uniform has in this country.

SANTACRUZIN-4-BRUIZIN

The Santacruzan celebrates St. Helena's journey to the Holy Land of Jerusalem. Mother of Constantine the Great, Emperor of Rome, she conducted an excavation project that led to the discovery of the Holy Cross. Legend has it that after she, in her seventies at the time, ordered one of her slaves to lie on the Cross, the chains around his ankles broke free.

With a flair for colors and music, the Indios embraced the Santacruzan festival immediately. "Coercion played a key role in converting the pagan

Filipinos to Roman Catholicism," Dumpit writes in *Decolonization for Beginners*. "Pageantry insured it."

Since then, the Santacruzan has undergone numerous appropriations. As a colorful novena procession, with a movie star or a daughter of a politician invited or chosen as Reyna Elena. As a nightlong gay beauty pageant called "Santacruzin" in the province of Pasuquin in Northern Luzon. And as an opportunity for celebrities, politicians, elites, and their social-climbing sidekicks to have their photos appear once more in the lifestyle sections of newspapers that make up ninety percent of their contents. Newspapers like the *Philippine Bulletin*, aptly named because it really is nothing but a bulletin board crammed with ads and info on the latest parties; *Daily Star*, with its focus on the glamorous, complicated lives of the rich, famous, and wannabes; and *National Inquirer*, the only circulating newspaper with a semi-interest in reporting facts with matching typos.

HAUTE COUTURE VS PRÊT-À-PORTER

Am I in a Halloween party sponsored by Geritol and Ensure? Vince thinks as he passes two matriarchs gossiping near the entrance. One is dressed in a bikini, the other a unitard too tight for her lungs; both are wearing eight-inch heels. Another in a Catalina swimsuit approaches them, flaunting science's latest achievement. "Only three thousand for each," she brags. "Silicone na, leak-free pa."

"They look so natural, Mare," the woman in the unitard says.

"As they should. I had them made in Canada." Then, soon as she leaves, the other woman quips, "She's all nipples but no heart."

Everyone but Vince is in costume. A statuesque woman in a toga and blindfold, holding a scale, is guided by a dark-skinned chambermaid. Several of them are passing off as Little Bo Beep or Mary. One looks older than Death—she is pushing a walker while her team of maids closely follows her. A woman walking around with chains around her neck, wrists, and ankles is practically naked except for a leopard-print thong and nipple-covers. Three men trying to look like Charlton Heston as Moses are carrying faux stone tablets. A couple with well-sculpted bodies in G-strings catches everyone's attention. The guy, who is a full head shorter than his companion, is wearing a feathered head-band while the woman balances a clay pot on her head.

Vince heads toward the bartenders in white long-sleeve shirts, cummerbunds, and black pants. While standing in line, he eyes one of them stacking crates of empty San Miguel bottles.

Someone taps him on the back. "Excuse me, you dropped this back there," says a voice belonging to a wispy man in a sunflower-print housedress and horn-rimmed glasses. On his head are a swarm of yellow curlers. He could be President Aquino's doppelganger. In his hand is Vince's sash, smudged with dirt and muddy footprints.

"Thank you," Vince says, folding the sash and stuffing it back into his coat pocket.

"I'm Bino Boca."

"As in the director?" Vince asks.

"One and only," Bino says. "And you?"

"Vince. Vince De Los Reyes," he says, pretending not to be starstruck.

"Thank god she's wearing a mask," Bino says, pointing his mouth to a woman wearing an off-the-shoulder flowing dress, her hair pulled back into a sumo-wrestler knot. "She's had so many face-lifts she's run out of skin."

"Who's she?'" Vince asks.

"Wife of a Chinese billionaire," Bino answers. "A recluse uglier than sin. Sad part is he knows it too. Otherwise, he'd be here barking with the mongrels. The Elephant Man saw more of the world than him."

According to Bino, she and her husband belong to the highest echelon of Manila's high society. "A is for the embarrassingly rich, ill

gotten or not," he tells Vince. "They practically own the whole country, their workers included. B is for the old rich. Many of them are
landowners who live in Tara-inspired mansions in the provinces, with
maids who come from eighteen generations of servitude. They come
to Manila now and then to remind everyone that they were the original rich, and that though they may not be as wealthy as they were in
1521, and lost the war in 1898 against the Americans, they still perpet-
uate inbreeding.

"Think of Tennessee Williams's self-deluded heroines and loboto-
mized, repressed, or cannibalized fags," Bino continues. "In fact, there's
our Bacolod version of Blanche du Bois." He points to a woman wearing a strapless dress that makes her look as if she's stepped into a sausage
casing, with French fry–like tassels peeking out of her neckline.

Vince asks who she is and for an answer gets: "A daughter of a sugar
baron. She owns the biggest collection of fake lashes in the universe.
Lashes with rhinestones, with feathers, with leather, with ceramics, with
crystals, with acrylics, with cum. The guy she's talking to is Sotto Voce,
make-up artist. If he looks like he's high on cocaine it's probably because
he is. His father's über-rich, like his über-bitch mother. Together they
own businesses from A to Z. Airlines, banks, country clubs, dampa, elec-
tronics stores—"

"Dampa?" Vince cuts in.

"Seafood market with built-in restaurants that prepare the dishes to
your liking," Bino replies.

An x-ray-thin woman with long, stiff hair and kabuki-like make-up
greets Bino with a peck on both cheeks then, absentmindedly, walks
away with her escort, a dark, tall, and handsome young man elegantly
dressed in a tuxedo.

"Bald underneath all that horse hair," Bino says. "She's from the C
group, or that frightening word 'nouveau riche.' Mostly Marcos cronies

and mistresses, like her, of men from the A or B groups. She used to be very beautiful, until she caught her six-million-dollar man sleeping with her maid, who belongs to a mountain tribe in the south. She never got over it. Now, she's just an Alzheimer's case waiting to happen."

"Who's the young guy with her?" Vince asks.

"Her son's ex-lover—a social climber," Bino says. "Belongs to the E group."

"What about the D group?" Vince asks.

"They're the untouchables," Bino says, "nobody talks or cares about them. Duller than lead. Uninteresting people, unless the issue is money. They're the professionals, managers, and entrepreneurs who run or own small-to-midsize businesses that A, B, or C would never be caught or confess to owning. Food stalls in malls, fast-food wagons, boutiques specializing in designer brands purchased from u.s. outlet malls."

An entourage all clad in black with raccoon eye make-up passes them by, smiling at Bino, who returns their greeting with a nod. "More social climbers," Bino whispers to Vince. "They're the Armani Exchange Gang. Too cheap and too poor to afford an Emporio or a Giorgio. Many of them are trying-hard wannabe newspaper columnists and fashion magazine editors. Think remora to a shark, or those doctor fish in Bangkok beauty salons that live off of the dead-skin feet of A, B, C, and D."

Vince watches them exchange kisses with the gorgeous couple garbed in his-and-her headhunting costumes. "Nothing is more spectacular than watching social climbers flock around the current mother and father of social climbing," Bino says. "Meet Charlene and Jojo Rosales, who's gayer than a Miss Universe trivia freak. That couple rewrote the book on social climbing, from the chapter 'Paris on Twenty Pesos a Day' to 'Gonorrhea Today, Rectal Bleeding Tomorrow.' You can spot the giant wife from a mile away by her fake designer bags; Muslims sell them in Greenhills, counterfeit capital of the world. Her mother's a putang klepto who makes 'mania' a tame word. Cheaper than brand X, she forced herself on a congressman who dumped her after she was caught stealing a ruby necklace at Rustan's. She was on every blind item for months as 'Ruby.'"

"And Jojo?" Vince asks.

"Jojo comes from a very interesting assembly line of social climbers. Mother's a former child actress turned mistress of a diplomat from another turd world. Sri Lanka, I think. That's why he looks Bombay. Father was a famous basketball player, hailed from the squatters of Smoky Mountain. Boy toy of Caloy Romero and Soxy Sarmiento, rival fashion designers and close friends of Imelda. Showdown took place, of all places, at a party hosted by Madame. It was so haute couture versus prêt-à-porter. Imagine two skeletal queens, one with a fork, the other wielding a butter knife, trying to stab each other, with Imelda and her upswept hair acting as referee? Truly one of the highlights of the seventies, next to the torture chambers of martial law."

"That fight was real?" Vince asks. "Didn't you put that in one of your movies?"

"Hijo, nothing in my movies is made up," Bino remarks. "That's what makes this turd world of ours so great. I don't need to stretch my imagination because imagination stretches out to me.

"Jojo used to be a model slash actor before he turned into a social-climbing polo player slash fencer slash Alliance Française member. Hopped from one CEO to another, until he bottomed for an executive— or was it his hung and hunky son? The rumor, which is really the truth passing off as a rumor, is that he almost bled to death. Had to be rushed to Makati Med. One floor closed off. He and the hospital staff who tended to him were paid off to hush the incident. While in the recovery room, he supposedly saw Jesus. That's when he became a full-fledged lesbian, which is what happens to every gay man in this country who turns Born-Again. He married that giant over there and together they sired a child who's allowed to stay home for weeks during the school year so they can tell the teachers they were on a European vacation. But to this day, he still suffers from rectal bleeding and irritable bowels. His farting and shitting can be heard in Taipei."

Vince laughs.

"I'm not kidding," Bino says. "If you don't believe me, sit in the sauna with him."

"I believe you."

Bino looks around. "Practically everyone in here is, or once was, a social climber. A, B, C, and D usually stick to their own kind. They seldom marry outside their endangered species. But these social climbers suck up to all levels. They don't discriminate because they don't know how. To them money, dirty or laundered, is money. Louis is Vuitton whether it's made in Paris or Korea. And coke is cocaine, whether it's crack or crushed aspirin. They have no prejudices because they have no shame. But, take note: they are the future of Manila's high society."

"How so?" Vince asks.

"They control the media, which means they control the image of the rich," Bino says. "You see that half-baked transvestite over there, the one wearing fake Mikimoto pearl earrings and frantically waving a fan to shoo the flies and mosquitoes he attracts? The rich, particularly the nouveaux, love him. He's the lifestyle editor for the *Philippine Bulletin*. They pay him big bucks, invite him to their homes and VIP-only parties, bring him along on their U.S. and European trips, religious ek ek pilgrimages to Medjugorje and Lourdes, Hong Kong shopping sprees, so he can feature them full-page in his paper. Perfect zero in grammar and creativity. Ergo, his section is called "Vanity Far." But gotta hand it to that faggot: he knows where to read the *New York Times* and *Vogue* for free—at the Shangri-La—and knows how to cut and paste articles.

"There's one more group left, and that's F—the mountain climbers," Bino continues. "All social climbers start off as mountain climbers. They're so desperate to be on the A-list that they're willing to climb Mount Everest naked and barefoot. You see them during typhoons rowing a kayak, or swimming in floodwaters to attend a golden wedding anniversary or the wake of a matrona. To them, ain't no mountain high enough, ain't no river swollen enough. A famous mountain climber is that faggot over there." Bino points to a man wearing a shoulder-baring magenta sweatshirt à la Jennifer Beals in *Flashdance,* long flowing pants, and so much foundation he looks embalmed. "He's the society columnist for *IN* magazine, the *Harper's Bizarre* of Manila. A photo album full of faggots and their haggots, tragic and comic reliefs."

"Is that the difference between social and mountain climbers?" Vince asks.

"No," Bino responds. "The difference is that social climbers will sleep with the rich. Mountain climbers will sleep with their pets." Pause. "You know, you could be part of the A-list. In fact, you've already got one foot in the door by virtue of being here. You really don't need much. Fair skin; an accent, preferably Australian, British, or MTV; and a couple of authentic IZOD shirts. And with your tisoy features, hijo, they'll welcome you, even in your boxer shorts, undershirt, and rubber slippers."

MASSACRE QUEEN

"Tito Bino!" It's Kris Aquino, the nation's First Daughter, wearing a gold headband, a red-white-and-blue bikini, and purple knee-high boots. She brushes past Vince, assaulting his nose with hair spray and perfume. A dozen bodyguards follow her, carrying enough ammunition to start a coup d'etat.

"Hija, why are you dressed like Wonder Woman?" Bino asks after their cheek-to-cheek greeting. "I thought we agreed on Little Orphan Annie."

"I know, but Mommy disapproved," she whines.

"Pero por que, hija?"

"She said Wonder Woman was much more appropriate and patriotic. Plus it goes great with our pro–u.s. military base stand."

"Just pray the volcano doesn't erupt. Otherwise all that ass-kissing will amount to a heap of ash," Bino says.

Vince looks at Kris and remembers the time he saw her on *Nightline,* stealing the spotlight from her mother while Ted Koppel tried to interview the housewife-turned-president on the night Marcos and his family fled the Philippines for Hawaii.

"Kris, I want you to meet Vince. I guess he's the lucky guy who'll be escorting you this year."

"Welcome to Manila Zoo," Kris says. "When did you arrive?"

"Yesterday," Vince answers.

"Vince, as you may already know, Kris is the daughter of our beloved president and the most in-demand actress in the country," Bino says.

"And I owe it all to you, Tito Bino," Kris says.

"She's also our Reyna Elena for the third consecutive year," Bino adds.

"Oh, my god. It should be I who is the lucky one. Guwapo si Vince; may dating siya. Last year's titleholder was not even half a head turner. Plus he was not a straight-acting gay," Kris says. "This must be my lucky year talaga. First, a blockbuster film, *In the Name of Shame,* and now, a cutie-pie from *Hawaii Five-O* as my escort. I'm so blessed talaga."

A woman with red hair peeking from underneath a habit approaches them. Vince recognizes her immediately.

"Hi, Sister Marie," Tito Bino and Kris say in unison.

Besso, besso. Vince gets introduced to Sister Marie. More besso, besso.

"Have you seen Jolie B?" Sister Marie asks.

"Did you try asking the Virgin Mary?" Bino laughs.

"Do you know Jolie B?" Kris asks Vince.

Vince shrugs. Too jet lagged, too uncaring to search his memory for the identity of Jolie B. Plus he still can't believe that the lead stars of the movie he saw less than two days ago are standing so close to him he can smell their hair spray. It feels more surreal and melodramatic than the movie they were in. And though he's heard from Edgar, Jing, and just minutes ago from Bino, how easy it is, especially for fair-skinned people, to hobnob with the who's who in Pinoywood, he didn't expect it to happen so soon.

"Lucky for you Jolie B isn't here yet," Sister Marie says. "She'll drive you up the wall with her British accent, imported all the way from Cebu."

"So pretentious," Kris says. "Worse than Lea Salonga."

"My dear, Lea is pretentious, yes," Bino says, "but at least she lived in the West End for a year, is currently the toast of Forty-Second Street, and is rumored to play the lead in Oliver Stone's upcoming movie about Vietnam."

"Vietnam again?" Sister Marie says. "Why does Hollywood keep hiring us to play Vietnamese whores?"

"Because their whores can't sing like ours," Bino says.

"Tito Bino, why don't you cast Vince in *Machete Dancers II*?" Kris asks. "He's got the right complexion, and the looks of an Amerasian hustler, di ba?"

"Now that you mention it Kris, yes, I can picture him as Emilio Van Nostrand, or Jeremiah Hagedorn," Bino says. "Have you done any acting, hijo?"

"Only high-school plays," Vince answers. "I played Peter in *Diary of Anne Frank* in eleventh grade, and in my senior year I was in *Guys & Dolls*."

"Wow! So you sing too?" Bino says.

"Not professionally," Vince says. "Only karaoke."

"Karaoke is good enough," Sister Marie says. "That's more than many actors here can say."

"Here's my business card," Bino says. "Call me and let's set something up."

"You mean like an audition?" Vince asks.

"Not exactly," Bino says. "More like a cold reading."

"Thank you, Mr. Boca, but—"

"Never say 'but,' hijo, until you see your paycheck," Bino says. "Besides, for all we know, you've got hidden talents."

"He's right, Vince," Kris says. "Me, myself, and I didn't know I could act until Tito Bino cast me in the lead for *Magdalena Ortiz*." Vince knows the movie because the title was so long: *God, Help Us: The Magdalena Ortiz Tragedy,* followed by a case number. He saw it with Alvin and Jing, who keeps track of the latest Tagalog films. Jing borrows them from the Filipino video store around the corner from her apartment, invites her brothers over for dinner, and makes them watch them with her.

In the movie, Kris plays a promising recording artist who gets abducted by the Ativan Gang, raped, then hacked into pieces and thrown into Manila Bay. It was a ninety-minute screamfest interrupted now and then by what would become Kris's acting trademark—a blank facial expression that contains a thousand and one conflicting emotions. She's perfected the look of a catatonic, so that one never knows if she's happy, terrified, or ecstatic, getting gangbanged or chopped. But the movie was a box-office smash and it popularized the massacre film genre, many of which starred Kris in the lead role, earning her the title "Massacre Queen of Philippine Cinema."

I THINK I'M READY FOR MY CLOSE-UP, MR. BINO BOCA

Go for it, Vince.

Why? To make an ass of myself again? No thank you. Mister Pogi was enough.

Water under the bridge.

It happened a week ago.

I know. C'est Si Bon ballroom. Pagoda Hotel. Five contestants, four titles.

It was so humiliating.

Not as humiliating as kicking a hacky sack, or boring the audience with a grueling forty-five-minute butoh dance number.

Am I trying to make myself feel better?

I wowed the crowd with my dramatic reading of Langston Hughes's "Let America Be America Again." Even the blacks, who went there to cheer for Art Johnson, gave me a standing ovation.

I still can't believe I let Edgar talk me into it.

But if I hadn't, where would I be right now?

Back in boring Honolulu, boring myself with other people's melodrama and indulging in SPAM.

I wanted to get the hell out of Hawaii.

And here I am.

In Third World Technicolor Manila.

But think of the money.

Yes. In pesos.

So? How many guys are given the chance to be in the movies?

. . .

How often do I meet a director who, upon introduction, offers me the role of an Amerasian hustler in his next movie?

He's not offering me the role. He just wants me to read for the part.

It's practically the same thing. And Bino Boca is not just some up-and-coming director. He's one of the most respected directors in the world. Even Cannes kisses his big toe.

These people come from power. They can make my stay in Manila paradise or a living hell.

So loosen up. Dreams aren't all bad.

"Maybe Vince is camera shy," Sister Marie says.

"Doesn't look it," Kris says.

"Well, there's only one way to find out," Bino says. "Kris, why don't you have Vince as a guest on your talk show?"

"What?" Vince asks.

"We really must be surfing the same waves today, Tito Bino," Kris says. "I was thinking the same thing."

"How about you put Vince on the same day as me?" Sister Marie tells Kris.

"That's a thought, Sister Marie," Kris says. "Vince, I'll have my assistant call you tomorrow or Sunday to set up a pickup time for you. Are you staying in the townhouse in Parañaque?"

"How did you know?" Vince asks.

"It belongs to Kris's uncle," Bino says.

"It's the designated lodging for balikbayan guests and pageant title-holders," Kris says.

Vince is about to turn down Kris's invitation when Sister Marie cuts him off. "Don't worry, Vince, Kris and I will guide you through."

BIO-PIC

Sister Marie E (for Espejo) gained (inter)national recognition when she defiantly marched head-on against an army tank during the EDSA Revolution (aka People Power), which led to the downfall of the Marcos regime in February 1986. A photographer for *Life* captured what eventually became the symbol of the peaceful revolution: Sister Marie charging the tank with a rosary dangling from a clenched fist. Since then, she's made headlines and done countless interviews on radio and TV programs in and outside the country, speaking against war, gender oppression, graft and corruption in the government, poverty, and capital punishment.

"I have nothing to hide. Ask me anything, Kris. And I mean anything," she told the First Daughter on her talk show. "I don't believe in secrets. I believe in one God, the Father Almighty. I believe everyone has the right to voice their opinions and concerns, to express themselves. I believe every Filipino, regardless of sexual orientation or gender, has the right to life, liberty, and the pursuit of happiness. Unfortunately, this right is exercised only by the elites, politicians, showbiz personalities like you, like me. You know, our government is always bragging that we are one of the few democratic nations in the world that still believes in freedom of speech, in equality, but really, Kris, I ask you, do we really have the right to speak our minds without a gun pressed against our temples? Are we really as equal as it says on paper?"

A strong advocate for women's and gay rights, Sister Marie is the number-one nemesis of the Roman Catholic Archdiocese in Manila, under Cardinal Jaime Sin. It all started soon after the People Power fervor died down, when she and six other Benedictine nuns joined the militant group Babaylan, headed and co-founded by novelist and leftist activist Tatyana Tolstoya (née Maria Theresa "Matet" Tolentino). Alongside über-feminists, the nuns protested outside the Japanese embassy for the war crimes committed against Filipino comfort women; the Hong Kong and Singapore embassies for the inhumane treatment of Filipina maids; and the u.s. embassy for the series of rapes of bar girls committed by American servicemen stationed at the Subic Naval and Clark Air Force bases.

"The seven feminists with loud habits," as they came to be known, gained greater media coverage when, during a radio interview about the then-controversy over condom use to fight AIDS, all said they were pro-contraceptives. The rift widened when the seven nuns, headed by Sisters Marie Espejo and Mercedes Manzano, appeared in TV commercials advocating prophylactics. This sparked a nationwide debate on the role of nuns, not only in the Catholic Church but in Philippine society.

Under extreme pressure from the Archbishop of Manila, Mother Superior Joaquina Antonio, who had served as spiritual counselor, inspiration, and role model for the seven nuns, told them, per order of the Roman Catholic Archdiocese, to either return to their vows of silence and servitude to God or, much against her wishes, leave their vocation. They chose the latter. Bidding goodbye to the elderly abbess who had infused in them the vigilant spirit they thought they never possessed, they quietly left the Benedictine girls' school that had produced the country's first female president, first female Supreme Court justice, and first Miss Universe.

They moved into a two-story house located in the university district of Pedro Gil and turned the downstairs room into an office and the three rooms upstairs into sleeping quarters. As with Philippine politicians whenever they got tired of switching parties, the seven feminists in habits, with financial backing from their followers (comprised mainly of gays, old maids, and the embittered wives of philanderers), created their own order: JOAN, after Joan of Arc, Patron Saint of Warriors.

Released from the fetters of the Catholic order, they became even more aggressive in their drive against oppression, poverty, corruption, and human rights violations during the Marcos regime as well as the current Aquino administration. Once pro-contraceptive, now pro-choice; once gay-friendly, now staunch supporters of gay rights. They formed alliances with a sister organization, the U.S.-based Leadership Conference of Women Religious (LCWR), known for their leftist leanings, radical definitions of love, empowerment of women, and endless anti-war and anti–capital punishment protests. And though they are not—and will never be—recognized by the Vatican, the Joans have amassed a strong and devout following for their three-year-old order.

"Oh, we can't be bothered with Cardinal Sin," Sister Marie told reporters in response to the rumor that the Archdiocese of Manila was going to excommunicate her and the six other nuns. "Please lang. I'm not scared of anybody. I eat death threats for breakfast, for crying out loud."

Against the advice of President Aquino, a staunch supporter of the cardinal, her daughter Kris invited the nun to guest on her daytime talk show *PM Talking with Yours Truly*. "From Province to Providence" was the title of the segment in which Sister Marie shared her harrowing experience of moving to Manila from her province up north. "I had just graduated from high school, Kris. I had just turned sweet sixteen," she smiled. "For months I was jobless, roofless, a faceless wanderer in Manila. I thought I was going to die from hunger or go crazy."

"Ay, how sad naman your past life, Sister Marie," Kris jumped in.

"I couldn't return to my province empty-handed. I didn't want to disappoint my family."

"So you sold your soul to the expats and Japanese in Ermita?"

"My body, but not my soul. I had to, Kris. I was surviving on Juicy Fruit and Mentos."

"And then you met Mother Superior Joaquina Antonio from Saint Scholastica."

"She saved my life, Kris," she said, pausing to look up. "Mother Superior, I know you are watching me from above. I just want to say thank you."

On the day of her guest appearance, Vice President Salvadore "Doy" Laurel also dropped by Kris's talk show to bid farewell to the tens of thousands of overseas contract workers leaving the country that week. "And for you young Filipinas who are preparing to embark on a dirty, difficult, dangerous, and maybe even demeaning journey, keep Sister Marie in mind. Imbibe her fighting spirit and know that you are not alone. God bless, and more power to you."

Sister Marie's personal narratives inspired artists throughout the country. Playwright/screenwriter Rimbaud Woo penned *The Mirror in Ermita*. The play became an instant hit—one of the most successful in Philippine history, second only to Severino Reyes's *Walang Sugat*. Sister Marie's life was an open book. Serialized in komiks; adapted into a telenovela; made the subject of student theses and official entries to international film festivals, docudrama division.

The masses idolize Sister Marie and view her, like Dr. Jose Rizal, Senator Ninoy Aquino, and other martyrs that came between them, as a saint, for she too is willing to die fighting for equality and human rights in this upstairs-downstairs country, where justice is owned by the privileged few and the average daily wage is equal to the price of a McDonald's Happy Meal.

NUNCHALANT

Sister Marie will lead the Santacruzan procession minus Jolie B Rizal, the British-accented actress, who paged the nun at the last minute to tell her that she couldn't make it because she had to investigate a possible Virgin Mary sighting, so go ahead and start the procession without her.

"We love you, Sister Marie!" The nun waves to her fans crammed onto the narrow sidewalk, their view of the living legend blocked by the Philippine National Police force hired to protect the country's First Daughter. Above them, from behind the iron-barred windows of pensiones and Spanish-influenced colonial mansions, more fans and potential assassins wave, take pictures, throw confetti.

There are two columns of men, women, and children with strapped-on wings. They're all holding lit candles. Between them are teenage boys carrying wooden arches festooned with flowers for the Santacruzan beauties and their escorts to march under.

"In the name of the Father, and of the Son, and of the Holy Spirit. Amen. I *believe* in God," Sister Marie prays as she heads the procession.

"*Hail!* Holy Queen, *Mother* of Mer*cy,* our life, our sweetness and our hope. To you do we *cry,* poor *ba*nished chil*dren* of Eve," the marchers answer.

At the tail end of the procession are Kris (as Reyna Elena) and Vince (as her son Constantino, Emperor of Rome). They are surrounded by a dozen bodyguards surveying the area and aiming their Armalites at people armed with rosaries and cameras.

Vince pretends to lip the Joyful Mystery—the Hail Marys, the Our Fathers, and the Glory Bes that get repeated numerous times throughout the rosary. When he was an altar boy in San Vicente, he memorized all the prayers and sometimes led the novena. He could explain the difference between Joyful and Sorrowful Mysteries. Which mystery involved the agony in Gethsemane and which dealt with a coronation.

When he moved to Hawaii, he got hooked on disco, worshipped the lord of two-toned polyester suits, John Travolta, spent Friday and Saturday nights dancing with Edgar at America, a discotheque for young kids. He conversed in standard English with a minimal Filipino accent, so he could talk his way out of the plantation of stereotypes and discrimination.

The eighties arrived and everything changed. Travolta was revolting in *Staying Alive.* Gonzo was elected the fortieth U.S. president. AIDS magnified Americans' bigotry and hatred for each other. In the De Los Reyes' residence, Vince's parents continued to show Vince, Jing, and Alvin the different ways to hate and hurt people you once cared for.

The days of touch dancing were numbered.

And now, it's the dawn of the nineties and where is he? Right back where he started, in the Philippines, holding the First Daughter's clammy hand, lipping a fragmented prayer, and wondering what the hell he got himself into, and how in the world is he able to recall the past and avoid potholes at the same time.

"Turn then, O most gracious advocate, your eyes of mercy toward us; and after this our exile," Sister Marie prays.

In the middle of Taft Avenue, the procession is disrupted by the sight of a jeepney smashed against a post. Vince is ready to give up the spotlight and either go cool himself in the walk-in freezer of the nearby Goldilock's bakery or hire a pedicab to take him back to the Circle, where he'll conclude his praying over a cold drink, straight up, anything on the rocks, followed by a night of dancing and, hopefully, sex.

With all the Hail Marys, Our Fathers, and Glory Bes he's muttered, he should at least be granted a drink, a dance, and Dante as a nightcap. Yes? Yes.

After the procession, they return to the Circle to drink and dance the night away. Marky Mark's "Good Vibrations" is pounding the hi-fi speakers. On the dance floor are gyrating bodies, eyes rolling back into whiteness, mouths opened wide enough to receive a communion wafer.

Kris rubs against Vince, rolling her hips against his while her bodyguards, caught in the music, circle them, snapping their fingers and wiggling their hips. The song changes. Salt-N-Pepa's "Let's Talk about Sex." Bino elbows the guards aside and taps Kris on the shoulder. She and her bodyguards head for the bar as Bino rubs against Vince.

"Are you all right, hijo?" Bino asks.

"Excuse me, Mr. Boca," Vince says.

"Where are you going?"

"I need to go home now." Vince stumbles off the dance floor.

"But the night is just beginning," Bino says. "Come back. Enjoy the party. We'll go to Leche in an hour."

"Thanks, but I'm very tired and my ride is waiting outside," Vince says.

"Don't worry. I'll take you home."

"No, it's o.k. Thank you. Really."

Tipsy, Vince wobbles his way out of the Circle and back into the sullen hands of street kids who, just seconds ago, were on each other's shoulders, trying to get a glimpse of the party inside. "Joe, Joe," they call Vince, tugging and smudging his Armani with their dirty hands. He shoos them, and the cabdrivers too, who try to accost him. He looks around at the parked cars and cabs blocking much of Adriatico Street. Where the hell is Dante?

Probably got tired of waiting and went home to his wife and kids.

But he said he'd wait; I'm sure he's around here somewhere.

Then where is he?

"Sir Vince," Dante says, waving his arms as he squeezes in between vehicles.

"Where are you parked?" Vince asks.

"By Aristocrat's, sir."

"How far is that?"

"Near where I dropped you off, sir."

Three blocks later inside the cab, which is partially illuminated by lights coming from the restaurant, Vince, sitting in the front seat, tries hard not to stare at Dante's mouth, where a thread of spit hangs. He lowers his gaze to Dante's Adam's apple, then down to the strands of hair peeping out of his armpit before resting it on the gold crucifix medallion against his chest.

"You o.k., sir?" Dante asks, as he starts the cab.

"I stink like hell," Vince says, unbuttoning his shirt and burying his face inside it to smell Bino's cologne, Sister Marie's perfume, Kris's hair spray, gin and tonic, tobacco, barbecue smoke, diesel fumes, as well as subdivision-wall piss and burning trash. "Is there someplace around here where I can shower?"

"Only motels, sir," Dante says, "and they're expensive. Don't worry, sir. I can get you home in twenty minutes, maybe less."

"What about at Leche? Do you know where that is? There's gotta be a shower room there."

"There is, sir."

"You've been?"

"Only once, sir," Dante says.

"Only once?"

"Not my kind of place, sir," Dante says. "Too expensive for me."

"Don't worry," Vince says, "I'll pay for you."

"But you look like you're ready to sleep, sir," Dante says, then, in Tagalog, he tells Vince he'd only be wasting his money.

"Dante." Pause. "Thank you."

"For what, sir?"

"For waiting."

BOOK IV

Who's Afraid of Cat Stevens?

Morning has bro
ken
like the first da
aaa
wning . . .
And the blackbird of consciousness is telling Vince, Hoy, wake up.
Go away.
Get up.
Go away.
Long night?
Leave me alone.
Dante's gone.
Who?
Dante. Taxi driver with a wife, three kids, wears a crucifix medallion,
has a cockfight tattoo on his arm.
What are you talking about?
Dante's gone. Split, poof, vanished.
"Aning." Vince calls out, pressing his palms against his eyes to alle-
viate the throbbing in his head.
Damnit. Where is she?
Vince opens his eyes to an empty bottle of mineral water on the
nightstand and remembers that, on the drive home, Dante made a quick
stop at 7-11. He picks up the bottle, twists it open, and smells the rim for
Dante's breath. None, so he shuts his eyes to summon more scenes from

last night's tryst. Nothing emerges, so he forces himself to get up and walk over to the dresser to get the bottle of Tylenol Extra-Strength that's mixed in with plastic vials of antibiotic, anti-diarrhea, and anti-anxiety pills. Head drooping, he crosses the living room and enters the kitchen, where he almost throws up at the sight of a huge roach crawling out of an untouched plate of re-fried chicken and fried rice with SPAM. He opens the refrigerator, which stopped humming early this morning, and finishes the entire pitcher of lukewarm water. He re-enters the living room and, seeing his pair of neatly folded Armani trousers placed carefully across the plastic-covered couch, goes into panic mode.

My wallet!

He snatches the pants and, seconds later, pulls it out of his back pocket. He checks its contents, is relieved to find his dollars, Social Security card, Hawaii driver's license, fruit-flavored condoms.

My passport!

He runs back into the bedroom, rifles through the drawers and bags, is surprised when his hand pulls his passport from the inside pocket of his backpack, exactly where he stashed it the night before.

See, Vince, everything's there.

Lying on his side, he sweeps his hands over the sheets, brings them to his face, and sniffs them for traces of Dante.

Nada. So he checks the floor, crawls on his knees, and looks under the mattress for crumpled tissues. Nada.

SING IT AGAIN, SAM

Vince could've slept another day had it not been for the loud singing coming from the kitchen. Whoever she is, she is definitely not Aning. Her accent identifies her as from the south, somewhere in the Visayas, where the vowels are hard and the r's never stop rolling. Sam-how. Sam-pleece. Sam-weeerrrr.

"Excuse me," he says, looking at a woman perched on a footstool, frying drumsticks in an oil-popping pan.

"Ay, good ebb-ning, surr," she says, dodging splashes of hot oil. She lowers the flame and steps off the footstool.

"Who are you?" he asks, noticing the black dot in her right eye. His grandfather had one on the same spot.

"Burrnadette, surr," she answers.

"Where's Aning?"

"Blak-jak, surr."

"What?"

"Blak-jak, surr. Casino Filipino, surr."

"Who sent you here?"

"Ma'am Aning, surr."

"You her daughter?"

"No. Assistant, surr."

Vince nods. A maid's maid?

"Did you sleep here?"

"No, surr. I live in kondominyum of Ma'am Aning, surr," she says, picking up a drumstick with a tong and putting it on a plate to complete Vince's high-cholesterol, high-sodium dinner, which consists of fried chicken, garlic rice, two salted duck eggs, and a panfried pepper-seasoned milkfish.

"Ready to eat, surr," Burrnadette says.

"Not hungry," Vince says. "Could you boil water? I wanna take a shower."

"My pleasure, surr."

"Thank you, Burrnadette."

A SHOWER OF MEMORIES

As he scrubs himself with soap and a washcloth, he remembers Dante. Dante saving him just in time from street kids, aggressive beggars, taxi drivers, gun-crazed guards. Dante guiding him past Dunkin' Donuts to get to the cab parked in front of Aristocrat's plate-glass window.

He remembers stinking of Manila and asking Dante to take him to Leche to shower. "You know where that is?" "Yes sir, but it's expensive to get in." He remembers the air conditioner blowing on his face, the music, Madonna's "Like a Prayer," playing on the radio, Roxas Boulevard with its neon signs flashing so fast he had to shut his eyes and didn't open them again until he was back in his bed, lying naked, no, he had briefs on, and Dante?

Dante was sitting on the edge of the bed, wringing a hand towel over a bucket of water. "What are you doing?" "Giving you a bath, sir." "You don't have to, Dante." "I want to, sir." "What happened to Leche?" "You passed out, sir." He remembers trying to sit up in bed so he could watch Dante wash his feet, the cloth moving around his toes. But he was too tired. "How old were you when you got that tattoo?" "Twenty, sir." "May I touch it?"

He remembers running his fingers over the punctured throat of the rooster, his heart beating so loudly that . . .

That?

I . . .

And?

Then he . . .

He?

I don't . . .

What?

I . . .

Don't remember.

Did we make it to first base?

I think.

I think? It's either a yes or a no.

Shit!

What?

He rinses himself. Towel in hand, he rushes to the mirror to examine his neck, chest, groin, butt for kiss marks, abrasions, open sores. None. He presses down on his coccyx.

Harder.

Deeper.

No pain.

No pain?

Oh. my. God.

What?

Did I dream it?

Don't know.

Did I make everything up?

Don't know, but I can make it up tonight.

What about Dante?

What about him?

Did he give me a bath? Show me his tattoo? Wash my feet? Did he guard me from my dreams?

He must've.

He must've?

He must've.

THE CADAVER OF MR. SIA, ONE OF THE
OFFICERS OF THE MASONIC TEMPLE

Jing,
Mid-morning nap interrupted
because of loud singing coming
from the kitchen. I couldn't
understand a word, the accent
rewrote the lyrics. But the
melody was pure Sondheim.

Why am I writing so big?

Jing De Los Reyes
513 North Kuakini
#6
Honolulu, HI 96817

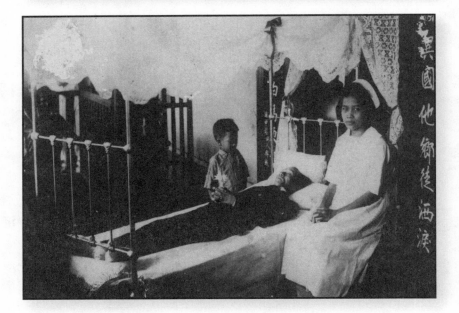

DEPARTMENT OF TOURISM, MANILA

#2 Cont. In the kitchen, in lieu of Aning, my part-time maid, was her maid, standing on a stool and frying chicken. Burrnadette, spelled just the way she pronounced it. "With two r's, surr." She's short, but has big, dark eyes that tell you she knows so much more than you think. Tonight, I asked her if Pagsanjan Falls, where Apocalypse Now *was filmed, was close to Manila b/c I plan to go there. You know what she said? "What for, surr? So you can get heart attack like Martin Sheen? The jungle is not for everybody, surr."*

From the wrong island,
Vince

Jing De Los Reyes
513 North Kuakini
#6
Honolulu, HI 96817

MANILA CHINATOWN

#3 P.S. I spent Friday night with your idol, aka "Massacre Queen." She's more caffeinated and annoying in person than when she's screaming or getting chopped or gangbanged in her movies. Someone should scan her brain because I swear it's more scattered than a Jackson Pollock canvas. Her tongue's looser than a cannon, with a sting more lethal than a scorpion's. That said, she has a commanding presence when she's not demanding it. And, like the Sphinx of Egypt, she is one of those people you'd just have to meet in person before you o.d. or have a seizure from watching her act.

Vince

Jing De Los Reyes
513 North Kuakini
#6
Honolulu, HI 96817

DIRTY ICE CREAM

Alvin,

I met your favorite nun—Sister Marie. Very spotlight-driven. She's beautiful and knows it. Big, expressive eyes. Like Judy Garland's. Like Mom's. Too bad she had to cover them up with blue contacts. Met Kris Aquino too. Talk about ADD. The best though is Bino Boca (as in the premier director of the turd world). That's how he refers to his country. He hates the upper class, which explains his negative depiction of them in his soft porn. Gave me a crash course on Manila's high society. In one word: vulgar. No, tacky. No, tasteless. No, cheap. No, queer.

Vince

Alvin De Los Reyes
430 Keoniana St.
2D
Honolulu, HI 96815

Tourist Tips

- Filipinos make passionate lovers. They are more Latin than Asian in this regard.

- 1% of them use prophylactics.

- Annual birth rate is 2.4%.

- Love, like noise, is always in the air.

- Three out of five Filipinos fall in—and out of—love every day.

- "Mahal kita" in Tagalog means "I love you."

- "Mahal" is "love" or "expensive"; "kita" can either be a pronoun ("me to you"), a verb ("to see" or "to show"), or a noun ("income").

- Divorce is illegal in the Philippines; Filipinos have annulments instead.

- Filipinos point with their mouths to indicate directions and raise their brows when they mean, "Yes, baby, you and only you are the one that I want."

- Use polite language when speaking to them. Get into the habit of inserting the honorific "po."

- When in doubt, use body language.

- Fact: 60% of human communication is via gestures. For Filipinos, it's 90%.

- Avoid asking direct questions.

- Don't use Spanish on them because their Spanish is not your Spanish.

- "Siyempre" is not "always" but "of course"; "grabe" is not "serious" but "too much"; and "siguro" is not "certainly" but "perhaps."

- English is more common and preferred. But know that a Yes and a Maybe can also mean a definite *No!*

Paste & Cut

Everything requires labor in Manila, from crossing the street to getting a cab to breathing, which feels more like catching up with one's breathing. And on a hot and sticky night like tonight, where the only breeze is coming from a fan oscillating weakly at top speed, Vince only has sufficient energy to remain in his vegetative state, glued to the couch that's still wrapped in the manufacturer's plastic, seesawing between the only two TV channels with clear reception. One has a program devoted to the much-anticipated Film Academy of the Philippines Awards, in which *In the Name of Shame* is predicted to take home the major awards, including Best Actress and Best Supporting Actress for Kris Aquino and Sister Marie, respectively. On the other station is an interview with another Best Actress nominee, Jolie B Rizal, who looks familiar, but he can't match the face or the faux British accent with a Tagalog film he's seen.

Unable to bear the humidity, he gets up, the back of his thighs burning as they peel from the plastic, and walks to the bathroom to take another shower, his third in two hours. Too lazy to transfer the fan to the bedroom, he returns to the living room with a white sheet and spreads it over the couch.

This is only his third night in Manila and already all his water weight is gone, from sweating, from running away from street children, and from nonstop dreaming. He's been mistaken for someone's dead son, surprised to learn that the "free accommodation" part of his prize was not at a five-star hotel but instead in an air-sealed townhouse in a subdivision run by gun-toting security guards. He's also had two maids, one of them an assistant of the other. He's hobnobbed with movie stars, and an internationally renowned director asked him to read for a part in his upcoming film, which will probably have its world premiere at Cannes. A project he might have considered had the director not turned him off by trying to grope him on the dance floor. But he might still change his mind, depending on what happens on Kris's talk show.

And then there is Dante, who is fast becoming an obsession. Who kept his word and drove him safely home, gave him a sponge bath, and sat up until daybreak, guarding him from his dreams and his memories. Dante—his Virgil.

NOTORIOUS BBG

Vince looks at the label on the TV, is tempted to peel it and the cellophane over the wall clock, and the plastic cover on the couch that crackles at his every move. But an anchorman's good looks draw his attention back to the screen.

"A jeepney carrying five people and two balikbayan boxes was ambushed along MacArthur Highway early Friday morning by the notorious BBG, or Balikbayan Box Gang. This is their eighth attack this month." The anchorman pauses. "All five passengers were shot to death."

Full shot of a jeepney riddled with bullet holes followed by close-ups of the slain bodies. "Oh my God," Vince says, sitting up and turning up the volume.

"Everyone knows that balikbayan boxes invite crime," says Harold "Dirty Harry" Piñeda, director of the National Bureau of Investigation.

Full shot of two balikbayan boxes, their contents scattered around the victims. "People are getting massacred because of these boxes," Piñeda continues. "They are targets for criminals and drug addicts, who commit unspeakable crimes because they think there are golden

Buddhas stashed in every one of them when they're usually only filled with canned goods, hand-me-down appliances, and discarded clothes and library books."

A close-up of Esther's passport photo confirms Vince's suspicion. What about the two boys? The reporter mentioned five victims. What about Benjamin and Jasper?

Close-ups of five corpses in their coffins.

"That's why I keep emphasizing to balikbayans, especially from America, and especially those who have to make the long trip home to their provinces, to think twice about coming home with balikbayan boxes," Piñeda continues.

Vince flinches as more graphic images appear on screen, followed by an old woman wailing over a coffin.

"It's tragic what's happening to this country," Piñeda concludes.

Anchorman: "Esther Lopez, co-owner of the jeepney, had just arrived from Hawaii, where she worked as a caregiver. The other victims are Esther's two sons, her sister—"

"Shit," Vince says as the TV and the lights go out. He leans back on the couch, trying to remember where Aning told him the flashlight was.

Vince stares at the blacked-out screen and sees a blue dot the color of his grandfather's eyes, gradually shaping into his face, the dot in his right eye, his widow's peak, his square jaw.

"Don't be afraid of the dark, hijo," his grandfather told him as a child whenever the lights went out in San Vicente. "God needed darkness so he could build our world. Without darkness, there wouldn't be any light. Everything comes from darkness, hijo. Spirits, ghosts, dreams, even the stories in your komiks and the movies we watch. Remember that, hijo."

CITY LIGHTS OUT

The martial law years, from 1972 to 1981, were marked with frequent blackouts and curfews, particularly during election time when ballots and candidates vanished with the light. If they were fortunate, the candidates' bodies resurfaced days, weeks, months, or a year later—in rivers, along roadsides, in sewage drainage pipes, in middle-of-nowhere fields, their bodies disfigured, resorting to belt buckles, handkerchiefs with embroidered initials, birthmarks, or teeth to identify them.

No one dared to print, let alone discuss, the who-what-where-when-and-why of the monthly, weekly, then daily disappearances and arrests. To speak and write critically of the Marcos regime led directly to the dungeons of Camp Crame and Fort Bonifacio, where all-night interrogations took place. This is how the martial law years came to be known by many as the Bangungut Decade, when the waking hours were as frightening as the killer nightmares.

One common occurrence was "hamleting," or the expulsion of villagers suspected of sympathizing with the Communist National People's Army. It happened in the outlying barrio of San Vicente, near the Sierra Madre range, purported to be a hotbed of Communist guerrillas. One day the military arrived and rounded up the suspects, many of whom were farmers and their families, took them to Camp Crame and Fort Bonifacio in Manila, where, before they disappeared, they were forced to confess that they were supplying food and arms to the rebels hiding in the mountains.

A few escaped before the soldiers arrived in San Vicente, seeking refuge in San Vicente Church, where Father Mendoza took them in, feeding them food donated by the Knights of Columbus, which included Vince's grandfather, Don Alfonso. The fraternal organization, whose members had fought in the second world war, also provided the victims with temporary lodging and transportation to their nearest relatives. Don Mario, the owner of the outdoor cinema and also a Knight, held benefit screenings to aid the dispossessed.

Vince associated martial law with his favorite Chaplin flick, *City Lights,* whose ending he and the people of San Vicente had never seen because it kept getting interrupted by blackouts. Only once was it screened without the power shutting off, when the incumbent mayor, who was seeking re-election, promised the people one blackout-free night; that time, the film stock burned. In fact, Vince cannot recall ever seeing an entire movie at the outdoor cinema in one sitting. He kept going back, usually with his grandfather, until he'd pieced together the story. Jing and Alvin, too tired of seeing the same old scenes, stayed home with Yaya Let and the maids.

"Watching a movie in San Vicente was like putting together a puzzle, except the pieces were given to you in installments. You had to keep going back," Vince told Edgar. "It was so frustrating. It kept everyone in suspense. I remember there were even bets made on how *City Lights* ended, on whether the tramp would reveal his true identity to the blind girl, or where he was going to get the money to pay for her eye operation. It took five nights just to see an eighty-minute silent movie, sometimes more."

"Imagine if it was *Gone with the Wind* or *Lawrence of Arabia,*" Edgar said. "You lucky you migrated, Vince."

"*Gone with the Wind* and *Lawrence of Arabia* never made it to San Vicente, thank God. Or if they had, it would've taken a lifetime and the afterlife to watch them. But we did see *The Ten Commandments* every year," Vince said.

"And how long wen' take you to get to the Sodomy and Gonorrhea part?"

"The entire Lent season. But nobody minded the blackouts or cared about the no-refund policy because everybody who was somebody, or who wanted to be somebody, or who wanted to see somebody, went to the outdoor cinema."

"Sounds like the men's toilet in Kapiolani Park and Thomas Square on Friday and Saturday nights," Edgar said.

"Most came by foot, but people from the barrios, who were mostly farmers and less-to-dos, if they could afford the fare, piled up inside jeepneys. They brought their produce with them to sell."

"How two-for-one!"

"You mean four-in-one. The movie theater was also an open market, a social hall, and a place for secret rendezvous."

"You went to the movies to do your groceries? No wonder you're so good at multitasking," Edgar said. "Did you ever get picked up by a perv?"

"Of course not. I was right next to my grandfather and his kumpadres," he says, remembering the rock-hard chairs for the VIPs. Alvin and Jing sat on blankets spread out on the ground with Yaya Let and the other maids, who, when they weren't crying their hearts out, were holding yak-a-thon contests.

"What else did they show besides Chaplin and *The Ten Commandments?*"

"Cowboy-and-Indian bullshit, old World War II movies, Tagalog melodramas, and Darna," Vince said, referring to the Philippines' version of Wonder Woman. "The sound quality was usually muffled and the picture was grainy or scratched. I think the film went around the world first before it reached our town. But during fiesta, the screenings were shown on the side of the town church and were free."

"How fun!" Edgar said.

"Yes," Vince said. "Beats having to deal with locals propping their stinky feet on the seat next to yours."

CORTEGE

When Vince was in first grade, he, as one of Father Mendoza's altar boys, ushered a funeral procession to San Vicente Campo Santo. The hearse contained a coffin without a body. It was a funeral for Don Guillermo Martinez, his next-door neighbor, a staunch supporter of the Liberal Party and a journalist critical of the Marcos regime.

The story that circulated around San Vicente was that Don Guillermo had gone to Manila to attend a Liberal Party campaign rally held in Plaza Miranda, which faces Quiapo church, home of the Black Jesus. The Liberal Party was hoping to win back the majority of the House seats from Marcos's Nacionalista Party. Among the attendees were seven of the senatorial candidates and four thousand of their supporters. Incumbent Senator Benigno Aquino, surprisingly, was not present; later, rumors abounded that, on his way to Plaza Miranda, he had received an anonymous phone call informing him about the bomb.

According to an eyewitness, hand grenades had been tossed on stage, instantly killing a child and a photojournalist and injuring hundreds. A senator was blinded in one eye and a Manila mayoral candidate lost his leg.

Marcos blamed the Communists for the Plaza Miranda bombing, as well as for the assassination attempt a year later on his right-hand man, Secretary of Defense Juan Ponce Enrile. By that time, the Marcos regime had performed enough dress rehearsals to stage His Majesty's magnum opus: martial law, which went into effect on September 21, 1972.

Don Guillermo, his sixteen-year-old son Giovanni (whom Vince and Jing had a huge crush on), and the family driver were spared from the bombing because they were stuck in traffic several blocks away. The next day, their vehicle was found riddled with bullet holes in a ravine in the province of Tarlac. The driver, his face blown off, was slumped over the wheel, the seat covered in blood. Giovanni was in the backseat, his throat slit, his eyes cut out and left on the floor. But Don Guillermo was missing.

A year passed, and the only stories about Don Guillermo and his whereabouts were hearsay passed on to the townspeople of San Vicente by traveling vendors, like how Don Guillermo's ghost was seen wandering around the country like a stray dog. Some claimed he'd traveled as far north as Ilocos Norte in Luzon and as far south as Basilan in Zamboanga, knocking on people's doors and asking for water and directions to a town whose name he couldn't remember. Some said they saw him hitching rides from jeepney and bus drivers in the wee hours of the morning, getting off at cemeteries, where he searched one gravestone after another for a name that would help him remember who he was.

"You're going to go crazy if you don't bury him," Yaya Let told Doña Priscilla, Don Guillermo's wife. She and Yaya Let had been best friends since childhood. "Bury him, Doña Priscilla, even if you don't have his body."

"But he isn't dead, Leticia," Doña Priscilla said.

"His spirit is lost, Doña Priscilla," Yaya Let said, "that's why he's wandering all over the country. Burying him will at least summon his spirit and put it to rest."

Doña Priscilla waited for another year before she took Yaya Let's advice. On the morning of the second anniversary of his disappearance, she and Yaya Let went to San Vicente Funeraria and bought the most expensive coffin for Don Guillermo. At the wake, Vince sat beside Yaya Let and watched her console her good friend as mourners lined up to peer into a coffin containing only the favorite possessions of the deceased, as was the custom in San Vicente. Every night, Father Mendoza conducted a short mass for Don Guillermo in the prayer room of the Martinezes' residence.

Nothing extraordinary happened that first night of Don Guillermo's wake. No dogs in San Vicente howled, no church bells rang, no lizards clucked. But Vince couldn't sleep; he kept smelling burning candles in his room and imagining Don Guillermo by his bed, trying to drag him to the cemetery and into an empty coffin.

On the second night, Vince didn't go back to the wake, nor did he sleep in his room. Rather, he stayed up reading a stack of komiks in his grandfather's bed. A maid was assigned by Don Alfonso to keep him company in the old man's room, until he returned home from the wake.

Later that night, Jing (who, like Don Alfonso, had a dot in her right eye), told Vince that Don Guillermo's ghost had finally come home.

"I saw him, Vicente," Jing said.

"Me too," Vince said.

"No you didn't."

"I did too."

"How could you?" she asked. "You weren't at the wake. Plus you don't have a dot in your eye like me and Lolo Al."

"But I did. He stood by my bed all night."

"That's just your imagination talking, Vicente."

On the third day, Doña Priscilla wrote a letter of apology to her husband for the long delay and buried it in the coffin, along with his favorite hat, an Aloha shirt, khaki trousers, leather sandals, the Bible, and reading glasses.

A woman's voice from next door barks orders to a maid, summoning Vince back to the present. "Ano? Sira? Broken na naman! Cannot be. What do you mean? I just had the generator fixed. Oh, my Lord. Malas naman! Go call the repairman! Hurry before I starve your family in the province to death."

It's been almost twenty years since Marcos first implemented martial law. Some things never change. Different government, same story: the Philippines is still spending a good part of its time in the dark.

Tourist Tips

- Filipinos love playing with language. To them, language is like a machine that can be taken apart, tinkered with, reassembled, decorated, and given a face-lift for that Filipino French-twist effect.

- "Fake" is "fay-kee"; "preface" is pronounced "pray-fahz"; and "façade" is "fa-kayed."

- Words with s are given a hard z. Yezzz.

- In the Philippines, English words can take on the complete opposite of their original meanings. "To salvage" is "to kill" or "to exterminate." As in "Salvaging bodies was common during the Marcos dictatorship."

- Filipinos are known to shift political parties and allegiances faster than they can change their underwear.

- EDSA, the main highway that connects north and south Metro Manila, is synonymous with traffic jams, sidewalk urinals, and the People Power revolution.

- There are thirteen golf courses in Metro Manila, all with English-speaking caddies.

- "Until now" is interchangeable with "up to now," as in "Your bank account is still good until now."

STATUE OF REVOLUTIONARY HERO ANDRES BONI-
FACIO AND THE KATIPUNAN

Alvin,
Thank god for Export-A cigarettes. I've been
chain-smoking since I opened my eyes, my
mouth, my nose, my ears this morning. I
should feel right at home since everybody
here smokes. The difference is I don't carry a
gun. The place I'm staying at is garrisoned by
guards ready for frontline combat. Don't
laugh yourself into convulsions; even Ronald
McDonald carries a gun. Charlton "Moses"
Heston should retire here.

Vince

Alvin De Los Reyes
430 Keoniana St.
2D
Honolulu, HI 96815

THE PHILLIPINES FIRST FIVE-STAR HOTEL, 1912

#2 About Manila: It breathes, belches, farts, grabs, and begs every second you're in it. There's no escaping the madness and sadness. You have to be in sync with the place or it'll kick you in the ass. NO PISSING signs and vendors everywhere. Manila gawks, steals you by surprise, smokes, hacks, sings, smiles, brings back memories and the smell you thought you had lost or never had. Manila burns, stings, spits, licks, laughs, rains, boils, bleeds, honks, barks, dances, chants, until your dreams bust. Vince

P.S. Didn't Mom and Dad honeymoon at this hotel?

Alvin De Los Reyes
430 Keoniana St.
2D
Honolulu, HI 96815

CORPSES OF FILIPINO REVOLUTIONARIES,
PHILIPPINE-AMERICAN WAR, 1899–1902

*Mom: I need five pairs of eyes to cross a
street. Ten if it's a major intersection. I'm
going cross-eyed just trying to get from Point
A to Point B. To the motorists, I am their
blind spot. Sometimes I have to pretend I'm
a pothole just to keep from getting hit. I
finally figured out the fastest and safest way
to get to the other side—follow the guy selling
Zest-O fruit drinks and try not to lose him
as he cha-chas between cars. Even if it means
stopping beside him to see if commuters are
thirsty. Hope you're well.*
Vince

Carmen Formoso
1519 Kaumualii St.
#310
Honolulu, HI 96819

After the Battle—
Ravine Where the Dead
Have Been Thrown

AnthrApology

Vince is poring through the sea of details in his spiral notebook. "House ele-vated. Below, on the packed earth—pigs, dogs, ducks, chickens. No furni-ture. At the center, three mats. Woven by women. The intricate designs came from their dreams. But difference in patterns hardly noticeable. As if women shared the same dream. Women go into a trance-like state while weaving. Men, incl. husbands, forbidden to speak, see, touch the women. Otherwise, Death will snatch them in their sleep.

Human skulls hang in every corner, window, door. To keep evil spirits away. Photographs cover the walls. In each frame, beside the picture, are strands of hair and a tooth. Beneath it—date of the person's birth and death. All bearing the same penmanship."

Vince jumps back, drops his pen and notebook. The face in one of the portraits belongs to him—square-jawed, thick eyebrows, a mouth reveal-ing perfect teeth with a slight overbite. Above his left brow, a line caused by too much brooding. But the penmanship records his birth as 1880 and death as 1931.

He runs for the mirror and sees a reflection with a trail of teeth running from his neck down to his chest. Behind him, his grandfather is drying his hair with a towel. He is in his pajamas and an undershirt that exposes a stab wound on his back.

"I want to go home, Lolo," Vince says. "They're eating me alive here. I must leave."

"You can't," his grandfather says. "You have to find my dentures first."

Vince checks the medicine cabinet, under the bathroom sink, inside the shower, the drawers.

"Here, sir," a man says to him. Vince turns. It's Dante, gesturing for him to lie on a massage table in the center of the room. Vince is naked, except for a towel wrapped around his waist.

"Swedish or shiatsu, sir?" Dante asks.

"Doesn't matter."

"Relax, sir," Dante says, rubbing oil on Vince's back, then applying pressure on his neck, along his shoulder blades and lower back.

"You have many knots," Dante says.

Vince cries out as Dante pushes his thumb down on a ligament in his right buttcheek.

"You want more gentle, sir?"

"No," Vince says, "I like it hard." So Dante presses down harder, until all Vince feels are the nerves below his tailbone twitching.

Dante asks him to roll on his back.

Eyes closed, Vince takes deep breaths as Dante begins gently massaging him on his chest, his groin, the insides of his thighs.

Vince throws his head back as all the blood in the world rushes to his head. He reaches down to grab a fistful of Dante's hair. But there is nothing to grasp. He sits up, finds only an empty room lit by bits of the moon passing through the holes of a latticed window.

BOOK V

Are You There God? It's Me, Margaret Mead.

As Vince lathers his head, the water from the faucet stops dripping. "Leche," he mutters, squinting so as not to sting his eyes. He calls out for Aning. She doesn't respond. So he tries Burrnadette, until he remembers that today is Sunday, and on Sundays, maids and their maids have the day off.

He snatches the towel from the rack, wraps it around his waist, and, dripping wet with his butt still covered in soapsuds, dashes out of the bathroom and into the kitchen, where he turns the knobs of the sink to make sure that he's not hallucinating: the city of Manila is once again dried up. He releases an endless torrent of cusses. For not refilling the bucket after using it up last night and this morning. For coming to a third-world country that didn't have water but was surrounded by it. For having to resort to the last option—the pitcher of drinking water in the fridge, which hadn't hummed since the electricity went out the night before. He opens the freezer and pours the four trays of melted ice into the half-filled pitcher.

Water—purified, filtered, or freezing—refreshes the body, brings clarity to the mind, plants brilliant ideas, like checking into a five-star hotel. He dials 411 and asks the operator for Nikkon Hotel, which he read about in the in-flight magazine.

"You don't want to stay there, sir," the operator says. "It's so overrated, plus too many Arabs. Better to go to Manila Hotel. General Douglas MacArthur stayed there, you know. With his Filipina mistress."

"What?" Vince asks, trying not to sound irritable.

"Yes, Isabel Rosario Cooper, the mistress also known as 'Dimples,'" the operator continues. "She was an actress. The first one to kiss on the silver screen."

"That's nice," Vince says. "But the Nikkon will do, thank you."

"What's your budget, sir? Five star or no star?"

"No star?"

"You know, drive-thru motels. 'Make fast love, not fast death.'"

"Could I have the number now, please?"

"How long are you planning on staying in our country, sir?"

Vince slams the phone down, stares at the couch cocooned in plastic, and beside it, on a table, the lamp, its rice-paper shade also covered in plastic.

He dials Philippine Airline's main office, gets an epic bilingual recorded message that basically translates into "Mabuhay. Office closed Sunday. Call back Monday."

He dials 411 again, asks for the Nikkon Hotel's number.

Seconds later . . . "New World Hotel, how may I book you for today?"

"New World?" Vince says, confused. "I wanted Nikkon."

"Not after you've tried our hotel, sir. We're brand new and centrally located, right in the heart of Makati. And right now, sir, you can avail of our promo."

"Avail? Promo? What do you mean?"

"Are you a balikbayan, sir?"

"Yes," Vince says.

"Stupendous! From where, sir? Carson City? I have cousins in Carson City."

"Hawaii."

"Oh, Paradise Park. How lucky. I hear it's very nice there, like Boracay. Our modern-day Eden. Have you been to Boracay, sir?"

"No." Though Vince has heard of the hot spot in the south, seen it in Tagalog movies. Boracay. One of the world's best hideaways. Powder-fine sand, warm water, beachfront massage-pedicure-manicures, high-end resorts like Fridays, where the air-conditioned rooms are paneled in woven bamboo mats, and there's dirty dancing at a discotheque with a Spanish name, Basura, meaning "garbage." Where every room has a workable shower and water you can drink. Paradise, Vince thinks, and only an hour away by plane from the hell he's in.

EIGHT WONDERS OF VINCE'S WORLD

"Do you have an unlimited water supply?"

"Siyempre."

"Hot and cold water?"

"Por su puesto."

"Air conditioning?"

"Centralized."

"How about room service?"

"With a wake-up call, compliments of the hotel."

"Hair dryer?"

"Dual voltage."

"Fitness room?"

"Jacuzzi, steam room, and sauna too."

"The nearest hospital?"

"Ten-minute walk, or forty by car."

"How much?"

"Only four hundred dollars a night."

"Don't you have anything cheaper?"

"No sir."

"What about the promo?"

"That is the special, sir. Would you like to reserve a room?"

"No, thanks," Vince says. Four hundred dollars! His cash prize of a thousand dollars isn't even enough to cover three days.

What now?

Go shopping.

Get a deep-tissue massage.

Deep-cleansing facial.

Look good, feel good, think good.

Who knows? I might run into Dante.

BUDDY DOUBLE

The five-minute walk to the front gate becomes a trip to hell because Vince makes the wrong turn onto Gemini Street, which branches out into several dead-end streets named after martyred heroes of the Philippine-American War. It isn't until he uses his nose as a compass— the sweet aroma of the barbecue stand right outside the main gate— that he is able to find his way out of the subdivision. A guard greets him with a nod. Vince asks if he could get him a cab. The guard tells him it's faster if he hails it himself. "Or try the jeepney, sir," he adds, pointing to the mad rush of commuters dashing out of the waiting shed and clambering into the jeepney named BUDDY DOUBLE while a greasy-haired man—also called a "barker"—shouts out its destination. Once it's filled, it speeds off as two teenage boys jump on the rear step, tightly gripping the steel bars on the roof.

Beside the waiting shed is a vendor fanning the smoke rising from a barbecue grill. Her stand is covered with pans of skewered pig and chicken parts marinated in soy sauce. Stepping into the shed, Vince waits behind a middle-aged Asian couple and a girl in a school uniform. He eavesdrops on their conversation, about progress and why it has stalled in the Philippines. "Because," the girl says, "we rely too much on fate. We have a word for that in Tagalog: 'Bahala na.'"

> **From** *Decolonization for Beginners: A Filipino Glossary*
>
> **bahala na**, *noun*. 1. the Filipino attitude of entrusting one's problem to God. 2. bahala is from Bathala, the supreme being of ancient pagan Filipinos; na is "already." 3. Que sera sera.

Vince wants to butt in and say, "It's kind of like herpes. Leave it alone because there really isn't anything you or anyone else can do. Eventually it will go away on its own."

"Buhay mahirap talaga, no?" the man says in broken Tagalog. "Mundo natin palagi sakit." Which translates to "Our world is always sick" or "Our world is a pain."

Vince detects an accent, wonders where the couple is originally from.

"But Philippines very good for us," the woman says in English. "Better life me and my husband have over here than back home."

"How long have you lived here?" the girl asks.

"Long time already," the man says. "Since 1975. First, in Palawan. Many refugee camps there. We learn English there."

"Very big camp," the woman says, "almost a town. Many Vietnamese still there, you know."

"But Philippine government want close down camps," the man says, "and send them back Vietnam."

"Why?" the girl asks.

"Because many who in camps now, they not political refugees," the man answers. "They here illegally because no work for them back home."

The man's remarks catch Vince offguard. He didn't know that Vietnamese people were migrating to the Philippines to find employment. Just as he didn't know they had come after the fall of Vietnam in 1975. He's always thought of the Philippines as a point of departure, a place many leave behind to seek employment, a better tomorrow elsewhere.

"You come eat at our restaurant in Quezon City," the man says. She nods before joining the other commuters hunching their way inside the cavernous interior of EMOTION SICKNESS.

"I see R & E coming," the man says, referring to the company that owns the cab Dante drives.

Vince bolts out of the shed and flags it down, his heart beating faster and faster, his eyes straining to make out the face of the driver. Definitely a male; white undershirt; hand towel draped over one shoulder. Any gold crucifix? Tattoos? Brakes screech, and a one-second peek is all that Vince needs to open the door and offer it to the Vietnamese couple.

BROWN VS FAIR

Alone once again in the waiting shed, littered with fliers for the upcoming election like "V IS FOR VICTORY, SO VOTE FOR VI." As in Vilma Santos, known for her dramatic roles, mestiza complexion, and TV commercials endorsing ESKINOL skin-care products.

Vince will deny it now, but he was once a Vilmanian, meaning he was part of the multitude of hopelessly devoted diehard true-blue-'til-death-do-us-part fans who didn't live a single day without thanking the Lord for bringing into their rich or wretched existence Vilma Santos. Aka Star for All Seasons.

Expect to see a horde of Vilmanians camping outside theaters days before her movie premieres. To buy out the entire issue whenever she graces the cover of a magazine. To make her records go platinum in a week. To go on pilgrimages to Manila and stand outside the gate of her home on her birthday. To hold a novena when she's up for an acting award. And to pore over their scrapbooks whenever they come down with Vilma-itis.

Vince had such a scrapbook. Scribbled on its front cover, in his first-grade penmanship, was: ATE VI & ME. In it were articles and pictures that he cut out from magazines with the precision of a surgeon and pasted onto the pages. A piece of memorabilia that, because there was no room in his suitcase and box, his grandfather had asked him to leave behind, along with his collection of komiks, books, and Charlie Chaplin movie posters. He agreed, thinking he would return soon.

While Vince, like half the country, was a bona fide Vilmanian; the other half were Noranians, like Jing and Alvin. As in Nora Aunor, Vilma's showbiz rival for the past two decades, though the two super-stars claim to be very good friends ("We're as close as wall-to-wall car-peting."—Vilma). Whereas Vilma is mestiza, which means she can enter through the front doors of Pinoywood without getting stopped or mistaken for a maid, Nora, on the other hand, is petite, olive-skinned, barely speaks English, prefers to converse in Tagalog, and is likely to be mistaken for a nanny or a squatter. As a young girl in the province of Camarines Sur, Nora helped her poor parents by peddling water in train stations. Her impoverished existence came to an abrupt end when she entered the country's amateur singing contest. She sang a Barbra Streisand chart-topper, "People," and from then on, Nora (who also goes by "Ate Guy") became one of the luckiest Filipeoples in the world.

Except Nora wasn't just lucky; she was talented. Her eyes could evoke a thousand and one emotions—she could tear your heart with one look—and her singing voice catapulted her to overnight stardom, breaking rules and records in Pinoywood, where whiteness was—and still is—used to judge one's beauty and talent and determine the num-ber of digits in contracts. Like Vilma, she too broke box-office records, in movies such as *Atsay* and *Bona,* where she usually played an under-dog—the maid, the poor girl, the maid, the provincial, the maid, the pariah, the maid, the lesbian, the maid.

Gazing at the flier of his former idol Vilma, Vince listens to the voices of his childhood and remembers the endless Nora-Vilma catfights with his siblings. "So? Ate Vi dances better than Ate Guy," Vince said, in response to Alvin's, "At least Ate Guy's boyfriend isn't fat."

"So what? Ate Vi is Darna," Vince retorted.

It was Vilma as Darna who made Vince believe that heroes on the screen were as real as the lights that made them. In the open-air cinema of San Vicente, underneath the stars and seated right beside his grandfather, Vince watched his childhood idol bring the komikbook heroine to life. When she wasn't championing good over evil, Darna was Narda, a provincial lass who got her superhuman powers from a white stone that fell out of the sky. Inscribed on the stone was "Darna," which she yelled out whenever she needed to fight her enemies, like the snake-coiffed Valentina, who turned people into stone.

Vince read about them in the komiks and watched the film adaptations in the open-air cinema, as well as on TV. He'd even feigned illness in school ("Ma'am, I think I have tapeworms!") just so he could go home and watch *Isputnik Versus Darna* on Sine Sa Siete (Movies on Channel Seven). And today, here she is, Vince's childhood screen idol, running for a mayoral seat in the province of Lipa, Batangas, where, in the sixties, the Virgin Mary had appeared through a rain of roses.

"Nora can't dance to save her left foot, but she sings like an angel," Jing told Vince. "But Vilma can't sing for shit."

It was true. Vilma couldn't tell the difference between sharps and flats, do from fa, mi from la, like ninety-nine percent of the movie stars in Pinoywood who insist on staging concerts in big arenas and releasing one album after another, relying on their tone-deaf fans to turn them gold or platinum. Alvin described Vilma's singing most accurately. "She sounds like Astrud Gilberto on morphine."

ALL SOUL'D OUT

The sight of a boy in a Montessori school uniform and an old man in a Panama hat approaching the shed keeps Vince in memory mode. Of those Sunday afternoons in San Vicente when he and his grandfather Don Alfonso went to the Campo Santo to visit the graves of Doña Aurora Del Rosario Lewis and William Lewis, Don Alfonso's parents; Don Alfonso's sister, Maria Lourdes Del Rosario Lewis; Don Alfonso's aunt, Marian Lewis; and Don Alfonso's wife, Doña Juanita De Los Reyes Lewis, who died from cancer when Vince's father was only a teenager.

Throughout the year, Don Alfonso made certain that the family mausoleum with "Lewis–De Los Reyes" etched above the entrance was well maintained. A caretaker was hired to cut the grass weekly, water the plants, and polish the marbled epitaphs and altar that had been built into the wall. Many only tended the graves of loved ones once a year, for All Soul's Day, which falls on the first of November. This was when the cemetery underwent a major makeover, with people flocking there to weed the surrounding areas and scrub and wash tombs or repaint them days before the dead were honored.

On this religious holiday, practically the whole country was there, spending an entire day eating with and talking to the dead, offering them food, candlelit prayers, music, laughter, and the latest memories. As ceremonious as Holy Week and Christmas, it was the one time of the year when the living surrendered their day to the dead, regardless of whether it was sunny or flooding, as it happened once in San Vicente. A procession of people wading in waist-high water to the cemetery, flowers and candles held high in the air, while the more fortunate ones, like Vince's family, were ferried to their loved ones in dugout canoes.

EYDIE GORME BBQ

Vince looks at the old man's eyes, then his right eye, then his earlobes, then down to his hands for freckles, thin veins. He wonders if the old man has a widow's peak under the hat, or a stab wound from the war on his upper back, or a black dot in his eye.

"Good morning," the boy greets the vendor, who waves to him with the cardboard she fans the smoke with.

"Lolo, Lolo," the boy addresses his grandfather. "I want to eat Adidas."

"O.K. You can have one," the old man says, "but only one."

Oh my God, Vince thinks. What am I going to say when I get back to Hawaii? That Filipinos are not only eating man's best friend but their own sneakers too?

"May I have one Adidas, please," the boy says. "And also a Walkman."

"Hijo," the old man says.

"I'll eat them all, Lolo. I promise."

Does *National Geographic* know about this? The Discovery Channel?

"Naku, believe na believe ako talaga sa pag-i-ingles mo." The vendor tells the boy his English is flawless. "Para kang galing sa Estates." As if he were from abroad.

The boy's grin broadens as his grandfather pats him on his head.

"Oh, your Walkman is ready now." The vendor hands the boy a stick of pig's ears, which he dips into a jar of sweet-and-sour sauce.

"How about you, Anak, you also want Adidas?" she asks Vince, pointing to the skewered chicken feet. "How about IUD?" she adds, referring to chicken intestines.

Vince declines with a tight-lipped smile that widens as he makes the connection between chicken intestines and their coily resemblance to the birth control device.

Tourist Tips

• Warning: not all Filipinos eat dog. But almost all Filipinos eat balut.

• Balut is a fourteen-day-old duck.

• The proper way to eat balut is to season it with salt then, without looking, suck out its veins, bones, feathers, and huge eyes.

• If you want to be accepted into the tribe, you have to eat balut, dinuguan (pig's blood stew), or bayawak (monitor lizard).

• Filipinos love to eat, and when they're eating, they want you to eat with them.

• Never turn down Filipinos who invite you to dine with them. You might injure their amor propio (self-esteem).

• Balut is an aphrodisiac.

• Balut + Beer = Bangungut.

Ride Me, Baby

RIDE ME BABY in huge yellow letters crowns the jeepney that Vince, after waiting in the shed for over an hour for a cab and starting to smell like barbecued chicken intestines and pig's ears, is forced to take to the malls of Makati. Shining on its hood is the star of Mercedes Benz. The antennas that are not connected to the radio are decorated with blue and yellow plastic strips. The parking lights that flash in red, yellow, green, orange, and blue adorn the Ford-inspired grille. And fastened onto the bumper by wires is the license plate: IN2U.

Vince is at the front passenger seat, watching with wonder as the driver transforms himself into a Hindu god with three eyes and eight hands. One eye looks out for potholes, peddlers, and pedestrians, another is in the rearview mirror asking passengers where they've gotten on and where they're getting off, and the third is on the odometer, which reveals the same numbers as twenty years ago.

As for his hands: one busily navigates the wheel, the second reaches back to accept the fare, the third counts it, the fourth drops it in the cashbox, the fifth hands back change (the change traveling from one passenger to the next inside the oxygen-deprived box until it lands in the palm of the one who paid), the sixth is in charge of the tape deck, the seventh wipes off perspiration, and the eighth is smoking a cigarette.

The bumpy ride to the mall reels Vince back to his first year at the University of Hawaii in 1986, when he had to attend a talk by Bonifacio Dumpit then write a reaction paper for his Political Science 100 class, taught by none other than the speaker himself. Entitled "How I

Traveled from the Rice Fields to the Moon," the lecture was part of a week-long symposium addressing issues of Filipino identity. Highly publicized and well attended, the event was organized and sponsored by the Center for Philippine Studies to commemorate the eightieth anniversary of the arrival of Filipinos in Hawaii.

Dumpit began by explaining how the Philippine jeepney had come about, this collage in motion powered by a four-cylinder engine. "Shortly after World War II—the war that claimed three hundred thousand Filipinos and reduced the country to a pile of rubble—the Americans were stuck with a surplus of six-passenger U.S. Army jeeps, or Original Willys, as they were called," he said. "So they sold them to the Filipinos who, not satisfied with the jeeps' drab look, repainted them with an explosion of colors to highlight the dizzying hues of Philippine colonial history. They then decorated them with an assemblage of folk, Catholic, and pop-Americana ornaments. A metamorphosis reflecting the Filipinos' pastiche-driven psyche. Or what I refer to as the 'Filipino flair.'"

According to Dumpit, these boxes-on-wheels plying their services across the war-torn country soon became the most popular commuter transport, turning jeepney production into a booming industry and making it the most spectacular invention to hit the road since the Spaniards introduced the horse-drawn carromata. Sarao Motors, for example, began building their jeepneys with bigger bodies to accommodate as many as twenty-four passengers.

The most amazing thing about the Philippine jeepney is that no two are alike: They may share the same shape and entrance, which is in the back. They may reach the same destination. But their similarities end there. For what sets one apart from the others lies in the artwork. One may brag about its discotheque-like interior with miniature spinning silver ball, pulsing lights, and a matching soundtrack blaring from speakers beneath the two long seats. Another may boast artwork that pays homage to the hallucinations of the sixties, the banana revolution of the eighties, or a cloud of galloping horses. Another may prefer a postmodern salute to installation art by showcasing a dazzling display of burloloys across the dashboard—strands of day-old jasmine, holy water inside a plastic bottle molded into the shape of the Virgin Mary, cartoon stickers of naked blondes, pictures of Pope John Paul II. The et cetera of our lives the jeepney cannot live without.

"Regardless of his birthplace, current residence, or nationality, a Filipino is not a Filipino until he has climbed into a jeepney and paid his share of the ride," Dumpit concluded, pausing to make room for the silence that had spread across the crowded room—mostly students, scholars, and faculty members who had spent an entire week arguing in circles about definitions, representations, and authenticity. A silence broken by gasps of astonishment: astonishment at how much truth was in Dumpit's definition of a Filipino. Astonishment at how much one's identity could depend solely on a Technicolor ride Dumpit described as "part lounge, part church, part historical museum, part kitsch, part kunsthaus, but purely Filipino. One hundred percent certified Pinoy."

Vince, like the many Filipinos in the room who had been transported back in time to their first jeepney experience, also recalled his first—and only—jeepney ride. He was five, maybe six. With Jing, Alvin, and Yaya Let. They were going to the barrio, to visit one of Yaya Let's relatives.

Boarding the jeepney from the back, they hunched their way into a tunnel of human sweat and breath. Throughout the entire trip, he tried to ignore the people who, sitting face to face, knee to knee, hip to hip, elbow to elbow, shoulder to shoulder, stared at him. He held his breath while Alvin and Jing peered out through the side window and took in the pastoral view of rice fields and water buffalo bathing in the mud—

a scene typical of a Fernando Amorsolo painting. On the way back, he could smell traces of the barrio on him—its heat, dust, burning trash, and twigs and leaves. It made him so nauseous that, compounded by the bumpy ride and the claustrophobic feeling of being trapped inside a box reeking of perspiration, he dashed out of the jeepney the moment it stopped in front of their house and puked all over the bougainvilleas. After that, he refused to ride in one again.

SKYWAY VIEW

Stuck in gridlock on a two-lane highway that's been converted into seven, Vince continues to explore the doily-covered dashboard cum makeshift altar. Laminated images of Christ with a wounded heart, Christ on the cross, the Mother of Perpetual Help next to a can of grape-scented odorizer. Coiled around the rearview mirror are rosary beads. A tiny battery-operated fan whirs at top speed.

Beside the altar, and within easy reach of the driver, is the cashbox. Stickers on the windshield remind passengers that the driver prefers small bills in the morning and that "Honestly Is the Best Policy."

Vince looks out at the series of shanties. Children bathing, women beating soiled clothes with wooden paddles, a crowd congregating in front of a television.

The knot of the traffic loosens and for a moment, it seems as if the road is gridlock-free, until it comes to a dead stop on the peak of an overpass, vis-à-vis billboards that at night light up the electricity-deprived city in neon. There's HCG, "World's #1 Makers of Toilets and Toilet Fixtures" so "Sit Back & Just Relax."

"Oh my God, she's everywhere," Vince says as a billboard of Sister Marie stretching a condom with her fingers invades his vision. The bubble reads: "Get into the habit. Be Pro-active and Protect yourself with Pro-phylactic."

Below him are Makati's Forbes Park and Das Mariñas Village, posh enclaves designed after American suburbs that, like all subdivisions, have wide streets canopied by acacia trees, landscaping, high walls topped with glass shards and barbed wires, *Architectural Digest*-designed homes, and, last but not least, Mad Max security guards to protect the country's wealthiest families, government officials, foreign investors, ambassadors, and consuls.

On the radio comes the harsh, crying intro of a song. "I Would Die for You" by Prince.

INCHES

Once upon a 1990 in Hawaii, in a twin tower with wraparound lanais, there lived on the edge of Waikiki two very single men. One was from San Vicente in Luzon, Philippine Islands; the other, Hollywood. One November night, they decided to bang a gong, get it on. But no one was surprised, or dropped dead, or threw a fiesta. Door-to-door humping was a common occurrence in gay Honolulu, as common as rain on one side of the street and sunshine on the other.

Everyone knows your name in Honolulu. And if you're out or closeted, it isn't only your name that's public knowledge, but who and when and where and how big and how long and why. So be on guard: BIG MAHULANI IS WATCHING. No kidding. Ask how small gay Honolulu is and you'll be told it can be measured in inches rather than blocks. As for the annual Pride parade, don't blink or you'll miss the dykes on bikes and three pickup trucks carrying drag queens with more body piercings than San Sebastian.

Gay hangouts are as easy to spot as historical landmarks. They're usually located on corners of busy intersections where you're bound to hear drive-by phrases like "Go back to San Francisco," or "Burn in Gomorrah," or "Holy shit, you're a chick with a dick!"

At the center of it all is Hula's Bar & Lei Stand, Honolulu's gay mecca and its only outdoor gay bar. Trolls and closet-cases congregate around a huge banyan tree. Part discotheque, part billiard hall, part café, where the future is read every Thursday for twenty dollars and dates are made every Wednesday, when all clear drinks go for two bucks. And happy hour is every hour on the hour, so drink as much as you want as fast as you can, because the lot it's squatting on is on the market, up for grabs, to anyone who can afford to convert a gay mecca into outlet stores, boutique shops, sports bar, a cineplex.

As for the two single men living in identical wraparound lanais . . . what baffled their neighbors was the news that spread like hives the morning after they exchanged grunts and spit.

"Are they nuts?"

"Who do they think they're fooling?"

"Sounds too fishy."

Predictions and bets were made:

"I give them a month."

"Make that two weeks."

"One day."

"Six hours."

Even Edgar Ramirez, the best friend of the one from P.I., flipped out. "Ten days max, Vince," he said. "You really honest to goodness think it's gonna last? Open your eyes. The guy's a rice queen who gets a hard-on watching *The Last Emperor*."

GUESS WHO'S COMING TO DINNER?

The men in Vince's life . . .

Seth Kahanu: four months if you don't count the two months they dated before Seth mustered the courage to confront Vince about the state of their whatevership. They were in Seth's truck, waiting for the light to change at the Kapiolani–Date intersection. Seth turned to Vince and asked him in Pidgin-English, "Eh, you like go with me or what?" "Go where?" Vince asked, looking lost as a poster child for Special Olympics. Seth pulled over to the curb to squeeze the words out from his brain: "Go steady."

There was Russell Takeshi Tanaka: one year, on and off, plus a three-month trial "engagement" period.

If one-night stands matter, then Carl Yamagita matters.

If fuck buddies count, then count the three months with Albert Kekoalani Ching (Cheung?). Albert was a super-duper guy, a great lay, and Vince would've continued doing him had the Hapa-Hawaiian-Haole babe not confessed that he was a bisexual on parole, had a restraining order from his ex-girlfriend, and had to attend mandatory anger management classes.

Christopher Velasquez was nine months of domestic partnership, which is equivalent to forty-five heterosexual years.

After Christopher came Vince's shortest relationship ever. A Guiness-record-breaking time of six days. And Vince has his mother to thank for it.

When Vince told his mother that he had finally dumped Christopher after a near fist-fight quarrel at Star Market over toilet paper brands—Vince preferred Charmin, for its scent; Christopher insisted on three-ply unscented Scott—the former Mrs. De Los Reyes took it upon herself to play matchmaker.

"I thought it was just the two of us, Mom," Vince said, seeing a third plate setting one November night. It couldn't be for his brother. He was in Paris, trying to seal a relationship with a Northwest flight attendant. "Is Jing coming?" he asked.

"Oh please," Carmen, his mother, said. "Your sister would rather pull a double-shift in the hospital wiping her patients' butts than have a Thanksgiving turkey with us."

"Dad?"

"Your father had his last supper here eons ago."

"Then who?"

"Dave," she answered casually.

"Dave?" Vince conjured up the Daves in his mother's life. Then, "No, you didn't. Why?"

"I happen to like Dave. He's a really nice guy. On top of that, he's got a successful modeling career and gets asked to emcee a lot," she said, referring to Dave Manchester. Irish American model. Kramer's Hunk-of-the-Year. Dave had graced the covers of fashion magazines in Hawaii and Japan, and was currently TV host of Hawaii's longest karaoke singing contest, *Sing Me to Stardom*.

"Plus he always helps me out with the fancy aerobic foot moves," she continued, "and you already know how our instructor enjoys watching us break our bones."

Carmen and Dave were gold members at the same fitness center. They saw each other three times a week at six a.m., for high-impact step aerobics.

"Mom, stop setting me up," Vince said. "I can find my own date."

Vince's words went in one ear and out the other. "Give Dave a chance," she said. "He's very sweet. Next week he's going to show me how to use free weights."

"I can't believe what I'm hearing," Vince said.

"And stop snubbing him. Dave told me that you give him the cold shoulder whenever he tries to talk to you."

"So?"

"Snubbing isn't good. You've always been a snob, and you have to stop. It's not healthy; only gives you wrinkles. If you're not careful, you'll have your midlife crisis before I menopause."

Vince's "I'm leaving" was punctuated by the doorbell.

"Oh, be a good sport and go answer the door, Anak," she said. "I'll go and carve the turkey."

Vince wished his mother would stop interfering with his affairs, driving him nuts with her determination to find him a good and reliable partner. But no matter how close he came to snapping at her, to unleashing invectives he'd regret for the rest of his life, he couldn't. He knew why she did it, why she continued to impose her idea of security and stability and happiness on him, and it wasn't because she herself was stable or happy—she was far from either—or impulsive, like Vince, or purely acting out maternal instincts. It was guilt, guilt that she had disappeared from her children's lives in exchange for a second chance to live in another country with a man who no longer loved her or meant anything to her. So when an opportunity like matchmaking opened up, she dropped everything on her plate and devoted her time and energy to relentlessly pursuing the possibility for security, stability, and happiness for her children, whether they asked for her help or not. Either way, she didn't care: she was making up for those years she'd been absent in their lives, which is why coming out was anticlimactic for Vince. All she told him was, "I know. I've always known. Just don't dump your love on anybody who doesn't care for it."

DIAL M FOR MO.NO.GA.MY.

After dinner and two bottles of red wine, Vince's mother said, "Why don't you hitch a ride home with Dave, Vince? That is if it's O.K. with you, Dave."

"Don't be ridiculous, Carmen," Dave said. "Vince and I practically live next door to each other."

Merlot-tipsy, Vince found himself in Dave's apartment, with Dave uncorking another bottle of wine.

"He opened a what?" Edgar yelled when Vince phoned him the following night.

"The wine wasn't that bad," Vince said.

"You losing your mind or what? He made you drink Vendage, Vince. You never drink wine that's under ten dollars, on sale or not." Edgar continued, "That motherfucking cheapskate rice queen. This is a sign, Vince. Pay attention to what that bottle of Vendage is telling you."

"What are you talking about, Edgar?"

"If he had any respect for you, he could've gone to Longs Drugs or dragged his bubble butt to the ABC store, which is only a stone's throw from your street, thank you, and soaked your high-maintenance ass in Robert Mondavi or Kendall Jackson."

"Never mind, Edgar."

"I'm telling you, Vince. It's a sign."

What Vince didn't tell Edgar was that the morning after he and Dave had brushed their teeth, kissed, and exploded into each other's mouths, Dave had wrapped his arms around Vince and said, "Babe, do you have any soy sauce?"

Baffled, Vince asked why.

"I want to cook us breakfast," Dave explained.

Dazed, Vince stuttered, "Kikkoman or Aloha?"

"Surprise me."

Vince spent that morning in Dave's tub, lathering with Neutrogena while Dave was in the kitchen frying eggs and SPAM, and brewing Lion's Kona coffee. After breakfast, they called in sick, and spent the entire day kissing and taking turns bottoming for each other to Prince's *Purple Rain,* the CD on repeat. After the dove shed its last tear, Dave popped the question.

"Yes," Vince said. "I'll even walk your dog."

"You will?" asked Dave.

"Under one condition."

"Name it."

"Mo.No.Ga.My," Vince spelled out.

For six days, Vince walked Dave's doberman Sally around Kapiolani Park. For six days, he ate Dave's breakfast—crispy-burnt SPAM, Reno Portugese sausage, Libby's corned beef hash, Island eggs cooked over easy, Hinode rice with Aloha soy sauce, and Lion's Kona coffee. For six days, he went straight to Dave's condo after work to get a cheap buzz from two bottles of Vendage Merlot, then fucked the night away to Wendy, Lisa, and the rest of Prince's revolution.

But all good things must come to a close, whether one is ready for it or not. By the sixth—no, the fifth—day, Vince was getting sick from eating Dave's SPAM and Portuguese sausage. By the fifth—no, the third—day, he had cultivated a deep hatred for Sally, who caused him major embarrassment at Kapiolani Park by trying to hump every dog she saw. Like master, like bitch.

And Dave Manchester's monogamy was nearing its expiration date. If it hadn't, in fact, already passed.

"What you expect, dumbass?" Edgar shouted over the phone on the seventh day. "Monogamy to guys like Dave is like a loaf of Wonder bread. It only lasts for a couple of days and then—mildew."

Six months later, Vince found himself sharing the spotlight with Dave, on the stage of the crowded ballroom of the Pagoda Hotel, where five contestants of Philippine ancestry competed in the third annual Mister Pogi pageant. Surprisingly Dave had only slept with two contestants; two of the other three were Born-Again and the third was closeted in the military. Even more surprising was how calm and civil Vince was to Dave throughout the evening, answering whatever questions Dave tossed at him for the sake of a plus point or applause. He spoke to Dave as if for the first time, as if they had no memory to compare with one another. As if neither history nor desire had ever nestled so comfortably between them.

BOOK VI

Islands in the Stream

Sunday in the only Catholic English-speaking country in Asia leaves Vince with only three options: go to church, shop, or attend mass in a mall. Manila is the church-mall capital of Southeast Asia, a religious shopper's fantasy come true.

Say, for example, that you are one of the formidable matronas de Metro Manila. Your marriage to a senator has outlasted most of your friends because you and your hubby have agreed that estrangement is cheaper than annulment. You let him live his philandering lifestyle so long as he doesn't interrupt your tango lessons with your straight dance instructor.

Being a Manila socialite, you're accustomed to attending weekly groundbreaking and ribbon-cutting events, including the one coming up this week—the opening of the country's first Hard Rock Café. It will be televised live by the two warring TV networks, GMA-7 and ABS-CBN 2. Everyone in Manila's high society will be there. So you accept the invitation.

You disappear into the wardrobe closet, rushing out a minute later, screaming in agony. Not from the puppy-sized rats that have managed to skitter under the glass-capped walls of your Forbes Park comfort, but from a sudden attack of midlife fashion crisis. And there's no way, not a fat chance, that you're attending this ribbon-cutting ceremony dressed up like every other socialite matron—shoulder-padded blouse and elastic waistband pants, or off-the-shoulder flowing dress with matching face-lift, liposuction, fixative brows, and typhoon-proof hairdo. No way. You promised yourself that you would not, over your dead body, start looking like your friends and enemies. You're different, a risk-taker, a trendsetter. So what are you gonna do? Here are your choices:

You could go Gucci, Dior, or De La Renta. Go to Rustan's or boutique-hopping along Ayala and Makati avenues. If you're looking for something with an ethnic twist, perhaps a fitted pink butterfly-sleeve gown, go to Divisoria and have it sewn while you practice the rhumba with your dance instructor. But if it's a Nancy Kwan-inspired cheongsam dress that your heart desires, go to Binondo, Manila's Chinatown. If Binondo disappoints you, make the sign of the cross and cross the highway toward Quiapo.

Flanked by Muslim-staffed bazaars, Quiapo is usually riddled with puddles and infested with flies and pickpockets, but you're willing to take the risk in the name of fashion. Besides, what you wear might make the U.S. ambassador's head turn. Try on the G-strings of the indigenous tribes displaced across the country, richly woven or embroidered, with matching accessories, like the single-feather head ornament of headhunters. But if you really want to be the talk of the night, step into the spotlight wearing a necklace, bracelet, and anklets made from filed human teeth.

NO ONE IN BETWEEN

Lancôme counter. Rustan's department store. Vince approaches a saleslady spraying the air with Chanel No. 5 and walking through it as if in a trance.

"Good afternoon, sir," she says. "Do you want to smell like the French?"

"I'm looking for the restroom," Vince says.

"It's in your house, sir," she says with a smile. Then, "How about some cleansing products, sir? You know, we have a special promo right now. If you spend the equivalent of fifteen dollars or 1,250 pesos, you can avail of the gift pack."

"No thanks," Vince says, growing impatient.

"He means the comfort room," an American lady intervenes on his behalf. "That's what they call restrooms here. Or CR."

"Thank you," Vince says, wondering why they don't tell you shit like this in tourist guidebooks and brochures.

The saleslady spews out an epic-length direction that leads him smack into the middle of Home Furnishings.

"CR, sir?" The salesman redirects him to the escalator, which takes him back down to the ground floor, where a grocery clerk bagging iceberg lettuce tells him to take the elevator, get off on the second floor, turn left, and it should be right there, sir, right by the Drakkar cologne display, only your eyes can miss it, sir, have a nice day, sir.

Arriving at the Toys-4-U section, Vince is ready to bring down the display of Cabbage Patch Kids. His bladder would've burst by now, but his bladder is not what's at stake here.

Hey, don't need to get worked up.

It's not worth it.

The workers are probably having a bad day.

They don't earn much.

At least the A/C is working.

At least I now know it's called CR.

Be patient.

That's right. I'll find it.

If I had only availed of the promo, perhaps . . .

Too late now.

Just laugh it off.

Look at yourself in the mirror; every vein in your body is bulging.

Stop it.

Anger leads to anxiety, which only speeds up the urge.

And I'm already breaking out in a sweat.

The nearest department store to Rustan's is Landmark. But it's jam-packed with aggressive shoppers because of the Afternoon Madness sale from two to four p.m. only.

So he heads over to Park Square, holding his breath and trying not to release any gas for fear he'll shit farts—or fart shit—in his pants. Luckily for him, an Odyssey Records salesclerk, bless her heart, properly directs him to a comfort room that is far from comforting—all stalls are occupied. He unbuttons his trousers, ready to burst into the next available one.

A minute passes and the poopers are still grunting, farting, splashing. Vince raps on all doors and receives no response. The contractions resume.

Vince sucks in air, Lamaze style.

Slow

ly

Now hold

It

Long

And gentle

Then squeeze

The sphincter inward

Clench

The buttcheeks

Hard

Harder

Good

One more time

Slow

Ly

Oh, oh, a flush

Door opens

Vince runs into the stall, nearly knocks down the kid, who leaves him a souvenir.

I can't sit on this.

Why not?

There's no toilet seat.

Then squat! It's not like I never sat on faces before.

No fucking way.

Poopers can't be choosers.

And the toilet paper.

What about it?

There's no toilet paper.

Of course not. What do you think the bucket of water in front of you is for?

But it's empty.

Oh, shit!

Holy shit.

Deep shit.

Like a golden geisha, Vince skitters out of the restroom and halts in front of a window display of toilet-paper rolls stacked up like pyramids. Mercury Drugs is having a special on MD and Kleene two-ply, but the lines to the cashiers are a mile long. Near tears, he passes Kenny Rogers Roasters then Dunkin Donuts then retreats to Kenny Rogers Roasters to make certain he's not hallucinating. He isn't. The sign on the two doors read: CM and CW.

Vince enters the crowded restaurant, where all go to eat the country singer's famous rotisserie chicken while gawking at his achievements and contributions to the U.S. recording industry. Gold discs, album covers, and photographs of Kenny and his ladies adorn the walls. Kenny with Dottie West. Kenny with Dolly Parton. Kenny in Sheena Easton's arms.

"Hey, stand in line, buddy," an American man shouts. Vince ignores him, rushes up to the counter, and asks for napkins. Kenny's employee gives him a sheet so thin he can only use it to dig into his right nostril. Vince holds up two hands. "Ten," he says, "give me ten. Please." The worker nods, begins carefully separating the napkins one by one from the inch-thick stack.

"Jesus Christ," Vince mutters, about to ask why he couldn't just have the whole stack when the worker cuts him off with "SOP sir."

"What the hell is SOP?" Vince says, struggling to express his anger and frustration while at the same time concealing his discomfort.

"Standard Operating Procedure, sir."

"I'll remember that," Vince says, tacking it onto his mental list of useful acronyms that's now as long as a roll of toilet paper. Snatching the ten sheets, he dashes straight for the door marked CM, Comfort Men. In the stall, he parks his ass on the porcelain throne and braces himself for the most unforgettable dump of his life. Accompanied by the piped-in music of Kenny and Dolly singing their number-one hit, *Islands in the Stream*. But he's too humiliated to make this moment memorable and too pissed off at Edgar and at himself, for letting Edgar talk him into joining the pageant.

Stop blaming Edgar and start owning up to my actions.

But it was *his* idea.

It sure was. And I executed it.

AND THE MANILA ENVELOPE, PLEASE

Less than a month ago, Edgar had invited himself over to Vince's Waikiki condo. "Here," he said, shoving a manila envelope under Vince's nose.

"What's this?" Vince asked.

"Your passport off this rock."

Vince opened the packet containing an application form and the guidelines for the Third Annual Mister Pogi Pageant. "Pogi," as in "cutie-pie."

"You fuckin' kidding me, right?"

"I thought you sick and tired of this place," Edgar said.

"I am."

"I thought you like change of scenery."

"I do."

"I thought you like repeat your mistakes in a foreign language."

"I will."

"Then what you waiting for? This your easy way out of here."

"But Mister Pogi?"

"Oh Vince, just fill it out and get it back to me ASAP," Edgar said.

Vince skimmed the guidelines, read them out loud. "The applicant must be at least twenty-one years old . . . of Filipino descent (send a Xeroxed copy of birth certificate for proof of authenticity . . . a resident of Hawaii . . . of good moral character . . . never engaged in any activity which could be characterized as dishonest, immoral, immodest, indecent, or in bad taste. This is a joke, Edgar."

"It flew me to the Big Apple on first class," Edgar said. "It made me feel like I own carte blanche. It gave me twenty-four-seven networking privileges, not to mention sleeping with three cast members of *Miss Saigon*, including the Eurasian pimp understudy."

"But that's you, Edgar," Vince said. "I don't need the spotlight as much as you do."

"Look, Vince. Right now, you only get two options: shoot for the Statue of Liberty or rot on Gilligan's rock," Edgar said, reminding Vince again of his New Year's resolution: that before 1991 ended, he'd wrap up his thirteen-year relationship with Honolulu and move to a place far, far away. Away from the Aloha spirit and extended family dramas. Away from the locals, whose idea of a dream vacation was Las Vegas, Hawaii's second capital. Away from SPAM-themed luaus.

"No worry, chicken curry," Edgar continued. "All you gotta do is stay focused, stay confident, and believe in all the clichés about believing in yourself. And you'll go home a winner. Relax. Live this moment up. Because not many get the chance for shine."

MERCURY RETROGRADE

Inside Mercury Drugstore, Vince is trying to find a line that leads to one of four pharmacy clerks manning the counter. Realizing that the only queue that exists in the country is a curly-Q, he joins the army of aggressive customers pushing their way to the front—many of them coughing, hacking, and sneezing on each other.

At the counter, Vince listens in on the other customers as they describe their symptoms to the clerks.

"I've been coughing up phlegm for over a week now," one says.

The clerk asks for its color.

"Red," he says.

"When was your last chest x-ray?"

"Last year."

"And?"

"Negative."

"Take Augmentin, five hundred milligrams three times a day."

"I have high blood pressure," says another.

"How high?"

"One fifty over one hundred."

"Take Norvasc."

"Is it true that tomatoes are good for you?" a man from the back shouts.

"Yes. They contain lycopene, number-one killer of cancer cells. It also helps prevent cardiac diseases."

"What about split ends?" the girl behind Vince asks.

"Sunsilk."

"Not Head & Shoulders?"

"No. Sunsilk contains Frutamens."

Finally it's Vince's turn. He hands over his slip of self-prescribed medication.

"Immodium?" the clerk reads out loud. "Sorry sir, we don't carry this brand."

"What do you have?" Vince asks.

"Loperamide," the clerk answers and triggers a tsunami of reaction: "Ay, ka diri!" "Gross." "How tragic!" "That's what he gets for drinking tap water."

"Give me whatever you have. Quickly, please," Vince says, ignoring the insipid remarks, though the thought of dropping a bomb right there and then has crossed his mind several times.

"How long have you had LBM, sir?"

"LBM?"

"Loose bowel movement, sir."

"First episode was fifteen minutes ago."

"Any cramping?"

"A little."

"Take two capsules now, then one after each bowel movement. But do not exceed four capsules in a twenty-four-hour period," he says. "And drink lots of Wilkins."

"Wilkins?"

"Mineral water. Good for dehydration," the clerk explains. "And lots of chiquitas."

"Chiquitas?" Vince asks.

"Small bananas. They're excellent for binding stool."

Tourist Tips

- Fight dehydration: always carry a bottle of mineral water.

- Fight diarrhea: don't drink from taps or drinking fountains.

- Don't order drinks on the rocks, unless you made the ice cubes yourself.

- Fight dengue: stay away from pools, flowerpots, or discarded tires with stagnant water in them; they are breeding grounds for mosquitoes.

- Dengue fever is one of the leading causes of death in the infant to twenty age group.

- According to the DOH (Department of Health), dengue cases quadruple during the rainy months, overcrowding ERs, hospitals, and funeral parlors.

- Beware of filariasis, an infectious tropical disease caused by roundworms in the lymph nodes. Transmitted by mosquitoes, these parasitic worms can lead to elephantiasis and inflammation of limbs and male genitals, sometimes swelling a scrotum to the size of a bowling ball.

- Fight elephantiasis: use insect repellant that says DEET, or diethylmetatoluamide, on it. Recommended dosage is 30%–35% strength for adults and 6%–10% for children.

- Wear long-sleeved shirts and long pants when stepping out.

- Manila is full of stray cats and dogs.

- Screen all windows and dome sleeping quarters with nets.

- Drowning is also a leading cause of death among children, usually during flash floods, ferry and boat disasters, and fluvial processions.

- Fight leptospirosis: do not wade in floodwater; it might be teeming with the bacterial disease, transmitted from the urine of infected rats.

- Protect yourself: use Safeguard. Recommended by nine out of ten doctors.

- Avoid going to hospitals, unless it is extremely urgent. The treatment is comparable to the first world but the paperwork is a nightmare. Too many windows, too many receipts, and too many employees, oftentimes with conflicting information. It is not uncommon to be admitted for a mild case of diarrhea and discharged with hypertension.

Vince on the Verge

Inside National Bookworms, on the ground floor of Greenbelt Mall, Vince asks the half-asleep salesclerk for the postcard section. She points a copy of *Cat's Eye* to three rotating stands next to the Filipiniana and Danielle Steele sections, then shelves Margaret Atwood's novel alongside Jessica Hagedorn's *Dogeaters,* James Herriot's *All Creatures Great and Small,* and *Chicken Soup for the Soul* in the section marked PETS.

Minutes ago, he found Salman Rushdie's *The Satanic Verses* in OCCULT, Garcia Marquez's *One Hundred Years of Solitude* in SELF-HELP, Sandra Cisneros's *The House on Mango Street* in ARTS & ARCHITECTURE, and Jean Genet's *Our Lady of Flowers* in RELIGION & MEDITATION, right beside biographies of Mother Theresa, Pope John Paul II, and Sister Marie.

A tall mestizo guy walks over to Vince and stands opposite him, excusing himself as he slowly spins the carousel, stopping at a postcard of two early twentieth-century American soldiers posing with native children and a pair of barbers cutting hair in front of a bamboo hut.

An optic collision occurs, and Vince drops his postcard of an American schoolteacher being carried in a chair by two Igorot men from a mountain tribe in Baguio.

The guy bends to pick it up, but Vince beats him to it with a "Thanks." The guy smiles, pockets a postcard of a soldier and a monitor lizard, then walks away, turning around once to nod at Vince, still ogling him.

CHANGING TIMES FIVE

At the 10 ITEMS OR LESS CASH ONLY express line, Vince hands the post-cards to one of four female employees fighting post-lunch narcolepsy behind the register. One of them takes the postcards from Vince.

The disturbing image of a slain Filipino who, as the caption says, had run amok and killed an American soldier wakes her from her noon-day trance.

"And they say martial law was bad," she says, showing it to her coworkers.

One by one, she looks through Vince's postcards.

"Is that Emilio Aguinaldo?" the one beside her asks, pointing her mouth to the portrait of a Philippine president with a top hat, white gloves, bowtie, and tasseled cane.

"Yes." She gives it to the cashier, who says she's appalled that her ancestors elected a dog for a president.

"No wonder we lost the war against the Americans," she says.

"Excuse me," Vince says, "I'd like to pay for them now."

The one closest to the cash register says, "Ang sungit," which trans-lates to: "What a dick!"

The postcards are handed back to the salesclerk farthest from the register. She begins counting them.

Vince is about to say ten when she silences him with her palm. After a recount, she brings a thick book marked POSTCARD RECORDS out from under the cash register and copies down the caption of each card while the others watch her beautiful penmanship appear across the page.

"Chocolate Hills, Bohol, Philippines."

"Seminarians, Vigan, Ilocos Sur, 1929."

"Tarsius Philippensis is the world's oldest mammal . . ."

"One-sixth of the Filipino population was killed in the Philippine-American War."

"Emilio Aguinaldo signing the Declaration of Independence on June 12, 1898, in Malolos, Bulacan."

"First bred in Manila Zoo in 1962, the zebronkey is half-zebra, half-donkey."

Once she's done writing her epic, she passes the postcards to the checker, who hands them over to the bagger, who gives them to the cashier, who scans them one by one across the barcode detector.

"Fifteen pesos," the cashier says.

Vince hands her a twenty-peso bill.

"Do you have any change, sir?"

"Yes," Vince says.

The cashier holds her palm out to Vince who, by this time, is ready to run amok himself. He shoots her a murderous look that quickly develops into a staring contest, with the other clerks fastening their eyes on him as well. The contest would have lasted until closing time but Vince, unable to control his temper any longer, says, "What are you talking about? I gave you a twenty-peso bill and you said the cards add up to fifteen pesos."

"That's right," the cashier says. "And I asked you for change."

"Let me start again," Vince says. "Twenty minus fifteen is five, right?"

Offended, the cashier tells him she's not stupid, that she passed the entrance exam at Saint Benilde.

"I didn't say you were," Vince says. "You did."

The cashier glowers at him. The other salesclerks exchange puzzled looks.

"I just want to know why you have to make something simple so damn complicated," Vince says.

"It's not, sir," the cashier says. "It's actually very simple. You're the one who's getting high blood pressure for nothing."

"Then why are you asking me for change when you should be giving me change?"

"Because a change for a change, sir. You give me a five-peso coin and I, in return, will give you a ten-peso bill."

"You don't carry change in your cash register?"

"Change for a change, sir," the cashier repeats.

Vince takes out dollar and peso bills. "I don't have any. See? Never mind, just give me my postcards. You can keep the damn change."

"Next time bring change with you, O.K.?" She hands him a five-peso coin from her purse.

The postcards then travel to the checker, whose job is to match the items with those on the receipt. She doodles all over it with her red pen, then hands the cards to the fourth body in the assembly line—the bagger, who slips the postcards into a plastic bag before delicately Scotch-taping its neatly folded top.

"Thank you, sir," they all say in unison. "Come again."

Vince rides the escalator up to the cinema house. What's playing? A mob is rushing in and out of *In the Name of Shame,* so far the most-awarded movie in Philippine film history. Also showing: a Hong Kong martial arts film starring Cynthia Rothrock (who?); a Brooke Shields romantic flick that went straight to video; and Mike Nichols's *Regarding Henry,* starring Harrison Ford.

Vince searches the crowd in front of the snack bar for the postcard thief. He's not there, so he approaches the ticket booth to buy an orchestra seat for *Regarding Henry.* The next showtime isn't for another hour, but people are already walking into the theater.

Standing in the aisle with his back against the wall, Vince waits for a well-lit scene so he can scan the crowded and noisy room for a vacant seat. In the movie, Harrison Ford, an overworked lawyer, has already survived a gunshot wound in the head, spent months in a rehab hospital, regained his speech, befriended a black physical therapist, and is back home, fighting the biggest battle of his life—reclaiming his memory.

But Vince, like Harrison Ford, has difficulty concentrating. Too much active interference: potato chips being munched, pagers going off, ten thousand conversations going on at once, bodies shuffling along the aisles, seats creaking, heads bobbing.

"The movie's not bad." It's the postcard thief. "But you'll only get a handjob here at the most." He pauses to squeeze Vince's arm. "Meet me outside in five minutes if you're interested."

Twenty-four seconds later, Vince goes out to look for him amidst a crowd that has come from nowhere, all going to see *In the Name of Shame*. Vince spots the postcard thief using the payphone. "Business call," is the explanation he offers Vince in the parking garage where he leads him.

"Where are we going?" Vince asks.

"That depends." The postcard thief scans the lot, then unzips his pants. Vince gets an instant hard-on.

"You like that?" he asks, then begins stroking himself. "It's yours for three hundred pesos."

"You want me to pay you twelve dollars for sex?" Vince asks, stunned.

"You think I'm free?" The postcard thief zips up his pants. "Pucha, Pare, this is not America. I'm giving you the best deal pero kung ayaw mo, e di huwag." Translation: no money, no honey.

Vince is speechless.

"So? Do you want it or not?"

"Of course, I do. But not for twelve dollars," is what Vince wants to say.

"Here." The postcard thief hands Vince the stolen postcard then struts off, his pager beeping as Vince watches him disappear into the afternoon light. On the postcard is an address somewhere in Pasay City. He flips it over and looks at a famous turn-of-the-century gag picture of a monitor lizard propped on the belly of an American officer feigning surprise. The caption reads: WELCOME TO THE JUNGLE!

THE JEEPNEY, KING OF THE ROAD

Edgar,
Garcia Marquez was right: no such thing
as magical realism in Macondo, or Manila.
Mention magical realism and people here will
think you're magically retarded. What you see
is what you get, and it comes to you at 100mph
and smelling of diesel fumes. All that crap about
Western metaphors, signs, and symbols is useless
here. Now I understand why Martin Sheen had
the heart attack and why the film crew kept
tripping on acid while filming Apocalypse
Now. *Like the maid of my maid said, "The*
jungle is not for everybody."

In a shithole, Vince

Edgar Ramirez
1586 Murphy St.
Honolulu, HI 96819

#2 Remember Nelson Ariola, the prick in 5th grade who thought he was more white than Stephen Bean, so he transferred to Punahou School? He should've just come here. There's an entire aisle in Mercury Drugs especially for him and his kind. Skin-whitening cream, skin-bleaching lotion, skin-lightening gel for dark armpits, skin-whitening plus anti-aging cream. Or he can just drown himself in a pool of papayas. Green papayas, according to the salesclerk, are supposed to be more effective than orange ones.

Vince

Edgar Ramirez
1586 Murphy St.
Honolulu, HI 96819

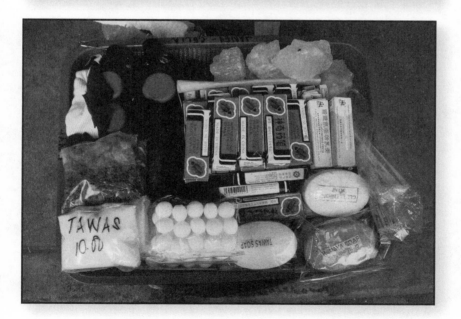

INTRAMUROS, THE OLD WALLED CITY OF MANILA

Alvin,
Today was really nice. Too bad I had to spend
it here. The sky was so blue I wanted to look
up but I didn't, afraid I'd fall into Hades, like
what happened to a scholar from Ohio who
was here to research, of all topics, rice! He was
admiring the sky when he fell into a hole. His
chin got caught on the edge as he was falling.
Fractured jaw, lost all of his teeth. He's suing
the city. I wish him all the luck. I saved the
front-page article to prove I'm not making this
up. Shit. Gotta run. Vince
P.S. Dreamed of Lolo Al last night. He was
asking me for his dentures. What does it mean?
I miss my room.

Alvin De Los Reyes
430 Keoniana St.
2D
Honolulu, HI 96815

Tao of Cartography

Red light means "Gas it!"

    One way equals four-way.

    Motorcyles speeding on sidewalks.

    People living off garbage.

    People living in garbage.

    Komiks vendor gives birth to mudfish.

    Brownout is blackout.

    Diarrhea is an acronym.

Where are all these metropolitan hyperrealities exploding from? Where else, but in the Metro Malignant mind of Vince; Vicente; Vincere. El Conquistador. Constantino to the nation's First Daughter. First-class passenger to the city of contrasts and blackouts. The capital of collapsing metaphors and memories.

On the toilet, Vince meditates on Manila, the meaning of Manila, the city that housed his childhood Christmases and summers, when his grandfather whisked him, his siblings, and Yaya Let away from the heat and their routine lives in San Vicente and brought them to a mansion tucked in the cool mountains of the very exclusive Antipolo, a getaway spot for the rich and the infamous who wanted to leave Manila without leaving Manila. The mansion, with its matching tennis court, garden, and swimming pool, belonged to Don Alfonso's childhood friend, the widower Don Renato de Guzman, who, before his death in '76, was one of the most in-demand architects in the country. Some of the buildings he'd designed, such as the Central

Bank and the U.S. ambassador's residence in Forbes Park, are now considered historical landmarks.

Vince remembered Don Renato as a high-spirited man who lived to laugh, at himself and at the circus freaks who ran the country to its grave. He downplayed his success by insisting he was only famous because he chose the perfect master and the right enemies: he had studied under Frank Lloyd Wright and had turned down Imelda Marcos when she asked him to design her film center.

During their vacations, Don Alfonso would take his grandchildren around the city. One summer, they spent an entire day at the Manila Zoo and at the mall across the street, Harrison Plaza. They dined in fancy restaurants like Aristocrat's and had pizzas at the newly opened Shakey's in Cubao, where they also shopped for clothes and school supplies. They strolled around Luneta Park, rode slides and climbed statues in the shapes of dinosaurs, ate hot dogs and drank Coke, and circled the Jurassic-themed playground on a train. Then, before heading to the bay to watch the sunset, they strolled to the skating rink and watched people skate around a spinning globe fountain that released water from the top, trickling over continents lit in bright colors.

In December the ritual was repeated, with the addition of a midnight mass on Christmas Eve and frequent trips to C.O.D., where Vince, Alvin, and Jing reverently watched the display of mechanical toys from the second-floor façade of the department store, reenacting a scene from the book of Christmas. One year, it was Rudolph and the reindeers pulling a lifelike Santa Claus on a sleigh across a snow-covered street, going from house to house to deliver presents to children who went running to their front doors to receive them. Another, it was the three kings following a traveling star that led them to Mary, Joseph, and Jesus in a stable in Bethlehem. Yuletide tunes played throughout the night. A new Christmas meant different scenery, another story. But each was as beautiful and electric as old reveries.

It was also in Manila that they caught up on movies. First-run Tagalog melodramas for Yaya Let, Jing, and Alvin, and American films for Don Alfonso and Vince.

Manila. The sprawling metropolis that, after being back in it for only four days, is becoming more and more the capital city of Vince's frustrations, daydreams, nightmares, reflections, and wonderment. It overloads his senses, wakes up tastebuds he thought he never had, or had lost, guides him from one darkness to the next, from one window of sadness to the next, from one reverie to the next. It shocks him with what was once familiar. It assaults him with memories that pull him, break him. It floods him with dreams, his grandfather appearing in all of them, first as apparition then as cameo, with a face, body, voice.

If Vince believed in the Tao of cartography, he'd go straight to a map, point his middle finger at the 180-degree longitude line, in the middle of the Pacific Ocean, and say, there, right there is where it all began, that series of lines that splits the ocean in half and propels him into the next nightmare and memory, that part of the world where yesterday suddenly merges with tomorrow.

CHOCOLATE HILLS, BOHOL, PHILIPPINES

Alvin,
You want madness and malaria? Forget
Conrad's Congo. The horrible heart of the 20th
century is right here in Metro Malignant. So
many contradictions, so little room to vent. I
feel like a squatter, squeezing myself inside
boxes. I don't know where to begin, except I
still can't believe here is where we all started.
Smaller. I have to write smaller. I'm running
out of space and my stomach's turning again! It
feels like I came here just to take a dump. Did
I? Gotta run, Vince
P.S. Still trying to figure out why
they're called chocolates. Hershey's kisses?

Alvin De Los Reyes
430 Keoniana St.
2D
Honolulu, HI 96815

THOMASITE SCHOOLTEACHER BEING CARRIED
IN A CHAIR BY IGOROTS

*#2 The longer I'm here the more I'm convinced that
everything in this city conspires to vex me. Either
that, or this is where Mercury goes retrograde. I
can't buy a pack of AA batteries without popping a
blood vessel. The cashier put the batteries on a tray
behind the others and told me I had to wait, but I
was the only one ready to make a purchase. I lost it.
I started shouting. Two guards with guns had to
escort me out. Had to take an Ativan. In the
dump, Vince*
*P.S. Better cherish this postcard. I nearly strangled
the four cashiers for it.*
*P.S. The schoolteacher reminds me of our
great-great-aunt. Didn't she take a similar photo?*

Alvin De Los Reyes
430 Keoniana St.
2D
Honolulu, HI 96815

MORO AMOKED AT ASTURIAS

Mom,
Did you know the Virgin Mary has a TV
commercial where she walks out of her grotto
and asks everyone to pray the rosary? There
are billboards of her everywhere and shrines
in the mall. Last month she appeared in Agoo,
La Union, to a teenage transvestite. Everyone
went there to faint. Some went blind from
staring at the sun too long. See what you've
been missing out on all these years? Time for
you to come home, and experience it live.

Vince

Carmen Formoso
1519 Kaumualii St.
#310
Honolulu, HI 96819

BOOK VII

Sexxxy

Vince, once again, is in a cab, meandering through narrow, labyrinthine streets in Pasay City, one of eight cities that make up Metropolitan Manila, or, as Bino Boca dubs it, "Metro Malignant." He's seen it through the lens of the controversial filmmaker, in sociopolitical flicks like *Taste of P* and, most recently, *In the Name of Shame:* a squalid city, overcrowded with squatters, vendors, love motels, auto and electronic repair shops, gambling parlors, and strip joints, like Chicks O' Clock, one of the locations where Boca shot *In the Name of Shame*. It is where Mia (Kris Aquino) worked as a stripper/karaoke hostess before she went to live illegally in Japan, making ends meet as an underpaid sushi maker by day and bar hostess at night.

"Pasay City can live on sex alone," the neo-realist director once told Kris on *PM Talking with Yours Truly*. And Boca is not far from the truth. If Pasay's not fucking, it's playing twenty-four-hour blackout bingo or holding the next assassination of an international figurehead. In the early seventies, Pasay City made headlines twice. The first was on November 27, 1970, when a surrealist painter from Bolivia lunged at Pope Paul VI with a knife, just hours after the pope had landed in the Philippines. It was the first time a pope had visited the country. Two years later, shortly after martial law went into effect, an assassin tried to kill Imelda Marcos as she was handing out prizes to the winners of the National Beautification and Cleanliness contest, one of her many pet projects as governor of Metro Manila.

Boca came from an impoverished family. "We were poor, Protestant, but proud," he told Kris. Before he ventured into filmmaking, he was directing plays for the Philippine Unconventional Theater Association (PUTA), which he co-founded with playwright and screenwriter Rimbaud Woo. "He was making independent movies way before Island Pictures and Miramax," Rimbaud, who penned all of Boca's films, said. "In my opinion, he and Derek Jarman are the forefathers of the indies."

But it wasn't until Boca made *Taste of P* that the world took notice of the anti-Marcos director who, as a child, recycled bottles and sold tabloids to help pay for his education. Cineastes described him as the next Ingmar Bergman or the next Federico Fellini—two masters Boca credits as his influences.

Vince was a sophomore at the University of Hawaii when *Taste of P* had its premiere at the Hawaii International Film Festival. But he had no desire whatsoever to see it. He'd seen the previews—aerial shots of Pasay City, people stampeding as machine guns muffled their screams, semi-nude men getting arrested in front of brothels, close-ups of an issue of *Time* magazine with President Aquino on the cover, a man grinning as he holds up a severed head, a threesome between the film's lead characters.

"Forget it," he told Edgar. "I don't need any more melodrama in my life."

"And what you call the recent string of losers you've had? A one-night stand extended to four months with a bisexual, a closet case in dire need of an anger management class, and a three-month trial at domestic partnership with big bottom Russell Tanaka. Please, Vince. No even get me started."

"Shut up, Edgar. I'm just not in the mood to sit through a two-hour porno passing off as a sociopolitical flick."

"Come on, Vince."

"It has a close-up of a severed head, Edgar. And the head is real."

"Because Boca is a neo-realist! Besides, this one's supposed to be the most controversial film in the history of Pinoywood."

"That's just publicity, Edgar," Vince said. "You'd get more gratification from *Fritz the Cat,* or Japanese porn with the pubes blurred out."

"But it's free. And you're cheap," Edgar said. "Besides, I have the hots for the hustler. He so onolicious that I'm willing to risk third-world malaria, hepatitis, and diarrhea just to be in a threesome with him and that dirty old German."

"Too late. The hustler is already dead," Vince said, of the Amerasian and then-rising movie star.

"How you know?" Edgar asked.

"Jing told me. She read it in *Kislap.* He died in his sleep last week."

"Bangungut?" Edgar asked.

"Supposedly," Vince said. "Why don't you ask Jing to go instead? She loves that lead actress—Pooky Moreno."

"Nah. A movie date with Jing is worse than Portuguese torture," Edgar said. "Fags and full-moon-only lesbians should not slurp from the same straw. Look what happened to Richard Chamberlain after he made out with Barbara Stanwyck in *The Thorn Birds.* He was forced to come out."

"Yeah, to his lover," Vince said.

"Come on, Vince. Just go with me," Edgar said. "Anyway, it's 'cause of you I hooked on Tagalog melodrama."

"Me?" Vince asked. "No, it was Jing."

"No, was you, Vince," Edgar said. "Jing was the one who rented the Beta tapes at Sampaguita Video, but you was my translator. That's why you no more choice than to see *Taste of P* with me. Besides, I no trust subtitles. They always leave out the subtext."

Vince ended up going. He and Edgar stood in line for hours because the film festival was handing out free tickets to locals so they could give up a day at the beach to sit inside the cramped Kuhio and Varsity Twin Theaters and try and catch up with the subtitles. Honolulu's closet cases were also there; they'd heard about the raunchy ménage-a-trois that took up nearly a quarter of the film.

Taste of P had its world premiere at the 1988 Hawaii International Film Festival, where it received the Bird of Paradise Audience Award. It was later released in selected theaters in Manila as *Patikim (Can I Taste?)*, then banned, per the order of President Aquino.

SHAKE-A-BOMBA

The female lead in *Taste of P* was Pooky Moreno. Touted as a screen goddess from the early to mid-eighties, Pooky Moreno was a Visayan brown beauty who won a modeling contest on a daytime TV variety show. From there, she was chosen to be Tanduay Rum's calendar girl for two years in a row. Then Bino Boca took a risk and cast her in the lead of *Pooky Acts Up*, as a University of the Philippines student activist who gets incarcerated in an underground prison and repeatedly raped and tortured by soldiers and generals.

The movie, partly shot like a documentary with voiceover and lengthy monologues, focuses on the various torture methods the Marcos regime used on its female victims: punching and kicking and mashing their breasts, shoving a cucumber covered with chili peppers into their vaginas, electrocuting their nipples and genitals, making them lie on beds of ice. Grim as it was, it broke box-office records, making Pooky Moreno one of the hottest and most in-demand sex symbols of the mid-eighties, alongside actresses named after soft drinks—Pepsi Paloma, Sarsi Emmanuel, Coca Zobel, R.C. Araneta, Sasha Padilla, Fanta Elizalde.

Pooky Acts Up was the first Tagalog movie to show full frontal nudity. One unforgettable scene was Pooky getting gangbanged by soldiers in the background while actual female victims of martial law recounted their nightmarish experiences, comparing themselves to the comfort women of WWII and the Marcos regime to the Japanese Imperial Army during their three-year occupation of the islands.

A sequel, *Pooky Night Fever*, and a prequel, *Pooky Remembers*, were released a year apart from each other. The success of the three films, dubbed *My Pooky Trilogy*, pushed the marginalized bomba flicks into the spotlight of Pinoywood. Directors and actors who needed to revive otherwise stalled or flagging careers eagerly jumped onto the soft-porn bandwagon, willing to moan behind or in front of the camera.

Pooky Moreno's films continued to dominate the box office until the MTRCB, or Movie and Television Regulation and Classification Board, banned *Pooky's Lips Now*, a movie about a Filipino American CIA officer whose mission was to look for POWs in Vietnam and hunt down a colonel allegedly conspiring with the Vietcong. Using her brain and body, Pooky accomplished her mission in eighty minutes.

The movie was so demeaning to women that the Aquino administration took immediate action by banning it, saying it was nothing more than an eighty-minute advertisement promoting sex tours in the Philippines' virgin forests, disguised as a Vietnamese jungle. A committee was formed to head a "crusade against immorality in the arts and lifestyle section of the Filipinos."

Film critics and scholars protested the censorship and criticized Aquino for denying artists freedom of expression. One journalist said, "We kicked a despot out of the country and replaced him with a rosary-clinging housewife."

Pooky Moreno disappeared from the scene right around the *Pooky's Lips Now* controversy, only to reemerge two years later, newly christened as Jolie B Rizal, a Charismatic Catholic and a devotee of the Virgin Mary.

DRIVE-BY VIGILS

"What's wrong?" Vince asks.

"Lamay na naman, sir." The driver points to the street, which is blocked off.

"Lamay?" Vince asks.

The driver searches for its English equivalent.

"Patay, sir."

"A wake?" Vince asks. "Another one?"

It's the fourth they've encountered since Vince slid into the backseat an hour ago, making him wonder why people were dying faster than flies in Pasay City. In the second one, the road was so narrow the mourners were literally right in his face, wailing over a coffin.

"I drop you here, sir," the driver says.

"Here?"

"Bad sign, sir," the driver says. "This is the fourth one, and four is not a good number."

But you're not even Chinese, Vince was about to say, when the cab driver interrupts with: "Anyway, where you want to go is very near here, sir. Only two or three blocks away."

Vince gets out of the cab and into the noise of horns and yelling voices trapped in the pileup of cars. In the stagnant air, the dizzying smell of gas and oil fumes mixed with the pungent scent of flowers and candles makes him want to throw up. Nauseous, he sits on the curb in front of the house holding the wake.

When he was fourteen, Vince dreamt that his grandfather was eating candles from Vince's birthday cake. "So nobody can take away your years, hijo," his grandfather said, then began coughing. "Lolo Al," Vince, who in the dream appeared as a child, said. He watched his grandfather spit one cord of phlegm and blood after another into his hands, then braid them into a rope.

"Remember, Vicente," his grandfather said, "swallow the candles." He tied the rope around his chest, punctured a hole in the corrugated roof, and let it lift him up into the sky.

The following day, Vince had been in a daze, as if he'd sleptwalk his way through all his classes. His teacher sent him to the health room, where the nurse, seeing the dark rings around his eyes, asked, "Have you been sleeping?" "Yes," Vince said. "I don't think so," the nurse said. "Lie down for a while. I'll wake you up in an hour." During sixth-period Band, while he was practicing the pieces for the upcoming Select Band concert, his mother Carmen entered the air-conditioned room and whispered something to the conductor. She had been crying. Vince could tell by the Jackie-O shades, the tissue in her hand.

When she'd turned her head toward the clarinet section to search for her son, Vince had seen the black shades and sensed that his grandfather had passed away. In the car, on their way to the travel agency, his mother said, "I've already booked flights for us. I'm going, whether your father likes it or not. Tough shit if he doesn't. He can stay here with his second wife." She continued, clutching the steering wheel as she came to a stoplight. "I know Don Alfonso was his father, but he was also like a father to me."

"Mom," Vince said, "I can't go. The Select Band concert is in less than a week. I can't miss rehearsals."

His mother looked at him. "No, Vicente. You have to go," she said. "You were his favorite."

"I've been practicing for months, Mom. You know how important this is to me."

"You can't miss your grandfather's funeral. It's bad luck."

"Only the best in the state made it, Mom," he said. "Only the best. And I'm one of them."

Shaking her head, she loosened her grip on the steering wheel and rested her forehead against it.

Quietly, he sat there, looking at her, remembering the last time he saw his mother break down. It had been two years earlier, in the seventh grade. He had been on the #2 Waikiki-bound bus that had stopped in front of the post office and the King Kamehameha statue on King Street. He had been on his way to meet Edgar at Waikiki Twin Theaters, where they were going to see *E.T.* He had looked out of the tinted window and seen a woman fall on her knees and break into tears. A man in a business suit ran and knelt beside her. She shook her head no. When she'd lifted her head to smile at the man, Vince saw that it was his mother. She'd stood up and walked away as the bus started to move. That night, at the dinner table, his mother told him, Jing, and Alvin that she and their father were officially divorced, that she was never letting a man into her life again, that she could ruin it herself without his help.

"Mom," Vince says, "the light's green."

BACK TO PRESENT-NIGHT MANILA

A woman wearing a black dress and a black veil, and fanning herself, approaches him. "Jun?" she says.

Vince gets up from the curb, brushing the dirt off his pants.

"I'm sorry," she says. "I thought you were Jun. You look so much like him." The woman sighs and begins telling him who Jun is. "Jun is the pen pal of my niece Lilibeth." A color photocopy of a young woman in her college graduation cap and gown is glued to the fan she holds. Below the portrait is a quote from Ecclesiastes 3:1. *To every thing there is a season, and a time to every purpose under the heavens.*

"They've been writing letters to each other for ten years," she continues. "Imagine the money spent on stamps. Jun is an engineer in the states. New Jersey, I think, or New Hampshire? Anyway, it's New something. He was supposed to come here in July, you know, to propose to Lilibeth. That's what everybody says, so I guess it must be true, but—"

She pauses to sigh again. "I don't understand. I was just with her last month. We were shopping for her wedding gown in Divisoria. Life and death are so unpredictable." Pause. "How rude of me? Are you hungry? You want coffee, Goldilock's pastries—?"

"No, thank you," Vince says, looking past her at the mourners, who've turned a somber occasion into a fiesta with nonstop eating, drinking, socializing, and praying the novena, which is held for nine days, starting from the day the person expired. Another mass is said on the fortieth day, when the soul of the deceased leaves the earth for the afterlife. Throughout the novena, sweeping is forbidden because it's thought to chase away good luck.

The yard, lined with potted bougainvilleas, has been converted to a gambling den for mahjong and pusoy—thirteen-card poker. At the end of the night, a percentage of the proceeds goes to the family of the deceased.

"Jun was her first love," she says, as loud wails explode from inside the house. "Professional mourners," she explains, then adds, "with very expensive tears."

Vince has heard of them before—women who get paid to wail in front of the dead. It's a Chinese ritual practiced primarily by Ilocanos in the north. He'd seen them when he was young, at the wake of his neighbor, Don Guillermo: old women screaming and crying uncontrollably in front of an empty coffin. It had frightened and bewildered him. He had never seen any of the crying ladies before. He thought they were relatives, until Yaya Let explained to him that they had been hired to go into hysterics to attract a crowd, because a crowded wake showed that the man was loved, revered, and could afford to buy the tears of strangers. Still, Vince couldn't understand how someone could cry so much over someone they didn't know. The issue was put to rest years later when his sister told him, "It's called drama, brother, and it pays very well."

Wailing subsiding, Lilibeth's aunt looks at Vince more closely and asks him his name.

"Vicente," he says, then corrects himself. "Vince. Call me Vince."

"I'm Lita." She motions for him to follow her into the house.

"I can't, I'm sorry. I'm already late," Vince says.

"Late? Late for what?"

The first excuse to enter his mind is blackout bingo, then, "I'm meeting my cousin for a drink," he says.

Lita smiles at him, asks if something's been on his mind, a problem that won't go away.

"No," Vince says, startled. "Why?"

"You look like one of us. Like you've been sleeping with eyes wide open."

"What makes you say that?"

"Your face," she says, pointing to his eyes. "If you've got problems or worries, now is the best time to get rid of them."

Seeing the "how?" on Vince's face, Lita tells him, "Go inside and give them all to Lilibeth. Say a prayer, then ask her to take all of your problems, your worries, everything that's causing you pain, sleeplessness, trouble, and she'll bring them with her to the afterlife."

"Is this a Catholic practice?" Vince asks, trying to remember if people from his childhood had also attended wakes to surrender their problems to the deceased.

"I'm not sure. Baka folk superstition," Lita says.

Vince looks at the mourners queuing in front of the coffin, imagines them dumping their troubles onto Lilibeth, including sins, bahala na's, regrets, sorrows.

"I don't remember hearing anything like this before," he continues.

"Please, come." Lita touches his arm.

"I'm sorry, but I really have to go," he says, drawing back from her touch.

"Where are you going, anyway? Maybe I can have somebody drive you there. Pasay City is not exactly the safest place on earth at night."

From his pocket, Vince takes a postcard folded in two and shows her the address of the postcard thief. A smile of recognition appears on her face. "No wonder you're in such a hurry."

"What do you mean?"

"You're not really going to meet a cousin, are you?"

Vince blushes.

"It's O.K.," Lita says. "I go there too. On payday."

"You do?" he asks, wondering if she knows the postcard thief or has slept with him for cash.

"Yes, I do," she says. "You're looking for Leche, right?"

"Leche? That's the address for Leche?"

"Yes," Lita says, "Leche. As in lecheng laway."

"What's that?"

"Devil's spit," she says, then, whispering, adds, "Leche's a bar. I go there with my Japayuki friends when they're in town, visiting from Nagoya. But it's closed on Sundays."

"Japayukis?"

"Filipina hostesses in Japan."

"So it's closed on Sundays?"

"Sabbath—day of rest. I guess to give those guys a break," she says. "Oh, I have to go. They're calling me to start the novena. You sure you don't want to come in?"

"No, thank you," Vince says.

"Okay, but should you change your mind, come back. The burial isn't until Wednesday," she says.

"I'll keep that in mind," he says.

"But don't wait too long, Vince," Lita says. "Or else you'll get insomnia, or nightmares, or worse."

"Thank you, Lita," Vince says, then watches her rejoin the mourners in the house before walking to the end of the street to hail a cab he hopes will shuttle him home safe, sound, and bribe-free.

FOUR FILIPINAS

Jing
Remember your idol Pooky Moreno from Taste
of P? *She's now Jolie B Rizal, a Charismatic*
Catholic (think Born-Again, but Catholic)
who speaks broken English with a British
accent and is a Marian devotee, meaning she's
married to the Virgin Mary. She spends her
days and nights traveling to Virgin Mary
sightings. Most recent was through the hole of
a Mister Donut. I'm not kidding. Jolie's motto
is now "The more the Mary-er," a far cry from
Pooky's "I can never get enough of enough."
Remember how you used to go gaga over her,
and Dovie Beams?
Vince, getting smaller and smaller

Jing De Los Reyes
513 North Kuakini
#6
Honolulu, HI 96817

BLACK JESUS, QUIAPO CHURCH

Jing,
#2 If your tears touch the corpse, it means
you'll be the next to go. Dreaming of falling
teeth or hair means someone in the family will
die. Likewise for cutting toenails at night
(gross!), being in the middle of a group photo,
roosters crowing in the afternoon, and black
butterflies and moths flying into the house. To
break the cycle of death, I know you have to
cut the rosary beads placed on the chest of the
dead before burial. But have you heard of people
handing over their problems to the dead at
wakes? Did you do this at Lolo Al's wake?

SOS, Vince

Jing De Los Reyes
513 North Kuakini
#6
Honolulu, HI 96817

ALONG RECTO AVENUE, OLD MANILA

Edgar,
Turns out Leche is closed on Sundays. It also
turns out it's not the world's best-kept secret. The
maid knows it, cabdrivers know it, and the
woman who mistook me for an engineer from
Jersey City knows it. She said she's gone there
several times. So it might not be as Sodomy and
Gonorrhea as you think. Plus, getting out of
there was hell. I had to pay the driver extra to
take me home. Taxi driver must've been on
crack—"shabu" as they call it here. He kept
pushing me to go with him to Chicks O' Clock,
a pussybar. We passed by four wakes. The whole
night was so Emily Dickinsonian.
Vince

Edgar Ramirez
1586 Murphy St.
Honolulu, HI 96819

FORTUNE TELLER'S TABLE OUTSIDE QUIAPO CHURCH

Alvin,
I just watched an interview with Madame
Auring Borealis, a psychic who predicted last
year's Baguio earthquake and Oscar winners.
Her predictions for the rest of '91? More natural
disasters, coup d'etats, major crisis in the Aquino
administration, including her daughter Kris,
who'll become a mother; baby's father—"a
married actor." The film industry will be plagued
with scams and scandals. On the bright side:
more gory films from the Massacre Queen of
Phil cinema. If there's a purgatory on earth,
then it just got upgraded to inferno status.

Vince

Alvin De Los Reyes
430 Keoniana St.
2D
Honolulu, HI 96815

Filipinese

Broad daylight. Ono Hai International Airport. The light-deprived termi-
nal is supported by stacks of balikbayan boxes serving as posts, its walls and
roof made from sheets of corrugated tins.

Vince's mother showers deplaning U.S. *troops with leis, thanking them*
for nuking the Japanese on Johnston Atoll. She's so grateful she can't control
her smiling. "Most people live on a desert island," she sings. "With Gilligan
and Skipper too / Ono Hai / stay calling."

She pauses to greet more soldiers. "Welcome to Ono Hai." Her radiant
smile is so wide her eyes disappear. "Ono Hai means ono island. Means
sweet I am. You like smell? Onolicious to you? Listen." She points a finger
at her ear. "You no hear nothing?"

"Get your fat ass off this island!" It's Vince's father, wearing a grass skirt
and a coconut-shell bra. Sailing across his belly—a tattoo of Captain James
Cook's vessel, the Endeavour.

Vince's mother gives him the Filipinese evil-eye look. "Me Filipinese," she
tells him. "Here I live. Here I native. But you only son of Creole here."

A Filipinese headhunter in a G-*string approaches them. His face is tat-*
tooed in red and black stripes, his fat tongue pierced with silver studs.

"Brother," Vince's mother says, "can you get this loser away from my
sight?"

A handsome soldier steps off the plane. His features are so striking he
could be spotted in a hurricane.

"Regardez, Mama!" Vince says, tugging at her floral-print muumuu and
pointing to the blue-eyed man's widow's peak. "Il est ici! Il est ici!"

His mother jumps up and down, clapping her hands. "It really is you, Mr. Smith! We thought the jungle had eaten you alive." She rushes to give Mr. Smith a bear hug and suffocates him with kisses.

"Take it easy, Mama Mary," Mr. Smith laughs.

"I no believe is you for real, but is you, is really you, Mr. Smith."

"And who are you?" He glances at Vince.

"That my Yat-Bilat," his mother says. She motions Vince to stand still and smile big. "Pretty in the face, Mr. Smith? You like?"

Blue eyes wash up and down Vince's body. "Does he speak French?" Mr. Smith asks.

"Bien sûr."

"English?"

Vince's mother nods with pride, then adds: "But no helping verbs, Mr. Smith."

Finally, Vince says, "I believing in the Declaration of Independence. Egalité, liberté, fraternité."

Mr. Smith touches Vince's cheek and smiles. He is much more handsome in real life than in the komiks, Vince thinks, the hibiscus behind his ear melting as he stares into the bluer-than-blue eyes, then up at the combed-back silver hair that makes the widow's peak more pronounced.

The color around them changes from blue to menstrual red.

"As-tu peur de moi, Yat-Bilat?" Mr. Smith asks Vince if he's afraid of white men.

Vince pinches an invisible bug between his thumb and forefinger and says, "Un peu."

"Don't be," Mr. Smith says, then asks why life in Ono Hai is so wonderful.

"À cause / de toi," Vince sings.

"You have such a lovely face." Mr. Smith strokes Vince's cheekbone, brushes his chocolate lips with his middle finger. Vince quivers with fear and excitement.

"*Tu es très, très jolie.*" Mr. Smith takes Vince in his strong arms and, French-kissing him, drowns him in his saliva.

Forty seconds later: a sunrise. The room explodes in bright orange. Vince opens his eyes and the world is in soft-focus. On the tatami mat, Mr. Smith's naked body is spooning his, his right arm over Vince, his gray chest hairs brushing his back.

Vince turns to face him.

"*Bonjour, mon amour,*" Mr. Smith says, kissing Vince's bee-stung lips, his St. Theresa of Avila eyes rolling to the back of his head in Filipinese ecstasy. He sighs.

"*Tu es mon bébé?*" Mr. Smith asks.

"*Bien sûr,*" Vince answers, then adds: "*Papa.*"

Mr. Smith kisses his forehead.

"I am much older than you, too old for you perhaps."

"*Pas du tout, Monsieur.*"

"If we have children," he brushes Vince's bangs aside, "will you promise to bring them to America when I die?"

Vince begins to cry.

"*Ne pleure pas,* my Yat-Bilat," Mr. Smith says.

"*Ne parlez pas comme ça, Papa.*"

"*Pardonne-moi,* Yat-Bilat. I'm sorry."

The sound of seven ukuleles strumming in the background cues Mr. Smith to start singing: "Born in different worlds / We are as different as sun and moon / But down the aisle / we march and say—"

"I do / love you," Vince sings.

"You want marry Yat-Bilat, Mr. Smith?" His mother hovers over them, her unexpected presence darkening the room to piss-yellow. "If you love my Yat-Bilat, Mr. Smith," she says, "you must marry Yat-Bilat now."

"*Vous êtes folle?*" Mr. Smith says.

"You marry Yat-Bilat or I sell Yat-Bilat to British Museum," Vince's mother says.

"C'est impossible."

"Pourquoi pas, Papa?" Vince cries.

As Mr. Smith attempts to get up, Vince throws his arms around his neck.

"Me think Mr. Smith want make voodoo witch girl from Siquijor wife number four," Vince's mother says. "That's why he maki-maki in his dreams."

"Non! Not true! Not true!" Vince cries.

Mr. Smith breaks free from Vince. "If only the world were a better place, Yat-Bilat," he says.

"Jamais!" Vince's mother exclaims. "And you know why, Mr. Smith? Because you no like have Filipinese children. Because you think Filipinese not good enough for you and Philadelphia, PA."

"Arrêtez, Mama, s'il vous plait, arrêtez." Vince begs his mother to stop.

"Mais c'est vrai, Yat-Bilat," Mr. Smith says. "It's true."

"Non, je ne crois pas. After me give you everything," Vince says. "Me give you sky meet sea in Ono Hai, onolicious island. Come to me, come to me. Me show you how eat with bare hands. Me talkin' talkin' happy talk." Vince stands up and breaks into a song, pantomiming the lyrics à la hula. "Talk about the you / Swimming in the me / Loving bits and pieces / Of my sea."

"Stop, Yat-Bilat," Mr. Smith pleads, turning away.

But Vince continues. "Talk about the man / Saying to the boy . . ."

"I do love you, Yat-Bilat," Mr. Smith says as his legs begin to disappear.

"Je vous aime aussi, Papa," Vince says. "Vous êtes ma vie, mon destin, mon rêve, Papa."

"But I just can't. Don't you understand, Yat-Bilat? Je ne peux pas."

"Pourquoi, Papa?"

"Because you are going to cause an economic revolution," Mr. Smith says, his legs, arms, and trunk disappearing. "Forgive me, Yat-Bilat." And Mr. Smith vanishes completely.

"You stupid Filipinese kid, you no smile wide enough for Mr. Smith, that's why. That's why he not yours, ever," Vince's mother says, raising her voice.

"Pas vrai, pas vrai," Vince says. "Not true. He mine. All mine."

Suddenly, a tremor accompanied by dogs howling.

Another quake, this time stronger.

More dogs howling as faceless voices scream, cry, ululate so loud, so clear, they're no longer part of a dream.

THE PHILIPPINE ROOSTER

Jing,
Holy shit. The howling dogs and human
screams turned out to be real. I thought I was
dreaming. The newscaster reported a five on
the Richter scale. It felt more like the end of
me and Manila. Even he wasn't convinced.
It's coming from a volcano two hours from
here. We used to pass it on the way to Manila
from San Vicente. Dormant for six centuries.
Until now!

Vince, getting ready to explode

Jing De Los Reyes
513 North Kuakini
#6
Honolulu, HI 96817

WELCOME TO THE JUNGLE!

Edgar,
Newsflash: Get your Hawaiian Tropic butt
over here because this is where the next Big
Bang will take place. It's confirmed: Mount
Pinatubo, a volcano near here, has awakened.
Minor quakes for now (I felt them in my
sleep), but it's being closely monitored. It's near
Clark Air Force Base in Angeles City. Wasn't
Art "Mr. Pogi" Johnson born there? Does he
know his birthplace is the next Pompeii? He
should've gotten my
consolation prize.

Kita kits,
Vince

Edgar Ramirez
1586 Murphy St.
Honolulu, HI 96819

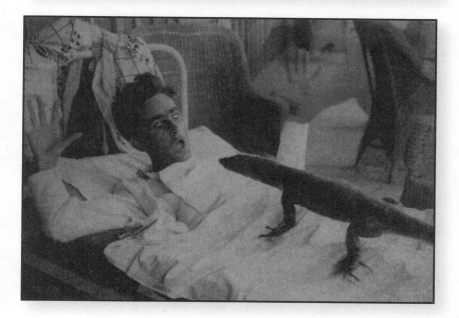

BOOK VIII

PM Talking with Yours Truly

KRIS: Hellooooo! Good afternoon, everybody. Welcome to another delightful afternoon of *PM Talking with Yours Truly* on ABS-CBN Studio, the only network in the country worth wasting your electricity on. That's why we're number one again. Oo. Truly. Number one. Thank you everybody for your continued support. Because without you, my show might be number two, or worse, cancelled. Pero huwag naman sana because I don't think I can bear another bad news.

(Pause. Camera closes in on Kris as dramatic music plays in the background. Kris, her eyes beginning to tear, opens her mouth but is too choked up for words.)

Napakasakit to admit but, yes, the rumors you've all been hearing since last night are true and nothing but. Break na kami ni Albert. He moved out of Malacañang three hours ago. It's for the best. Love burns talaga, but then again, who goes through it without hurting, di ba? I'd be lying to you right now if I told you that I don't love him anymore. Of course I do. He will always have a spot in my heart. But I have to let him go. He gave me no choice. I mean, you don't give someone you love venereal disease, di ba? Call me old-fashion, tanga, masochistic, but you just don't do that to the woman you love, especially if she's carrying your baby. (*A wave of gasps spreads across the studio.*) Yes, my beloved televiewers, I'm Madonna with a child, but without a Joseph. I think it was the poet Kahlil Gibran who said life is full of harsh lessons, but we must accept and learn from them so that we can continue to grow and become a little more caring, a little more compassionate, and I guess, a little more mature.

The cruel lesson this time is that I have to learn to live with love alone. Oh, my God, I'm making you all cry with my sob story. Enough na. Sobra na. Change the topic na. Let's go on a commercial break and when we come back, I promise you no more tears from yours truly.

* * * * *

KRIS: I have a double-treat for you today, as in hot fudge sundae na, cherry on the whip cream pa. My first guest is more super than a superstar, more brilliant than a diamond star, and more mega than a megastar. She's cofounder and head of JOAN, my favorite army of sisters, whose order has now increased to nearly a hundred since it was established three years ago. Like the other nuns of JOAN, she is a vigilant feminist and a warrior for the poor and the oppressed. And lately, she's added acting to her resume. Tonight, if she wins Best Supporting Actress at the Film Academy of the Philippines Awards show, she will be the first nun in the history of Philippine cinema to win awards from all five major award-giving bodies, Catholic

Mass Media excluded. Please help me welcome the one, the only, Sister Marie.

(*Close-up of Sister Marie sitting between audience members holding a WE LUV U, SISTER M! banner. She rises from the bleacher and, camera trailing after her, makes her way down to the mock living room set. An assistant hands her a microphone.*)

SISTER MARIE: Good afternoon, everybody. Good afternoon, Kris.

KRIS: Good afternoon, Sister Marie. (*Kris waits for applause to die down.*) What an amazing year, no? And we're not even in the "burr" months.

SISTER MARIE: Blessing from the skies talaga, Kris. But the same can be said about you. Your last three films were certified box-office hits. You were Takilya Queen for two years in a row, and, thanks to the success of *In the Name of Shame,* you might be Box-Office Queen again. Your *K.A. Drama Anthology* and this talk show are number two and number one, respectively. And this year, you didn't go home from an awards ceremony empty-handed.

KRIS: Pero on the dark side, Sister, my personal life sucks.

SISTER MARIE: O.K. lang 'yun, Kris. Basketball players come and go. It's a given. They're known to "double-dribble," as they say. I wouldn't worry about spending love alone. This country never runs out of basketball teams.

KRIS: Pero Albert is special.

SISTER MARIE: May I be frank?

KRIS: Please.

SISTER MARIE: That's what you said about Danny and Diego, remember?

KRIS: True, true.

SISTER MARIE: Albert is itchier than those women along Quezon Avenue at night. It's a tabloid fact. Everyone knows it. My cousins in Daly City, California, know it. You're better off without him, Kris. Trust me. If I were you, I'd focus all your energy na lang on your nine lives—acting, hosting, singing, endorsing products, Kahlil Gibran, your monthly book club, your weekly column in *National Inquirer*, motherhood, and being the Oprah Winfrey of the Philippines. Such a hectic schedule and I'm amazed you still find time for love with losers.

KRIS: That's exactly what Mom said.

SISTER MARIE: You see? Get your mind off the basketball court and start aiming higher. Find another kind of court.

KRIS: Tennis?

SISTER MARIE: Not quite. I was thinking more like the Supreme Court.

KRIS: In that case, never mind, Sister. I might end up in divorce court. Royal court na lang.

SISTER MARIE: That's the spirit, Kris. God, I'm so excited about tonight. Aren't you? You and I are about to become the first grand-slam actresses in the history of Philippine cinema, and you're wallowing over a guy who keeps committing fouls on you.

KRIS: You're right, Sister. He's not worth it. But I do hope you're right about us becoming the grand-slam actresses. Me, lead; you, supporting. I hope this is not only an open-ended dream, but one that will come true tonight.

SISTER MARIE: And it will, Kris. Have faith in God's will, and it will.

KRIS: And I have Bino Boca to thank for that. Without him, I wouldn't be where I am right now. He taught me how to channel my horrible experiences in Boston as the daughter of an exiled senator into my acting. I never knew I could be this good.

SISTER MARIE: You're not just good, Kris, you're grand.

KRIS: I can't wait to start work on Tito Bino's next movie.

SISTER MARIE: Which is?

KRIS: *Machete Dancers II.* I play a blind woman who makes ends meets working in rundown movie theaters. What about you, Sister? Do you have any other movies or telenovelas lined up?

SISTER MARIE: I think this is it, Kris. I appeared in two movies, starred in a *Remembrances* episode about the JOAN sisters. I enjoyed making them. But how many times can you play yourself? I don't know how the others do it, going from one movie to the next playing practically the same role. Sure, there were offers. One was to play Mother Miriam Ruth in *Agnes of God* for Repertory Philippines, another a Philippine version of *Song of Bernadette*. But I said no, no more films. I have to keep reminding myself why I even entered showbiz.

KRIS: Why, Sister Marie?

SISTER MARIE: It wasn't to win awards or attract attention or stir controversy. It was, as you already know, out of necessity. It was for the sake of JOAN. That's why I, and six other sisters, agreed to make *Seven Nuns & Six Days in February* and *In the Name of Shame*. We did it in case the donations stop coming, which, thanks to our supporters and the Lord, are still pouring in.

KRIS: Why do you think JOAN, even though it's not recognized by the Vatican or the Archdiocese of Manila, is still going strong after you and Sisters Benedicta, Evangeline, Mitch, Pura, Assunta, and Pinky left the Benedictine order?

SISTER MARIE: It's because people believe in us, in our struggle, what JOAN stands for. We're not just angry feminists in habits, as Cardinal Sin and his critics like to think. We're not angry, Kris, oh no, we're not. We're fed up. (*Applause*) Fed up with the system. (*Applause crescendos.*) There's no more justice in this country for the poor, because it's all been bought out. There are no more free elections because the ballots have been paid for, or stolen. And there have never been rights for women, for gays, that equal the rights of men. There's no more peace and order, because the rules and laws were written by and for the rich. And it's only going to get worse. But we must not give up hope. We must not let faith go. We must fight this hopeless and senseless battle, fight it to its very end. That's what Saint Joan stood for. That's what we as sisters of JOAN stand for. Three years ago, there were only seven of us who dissented from the Benedictine order, which is the most progressive, most forward-thinking. Now there are close to a hundred, many from the Dominican order. Next week, we're moving to a six-story building that was given to us by an anonymous donor.

KRIS: Caloy Moreno?

SISTER MARIE: No confirming that. But Caloy is one of our diehard supporters, one of our first believers. He was there from the very beginning of JOAN, because he knew what it was like to live on dried fish and rice without rights. Same for the other gay fashion designers, make-up artists, comedians, and parloristas who are now part of the A class but have not forgotten where they came from. There's so much work to do at JOAN, so much unfinished business. And that's what my sisters and I have to concentrate on. Lie low muna from the spotlight. Tagalog melodrama will never go away anyway. Next week, JOAN will be at the U.S. embassy, protesting against the military base lease extension. No more na, di ba? One hundred years of solitude is enough. We already have our own Hollywood. Plus it's time we fight our own battles. Then next year, there's the presidential election. We're monitoring it, making sure cheating is at a low level and no one tampers or runs away with the ballot boxes.

KRIS: Is it true that the sisters of JOAN have agreed to carry guns?

SISTER MARIE: No, it's not. But we're not opposed to the idea, Kris, especially for the nuns who are going to Mindanao.

KRIS: Oh, Sister, we have to go on a commercial break, but before we do, I want to thank Bench for my outfit, Rustan's for my shoes, Tita Fanny for my make-up, Tita Raffy of Felix the Cut for my hair, and Optical Illusions for my contacts.

SISTER MARIE: Kris, if I may?

KRIS: That's why you're my guest, Sister.

SISTER MARIE: I want to thank Kirei for my wardrobe, Rusty Lopez for my sandals, Tita Ricky for my make-up, and Optical Illusions for my contacts.

* * * * *

KRIS: My next guest is super guapo, as in super kilig me to death, and, judging by his looks, super smart. He escorted me last Friday at the annual Santacruzan gala in Malate.

His name is Vicente De Los Reyes, but he prefers to be called Vince. (*She reads the teleprompter as if hypnotized.*) He was born in the town proper of San Vicente, Philippines, and moved to Hawaii in 1978. He completed his bachelor's degree at the University of Hawaii at Manoa, where he graduated with highest honors. Please give a warm round of applause and a-lo-ha! to Vince De Los Reyes.

(*Vince appears from behind a curtain where, during the commercial break, he watched the set director remind the audience to applaud louder or he'll replace them with fans begging to be let in to the studio. The camera trails after Vince as he crosses the set. The audience gasps when he nearly trips over a spaghetti heap of cables. Stepping into the mock living room, he is greeted with hugs and kisses from Kris Aquino and Sister Marie. They sit and wait for the applause to die down.*)

KRIS: Welcome to *PM Talking with Yours Truly,* Vince. Thank you for squeezing us into your hectic schedule. Is this your first time on television?

VINCE: . . .

SISTER MARIE: Vince? Vince?

VINCE: Pardon?

KRIS: Are you nervous?

VINCE: Kind of. (*Kris motions for him to bring his mouth closer to the microphone.*) A little.

KRIS: A little is good. You're only a *Homo sapiens,* after all.

SISTER MARIE: Kris is right, Vince. I remember the first time I appeared on Kris's show.

KRIS: She fainted and hasn't been the same since.

SISTER MARIE: You know, Kris, Vince reminds me of that actor in *What's Eating Gilbert Grape?*

KRIS: Who? Johnny Depp?

SISTER MARIE: No, the other one.

KRIS: The mother who weighs more than an elephant?

SISTER MARIE: No, the one who's retarded.

VINCE: Leonardo DiCaprio?

SISTER MARIE: Yes, him.

VINCE: But I'm not blond or blue-eyed.

KRIS: It's your aura, Vince.

SISTER MARIE: Where do you get your mestizo features from?

VINCE: My mom is a quarter Spanish and my dad is a quarter American.

SISTER MARIE: No wonder you look like a Close-Up toothpaste commercial model. You should model, hijo. You have the right skin and the right height. Was your American grandfather in the military?

VINCE: He fought during World War II and his father was a lieutenant in the Philippine-American War.

KRIS: Of 1899?

VINCE: Yes.

SISTER MARIE: Very interesting. You're a product of interracial marriages.

KRIS: And a legacy of betrayals.

SISTER MARIE: And mongrels.

VINCE: That's right, I'm a zebronkey.

KRIS: Oh, zebronkeys. I miss them.

VINCE: They're real?

KRIS: Of course naman.

VINCE: I thought they were fake. Postcard gags.

KRIS: Of course not. Those half-zebra half-donkeys were as real
                as the Dr. Jose Rizal statue in Luneta.

SISTER MARIE: The last zebronkey died during the EDSA Revolution.

KRIS: I cried for weeks.

SISTER MARIE: Me also.

KRIS: So, Vince, this is your first time back in the Philippines,
                correct?

VINCE: (*Nods*) After thirteen years.

KRIS: You were still a child when you left.

VINCE: Ten.

KRIS: (*Counting with her fingers*): Which makes you twenty-
                two.

VINCE: Twenty-three.

KRIS: You're older than me. I just turned sweet twenty on
                happy Valentine's Day. I love it. People get to greet me
                twice on that day. (*Pause*) How does it feel to be back in
                the Pearl of the Oreos?

VINCE: Overwhelming.

KRIS: I'm sure. I live here and I feel overwhelmed every day.
                The pollution.

SISTER MARIE: The beggars.

KRIS: The squatters.

SISTER MARIE: The vendors.

KRIS: The BAWAL UMIHI DITO signs on the walls.

SISTER MARIE: The missing sidewalks.

KRIS: The blackouts.

SISTER MARIE: And brownouts.

KRIS: The noise.

SISTER MARIE: The rats.

KRIS: Stray dogs.

SISTER MARIE: Glue-sniffing children.

SISTER MARIE: The way people drive.

KRIS: Not to mention the traffic.

SISTER MARIE: The Ministry of Transportation reports it will only get worse.

KRIS: But you know Sister M, I'm not affected by the traffic. You know why? Because I found a way to beat the bottlenecks and gridlock.

SISTER MARIE: Really?

KRIS: Truly.

SISTER MARIE: What's your secret?

KRIS: I read Russian novels and plays. Oo. They're so powerful they have the power to take my mind off my personal issues and Mommy's problems in her administration. If people only read in traffic, there'd be less road rage and less crime and corruption in our country, and a higher literacy rate. I'm seriously thinking of starting my own televised book club. You know, Sister, before I leave the house every morning, I make sure that Dostoevsky or Tolstoy or Solzhenitsyn or *Doctor Zhivago* is in my gym bag. In fact, I actually look forward to getting stuck in traffic. If not for traffic, I would never have read *Anna Karenina* or *Heart of Darkness*. In fact, this morning, on the way to the studio, I read a play by Anton Chekhov. *The Seagull*. So depressing, I wanted to shoot myself. That's how powerful it was. I highly recommend it.

SISTER MARIE: You and I are soul sisters, Kris. I, too, read on the road. Scriptures and scripts.

KRIS: But for you, Vince, coming back here must be like get-
               ting stuck in a nightmare. I mean, I myself was shocked
               when my family and I returned to Manila after living in
               exile in Boston, MA. And we were gone for only—
               what?—three years. But you—thirteen years! That's over
               half of your life. I cannot even begin to imagine what's
               going on in your mind right now! I mean how do you
               say hello again to those wonder years you'd left behind?

VINCE: (*Shrugs*): I don't know. Sensory overload.

KRIS: Care to share?

VINCE: A moment doesn't go by without my eyes, ears, and nose
               getting bombarded. If it's not the smell of something
               burning, then it's horns blasting in my ears, or a jukebox,
               or someone singing their heart out. So many things to
               see, to watch out for. So many things going on or going
               off at once that it makes it difficult at times for me to get
               my bearings, to process, to breathe. It's like, I don't know,
               being sucked up by a tornado.

SISTER MARIE: It's called culture shock, Vince.

KRIS: *Reverse* culture shock.

SISTER MARIE: But, hijo, what I would like to know is why did you wait
               so long to come back?

KRIS: Yes, Vince. Why? When Hawaii's only—what?—eleven
               hours away via Philippine Airlines.

VINCE: I didn't feel the need to come back. Hawaii has a large pop-
               ulation of Filipinos, both immigrants and locals. We have
               our own mini-Manila, mini-Ilocos, mini-Davao in Hawaii.

KRIS: Oh my God, you left the Philippines for that? How tragic.

SISTER MARIE: But they're not the same as Manila, Ilocos, and Davao,
               Vince. I've visited these miniature Philippine versions in

the u.s.—Queens and Jersey City on the East Coast, and Daly City, Union City, and Carson City in California— and they're nothing but sanitized, trying-hard-to-copycat versions of the original.

VINCE: So a filthy version is better because it's more authentic?

SISTER MARIE: I didn't say that.

VINCE: But these versions are the closest we have to a Filipino community.

KRIS: It's not home.

VINCE: It is to many of them.

SISTER MARIE: They stand for nostalgia.

VINCE: If nostalgia's what it takes to bring Filipinos closer to the Philippines, then I don't see anything wrong with that.

KRIS: But it's not the Philippines. Just as Manila is not *the* Philippines.

SISTER MARIE: A mistake many foreigners make when they come here.

KRIS: True, Sister Marie.

SISTER MARIE: In fact, these Fil-Am communities are not much different from the mock Philippine villages that were exhibited at the St. Louis World's Fair in 1904, when Filipinos in G-strings, holding bows and arrows, lived in huts next to Geronimo.

VINCE: What? That's different.

SISTER MARIE: Is it? How so?

KRIS: Sister Marie?

SISTER MARIE: Sorry, Kris. And sorry too, Vince. I don't mean to harp on you like that.

KRIS: Back to me, Vince.

VINCE: Yes?

KRIS: So if you hadn't joined the Mister Pogi pageant and placed second runner-up—

VINCE: First.

KRIS: Mea culpa. First runner-up.

SISTER MARIE: Who won?

KRIS: Arturo Dwayne Johnson. African-Filipino; military brat. Born in Angeles City and one of the very few who was not abandoned by his G.I. father. Lived in military bases all over Asia and the U.S.

VINCE: How do you know all this?

KRIS: I'm the Oprah Winfrey of the Philippines.

SISTER MARIE: So if the first runner-up prize was a trip to the Philippines, what prize did the winner get?

KRIS: Vince?

VINCE: He gets to travel around the United States for three months and visit all the Filipino American communities.

SISTER MARIE: So if you had won the Mister Pogi title you would have gone to Jersey and Union and Carson and Daly cities instead of Manila?

VINCE: I guess.

KRIS: So you wouldn't have come back?

VINCE: Well, not this soon.

KRIS: Why not?

VINCE: My family's in Hawaii.

SISTER MARIE: You don't have any relatives here?

VINCE: I don't think so.

SISTER MARIE: I believe there's a deeper reason why you're back here, hijo. Just as I believe there's a deeper reason behind everything. Why things turn out the way they do, why we end up in places that are not part of our plans, why you placed first runner-up rather than winning the Mister Pogi title. Fate, Vince, and fate is God's mysterious way of telling us we don't have control of our lives.

KRIS:	Isn't it bizarre, Sister, that Vince came home at the same time that Mount Pinatubo decides to wake up after six hundred years?
SISTER MARIE:	Oh my God, did you feel the earthquake Saturday night?
KRIS:	How could I not? I live next to the Marikina fault line.
SISTER MARIE:	Nostradamus was right: this is the end of the world and we are at the epicenter.
VINCE:	So I woke up the volcano?
KRIS:	What other reasons can you think of why, after six centuries, Mount Pinatubo would start to act up?
VINCE:	Could it be because of the geological excavation that's been going on there? That's what it said in the *Philippine Bulletin*.
KRIS:	That's not a newspaper, that's a bulletin board.
SISTER MARIE:	Vince, you were meant to come back. Whether you wanted to or not, you had to come home. And it had to be now.
KRIS:	Home? Do you still consider the Philippines your home, Vince?
VINCE:	No . . . well . . . yes . . . in a way . . . I guess. I mean, I was born here, but . . . no . . . Hawaii is where I've spent most of my life.
KRIS:	I'll make it simpler. Do you identify more as Asian American or Fil-Am?
VINCE:	Neither.
KRIS:	Then what?
VINCE:	Filipino.
KRIS:	Cannot be. You just said you've lived most of your life in America.
VINCE:	Yes.

KRIS:	Do you still speak Tagalog?
VINCE:	No. But I understand it.
SISTER MARIE:	He who does not love his language is worse than a smelly animal and a smelly fish.
KRIS:	Amen times ten to that, Sister.
VINCE:	Isn't that redundant—a smelly animal and a smelly fish?
KRIS:	Not if you're José Rizal.
SISTER MARIE:	But, hijo, is it in your heart to speak it?
VINCE:	My brother and sister speak it, so does that make them more Filipino than me?
KRIS:	I didn't say they were Filipinos. Are they willing to live here for the rest of their lives?
VINCE:	I don't think so.
SISTER MARIE:	How about you? Are you willing to give up your U.S. citizenship?
VINCE:	No.
SISTER MARIE:	Then you're not a Filipino.
VINCE:	What about those overseas workers who go abroad to work and stay there for many years, are they still Filipinos?
SISTER MARIE:	Filipino overseas workers are an exemption to the rule. They leave the country because they have to, Vince. Unemployment is at a record-breaking high. Ninety percent of the country is living beneath the rodent level, and, as you already know when you go to Shoe Mart to change your dollars, not even a miracle can revive the economy. We have the human resources, we have the strength in numbers, but we do not have jobs for them. That's why they are forced to leave the country to work as maids, drivers, caregivers, and entertainers. Many of

	them are college graduates, with degrees in engineering, nursing, physical therapy, med tech, and accounting.
KRIS:	And, in my opinion, which I'm entitled to, these Filipinos are our heroes because of their daily sacrifices and the monthly money remittances they send to their families.
VINCE:	What if they don't come back? What if they decide to start another family, a new life elsewhere?
SISTER MARIE:	You mean like those brain-drainers who renounced their families in the sixties, when they left the country to work as nurses, doctors, and teachers in the U.S.?
VINCE:	Yes.
KRIS:	Then they're blank-blank-blankholes.
VINCE:	Yes, but don't their assholes remain Filipino? Once a Filipino asshole, always a Filipino asshole, right?
SISTER MARIE:	(*Makes the sign of the cross*) Ay, my ears!
VINCE:	Isn't your definition of Filipino too narrow, too specific, too literal?
KRIS:	Of course, otherwise it wouldn't be a definition, right?
VINCE:	I thought once a Filipino in the heart, always a Filipino in the heart.
KRIS:	I don't know. Let's ask our televiewers? What do you think? Once a Filipino, always a Filipino ba? (*Camera closes in on Vince.*) Does Vince have to live in the Philippines to be a true-blooded Pinoy? Must he give up his first-world privileges, U.S. citizenship, American slang? What does it take to be a true Filipino, anyway? Can you ever become one? Or, in Vince's case, can you return to being one? Send your comments to *PM Talking with Yours Truly* c/o ABS-CBN, Mother Ignacia Street,

Quezon City, Philippines. See you tomorrow. Don't forget to watch me and Sister Marie at the Film Academy of the Philippines awards show tonight. Telecast live, and only live, right here on ABS-CBN. Bye everybody. I love you. Forever as ever.

A MATRIARCH'S FUNERAL, ILOCOS NORTE, 1936

Mom,
My tolerance for this city just hit subzero.
Somebody has to do something with these
UNICEF rejects. They won't leave me alone.
"Joe! Joe!" "Who the fuck is Joe?" And they
answer with more "Joe! Joe!" Enough already.
Go away. Shoo, shoo. Dengue, malaria, take
them away. I tell you, my compassion for your
fellow brothers and sisters has sunk deeper than
the pothole that swallowed a jeepney.

Vince

Carmen Formoso
1519 Kaumualii St.
#310
Honolulu, HI 96819

PEPE & PILAR

Edgar,

*Appeared on Kris Aquino's talk show. Forgot to
ask when it's going to air. She said it was a
"taping," but it felt more like live. That's the
other thing about this place: Don't trust the
English language here. What a word means to us
means another to them, if not the exact opposite.
English is a subtext language here. Worse than
Japanese. Soon as taping was over, I got the hell
out of there, and as far away as possible from
her and that nunconformist. I'm now in a café,
inside the walled city of Intramuros. Just me
and two Japanese tourists. Took me two hours to
pass through ten traffic lights. URGH!*

Vince, waiting for the lonely tour to begin

Edgar Ramirez
1586 Murphy St.
Honolulu, HI 96819

LUNETA PARK

*#2 By the way, Kris knows about the pageant.
Just how much? Probably everything! Her
estranged uncle, a Marcos crony, owns Joji's
Kamayan Restaurant, proud sponsor of Mr.
Pogi. That's his townhouse I'm staying at.
Apparently, it's where all the runner-ups get
shoved. If Kris knew all the 411 on Art being
Afro-Pinoy and a military brat, she must also
know about the opening song-and-dance* West
Side Story*—inspired number you choreographed,
and Kenzo getting major deductions in the
talent portion for wasting forty-five minutes
dancing butoh. Shit, I'm running out of
space.*
Vince

Edgar Ramirez
1586 Murphy St.
Honolulu, HI 96819

TWO MEN SMOKING OPIUM

#3 Which can only mean she knows a lot about you, Edgar! And has the 411 on me and Dave! She is as terrifying as the massacre movies she stars in. I'm just glad she didn't drill me about the pageant, or ask me about the emcee formerly known as the rice queen named EX. Imagine me getting outed by the country's First Daughter. Shut up, I can hear you snickering. Oh, shit, a frightening thought just invaded my mind: <u>Kris is running the damn country from her dressing room at ABS-CBN</u>. Otherwise, how else is it possible for her mother to find all the time in the world to pray with the nuns and focus on her watercolor paintings?!
P.S. I guess I'm the guy on the left.

Edgar Ramirez
1586 Murphy St.
Honolulu, HI 96819

TARSIUS PHILIPPENSIS IS THE WORLD'S OLDEST
MAMMAL AT 40 MILLION YEARS OLD.

*#4 Aren't they cute? Pocket-size mammals with
thick wooly fur. They've been known to commit
suicide in captivity. Shit, another white troll with
a Filipina young enough to be his granddaughter.
I swear the ugliest white people come here!
They're either TB-looking, pedophiles, or both!
Can't blame them, though. This is probably the
last place on earth they can still feel revered.
Wonder when the tour is going to start? Sign
said two, but it's already two thirty. Read next
postcard to find out what Kris, the nun, and I
talked about. It'll be of great interest to you.*

Vince

Edgar Ramirez
1586 Murphy St.
Honolulu, HI 96819

STATUE OF CONQUISTADOR MIGUEL DE LOPEZ
DE LEGAZPI WITH DATU SIKATUNA, BOHOL.

#5 Marlon Brando is Okinawan in The
Teahouse of the August Moon. *Alec Guinness
is Hindu in* A Passage to India, *Japanese in* A
Majority of One, *an Arab in* Lawrence of Arabia,
a Jedi in Star Wars. *Mickey Rooney is a
bucktoothed Japanese in* Breakfast at Tiffany's.
Peter Sellers is Chinese in Fu Manchu. *David
Carradine is everybody's kung-fu-fighting
Amerasian in* Kung Fu. *Lea Salonga is a
Vietnamese whore in* Miss Saigon . . .

Edgar Ramirez
1586 Murphy St.
Honolulu, HI 96819

LUNETA PARK

#6 Anthony Quinn is Italian in La Strada, *Greek in* Zorba, *Gauguin in* Lust for Life, *and in* Back to Bataan, *the Filipino grandson of Andrés Bonifacio, first president of the Philippine Republic. In* The Year of Living Dangerously, *Linda Hunt is a man. But I, Vince De Los Reyes, cannot be a Filipino? You got an explanation? Save it for when I come home. Tour's about to start.*

Vince
P.S. According to Kris, the zebronkey is real!

Edgar Ramirez
1586 Murphy St.
Honolulu, HI 96819

Blow-Up

"Philippine colonial history begins here, inside the Old Walled City of Intramuros." The guide, Jonas, pauses to exchange introductions with Vince and a Japanese couple, Reiko and Masa. They make up today's walking tour, which begins in Fort Santiago, the northern sentinel of the Walled City, and concludes at the Dominican-run San Agustin Church. The Japanese couple's interest in the tour is ostensibly to educate themselves about the atrocities the Japanese Imperial Army perpetrated against the Filipinos. War crimes that are absent in their history textbooks. Vince's reason: Jonas is the cute guy he locked gazes with at the sidewalk café where he was venting his third-world frustrations on turn-of-the-century and Philippine wildlife postcards.

"Excuse me." Reiko points to the gold-plated footprints on the ground. "Who these berong to?"

"Dr. Jose Rizal," Jonas answers.

"Dr. Jose Rizar," Reiko and Masa repeat, struggling not to roll their *l*'s.

"He is our national hero," Jonas continues. "He was executed by Spaniards on December 30, 1896. He was blamed for inciting rebellion against Spain because of the two novels he'd written, *Noli Me Tangere* and *El Filibusterismo*, or in English, *The Social Cancer* and *The Insurrectionist*. He was imprisoned right here at Fort Santiago. We will visit his cell shortly."

Masa hands Jonas the camera while he and Reiko squat in front of the footprint, their fingers touching Rizal's size-six sole. Cheek to cheek, they smile directly into the eye of Fuji.

"One more time," Reiko says. "Domo arigato gozaimasu" (bow).

Reiko and Masa are not the only ones enthused about seeing themselves on three-by-five glossy prints. Across from them is a busload of students, posing in front of the fountain of Plaza Moriones, counting to three out loud in a dialect Vince recognizes immediately as former president Ferdinand Marcos's native tongue—Ilocano. Spoken by the majority of Filipinos in Hawaii, Ilocano sounds like a head-on collision between High German and Vietnamese: guttural, glottal, and nasal.

Reiko and Masa invite Vince to join them for photo ops on the bridge overlooking a moat of centuries-old water. He tells them no and volunteers Jonas instead.

Vince has had it with being in front of a camera. Just last month, he stood in front of one for the five-dollar program for the Mister Pogi pageant. The photographer, Jun, owner of Jun's Take One ("All it takes is one take at Jun's Take One Studio") took a thousand and one takes of him and another thousand and one for the group shots. The photo session ate up an entire day, but the hours flew by because Jun spoke and smoked and directed and clicked at the rate of ten espresso shots, stopping only to load films, light cigarettes, and teach Vince and others how to strike a pose. Jun's overcaffeinated personality, plus the succession of clicks and flashes, at times made Vince and the other four contestants feel like they were being hounded by a one-man paparazzi team.

Then, a week later, Vince was in front of the camera again, this time on television. A taping for *Emi's Island Moments,* where he and the four other contestants were interviewed by perky, pert, and petite Emi Dacuycuy-Paterson. The pre-pageant coverage, aired two days before the event, was how Vince's mother and siblings found out that he had joined a pageant.

But for all the embarrassment and humiliation the exposure had given him, it paid off. The black-and-white photos captured the elegant and charming side of Vince; Jun likened him to the actors of Hollywood's golden era—an Errol Flynn minus the tights, or a young Cary Grant, especially those of him sitting on a barstool and smoking a cigarette. Even hotter, surprisingly, were those of him in color, wearing black Speedos and an aquamarine polo shirt with the collar up—an homage to the eighties—and sizing the camera up with a one-sided smile that lit up his face once more when he was told he'd won Most Photogenic.

ONCE WE WERE MUSLIMS

"Come on, Vince," Jonas says. "Take the picture."

Vince takes a step back and presses the auto-focus button to magnify Jonas. Isn't that what blowing up is about? The power to enlarge the object of desire while erasing everyone and everything near it?

"One more time." Vince takes their photo under the stone arch bearing a wood relief of Spain's coat of arms, imagining the look on Reiko's and Masa's faces when they discover their limbs and parts of their faces had been lopped off. But Jonas, like a god, remains untouched.

Jonas leads them past Plaza Armas, a lawn shaped like a right triangle. He stops to point to the ground—more footprints of the martyred hero.

"Rizal spent his last night here," Jonas says.

"Where?" Masa asks as he and Reiko stare first at the ground, then up at the trees and the net of the driving range towering behind it.

"The building's not here anymore. I have to ask you to imagine it," Jonas says.

"Hai, so desu ne," the couple say in unison, sucking in their breaths and nodding their heads.

"Intramuros was severely destroyed during the war," Jonas continues. "First, by Japanese bombings."

Masa drops his head. Reiko takes her husband's hand and squeezes it.

"The Americans, too, bombed the city, in 1945, when General Douglas MacArthur returned to the country after three years. By the time the war ended, Manila was the second most-destroyed city, after Warsaw."

"It says here on the map that we're standing in front of Dulaang Rajah Sulayman," Vince says.

"'Dulaang' means 'theater' and Rajah Sulayman was a Muslim chief who ruled most of Manila when it was still called Maynilad. Maynilad is a plant that grew along the banks of the Pasig River," Jonas explains. "Unfortunately, the plant is now extinct."

"Excuse me, I rittre bit confused ne," Reiko says. "You mean before Spanish time, Firipinos were Musrims?"

Jonas nods. "In 1570, Miguel López de Legazpi, a Spanish conquistador, defeated Rajah Sulayman and took control of Manila. Legazpi died in 1572. We will visit his tomb inside San Agustin church at the end of the tour."

They stop to read a memorial plaque, then climb down a series of steps to a dungeon built alongside the Pasig River. Reiko clutches Masa's arm as they enter a room where the lighting is controlled by whatever sunlight passes through the barred windows.

"This is where the Japanese imprisoned American and Filipino soldiers during the three-year occupation, from 1942 to 1945," Jonas says. Vince inches closer to Jonas, brushes his hand against his. Jonas slides his hand over Vince's, guiding it into a fold.

"They weren't given food or water," Jonas continues. "Most of them died from starvation, disease, or drowned when the river flooded the room during high tide."

Suddenly, Masa falls on his knees. Reiko urges him to get up.

"Prease, forgive me," Masa cries, the walls echoing his plea. "I very ashamed to be Japanese. I herp destroy your country."

Jonas releases his grasp. "Masa, it wasn't only the Japanese. The Americans destroyed our country too."

"I know, I know. But." Masa bows his head in shame.

"Many times he thought of kirring hisserf," Reiko says.

"It's all history now," Vince says, omitting the adjectives "hidden," "censored," "edit," "selective," "amnesia," et cetera.

Masa wipes his eyes with the back of his hand. "You don't understand. You see—" Masa pauses to catch his breath. "I herp destroy histry. Your histry. My histry too."

"It's O.K., Masa. The war did it, not you," Jonas says. "War brings out the evil in all of us."

Vince throws Jonas a look of: Wait a minute, I've heard those words before, they came straight out of Kris's mouth as Lola Maria, the traitor in *In the Name of Shame*.

"I was stationed in Raguna during three-year occupation time," Masa says. "There, I ferr in rove with a Firipina, and I made her mine."

Vince looks at the dungeon walls, the supporting characters, the bad lighting. Am I in a Bino Boca sequel?

"We got married and, right after war, she jumped in river someprace near here and drowned," Masa continues.

"Because Japan rost war against U.S.," Reiko explains.

Masa walks toward the iron-bar windows; Reiko continues the story. "She kirred herserf because she said Phirippines good under Japan. Japan give Firipinos independence. But after war, when Japan rost war, she said Phirippines under U.S. forever."

Reiko and Masa decide not to finish the tour. All the sobbing has left them exhausted. They thank Jonas and give him a tip equaling a month's salary. "Domo arigato," Jonas says, bowing and closing the door of the cab destined for the Manila Hotel, right across the highway.

"Finally, I have you all to myself," Vince jokes.

"Shall we continue with the tour?" Jonas asks.

"No. Enough history and drama for today." Vince stares at Jonas's mouth, imagines nibbling his naturally moist lips. They cross the street and walk alongside a church. "Is that San Agustin?" he asks.

"No, Manila Cathedral."

A horse-drawn carruaje carrying a pair of tourists clops by. Jonas waves to the cochero, an old man in cotton trousers rolled up to his knees.

"Did you know that during Spanish time, coachmen like him were the only few Filipinos allowed inside the Walled City?"

Vince shakes his head no, then cuts to the chase. "Have you eaten?"

"No," Jonas says, "I was too busy with the morning tour. But I do need food soon or I'll faint."

Vince stops walking. "Are you diabetic?"

"No," Jonas says. "I don't know what it is. Something metabolic. I've had it since I was small."

"We can pick something up, then eat it at my place," Vince suggests.

"Where are you staying?"

"Parañaque."

"It'll take us an hour to get there," Jonas says. "And I still have to go to Bulacan."

"Bulacan? Isn't that outside of Manila?"

"Hour and a half by bus from here," Jonas says. "I have to drop off medicine for my mother."

A string of questions invades Vince's head: Is she all right? Isn't there a Mercury Drugstore or a hospital near where she lives? Why can't your father buy it for her? Where the hell is he?

They pass a banner that reads MCDONALD'S COMING SOON. Across the street from it are moss-covered steps that lead to ramparts, where rusty cannons are aimed right at the bars and hotels in the red-light district of Ermita.

"How tragic," Vince remarks, pointing to the sign.

"Sadder for me—I live here," Jonas says. "It's like watching my country commit suicide."

TOUCHÉ, CLICHÉ

My country.

My, not *our*.

It's obvious: to Jonas, I'm an outsider.

A foreigner in his formerland.

A cliché.

Because I don't speak Tagalog.

Can't code-switch without stuttering or tripping over the barbed wires of bilingualism.

Because I'm not an Oreo in the Orient.

Because I carry a U.S. passport I'm not ready to give up.

Or trade for a Philippine life.

My, not *our*.

Because I no longer live here.

Otherwise, I would know LBM, CR, DH, and GOLF—Gentlemen Only, Ladies Forbidden.

Because I don't read the Russians in traffic.

Or slave in Saudi.

Or send my Hong Kong earnings back home.

Because we may speak the same language and use the same words, but we don't mean the same thing.

Because Jonas's reality is my disorientation.

And my chaos is his order.

So stop resisting and surrender.

Surrender what?

My identity.

And what? Give up the first ten years of my life?

Vince's mind falls silent. Seems like he doesn't qualify to be a Filipino. All these years he's never questioned his Filipino identity. Because in Hawaii, a Filipino—whether he or she is born and raised there, like Vince's best friend Edgar, or migrated there from the Philippines, like Vince—is considered a Filipino. Sure, Edgar often made cutting remarks about Vince's hidden desires to reenact scenes from *Gunga Din* with Caucasian fags, but Vince always checked off the "Filipino" box on surveys, college grants, job applications, and affirmative action scholarship forms.

"Shut up, Edgar," Vince usually said. "You don't need to leave the Philippines to be a banana. You can become white through repeated injections."

"You took the words right out of my ass, Vince," Edgar answered. "And remember: You also a local of Hawaii. You also one of me."

But now that he's in the Philippines, the land of his birth, the country of his first memories, the ethnic ID Vince has been carrying around is no longer valid, dismissed by two showbiz icons and a metabolically challenged tour guide with an ailing mother.

"You grew up in America. You speak English. You shit on toilets with working flush, therefore you are an American" is what Kris and Sister Marie basically told him when they put him on the witness stand of ethnoracial authenticity. Jonas didn't even bother questioning Vince's Filipinoness. As far as he was concerned, Vince was an outsider. "It's *my*—not *our*—country." Simple as that.

GO ASK ALICE

The Walled City is crammed with canteens, colleges, and dormitories with signs advertising vacancies. Vince stops to read: ONE MALE BEDSPACER ONLY. NO MALE TO FEMALE WITH FEMALE AT NIGHT. He looks around for a nervous rabbit rushing to and fro with a waistcoat and a pocket watch, or the grin of a Cheshire cat hanging right above his head like a thought bubble, or a decapitation-crazed queen screaming "Off with his head!" None. Turning onto a narrow street and disrupting a basketball game, he checks to see if the basketball is a rolled-up puppy.

Unblinking eyes stare at Vince quickly covering his nose as he passes the stench of rotten food. He's entered another squatter community that, like the other ten million squattervilles he's seen, is built from scraps of wood and rusty tin, the roofs held in place by nails, tires, hollow blocks, and TV antennas. On the sidewalk, the squatters are doing precisely what the sign on the blackboard forbids them to: shampooing, brushing their teeth, washing their clothes, plucking lice from children's heads.

Vince concludes that not even Alice could navigate this underground, let alone comprehend it. No matter which side of the mushroom she ate.

Tourist Tips

- The Chinese are the backbone of the Philippine economy. Many of them were forced to renounce their faith and convert to Catholicism around the mid-eighteenth century, in order to conduct business in the islands. Ma-Yi was their name for the Philippine Islands.

- The Philippines is divided into 7,107 political, religious, class, ethnic, separatist, and criminal groups.

- Kidnapping Chinese businessmen and/or their children is a common occurrence.

- Crime in the capital is either on the HIGH or EVEN HIGHER level.

- Drug use, especially shabu, is also very high. Recent arrests included Taiwanese drug lords.

- Criminals are highly sophisticated, organized, and skilled individuals that can access top security data, including itineraries of foreign dignitaries and tour groups.

- Security is either a near hit or a near miss.

- Popular targets for terrorist activities include shopping malls, embassies, posh residences, hotels, hostels, food courts, cinemas, mosques, churches, bus terminals, kiosks selling contraband merchandise, spas, sports and cockfighting arenas, money changers, pawnshops, banks, beerhouses, pubs, spelunking caves, fiestas, airports, military bases, government buildings, religious processions, beach and spa resorts, movie premieres, piers, tollbooths, C-5 highways, trains, and sidewalk urinals.

- Hire a bodyguard with years of experience in combat fighting and sniffing terrorists.

- It is not uncommon for a disgruntled government employee to hijack a tour bus of Chinese foreigners.

- In case of a hostage crisis, the crisis management committee, along with the President and his secretaries, will closely monitor the situation from a TV in a nearby dim sum restaurant.

- It is recommended that hostages negotiate with their captors before the SWAT team and Philippine National Police arrive.

- In case a hostage crisis is botched, the Department of Justice will issue a gag order for three weeks, or until Philippine authorities are finished with their investigations.

- "Bintang," or "finger-pointing," is a popular sport among politicians, second only to golf.

- Whitewashing is interchangeable with skin-whitening.

- Media is invited to enter the scene of the crime.

- "Typhoon" comes from the Chinese word "tai fung," which means "big wind."

- The Philippines, along with Japan, is part of the Ring of Fire, meaning earthquake-prone.

- Always have a flashlight handy and an unlimited supply of bottled water.

My Dinner with Jonas

"Kamayan" means "to eat with the hands." So when Vince steps inside Joji's Kamayan Restaurant, he isn't surprised to see people doing exactly that. Jonas and he are ushered to a corner table near a window with a view of construction. Next to them are two Caucasian men who could pass for Max Von Sydow: tall, long, lean, translucent. Their companion, a Filipino man (their guide? driver?), has a toupee that juts out from his head like a cap. He's teaching them how Filipinos in the olden days used to eat.

"You put one foot up onto the chair, like this," the Filipino man instructs them. "Then you prop the elbow against the knee, like this. Okay, you try now."

Max Von Sydow's doppelgangers imitate him.

"Then you dunk your lumpia like this."

Vince watches them dip half-bitten fried rolls into a bowl of peppered vinegar.

"Then you crunch crunch crunch," the Filipino man says.

And that's how you catch hepatitis-A, Vince wants to tell Jonas.

The waiter hands him and Jonas menus and, seconds later, asks for their order.

"Could you give us a couple more minutes?" Vince asks.

"Okay, sir."

Jonas stops the waiter as he's about to walk away. "That's not how it works here," he tells Vince.

"So he'll just stand here for as long as we want him to?" Vince asks. "Yes."

"Are you serious?"

Jonas nods. "If we send him away, he might never come back. Do you eat dinuguan?" Pig's blood stew.

"I used to," Vince answers, "until I saw John Travolta dump that bucket of pig's blood on Sissy Spacek in *Carrie*."

Jonas laughs.

"How about hot-and-sour soap, sir?" the waiter cuts in.

With or without bleach? Vince is tempted to ask.

Don't be an ass. I was once in his shoes. If not worse.

Every syllable pronounced like Rita Moreno and Morgan Freeman in *The Electric Company*.

Por ex-am-pol:

Com-por-ta-bol / Comfortable

Fi-zee-ca-lee / Physically

Ak-twa-lee / Actually

Mu-zi-ka-lee / Musically

Ta-len-ted / Talented (accent on the second syllable)

Ay-pol / Apple

Mu-zles / Mussles

"Penny for your thoughts," Jonas says, placing his hand over Vince's.

"What?" Vince asks, blushing.

"Daydreaming?"

"No," Vince says, and smiles as he gingerly moves his hand away from Jonas's.

"How many order of muzzles do you want, sir? Full or half?" the waiter asks.

The waiter brings them green mango shakes, calamari, and a tray of fried lumpia rolls.

"Where are you from?" Jonas asks, biting into the egg-battered fried calamari.

"Hawaii." Vince dunks a spring roll into a bowl of vinegar, garlic, and pepper.

"You ever run into Imelda?"

"Only once. Shopping with her daughter Imee."

"They're coming back next month. There's talk of Imelda running for president. Her son Bongbong is already a front-runner as a congressman, and Imee as governor of Ilocos Norte. The children will most likely win, but not their mother."

"Exiled in '86, welcomed back in '91," Vince says, shaking his head.

"Filipinos are tired of Cory Aquino. She's done nothing to improve the country, except where the rich Chinese are concerned. I think she spends more time praying her rosary and painting landscapes on ceramic plates than getting the country back in order."

"Filipinos are so quick to forgive and forget," Vince says.

"Not true," Jonas says, "We're anything but the forgive-and-forget type. It just seems like it because we're desperate. We're sick and tired of this life. We want another life, another country. And we'll elect even the most corrupt who can give us that better life, even if it's brief. But we never forget, Vince. We remember everything. We may be a poor country, but we have our memory. That's why it's so hard for us to move on. We're still hanging on to every scrap of our past."

"But memory's fiction," Vince says, unleashing the phrase so fast that by the time he realizes what came out, it's too late to retract.

"You believe that?"

Vince shakes his head. "What I mean is that memory has a way of embellishing the past, so that it doesn't belong to us anymore."

"Maybe to you Westerners," Jonas says.

"It's important to Americans too," Vince cuts in. "If it weren't, Americans wouldn't have so much anxiety about Alzheimer's or amnesia.

I think we all have fears of losing our memory, regardless of what and who we are. I once read an interview with a writer—I forget who it was; I think he was an Israeli novelist—who lived with that fear every day of his life because Alzheimer's ran in his family. Every morning, soon as he opened his eyes, he went to his desk and wrote his name over and over, until he was convinced that he hadn't forgotten himself yet. Imagine living a life and just waiting for that day when you wake up and can't remember your name. It's the one thing I fear most."

"Same here," Jonas says. "I don't know about you Americans, but we Filipinos are governed by what and how much we remember."

Enough with the "you Americans" and "we Filipinos," Jonas. I know you see me as an American, but do you have to keep saying it? is what Vince really wants to say. But knowing the conversation will only be a regurgitation of this morning's *Spanish Inquisition with Yours Truly,* he tells Jonas instead: "What's so frightening—and fascinating—about memory is that I sometimes wonder if what I'm remembering really happened, or if I'm making it up. I know nobody can recollect the past exactly as it was, no matter how convincingly one describes it, but—"

"It's all we've got," Jonas cuts in. "Memory makes our lives more interesting and much richer. It's like giving ourselves endless chances to relive one moment. Each remembrance slightly altered," he continues, "but not all memories come from firsthand experiences. The stories that were handed down to you when you were young, like the stories about your ancestors, for example, they're memories too. Memories are what keeps us from being strangers to each other," Jonas says. "Take you and me, for example."

"Yeah?"

"It'll be hard for me to forget how you emptied that plate of lumpia in five minutes," Jonas answers, pointing to the plate of crumbs.

"Maybe in your next recollection, it'll be you who ate them all," Vince laughs.

"You want another order of lumpia?" Jonas asks.

"No," Vince says, embarrassed. "Do you?"

Jonas shakes his head.

"Where were we?" Vince asks. "I mean before we went off on memory."

"The Marcoses' homecoming," Jonas says.

"Is that a rumor?" Vince asks.

"In this country, rumor is the other face of truth."

"But do you really think President Aquino's going to let Imelda back into the country after what she and her husband did? Letting them come back would be a sign of defeat, wouldn't it? Won't there be a mass protest? Another People Power revolution? More coup attempts?"

"Aquino's term is ending in a year," Jonas says. "Once she's out of office, whoever steps in will lift the ban. Mark my words." He pauses to drink.

"Because this is more of a personal rather than a political matter?" Vince asks.

"Because personal is also political here," Jonas answers.

"Wasn't Imelda behind Ninoy's assassination?"

"There's no proof of that."

"Then why did Ferdinand throw a bourbon glass at her when he found out about the assassination?" Vince asks.

"That's a rumor," Jonas says.

"Which is your version of truth."

"One of several. Another version is that it was Marcos's right-hand man who was behind Ninoy's murder," Jonas says. "As for revolution, revolution will always be a part of this country, whether it's sinking or floating."

Vince is silent for a moment, then, "Are you for the Marcoses?"

"Of course not," Jonas says, emphatically. "They're the main reason why this country is so messed up. Did you know that they're the only Filipinos in the *Guinness Book of World Records*?"

"As the world's greatest thieves," Vince, nodding, answers.

Jonas takes a sip of his green mango shake. "After this upcoming election, the Philippines might be in the *Guinness Book of World Records* again, as having the only government with a basketball player, an action star, a former beauty queen, and Vilma 'Darna' Santos."

"I know. I couldn't believe it when I saw the fliers. The Philippines' own Wonder Woman is running for mayor," Vince says, sipping his shake.

"You know Vilma Santos?" Jonas asks.

"Of course," Vince says. "I'm not as American as you think."

"I didn't mean to offend you."

"Let's just say it's water under the Intramuros Bridge," Vince says, smiling at Jonas. "I grew up watching Darna movies. I remember how our small town would shut down whenever the outdoor cinema showed a Darna film. Do they still have them—outdoor cinemas?"

"Only in the provinces. Most of them closed down in the early eighties. Got replaced by Betamax."

"What about komiks?" Vince asks. "I tried looking for them on newsstands and in the bookstore but I didn't see any."

"You'd have to go to Recto," Jonas says.

"Where's that?"

"Near Quiapo. You didn't grow up in Manila, did you?"

"San Vicente," Vince says. "Halfway between Manila and Baguio."

Jonas nods, indicating he knows exactly where Vince spent his boyhood. "It's right on the Dig-dig fault zone," Jonas says, referring to the fault that runs from north to south of Luzon. Last year, it rocked the city of Baguio with an intensity of 7.7 on the Richter scale, ripping the Nevada Hotel in half and burying hotel guests of the five-star Hyatt.

"Really? Is it connected to Mount Pinatubo?"

"Yes. The next earthquake is supposed to be stronger. No wonder your town is called San Vicente."

"What do you mean?"

"You know what kind of saint San Vicente is, right?"

Vince shakes his head.

"He's the patron saint of Judgment Day."

"Shit," Vince says, helping himself to another egg roll.

"Better try the calamari before I eat it all," Jonas says.

"Be my guest," Vince says.

An unexpected moment of silence falls between them. "How many brothers and sisters do you have?" Vince asks.

"I have three brothers and one sister. All of them are working abroad. My brothers are in Abu Dhabi and my sister is a D.H. in Singapore. I had a job waiting for me in Seoul last year, in a factory. But my mother had a stroke, so I was forced to stay back."

"And be a tour guide to a bunch of tourists with repressed memories and guilt-ridden pasts?" Vince asks.

"I actually enjoy my job. Gives me the chance to make use of my college degree."

"What was your major?"

"History. You?"

"Film and literature," Vince says, then points to the pitcher of water. "Is the water boiled?"

"I wouldn't chance it," Jonas replies, flagging down the waiter and motioning for him to bring a bottle of mineral water.

"Who takes care of your mom when you're at work?"

"My nephews and nieces."

"Where's your dad?"

"In the States." Pause. "He left us a long time ago."

An "I'm sorry" leaves Vince's mouth and hangs in the air.

"It's O.K. I was too young to remember him anyway. I was only four or five when he left for the States to go and work as a doctor. That was around 1966 or '67. But when he arrived in California, he was told he had to retake the Boards. He wrote to my mother and told her that plans had changed; that he'd petition us once he passed the Board exams and started practicing."

Vince nods in silence; he's no stranger to Jonas's history. His own parents left the country to be teachers in Hawaii, leaving him, Jing, and Alvin in the hands of a widower and an old maid. This was 1971. Jing was four; Vince was three; Alvin, two. After a year of teaching at an elementary school on a sugar plantation community, his parents ended up working for the backbone of Hawaii's economy: the tourism industry.

In college, Vince had read about the brain-drain phenomenon in *Decolonization for Beginners*. How it began in 1965 when President Johnson allowed twenty thousand Filipinos a year into the U.S., many of them professionals who had been promised opportunities, better wages, and further training in their specialized fields. Prior to that, the Tydings-McDuffie Act of 1934 had limited the number of immigrants to fifty a year.

A brain drainer himself, Dumpit wrote about the racial discrimination Filipinos encountered upon their arrival in America; how thousands of doctors, nurses, teachers, lawyers, accountants, and scientists left the Philippines labeled as "professionals" by the Immigration and Naturalization Service and the Department of Labor only to discover that they couldn't practice their professions right away because of strict licensing laws.

Angel Cortez, a second-generation Filipino filmmaker from New York, made a documentary on the brain drain. It was screened at the Hawaii International Film Festival. Vince saw it twice. One of Cortez's subjects was a surgeon who ended up a butcher in a New York restaurant because he couldn't afford to go back to school and, at the same time, feed his family, who'd accompanied him to the U.S. Another was a pharmacist from San Jose who wasn't allowed to take the license exam because of state laws. California, as it turned out, had a law stipulating that only those who had attended the schools mentioned in the state's Board of Pharmacy list were eligible to take the test. She had earned degrees in pharmacy and biochemistry at the University of Santo Tomas in the Philippines, a university older than Harvard and that has one of the best med schools in Southeast Asia. But UST wasn't on California's list.

DIG-DUG

"When was the last time you heard from your father?" Vince asks.

"While he was still living in California," Jonas answers.

"Has he been back?"

Jonas shrugs.

"Sounds like you're over him."

Jonas gestures for Vince to hold his words while he flags their waiter to follow up on their orders.

"I don't really know him," Jonas says.

"You weren't angry?"

"Of course I was. I hated him for what he'd done to my mother, to us. It took me a long time to deal with the anger, to get rid of the guilt. But I'm glad he's out of our lives."

"You forgave him?"

"I forgave myself," Jonas says. "It's hard to forgive someone you don't remember. What about you? Do you have any brothers or sisters?"

Vince holds out two fingers. "A very crazy younger brother and an even crazier older sister. But I love them both," he says.

"And your parents?"

"No more."

"I'm sorry."

"It's O.K."

"How long have you been an orphan?"

"What?" Vince laughs. "No, my parents are still alive. They're divorced."

"Were you all born here?"

Vince nods. "In San Juan De Dios Hospital in Pasay City."

"How old were you when you left the Philippines?"

"I was ten, Alvin was nine, or he was about to turn nine, and my sister Jing was eleven."

"And this is your first time back?"

Vince nods.

"What about your brother and sister? Have they been back?"

"They visited once."

"How come you didn't come then?"

"Long story," Vince says, then adds, "school."

"So what do you think of Manila?"

"Chaotic, depressing, surreal." Vince catches himself and stops. He doesn't want to offend Jonas the way he offended Kris and Sister Marie. He has to be cautious with what he says, choose his adjectives carefully.

"There's nothing surreal about Manila," Jonas says, matter-of-factly. "It's only surreal because Manila's no longer part of your world."

Vince falls silent for a moment. "It's not only that, Jonas. I feel utterly hopeless here." In his mind, a litany is building:

Helpless

This city that's got one foot in the gutter and another in a volcano

With a palace wrapped in broken glass and barbed wire

And surrounded by cardboard sidewalks

Cardboard houses

Cardboard lives

In-your-face contradictions and

I-can-see-right-through-you gazes

This city where I can't cross a street without cars trying to kill me

This place obsessed with skin-whitening cream and nosejobs

This malignancy that drags down passersby who dare to look up at the sky to Hades.

What sky?

Where?

Show me

No

I want to leave

I want to give up

I want nothing to do with this place anymore

And just when I'm ready to surrender

Just when I'm gearing up to leave

Get the fuck out

Something comes and stirs me

A memory

Tenderness

Beauty

Hunger

Eye-popping signage

Another unwanted dream

BI THE WAY

The waiter returns with a tray of food: pork adobo marinated in vinegar and soy sauce; steamed mussels with ginger roots; fried rice seasoned with shrimp paste; and a special dish from the Ilocos called pinakbet—vegetable potpourri: eggplants, okra, bitter melons, pumpkins, string beans, and tomatoes—cooked in fermented fish sauce and sauteed garlic.

"Finally," Jonas says.

The waiter apologizes, tells them the chefs are busy preparing for tonight's Film Academy of the Philippines awards banquet. "Over twenty-five entrées," he says, then excuses himself.

"That's right," Jonas says. "I almost forgot it's tonight."

Vince watches him dip his hand into the bowl of vegetable stew.

"Don't you get tired of commuting to Manila?" he asks, scooping a handful of bagoong-seasoned rice onto his plate.

Jonas shakes his head, says, "I'm renting a room in a boardinghouse in Pasay City." He pauses to taste the ginger-flavored broth. "Near Libertad."

"I was there last night," Vince says.

"Doing what?"

"Looking for Leche."

"It's closed on Sundays."

"You know Leche?"

"I used to go there often. With my ex-girlfriend. She was the one who took me there."

"Before you dumped her for a guy?" Vince jokes.

"No," Jonas laughs. "She gets turned on by watching guys make out."

"Which makes you gay? Not gay? Semi-gay?" Vince asks, trying not to stare at Jonas's lips.

Jonas shakes his head. "'Gays' refers to transvestites," he says. "They don't see themselves as guys. Not like in America."

"Really?" Vince says. "What about the straight-acting ones?"

"They're in the closet," Jonas answers. "Usually A/B class."

"So you're—"

"Silahis."

"What's that?"

"Bi. AC/DC. One ten/two twenty."

"Oh, one of those."

"One of those what?"

"Jack of all holes, master to none."

Jonas laughs.

"So what's Leche like?"

"Exactly like Manila. Anything that can happen happens there," Jonas says, helping himself to another scoop of vegetable stew. "It used to be an orphanage a long, long time ago. Started by wives of Spanish generals. You should definitely check it out before you leave."

"What about tonight?"

"Tonight?"

"Why not?"

"I suppose I could. It's Lollipops and Roses night on Mondays."

"What's that?"

"Toro."

"Bull-and-matador toro?"

"Live sex show. Sixty-nine acts," Jonas says.

"Hot," Vince says. "I've never been to one."

"You're missing out."

"Then go with me."

"I already said yes, didn't I?"

"Great. Where should we meet?"

"Best to just meet there because I'll be coming from Bulacan. In fact, I better get going or I'll miss the bus. Here's some money."

"Don't," Vince says. "My treat. And tonight as well."

"You sure?"

Vince nods.

"Okay, see you tonight," Jonas says, squeezing Vince's hand.

Across from the restaurant is a construction site where a hotel is expected to open before the year ends. Vince stops to make sure he isn't losing his mind. Transfixed, he reads the sign again. And again. And again. Then adds SLOW MEN AT WORK to his growing list of Manila signs that continue to bewilder and amuse him.

Signs of the Times

PETAL ATTRACTION is a florist. **ELIZABETH TAILORING** is hiring experienced sewers. **CULTURE SHACK** specializes in native handicrafts. **MANG DONALD'S** makes the best **PRINCE FRIES**. The owners of **KAREN'S CARPENTRY** can't carry a tune, but they can make you a hand-carved four-poster bed in a week. **DEAR HUNTER** helps you find rich, old, white husbands. Need a new pair of running shoes? Try **FOOT LUCKERS**. **WALTER MART** carries designer labels like **CHRISTINE DIOR** jeans and **GEORGIO NOMANI** T-shirts. Having a bad hair day? There's FELIX THE CUT, SONNY'S SHEAR, **SCISSORS PALACE**, and MANE ATTRACTION. And when all is said and done, check in at *STAIRWAY TO HEAVEN*, **MAKE THE DEAD SMILE**, or VIVA FUNERAL & BEAUTY PARLOR, which also accepts laundry on Wednesdays and Sundays. And the latest one to make Vince smile: LOOK UP FOR FALLING DEBRIS.

JEEPNEY BARKER, QUIAPO

Alvin,

From a notice posted on a blackboard in
Intramuros: NO SIDEWALK LAUNDERING. NO
CURBSIDE HEAD & SHOULDERING EXCEPT
10P-7A. NO CURBSIDE COLGATE-ING OR
CREST-ING. ABSOLUTELY NO LICE-PICKING AT
ALL TIMES. NO PUBLIC JINGLING OR URINATORS
PUNISHED. KARAOKE WITH PERMIT ONLY.
PROMOTE SANITARIZATION & SOCIAL
CONDITIONING. REMEMBER: BEAUTIFICATION
OVER UGLIFICATION PER ORDER BY MANG
CARDING, BARANGAY KAPITAN, INTRAMUROS.

P.S. I am not on drugs.

Alvin De Los Reyes
430 Keoniana St.
2D
Honolulu, HI 96815

Carte Blank

"Welcome to Leche!" A waifish man sporting espadrilles, jeans, a shoulder-baring sweatshirt, a ponytail, and too much foundation but not enough lipstick greets Vince. "Call me Tita G. As in G marks the spot," he adds, snapping his fan open.

Vince glances around the room. No Jonas. Only Spanish antique furniture and a transvestite ensconced on a velvet couch, smoking a cigarette, his eyes glued to a television monitor.

"Am I the only one here besides him?" Vince asks. "Or is he a she?"

"That's Yermaphrodite, Manila's most endangered speciman, next to the tarsier," Tita G says. "Yerma works here. Right now, it's just you, shim, and the five Arabs upstairs."

Vince looks at his watch.

It's still early.

Jonas will show up.

He said so.

Give him time; he's coming from a thousand miles away.

Give him a break; his mother's ill.

Maybe he's on his way, just blocks away.

But stuck in traffic because of a wake.

He'll be here.

Relax.

"Don't worry," Tita G says, "this place will be humping before you know it." Tita G eyes Vince up and down. "You look so familiar. Have we met before?"

"No," Vince answers.

"Are you sure?"

"Yes."

Tita G shifts his eyes to the television, where Kris Aquino and Sister Marie are singing "Unforgivable"—one of the five songs nominated for Best Theme Song. Lyrics by Sister Marie. "My god, are they still at it? Ka loka!" Tita G says. Yerma hushes him as Kris and Sister Marie belt out the last notes.

"About fucking time." Tita G rolls his eyes. "This awards ceremony is worse than a drag queen pageant."

Tita G is not exaggerating. Over two hours have passed, and the Film Academy of the Philippines has only handed out six trophies. All to *In the Name of Shame*: Best Sound Editing; Best Sound; Best Lighting; Best Dubbing; Best Director to Bino Boca, his first FAP directorial award; and Best Screenplay to Rimbaud Woo, who adapted the film from a serialized komik.

"What's the entrance fee?" Vince asks.

"There isn't one," Tita G replies, hitching his sweatshirt up. "Too much paperwork. Too many receipts to write out. And as you may have already experienced, receipts eat up patience, get on everyone's nerves. Nakaka-buwishit, di ba? I don't know why we're so obsessed with receipts in this country. It's not like it's going to save our plummeting economy," Tita G pauses. "What we offer here at Leche are three types of membership plans. Eight hundred fifty pesos for a year, ten thousand for lifetime, or fifteen thousand for Carte Blanche."

Lifetime?

Carte Blanche?

Eight hundred fifty?

"You forenjers, talaga," Tita G says. "Always computing how cheap life is in Manila. Well, you're right. It is cheap. Just how cheap? You can feed a starving village on cans of 555 sardines or Pure Foods Vienna sausages for a week for the price of a one-year membership."

"But I'm leaving in a few days."

"And you have a year to come back."

Vince shudders at the thought.

"It's worth it even if you never come back," Tita G says, as if she's read his mind.

Vince hands Tita G eight hundred fifty pesos exact; he doesn't want to go through another transaction nightmare.

"Fill this out, then I'll give you a short tour of Leche," Tita G says, handing Vince a pen and a four-by-six index card.

"Tour?"

"It's part of the package. Don't worry, it'll be quick. Anyway, it's still early." Tita G stops to read over Vince's shoulder. "Vicente. Nice name."

Vicente? Vince rereads the card. That's what he's written. He puts the tip of the pen against the *V,* ready to scribble the name out and write Vince instead, but stops.

Let it go, Vince.

Just this once, let it go.

"Next time you come back, bring a passport-size photo," Tita G says. "And we will laminate your card for free. Claro?"

Vince nods.

"Don't lose it or you'll have to get an ALR."

"ALR?"

"Affidavit of Loss Report form," Tita G says. "You can get one from a licensed lawyer. It costs less than a hundred pesos."

ALR. Another acronym to add to his growing list, which includes LBM, GOLF, and NATO—No Action, Talk Only.

Vince sits on a chair that reminds him of the furniture in his grandfather's house in San Vicente—Spanish wooden furniture with cane backing and elaborate carvings. He browses through the how-to pamphlets on preventing STDs and AIDS stacked on the coffee table in front of him. There are travel brochures on Pagsanjan Falls in Laguna, where one can experience the ultimate boat ride of his life, visit the ruins that were once Marlon Brando's temple in *Apocalypse Now,* and mingle with the boatmen who worked on the set of Coppola's movie. Also, there are back issues of *Chika-Chika* and *Hot Copy* magazines featuring B-movie actors in thongs. One of them has a centerfold of none other than the postcard thief who tried to sell him sex for twelve dollars in the parking lot of Greenbelt yesterday. In the picture, he's wearing nothing but a surprised look on his face, his hands partially covering his private parts.

"You like?" Tita G asks, almost singing the words. "He lives here, you know. All eight inches of him. And very thick, thicker than a boxer's fist. He's already taken, but it can be arranged . . . for ten thousand pesos."

"I'm on a student budget," Vince says, putting the magazine back in the pile and trying not to react.

"You know Vicente, I'm certain that we've met before," Tita G insists. "Where did you say you're from?"

"I didn't," Vince says.

"But your face is so familiar," Tita G says.

"He was on TV," Yermaphrodite blurts, as if he's reporting recycled news. "Kris's balikbayan guest. The one who almost tripped on the cables."

"That's right," Tita G says. "Ikaw 'yun, di ba? The one who made that comment about Filipino assholes?"

Startled, Vince looks at Tita G.

"Yes, he *is* you," Tita G says.

"You mean it's already been shown?"

"Live at noon, honey."

"But Kris said—"

"Oh my Lord, hijo. You're in the Philippines. Everyone here speaks in subtitles. What is said is a translation of *what can be*. Intiendes? And of all people, Kris is the last person I would want to be interviewed by. That girl's mouth is wider than Lake Taal, plus the volcano inside it."

Vince is surprised—and yet, he isn't. He knows that, to Filipinos, "yes," "no," and "maybe" are interchangeable, regardless if they're uttered in Tagalog, English, or patois. The nuance is in the tone, and dramatic facial and hand gestures. So when Kris told Vince that her program was preempted, she actually meant live, but delayed by ten minutes.

"Ay, naku, hijo, you can't trust anybody nowadays. The only one you can trust is Leche. Because if there is one cardinal rule Leche preaches, it is confidentiality. Leche is the gatekeeper of secrets, and Yermaphrodite is the three-headed dog. And because two-thirds of the country is in the closet—or what they think is the closet—Leche will never go out of business. Why do you think the very popular and powerful come here? Why do you think everyone who wants to be somebody flocks here? To share and spill secrets. So, I hope that before you leave tonight, Vicente, you will have shared and spilled secrets with one, if not many."

TOUR! DE-TOUR!

Tita G instructs Yermaphrodite to page him when they're about to announce the winners for Best Supporting Actress and Best Actress.

"If I remember correctly, you're from Hawaii, right?" Tita G asks, leading Vince along a lit hallway. "Do you know Marlon Fajardo, the Concert King of the Philippines, who's married to Paloma Vargas, the Concert Queen, ek ek?"

"Yes, but not personally."

"You want to meet Marlon?"

"He comes here?"

"Secret," Tita G says.

They pass a wooden staircase with hand-carved balustrades reminis-
cent of upper-class homes during Spanish colonial times, then halt in
front of a glass door. A small sign reads: MUSEUM HOURS: OPEN 10A–2P.
THURS ONLY.

Tita G unlocks the door, switches on the light, and leads Vince into
a room with a chalkboard and rows of desks and benches. An entire wall
is covered with alphabet charts, flash cards, grammar lesson plans, and
other visual aids printed in Spanish, English, and Japanese—the lan-
guages of the colonial masters, which Filipinos spoke at one point or
another in their history.

"Leche was founded in the 1870s by wives of Spanish government
officials," Tita G begins. "It began as a milk distribution center for
young, poor Filipino mothers in the city. When the Americans took
over in 1899, they converted Leche into an orphanage for children
whose parents were killed in the Philippine-American War."

Tita G flicks his fan open. "This classroom was built at the turn of
the twentieth century." Tita G walks over to a glass cabinet and pulls a
book from the shelf. *The First Philippine Reader*. He hands it to Vince,
who looks at the copyright date. 1903.

Vince turns the page to the first lesson, accompanied by an illustra-
tion of two girls wearing sailor shirts and pleated skirts. One holds an
American flag, the other, a heart-shaped fan. Below it are the words "I"
and "You."

I have a flag.

You have a fan.

Have you a flag?

I have my flag.

"This is a collector's item." Vince hands the book back to Tita G,
who shelves it.

"I know," Tita G says. "If you only knew how many American scholars come here to bug me and Yerma, offering to buy these books for as much as one thousand pesos per title. One professor flew all the way from Wisconsin, made lambing-lambing to me and Yerma pa nga e, you would've thought he was going to marry us, spoke to us in broken Spanish because he thought we were Madrileñas, even slept with us, imagine!—but not at the same time, of course; Yerma and I aren't lesbians. He thought we would give in and sell the entire library for five thousand pesos."

The fan snaps open, the eyebrow arches. "Excuse me lang. What do these Kang-Kang Kanos take me for? I told them off, then I sent them away without a merienda. I wasn't born yesterday. I've been to London, to New York. I know about Christie's and Sotheby's. Excuse me lang. Go pillage somebody else's history. Mine is already on reserve. Leche!"

"Where'd you find these books?"

"Where else but in the private collection of Madame," Tita G says. "Got it on the night she fled the palace for your friendly neighborhood in Hawaii," he adds, referring to that February night in 1986, when Marcos and his wife ended their twenty-year conjugal dynasty to begin a new life in exile in Honolulu.

"I watched it live on *Nightline* and *CNN*," Vince says as images replay in his mind. Nuns cooking meals for rebel troops along EDSA Highway. Marcos's top two military advisors—Defense Minister Juan Ponce Enrile and Chief of Staff of the Armed Forces Fidel V. Ramos—switching their allegiances to Corazon Aquino at the last minute. Thousands and thousands of angry Filipinos praying amidst armed soldiers and tanks on EDSA. A woman holding a placard—I'M A MOTHER FIGHTING FOR MY CHILDREN. Filipinos stampeding the palace and showing the world how one family's extravagance had perfected one country's misery.

"The funny thing is that while the governor and his wife were welcoming them to Hawaii, u.s. customs officials were confiscating their dozen-plus balikbayan boxes crammed with dollars, jewelry, paintings," Vince continues.

"How far was your place from theirs?" Tita G says.

"Three freeway exits," Vince says. "So, were you one of the looters?"

"No," Tita G says.

"Then how'd you end up with these books?"

"Through a middleman," Tita G says, "which is what you do when you want something done in this country. A middleman's more efficient and faster than Federal Express. I had one of my boys do it. I knew exactly where Madame stashed these books: behind a wall in her private library, next to the music room."

"You've been inside Malacañang Palace?" Vince asks.

"Too many times. I could tell you who slept with whom in which room," Tita G says, matter-of-factly. "In fact, I was one of the very first to get a sneak peek of Madame Imelda's bulletproof bra and her three thousand pairs of feet. All custom made, by the way. She also kept a temperature-controlled basement for her gallons of perfume."

"Is it true Ferdinand kept a dialysis machine in his room?" Vince asks, remembering reading about it in the papers, how it was still running hours after they fled the country.

"Not one," Tita G pauses, "but four. Marcos's room hardly had any light. It was a combination of a kidney dialysis ward and the Vienna Opera House. Dialysis machines, a king-sized hospital bed, iv poles, steel carts loaded with medicine and feeding tubes. Velvet furniture, velvet drapes over stained-glass windows, velvet everything. And all-day, all-night chamber music by Bach. Napaka-eerily. Parang mausoleum. All you needed was a coffin in the corner with a white suit in it and the installation art would've been complete."

"How macabre!" Vince says.

"She and Ferdinand slept in separate rooms, you know," Tita G continues. "Ay, I better stop before that woman puts a curse on me. I really shouldn't talk bad about Imelda, because she does have exquisite taste in art and she is a dear friend of mine. But she's mad, mad talaga, as in the madwoman in the Malacañang attic. Did you know she hired one of the national artists to paint a reproduction of the Sistine Chapel on the ceiling of the music room? Oo. Truly-ly. A fresco a là Michelangelo. But instead of Adam, it is she who is touching the forefinger of God."

"Is it still there?" Vince asks.

"No more. President Cory replaced it with a reproduction of one of her landscape paintings. Those two widows talaga. Nakakabaliw! Nakakaloka Garcia Lorca! Different as night and day. One speaks French, the other thinks she's Marie Antoinette. But same under a full moon." Pause. "Where was I?"

"Somewhere between the early 1900s and the 1986 EDSA Revolution."

"Oh, yes. The Japanese. Come. Follow me." Tita G leads him to the second floor, where the bar is. At the end of the corridor is the video room. "In fairness to our bisexual patrons, we have straight and gay porn tapes, and over a hundred titles to choose from. The video room is self-service and is on a first-come, first-serve basis." Tita G pauses.

"When Japan invaded the Philippines in 1942, the Japanese wanted us to be Filipinos again. They were furious at us. What were we doing? they asked. Sleeping? For over four hundred years? How could we have allowed Spain and the U.S. to control us, brainwash us with religion and Hollywood?" Tita G says. "They shut down the orphanage and turned it into their main headquarters."

"What about the orphans?" Vince asks.

"They handed them over to the Catholic churches in and outside Manila."

SWITCH TO VOICEOVER OF MEMORY, 1975-ISH

"Yaya Let, what happened to Lolo Al during the war?" a seven-year-old Vince asked his maid as she readied him for bed one night.

"You already know, Anak," Yaya Let said, addressing him as "my child" in Tagalog, for if there were a person who could claim him as such, it was her. At age nine, she had gone to join her parents working for Don Alfonso's family. She nurtured him, along with Alvin and Jing, from birth until they left the Philippines. "I told that story to you na. Many, many times," she continued. She slid the capiz-shelled windows closed, leaving just enough opening for the breeze to enter the room.

"Tell it to me again so I don't forget," he said.

"You won't," she said. "You have the memory of an elephant."

"Please."

"Ay, naku, Vicente, you're just like your grandfather," Yaya Let sighed. "So persistent, so makulit." She sat on the edge of the mattress and turned her head toward Vince.

"When the Japanese arrived in San Vicente," began Yaya Let, "the first thing Doña Aurora, your great-grandmother, did was send your Lolo Al to the mountains to hide. For if the Japanese ever saw him, they would automatically, because of his blue eyes, take him for an American and arrest him." Yaya Let paused. "Napaka-puti niya. Much fairer than his father, Sir Lawrence."

"What was he like, Yaya Let?" Vince asked.

"Who?"

"Sir Lawrence."

"Well, like your Lolo, your great-grandfather was a man of few words."

"You mean when he spoke, the whole room listened," Vince said, remembering one of Yaya Let's adages about his grandfather.

"Yes," she smiled. "For a long time, we didn't see or hear from him. We thought we had lost him to the Japanese. Then one night, shortly after the war ended, an American soldier brought him back to us. The soldier said he'd found him in Camp O'Donnell in Pampanga, along with thousands of American soldiers who were imprisoned there. He was very thin when the war returned him to us. We could see the shape of his bones. We wanted to embrace him but were afraid he'd break. His own mother didn't recognize him. He himself didn't know who he was, where he was, who we were. For over a year, he didn't speak. The doctor told us there wasn't anything we could do, except leave him in the hands of God. Then, one Sunday morning, as I was walking out of the house to go to the market, he called me. He was sitting in his chair in the living room, the same one he spent most of his days in, looking out the window, smoking a cigarette, listening to the radio. 'Leticia, bumili ka nga ng pakwan,' he said. I couldn't believe my ears. It's just your imagination talking, Leticia, I told myself. 'Leticia,' he said again. I turned around. He was looking at me. Then, in English, he said, 'Buy me watermelons.' I nearly fainted. I shouted for Doña Aurora to come to the living room right away. He didn't know why we were crying. He'd forgotten about the war. Doña Aurora forbade us to ever bring up the subject of war again. She was afraid that resurrecting those times might take him away from us again. As far as Doña Aurora was concerned, God could keep that part of her son's life. It wasn't until years later, after your father was born, that pieces of the war returned to him."

Yaya Let paused, recalling for a moment the horror and sadness on Vince's grandfather's face when he told her of his memories about those hellish years that began with a sixty-mile march from an airfield in Bataan province to a prison camp that had been a former training ground for u.s. armed forces. Many of them had already been suffering from malaria or starving because the u.s. government, under Theodore

Roosevelt, had failed to send them the food and medicine they had been promised, along with additional troops. Too weak to fight, even if they had outnumbered their captors two hundred to one, they were forced to surrender to the Japanese after three months of fighting.

"The march lasted for six days," Yaya Let continued. "Six days of burning under the sun. Six days of walking in two columns, shoeless and in rags. Six days of dirt and dust. Six days of begging for water on an empty stomach. Six days of praying for strength, a miracle, some mercy. Six days of going from one death to another."

Years later, Vince would hear Yaya Let's voice replay in his head whenever he saw documentaries on the Bataan death march, or read about the Japanese war crime. How Japanese soldiers didn't spare a moment cleaving American and Filipino soldiers' heads in two or disemboweling them with their swords if they tried to escape. How American and Filipino soldiers were plowed over by trucks if they collapsed, or beheaded if they fell out of line. How Filipino bystanders watching the procession along the side of the road were shot or bayoneted if they got caught offering water or food to the prisoners. How out of the more than seventy-eight thousand soldiers, only fifty-four thousand made it to Camp O'Donnell. How by the time Douglas MacArthur had kept his promise and returned three years later only four thousand Filipino and American prisoners were left. Four thousand who lived under the most inhumane conditions, sleeping and eating on the same spot where they defecated, eating boiled tree bark, leaves, rags, and shoes.

"Your grandfather said he remembered being surrounded by dead soldiers talking to each other, helping each other, praying for each other," Yaya Let said. "And that he, too, was one of them."

LUST ON THE ROCKS

Tita G calls the third floor the Labyrinth of Desire, because of the multiple passageways that wind around booths and cubicles like a maze.

Vince peeps into a booth and wonders where in the hell he and Jonas are supposed to do it. There's barely room for lust in it. It would be like fucking inside a broom closet, or worse, an upright coffin.

As he follows Tita G through the maze, Vince feels like he's been inside Leche before. He searches the walls for clues, peeks into another cubicle.

"Did Bino Boca film *In the Name of Shame* here?" he asks.

"For four months," Tita G answers.

"You mean this is where the Lolas were kept?" Vince asks, remembering a scene where two of the former comfort women lead a cameraman through the maze and point out the cubicles they lived in for three years.

"Bino said the only way he could capture the nightmarish account of the comfort women was to film it exactly where the violation was committed. Right here in the former headquarters of the Japanese Imperial Army," Tita G explains. "He said it was the only way he could come closest to recording the factual events; otherwise, he had no business messing with history. He called it 'reciprocating memory.'"

"It must've been so painful for the Lolas," Vince says, "to be brought back here and reminded of their fears, the torture, the rape. Then, on top of that, giving their testimonies on film."

"Of course," Tita G says. "It happens to anyone who has to confront an unwanted past. It was super-intense nga e, with everyone breaking down into tears. Two of the Lolas had to be rushed to the hospital after recounting their nightmares. It's very heart of darkness talaga whenever the reel mirrors the real, and cruel memories get resurrected."

Vince remains quiet, but has a mouthful of words in his head: but young and innocent girls were raped and tortured in these rooms, and Boca has achieved nothing except to exploit the Lolas's ordeal, cheapen their suffering, capitalize on their sorrows by turning their victimization into a two-hour melodrama starring the Massacre Queen of Philippine cinema.

"Bino films in Leche all the time," Tita G continues. "This place is a feast for him, creatively and every-ly. It never runs out of material because it's always creating history no matter how much milk gets spilled, if you know what I mean. And for a consummate and perfectionist artist like Bino, this is the ideal, the home for many of his inspirations. Since the mid-eighties, he's been here almost every month shooting everything, from telenovelas to episodes for *K.A. Drama Anthology* to his controversial movies, including *Taste of P*. We have VHS copies of it for sale for five hundred pesos downstairs. Ask Yermaphrodite."

"*Taste of P* was shot in here too?" Vince asks.

Tita G's face beams with pride. "Including the ménage-a-trois scene that no Tagalog film since has been able to top."

"What happened to Leche after the war?"

"It curdled soon after the Japanese were defeated. Nobody wanted to touch it. It had too much mixed history. Plus the government had no money to maintain it. It wasn't until Marcos came along. That man was a genius. He was corrupt, but he was a genius. He knew how to milk Leche for what it was worth. He took the neglected property and had its interior repaired, but kept its deteriorating façade."

"For what?"

"This is where he kept his mistresses. Leche became his secret rendezvous, his bunker, his Antipolo, his rest home away from Imelda. Plus the house in Greenhills where he'd put up Dovie Beams was still being completed."

Vince's face lights up. "Dovie Beams?"

"You know Dovie?"

"Of course," Vince says. Then, more to himself, "Wait 'til Jing hears about this. She's going to die."

"Who's Jing?'

"My sister," Vince answers. "Dovie Beams was her idol when we were growing up," he adds. But Dovie Beams was more than his sister's idol—she was her femme fatale role model and her bombshell of a fantasy. What the blue-eyed bangungut victim, Mr. Smith, was to Vince, Dovie Beams was to Jing.

Though Jing was only five when the scandal broke, she found out about it three years later, when she and Yaya Let were going through her grandfather's old stacks of magazines for pictures for a collage project. She ended up making a collage of Dovie while Vince worked on his scrapbook of Vilma Santos.

"You mean Imelda didn't know about Dovie?" Vince asks.

"Of course she knew," Tita G replies. "She had an entourage of fortune tellers. But the straw broke the iron butterfly's back when the country heard her husband not only making love to Dovie on UP campus radio, but confessing to her that he and Imelda no longer had sex, because the Madame was as frigid as a Westinghouse Frigidaire."

LOVEY DOVEY

A busty, B-movie actress from Nashville, Tennessee, Dovie Beams had flown to Manila to audition for *Maharlika,* named after the guerrilla unit that Marcos had supposedly led against the Japanese during World War II. "Maharlika," which means "a noble warrior," was also Marcos's nom de guerre. The allegedly CIA-funded film project was to be completed in time for the 1969 election, in hopes that it would boost Marcos's image as commandeer of a 9,200-plus force and win him a second presidential term.

In the hotel suite, the producer had introduced Marcos as "Ferdy" to Dovie. Immediately there were sparks, and a couch. Before the night ended, she had won the coveted role of Evelyn, a Filipino American nurse and an informant for the Americans. As Marcos's wartime sweetheart, she supposedly died from a gunshot wound trying to stop a bullet meant for him.

Marcos's exploits during the Japanese occupation were sheer fabrication, as false as the name Maharlika, and as delusional as casting an American TV actor, Paul Burke, to play him. But because Marcos was so powerful, he could do anything, from sleeping with the wives of his generals to turning a jungle of lies into a metropolitan reality to writing his encyclopedic *Notes on the New Society of the Philippines* to romancing B-rated bombshells.

For two years, reel mirrored real. Beams lived the glamorous life among Manila's elite. As he made love to her, Marcos serenaded her with Ilocano love songs, like "O Narianag A Bulan" ("Oh, How Bright the Moon Is"), "No Siak Ti Agayat" ("When I Fall in Love"), and "Pamulinawen" ("Stone-hearted Lady"). He took nude snapshots of her, traded locks of pubic hair, taught her important Tagalog phrases and words—"mahal" means "expensive" as much as "love." Unbeknownst to him, Beams had hidden a tape recorder under the bed and surreptitiously recorded their lovemaking, conversations, and lovers' quarrels.

After winning the '69 election and becoming the first Philippine president to serve a second term, Marcos, at Imelda's insistence, ended his open-secret affair with the actress. "Get rid of that whore so you can finally do something about those students trying to run us out of our palace," Imelda said. She was right: anti-Marcos demonstrations were becoming a daily occurrence in the capital.

Dovie was furious. In front of Marcos and his top military officials, the actress called him a liar, accused him of manufacturing the war medals and manipulating the election, which many claimed was rigged and cost fifty million dollars, mostly from public funds. "Fucking murderer!" she screamed as a general and his men dragged her out of the room. They took her to the Savoy Hotel, where they allegedly beat her before dropping her off at the Manila Hilton.

Hemorrhaging, she cabbed it to San Juan De Dios Hospital in Pasay City and registered under a false name. She phoned the u.s. embassy; they advised her to leave the country immediately, especially since Imelda had threatened to have her killed for a hundred thousand dollars. Before she left for the airport, the very battered, bruised, betrayed, and bitter Dovie decided to hold a televised press conference, supporting her testimony with tapes and a cassette player.

In no time, everyone who could get their hands on the tapes duplicated them. Senator Ninoy Aquino, who led the Senate investigation hearing on the scandal, was said to have paid five hundred dollars for his copy. For a week the campus radio station of the University of the Philippines played a looped tape of President Marcos singing about the moon, enunciating Tagalog phrases, begging to be sucked, cussing, talking dirty, and announcing the arrival of Jesus.

Dovie Beams made it back to the United States miraculously, managing to evade her assassin, who had sat next to her on the outbound flight from Manila. During a stopover in Hong Kong, the Philippine Consul General, who tried to block her from boarding her Pan Am connecting flight to America, had stirred up such a scene that police were forced to step in and place Dovie Beams under their custody.

Maharlika never made it to the screen. Buried, some say, in Switzerland, along with the Marcos's Swiss accounts. Two years after the country confirmed his fetish for blonde pubic hairs, Marcos, the godfather of porn, who was the first—and only Filipino—to ejaculate over the airwaves, declared martial law.

When he, Imelda, and their children and grandchildren fled the country in u.s. helicopters on February 25, 1986, bound for Hickam Air Force Base in Hawaii, one of the souvenirs Imelda left for her countrymen to feast their eyes on was an October 3, 1970, issue of *Philippine Free Press* found on her nightstand. The cover story, "A Lovely Argument for a Special Relations," showed a side view of a dreamy-eyed Dovie Beams in a red bikini about to dip her foot in a pool, her head tilted at a three-quarter angle. Hand-drawn on the picture in red ink and measuring the size of a thumb was an erect penis with abnormally big balls, the small missile aiming for a rear entrance.

"Imelda, humiliated but not defeated, got even with Marcos before they left the Philippines," Tita G said. "He was still president, but she ruled the country with him as the second-most powerful leader. One of the first things she did was issue a ban on the film, ordered the banks to stop lending money to the production company. Then she proclaimed herself governor of Metro Manila, the minister of the Ministry of Human Settlements, Sacrifices, and other Che Che Bureches. On the waters of Manila Bay, she watched her cultural complex rise. She confiscated government properties like Leche, and turned her husband's whorehouse into a museum. Then she proclaimed it a historical landmark."

"But it's a sex club now, right?" Vince asks Tita G.

"Only at night," Tita G replies. "It's also a museum every Thursday, from 10 a.m. to 2 p.m. We're in the third world, Vicente, so we have to multitask in order to make it to tomorrow."

"But how did it go from a museum to a sex club?" Vince asks.

"Well, when Cory took over as president and discovered that Ferdinand and Imelda had left her only pebbles in the National Treasury, her administration's only recourse was to sell non-functioning government properties, like Leche."

"Who owns Leche now?" Vince asks.

"Secret," Tita G sings. "Oh, we're finish na with the tour. Do you have any last-minute questions?"

Vince shakes his head no. "Thank you very much, Tita G."

"You're very welcome. Just remember our cardinal rule: only milk gets spilled here and not what or who you see. The power of this place, hijo, can make you disappear faster than a finger snap. Or turn you into the brightest star overnight."

WHATEVER HAPPENED TO BABY JONAS?

One plus one equals two, but not for Vince, who is already on his third round of gin and tonic. By the time he's left the former set of *In the Name of Shame* for the bar on the second floor, there were already four Arabs in the club occupying two tables facing the stage. But still no sign of Jonas. Did he ditch me to stay home and watch the film awards? Vince wonders.

One of the Arab men tries to catch Vince's attention by winking, smiling, speaking to him with his hairy brows. Vince checks out their escorts: teenage guys dressed in baseball jerseys, moving their heads to the song bouncing off the walls, which are covered with egg cartons.

Double-doors swing open and a boisterous group of Chinese-Filipino matriarchs appear, smoking, talking loudly, and assaulting the room with hair spray and Tea Rose perfume. Dressed fashionably in shoulder-padded blouses with matching pants that were probably sewn by tailors in the garment district of Divisoria, they seat themselves at the front, shouting out their orders to the waiter standing an inch away from them while their escorts, who are young enough to be their sons, lean back on their seats and butch up their image by smoking their cigarettes marijuana-style—clipped between thumb and index finger.

Two Arabs and three Filipino youths walk to the rear of the room. Vince eye-trails them until they disappear behind what he thought was a wall but is really a VIP lounge made up of six adjoining rooms.

Vince retreats to the video room in case Jonas is there, looking for him. Empty, except for a troll slipping his hand inside the jeans of a young man whose eyes are glued to the monitor showing a Jeff Stryker porno. The Caucasian man nods at Vince, motions for him to join them. Vince returns to the bar.

While waiting for his drink, he checks his watch, wonders if perhaps Jonas's mother died.

Or his bus crashed or got hijacked, the terrorists taking him as a hostage.

Maybe he reconsidered the AC (or DC) part of his bisexuality and decided to have sex with a woman instead.

Or maybe he's blowing—or getting blown by—some guy in a movie theater, Luneta Park, a phone booth, a CR, or QMC (Quezon Memorial Circle, a park).

Maybe it was his SOP to make me think he's into me.

Shit, I could've had the postcard thief for less. He was only charging me what?

Three hundred pesos.

Or twelve dollars.

Stupid me.

Twelve dollars. My god, what is twelve dollars?

Six Big Macs.

I could've had the postcard thief, all eight inches of him.

He must've really liked me to charge only three hundred pesos, when his going rate is ten thousand.

My god. He was basically giving it to me for free.

But no, I had to listen to my pride.

Pride or principle?

Principle or principal?

That's what I get for being Mister High and Mighty.

And tight.

Except when it came to treating Jonas to dinner.

Bill came out to a thousand.

So what? It was worth it.

Jonas is a good man. A little too nationalistic at times, but I like him.

Just as much as I liked Dante.

That's right.

Dante's a good man.

A very good man.

He kept his word and waited up for me.

He drove me home.

Gave me a bath at bedtime.

He washed my feet.

And possibly even spooned me in my sleep.

Though I can't remember.

And it's not that a good man is not hard to find.

He just disappears.

Very, very fast.

WAITING

A girl in a skimpy dress and high heels approaches Vince's table. "Excuse me, O.K. ba if we sit with you?"

Before Vince can say anything, three chain-smoking women and a transvestite, all under the age of thirty, all so heavily made up Vince can't tell who is dragging whom, sit down. In rapid-fire succession, they introduce themselves as Lorna, Fe, Aida, and Bambi (drag?).

"I knew she was gonna win," Lorna says.

"Why wouldn't she? Even that fortune teller Madame Auring predicted her victory, di ba?" Aida says.

"I still think Kris should've won," Fe says. "It's hard to play two of yourself, you know?"

"Oh, pah-lease. Kris could play twenty of herself if she wanted to. She's like a broken mirror, willing to scatter herself so long as she'll reflect," Bambi says.

"Aba, mga puta-chings, magaling yata umarte si Jolie B. She deserves that award," Bambi remarks.

"Are you kidding me?" Aida says. "All she did throughout the movie was talk to a mango tree passing off as the Virgin Mary."

"Don't forget," Bambi says. "Jolie B was Pooky Moreno before she turned British wannabe on us with that facking Visayan accent. And it's not like this is her first acting award either."

"Bambi's right," Aida says. "She's won Best Actress before. Who among the actresses today can fuck an entire basketball team and, at the same time, deliver a dramatic monologue about the horrors of martial law?"

"You," Lorna says.

"Still, Kris deserved to win," Fe says. "After all, nobody can get beaten up and chopped to pieces better than her."

"High-five to that, sister," Bambi says.

"Well, you heard what Kris told the reporters after the awards ceremony, right?" Lorna says.

"Do you really think President Aquino will order the NBI to do an investigation?" Aida asks.

"Why not? Kris is so adored by the starving masses she could have her own People Power if she wanted to," Bambi says.

"Hello? Didn't President Aquino sue that columnist who said she hid under her bed during a coup attempt?" Fe asks. "If I remember correctly, she even held a press conference in her bedroom—di ba?—to show the reporters and cameramen that there was no way she could fit under her bed."

"Did she win?" Bambi asks.

"Case is still pending," Fe says.

"Like everything else in this country," Bambi says.

"Poor loser lang si Kris. Ever since she was a student pa in Ateneo,"

Aida says, then adds "Where's the fackin' waiter? We've been waiting forever."

SHOWBIZ NEWS UPDATE

Jolie B Rizal, the Charismatic Catholic artist formerly known as Pooky "Sex Goddess of the Eighties" Moreno, beat out Kris Aquino and two others in the Best Actress category at the FAP awards.

"What about the nun?" Vince throws out the question.

"You didn't watch it?" Lorna asks.

Bambi's answer "She won" overlaps with Vince's "I was busy."

"I don't care what anybody says, Sister Marie should've gone home with the Best in Costume award," Bambi says. "Very graceful Grace Kelly, talaga."

"And I love her forty-foot habit," Fe adds.

Changing the topic, Aida asks Vince if he's a regular at Leche.

"No," Vince answers. "Tonight's my first time."

"Oh, a virgin," Fe says.

"Doesn't look it to me," Bambi says at the same time as Lorna's "Not for long."

"Where are you from?" Aida asks.

"Hawaii," Vince says.

"Really? My aunt lives there," Bambi says. "In Hon-hi."

Vince is befuddled. "Hon-hi? What island is she from?"

Bambi shrugs.

A cloud of confusion hangs over them, until: "Gaga. Idiota. Stupida. Reyna nang mga bobita," Lorna tells Bambi. "Hon-hi is the abbreviation for Honolulu, Hawaii."

Embarrassed, Bambi apologizes. Their laughter disappears under techno music, multiple conversations, and waiters yelling erroneous orders to the bartenders.

A waiter, who has a "55" embroidered on his shirt pocket, arrives with their drinks.

Lorna takes her wallet from her bag. "It's my treat," she says, handing the waiter a five-hundred-peso bill. "You can keep the change if you don't fack up our next order."

"O, kaya niyo 'yan?" Bambi issues a challenge to the other girls to out-diva Lorna.

"Well, if I were engaged to a yakuza, I could afford to be a rich bitch too," Aida says.

"Excuse me lang. Hiromi is not a yakuza. He only works for them," Lorna corrects her.

"Aida is just jealous," Fe says, as if she isn't there.

"Hoy Impakta!" Aida turns to Fe. "Don't forget that I was the one who told you Tomo was facking Mylene behind your back."

"That's why you'll always by my true sister," Fe tells her, reaching over the table to give her a kiss.

"But don't forget, Fe," Bambi says, disrupting their Kodak moment, "I was the one who told you Kenji was a bisexual."

"Gaga!" Fe tells Bambi. "You found that out only after you slept with him."

As Vince suspected, Lorna, Aida, Fe, and Bambi, who are on vacation, have been living in Japan since the Philippine Overseas Employment Agency (POEA) granted them work permits. Of the group, the most Japafied is Aida—she's the one who's constantly bowing, covering her mouth when she laughs, and pointing to her nose to indicate "me." She's lived in Tokyo the longest—seven years. Lorna, who migrated there less than a year ago, will be getting married next month to Hiromi, who's not a yakuza but works for the syndicate. Like Kris Aquino's character Mia in *In the Name of Shame*, the four of them work in nightclubs, performing

Japanese, American, and Filipino musical and dance numbers. Their permits identify them as "cultural entertainers."

Ever since the demand for Japayukis skyrocketed in the mid-eighties, the profession has been plagued with negative publicity, ranging from prostitution to rape to murder to human trafficking to Yakuza affiliation.

"But not all Japayukis are puta-chings," Bambi tells Vince. "Fortunately, I am."

"Me too," Lorna says.

"But not me," Fe says.

"I used to be," Aida says. "But not anymore."

They all giggle, with their hands over their mouths.

Aida and Bambi return from the ladies' room escorted by two guys in baseball shirts numbered 89 and 85. Behind them is the waiter, 55. 89 is tall and mestizo, with a dimpled smile that belongs on toothpaste products. Vince fights off the temptation to walk over to him and lick the mole on his right temple.

Just as handsome is 85, the kind of guy that sent Oscar Wilde straight to Reading Gaol: raven-black wavy hair, dark brown eyes, innocent, princely, sensitive to poetry, and well endowed.

85 points to 89's watch. "Ten more minutes," 89 says.

Hasta la vista, Jonas, Vince thinks, and sends them both signals that he's interested in a threesome. Yes? Yes. Good. Now, all Vince has to do is find out how much it'll cost him and how he'll get them away from the Japayukis.

As he's planning his strategy, the two guys get up and leave. 85 heads for the bar, but Vince is eye-trailing 89, who turns back to gesture to the men's room. Wait for me, Vince's eyes say. He takes a sip from his drink and asks how long the show is.

"One hour with a fifteen-minute break," Bambi answers, then flags down the waiter to order another round.

Aida pulls a calculator from her bag.

"What's the total?" Fe asks her.

"Wait," she says, then, "2,225 pesos for number 89 and 2,125 for number 85. A total of . . . 4,350 pesos divided by four of us equals . . . 1,087 pesos each. Plus drinks plus motel plus breakfast plus cab fare plus tips."

"How expensive naman," Bambi says.

"What do you expect? Our economy is depressing," Fe says.

"Is that how much they cost?" Vince asks. "How'd you figure it out?"

Aida answers, "Multiply the numbers pinned to their shirts by twenty-five."

Twenty-five. The magic number for Americans. One dollar equals twenty-five pesos. Eighty-nine times twenty-five. Eighty-five times twenty-five. Multiply by twenty-five or divide by twenty-five, either way, Vince still wouldn't be able to afford them. Plus motel, meals, cab fares, and tips. Unless . . . unless . . . unless he brings them back to the townhouse.

Negotiating isn't that difficult. All Vince has to do is follow what Yaya Let used to do at the open market. Start from the bottom and stay there as long as possible. Don't surrender easily. In Vince's case, let 89 know that he and his buddy, 85, are not the only pricks in Leche that're for rent.

A stall opens, and out comes 72. In the mirror, Vince watches him shake hands. 72 exits, followed by the man Vince saw earlier from the video room. Vince follows 89 into the booth. Before he can lock it, 89 pulls him into a long, deep kiss.

"And that's just the preview," he whispers, then addresses Vince as "Pare." That machismo-loaded word that means he'll have sex with

Vince, because he's strictly queer for pay. Knowing this, Vince hikes up 89's shirt and kisses his chest.

89 pushes him back. "Not here, Pare," he says. "Tita G might catch us."

Vince cuts to the chase. "You and your friend wanna meet me later?"

"Not tonight, Pare. On Wednesday, if you want."

"Wednesday? That's two days from now. You sure you can't meet up later?"

"No can do, Pare, unless you want to pay the regular price."

"Can't afford it," Vince says, "even if I want to. How much you going to charge me on Wednesday?"

"Six hundred for each of us."

"Twelve hundred?!"

89 nods.

"How about eight hundred?"

"Thousand," 89 says. "Take it or leave it."

"Deal," Vince says. "Where do we meet?"

"Greenbelt McDonald's. You know where Greenbelt is?"

"Yeah, in Makati," Vince says, remembering that Greenbelt is where he'd run into the postcard thief.

"Six p.m. o.k. with you?"

"Make it seven."

"Deal."

Vince's timing for leaving the bar is perfect, as the spotlight shines on Tita G, singing with an exaggerated geisha accent. Outside, cabdrivers rush up to Vince. When he tells them "Parañaque," they either speed away or quote him an exorbitant fare. Vince haggles. They don't budge. He offers an alternative deal, to which one of the drivers yields.

"I-metro mo," Vince says, unleashing his first Tagalog words in years. It catches him off guard: the grin of the *i* followed by the fold of the *m,* then the trill of the *r,* and finally, the half-opened *mo.* It rolled out so effortlessly, so naturally, with the accent and the intonation in the right place.

In the backseat of a cab that's exiting the labyrinthine streets of Pasay City, he wonders if the Filipino language has ever left him. No, it hasn't. He just stopped speaking it. The last time he spoke it was in elementary school, just months after he arrived in Hawaii. He chose not to speak Tagalog, or Pidgin-English, which is what Edgar and many of his class-mates spoke, because thick accents and Pidgin from the plantation camps, as he had been taught, only led to a dismal future. But now, after all these years, the mother tongue that's been silenced by years of assimilation and school-enforced laws is waking up, waiting for him to transform a simple phrase into music.

SEMINARIANS, VIGAN, ILOCOS SUR, 1929

Alvin,

The G.I.s are seriously thinking of leaving the bases. Formula remains the same: the first to invade a country and the first to split when a volcano wakes up. Dormant for 600 yrs. Unimaginable. But the people aren't budging. They think it's only the media digging up stories from a dead mountain. "It's only snoring, for God's sake" is the general attitude. There's an indigenous tribe that lives along the slopes of the volcano—the Aetas. The gov't wants them to evacuate. They won't. The volcano is their god, they say.

Stay tuned,
Vince

Alvin De Los Reyes
430 Keoniana St.
2D
Honolulu, HI 96815

QUIAPO CHURCH, HOME OF THE BLACK JESUS

Jing:
Guess where I just came from? Hint #1: Bino
Boca shoots his movies there. #2: Marcos kept
his mistresses there, including your former
crush, Dovie Beams. #3: It's a museum, but
not really. #4: It's a sex club, but not really.
Might as well tell you because the hints are
never going to run out: Leche. That's right.
The place Edgar keeps talking about. The neither-
this-nor-that place, because it's all of the above.
A giant halo-halo. It's run by Tita G, a drag
queen, and her sidekick, Yermaphrodite. Two
of a kind. No one on earth like them. I'll
probably see you before you receive this postcard.
Love, your brother

Jing De Los Reyes
513 North Kuakini
#6
Honolulu, HI 96817

Coda

A feast in the ancestral home of the Lewis-De Los Reyeses, San Vicente.

Seated around the banquet table are the people who are in the photographs that cover the walls of the living room. They are wearing the same clothes that they wore in their portraits. Occupying one end of the table is a blond, blue-eyed man, square-jawed, broad shoulders, wide forehead, trimmed mustache, a pronounced widow's peak. He is Vince's great-grandfather, who went to the Philippines at the turn of the twentieth century to fight the Filipino revolutionaries in the Philippine-American War. Beside him is his sister, wearing a Mother Hubbard gown with long sleeves and a high neck; Vince remembers her from one of Yaya Let's bedtime stories because she was one of the first American teachers to arrive in the islands and introduce public education to the natives.

Vince walks around them, tries to interrupt their conversations, introduces himself to them. The intrusion fails. They continue dining, talking, laughing, toasting, indifferent to Vince.

Upstairs, he hears footsteps.

More voices.

Vince disappears into the dark corridor of the house, climbs the wooden staircase, his hand groping the wall for the switch. The pungent smell of boiled guava leaves invades his senses, makes him dizzy. From the room that had been his until he was ten years old comes a harsh, metallic sound. He walks toward it, sees through the opening Yaya Let, at the foot of the bed, washing his grandfather's feet.

"Did you call them?" his grandfather asks.

"I did, Don Alfonso," Yaya Let says.

"Why?"

"If you must go, Don Alfonso—"

Vince enters his room, sees on his bookshelf all his books and komiks individually wrapped in plastic. On the walls are black-and-white posters of Charlie Chaplin's movies and photographs of Vince and his siblings with their grandfather and Yaya Let at the botanical garden in Luneta. Of Vince and his grandfather in the open-air cinema, at the plaza celebrating the annual fiesta, in the crowded cemetery during All Soul's Day, at Vince's first communion, at the Manila International Airport. Of Don Alfonso looking refined as ever in his Barong Tagalog shirt, and beside him, Vince in a tattered suit, bowler hat, and paste-on mustache. Also, thumbtacked are the postcards he'd sent to his grandfather during his first year in Hawaii. "Lolo Al, I don't like it here. Everyone speaks funny but they're the ones laughing at my English," reads one. "Mommy and Daddy are fine. They do not belong together. Why am I here?" reads another. And the last one, "I want to come home. The movies are not the same."

"What about Vicente?" his grandfather asks.

Yaya Let's silence takes Vince's attention from the postcards.

"Vicente," his grandfather sighs.

"Yes?" Vince says.

But Don Alfonso does not hear him. He does not see him walking toward him, sitting on the edge of his bed. He does not feel Vince's hand rubbing his, massaging it, trying to wake up its thin veins. He does not see Vince's finger tremble as it brushes his brows, touches the lids of his half-closed eyes, his lips. He does not feel Vince's breath when he bends to kiss his forehead, his hair. He does not hear Vince say, "I'm sorry." Nor does he offer his hand for Vince to grasp, the grasp that guided Vince throughout his childhood in San Vicente, the grasp that Vince once could not live without. And now could not let go.

Lightbulb flickers.

A tremor, slight at first, not enough for Vince to discern whether the shaking is coming from within or beneath him.

Then a stronger quake sends him running out of the room, down the stairs, and out of the house.

BOOK IX

Fuseli Revisited

Vince opens his eyes and is startled by the sight of Burrnadette hovering over him. He snatches the sweat-soaked sheet and covers himself up. Within seconds, his senses bring him back to the cacophonous soundtrack of Manila: cardiac-arrest-causing horns from the morning traffic, crowing roosters, and the reverberant calls of vendors.

"Surr, are you O.K.?" Burrnadette says. "You were—how shall I put it?" She pauses, hunts the insecticide-sprayed air for words to match her thoughts. "Trapped in your sleep, surr. We call it bangungut, surr. You know bangungut? Deadly dreams."

Vince nods.

"My brother died from it, surr," she continues. "His soul did not return on time."

"His soul?"

"Yes, surr. You see, where I come from, we believe that when we're sleeping, our soul leaves our bodies. It travels, you know—the soul. It goes on a journey. And like many journeys, it runs into problems. The soul gets lost or gets tricked by spirits. When that happens, that's when the bangungut appears and drags us to hell."

"Hell?"

"Yes, surr."

"What about the soul? What happens to it?"

"The soul goes to Nowhere, surr."

"Nowhere?"

"Like purgatory, surr. Except it's here, surr. On earth," she explains. "Oh, it's terrible, surr, when that happens."

"Why?"

"Because the soul, surr, it just ends up wandering. Like it's homeless. But that's part of being Filipino, surr, because we are all wanderers. We're here, we're there, we're everywhere. Scattered like the stars. That's us, surr. Kalat kalat. Even in our sleep."

Vince remains quiet, listening intently as Burrnadette continues to talk in her sing-song voice, her roll of the *r*'s, her accent thick and lulling. Like a mother guiding her child toward wisdom.

"We're all wanderers," echoes in Vince's head. And whether it included him or not, it is true: Filipinos are wanderers, peregrinators, seafarers, scattering themselves across the world, as Burrnadette said, like the stars that first guided them out of Malaysia toward the islands of a thousand volcanoes before it was christened by the Spaniards as "Islands of St. Lazarus."

It is in the blood of every Filipino. It is in their nature and dreams to roam, to seek a better life, to adapt and adopt another country.

Migration is at the core of their existence and survival. It is inherent in their history. It is their legacy.

Seafarers then, overseas contract workers now, nothing much has changed. The Filipino is still going places, home-hopping, tongue-twisting. Whether in slippers, shoes, or barefoot, the itchy feet are constantly on the move—forward. And when sleep closes the nomad's eyes, the soul picks up where the body leaves off. Pursuing and preserving the never-ending journey.

"That's what happened to my brother, surr," Burrnadette continues. "One nightmare after another. We tried everything. My mother even went to a mananambal. "

Vince remembers encountering the word in his komiks. His sister Jing used to terrify him and Alvin with stories about the supernatural creature who, during the day, disguised itself as a beautiful woman, then, at night, transformed into a segmented flying monster, terrorizing the city, preying on victims by sucking out their intestines and organs with its long, hollow tongue. Though its preferred diet was the fetus of pregnant mothers. The only way to kill it was to find its lower half—usually hidden in the closet—and pour salt over it.

Burrnadette smiles. "That's ma-na-nang-gal, surr," she says. "I'm talking about the ma-na-nam-*bal.*"

"Ma-na-nang-gal," Vince says, "ma-na-nam-bal." Two more words that he'd confused. Like balikbayan and babalikyan. A Filipino who has returned home, as opposed to one who will return home eventually.

"Bery good, surr."

"What is ma-na-nam-bal?"

"Faith healers, surr," she answers. "There are many of them in Siquijor."

"Siquijor?" he says, hearing another familiar word from his childhood dictionary. Siquijor, a popular setting for tales that dealt with love, broken promises, and witchcraft.

"Siquijor?" Vince repeats, "as in the Island of Sorcerers?"

"You know Siquijor, surr?"

"Yes, but I didn't know it was an actual place," he answers, remembering that Siquijor was where Mr. Smith and his Filipina fiancée had gone on their honeymoon, visiting the oldest convent in the country, swimming inside one of the hundred caves, and making love on white, sandy beaches under a moonlit sky. They were a much-envied couple until the night Mr. Smith went to bed and never woke up, asphyxiated in his sleep by his wife, who turned out to be a bangungut.

"That's the wonder of Siquijor, surr," Burrnadette says. "It exists in the real and in your mind. During the time of Spaniards, Siquijor was called Isla del Fuego."

"Fire Island?"

"Yes. Because at night, the island was lit by fireflies."

"Are you also a ma-na-nam-bal?" Vince asks.

"No, surr," she answers quickly. "One doesn't choose to be a man-anambal, just as Christ didn't ask to be God's messenger. My mother used to tell me that the power of healing isn't something you can learn. It's a gift from God. And if you don't use it properly, it turns into a curse. My mother was a mananambal, surr. She was a very good Christian, very giving, very patient. She guided many of the young faith healers in Siquijor. They came during Holy Week."

"Why Holy Week?" Vince asks, then remembers that it was, in fact, during Holy Week when Mr. Smith's wife asphyxiated him to death with her cigar.

"Because Holy Week is when the most powerful spirits return to this world to share the secrets of their healing powers," Burrnadette answers. "Just about every faith healer in the country and albolario and mangkukulam are in Siquijor. The best day is Black Saturday, the day after Christ was nailed to the cross."

Vince imagines an archipelago of faith healers, folk medicine men (albolario) and voodoo witches (mangkukulam) journeying on crowded outrigger canoes and ferries to the enchanted island, conversing with spirits and learning from them the secret ingredients of the dead so they could reverse, multiply, plant curses, or heal the sick with tree bark, roots, insects, herbs, coconut oil.

"While my mother was alive," Burrnadette continues, "she healed not just the poor and the sick but the wealthy too. Many were corrupt politicians who were bewitched or cursed. Madame herself sought my mother," she continues, referring to Imelda Marcos.

"For what?"

"She had a strange skin disease; whenever she got excited, red blotches the shape of rose petals would appear all over her body and make her itch at night. I saw them bloom on her skin with my own eyes, surr. Madame believed that nakulam siya, that one of her husband's mistresses had put a curse on her."

The scent of a burning candle wafts into the room, then vanishes without a trace. Vince and Burrnadette exchange looks of surprise and awe, confirming the superstition that a ghost has just visited them.

"Did you smell that?" Vince asks.

Burrnadette nods. "Did someone you know die recently, surr?"

"No," Vince says. "Well, two nights ago I was in Pasay City, and the cab I was riding in passed by four wakes."

"Did you see any of the faces of the dead?"

"What do you mean?"

"You know, a photograph, a portrait. They usually have one beside the coffin or at the front of the house."

Vince shakes his head, then, remembering the portrait of the young woman pasted onto the fan that her aunt had held, says, "Yes. At the last wake, where I got off. I spoke with the aunt of the deceased, who mistook me for her niece's boyfriend," recalling his conversation with Lita.

"Did you go in and see the body?"

"No," Vince answers, "though she did invite me in. She even asked if I had any problems or worries to hand over, because that would've been the best time to get rid of them, to give them to the dead and let them deal with them."

"Next time, surr, you should do it."

"But I didn't know her."

"Even so, surr," Burrnadette says. "You should always pay respect to the dead, whether they are strangers or not. The dead know more about life than us. They know more about destiny, about eternity. They are the ones who guide us in and out of our sleep. And they know, surr, they know what is inside our shadow."

"You know, Burrnadette, when I was young, I had a neighbor whose husband had been missing for over a year. He was a journalist and was very critical of Marcos. He went to attend a rally in Manila, and the next day, they found his car with the bodies of his son and driver, but not his. Everyone was convinced he was murdered, except for his wife. She refused to bury him. She resisted until she had no choice because, they said, giving him a proper burial was the only way to call back the soul. Do you believe in that, Burrnadette?"

"Very much, surr. We have to honor the dead. We have to give them a proper burial, say mass for them. It is our duty, surr, to make their last day on earth as peaceful and beautiful as can be. It is also our way of accepting God's will, of saying goodbye to them for now." She pauses. "Did you know, surr, that we have two souls? Yes, you and me, surr. The first one is with us from the day we are born to the day we die," she says, then, pointing to her head, adds, "it's in here, surr. Where I come from, we call it kaluha. When we die our kaluha becomes kalag. That's our second soul, and that's the one that goes to the afterlife."

"That sounds like the belief of the people in my province," Vince says. "Except that when the person dies, his soul lingers around the house, shows itself in the dreams of his family and friends."

"That means that he or she is trying to tell us something, surr," Burrnadette says. "And we have to pay attention to the dream. Otherwise, he or she will not be at peace and will continue to haunt us. The dream can be as simple as blue pajamas."

"Blue pajamas?"

"My father's favorite pajamas," Burrnadette answers. "I dreamt about them on the night he died, and a week after we buried him. I told the dream to my mother, how my father had appeared twice in my sleep to ask for his blue pajamas. My mother broke down. She went to the aparador, opened the closet doors, and, from a pile of clothes, pulled out a pair of blue pajamas. 'Why didn't we bury them with him?' I asked my mother, and she answered, 'I wasn't ready to let him go.' 'But it was his favorite. You know that,' I told her. Because that's what you're supposed to do, surr—send the dead off to the afterlife with their favorite belongings so they have something to use or to do.

"'I know,' my mother said. 'I just needed something to bring him closer to me,' she said. So when a neighbor died later that year, my mother and I attended his wake late into the night and we asked him if he could please give the blue pajamas to my father because he'd been looking for them. We said a prayer, thanked him for the favor, and slipped the blue pajamas into his coffin."

From *Decolonization for Beginners: A Filipino Glossary*

kakambal, *noun.* 1. a twin. 2. soul on earth. See also *kaluha, kararua.*
kaluluwa, *noun.* 1. spirit. 2. source of inspiration. 3. what kakamba becomes after death. See also *kalag.*

NTH CIRCLE

"Burrnadette, are you married?"

"I am a widow, surr," she says. "But I won't remarry anymore."

"Why not?"

"Because of this, surr," she says, pointing to the dot in her right eye. "It makes me see my husband every day. As if he is not dead."

"My sister has one exactly on the same spot. My grandfather too," Vince says. "Strange," he adds, more to himself.

"What, surr?"

"My grandfather didn't remarry after my grandmother died," he says, wondering now if the reason was because his wife had never left him, because she was always there for him to see through the dot in his eye.

"Is your grandfather Lolo Al, surr?"

"Yes," Vince replies. "How did you know?"

"You were talking to him, surr," Burrnadette says. "In your sleep."

"What was I saying?"

"That you were sorry," she says. "When did he die?"

"A long time ago," he says. "In fact, earlier this month was the ninth anniversary."

"You two were very close no, surr?" she says, more of a statement than a question.

"He took care of me when I was young. 'Til I turned ten."

"And you love him very much," she says. "I can tell."

Vince falls silent. The muscles around his mouth tightening, his lips folding into an "embouchure," a musical term he learned from band class that refers to the proper positioning of the mouth over the mouthpiece to achieve the fullest, deepest sounds. Grandpa: Grandson. Flesh: Blood. Two: One. As inseparable as a violin and a piano in a sonata.

"Burrnadette?"

"Yes, surr?"

"What happens to those who *do* wake up from the nightmare? Does it mean that their soul has returned to their body?"

"That's what they say, surr."

"Then how come I'm still getting nightmares?"

Burrnadette looks at Vince with concern. "Maybe they're more than nightmares. These nightmares, surr. What are they like?"

Vince pauses to think. He doesn't know where to begin. A list of details is building in his head, but these are dreams and might reveal too much about him, his history, his desires and fears. Besides, some are just flat-out embarrassing.

"Well, lately, they've been mainly about my grandfather," he finally says. "World War II stuff. He was an American soldier in the war. Last night I dreamt about him, and for the first time, his father and his father's sister, who was a teacher. They came to the Philippines almost around the same time. He was a soldier and she a Thomasite teacher."

Burrnadette eyes widen. "Did they talk to you?"

Vince shakes his head. "That's the weird part," he says. "I tried to, but they wouldn't. Or they couldn't see me. As if I were invisible."

"A ghost."

"Yes."

"You mustn't talk to the dead in your sleep, Surr Vince," Burrnadette says. "Bawal 'yun." Forbidden.

"Why?"

"Because it means someone very close to you—or you yourself—will die."

"Oh my God."

"Surr Vince." Pause. "If this is your first time back since you left, that means you were not here to bury your grandfather?"

Vince does not reply.

"Not a good sign," Burrnadette says, breaking his silence.

"I had a feeling you were going to say that," Vince says.

"These bad dreams you've been having—they're not nightmares," Burrnadette says. "They're real. Your grandfather is talking to you. He's trying to tell you something very important. You must go and visit him, talk to him. Is he buried here in Manila?"

"No, in San Vicente," Vince says. "Couple hours from here by bus."

"What about his father and his father's sister—where are they buried?"

"There too."

"Then you should go visit their graves soon as you can, surr. Light a candle and make an offering of food and flowers. Your grandfather, what did he like to eat?"

"He was very picky when it came to food. He didn't eat much. Just as he didn't talk much. Everything was done through gestures. I could be in the same room with him for hours without exchanging a word and it was fine," Vince says. "Oh, he did like those buttered rolls and coffee. Yes, that's what he lived on. Coffee, buttered rolls. And cigarettes."

"Then that's what you will offer when you visit him at his grave. But you must go, surr. Even if only for a day. If you believe in what I believe, you must go. Pay your respects to your grandfather, surr, and to your ancestors."

Vince checks the digital clock on the bedside table. "Can you accompany me to San Vicente?"

"I wish I could, surr, but I can't. Not today. I'm sorry," she says.

"Why?"

"I have to stay here in Manila. Mister Pinoy is arriving in two hours from Daly City, California. I have to pick him up at the airport with Ma'am Aning's husband."

"Where's Mister Pinoy staying?"

"At the Shangri-La, surr."

"How come I wasn't given a room there?"

"I don't know, surr. Maybe because you are first runner-up and he is—how shall I put it?—Mister Pinoy."

"Burrnadette." Pause. "You think my grandfather is haunting me?"

"Oh no, surr. I don't think so," she says. "I think he's been watching over you all these years. And now that you're here—you must honor him, show him your gratitude. You owe it to him, Surr Vince. He's waiting for you in San Vicente. Go so you can finally bury him."

Burrnadette's last words are enough to convince Vince that he needs to return to San Vicente—his namesake, his genesis. Sister Marie called his homecoming fate, an inevitable return, whether by choice or not, providential or not. Is it?

Tourist Tips

- Manila is a never-ending, morphing city, constantly undergoing revisions and reversions.

- Your Manila is only one of the hundreds of millions of versions.

- Bring a balikbayan box full of open minds. Otherwise, Manila will kick you in the ass and trip your soul.

- Keep tourist tips where they belong: at the International Date Line.

- Remember: in Manila, contradictions are always welcome, including—and especially—yours.

Full Strings Attached

Ten a.m. Luzon Bus Terminal, Pasay City. It's hotter and more humid than yesterday's record-breaking Fahrenheit, which means the commuters are as edgy as a gun-toting son of a politician or Supreme Court judge. Crowding the terminal are the everyday characters that make this everyday cram-de-la-crammed city hypercharged to the hyperventilating degree. Aggressive vendors hawking anything and everything, from grilled chicken feet to potholders stitched from garment scraps to face towels to native brooms to purified bottled water; backpacking tourists making full use of their Tagalog via Berlitz on locals who were partially raised on pop Americana and Britannia; over-enthused commuters creating their own mini express lanes, convinced the queue originated with them way back there, at the entrance gate, where a team of security guards are poking through knapsacks and boxes for explosives with their dynamite detectors—drumsticks.

When Filipinos travel, they bring everything they've ever owned, including their dreams, memories, and disappointments. Which explains the larger-than-life balikbayan boxes, stuffed with enough objects and pasalubong, or gifts, to start a convenience store: imported cigarettes bought from the black markets of Ermita, marked-down Teflon pans haggled over in the bazaars of Baclaran, tubes of Pringles from Cash & Carry (Manila's version of Duty Free), Tagalog romance novels, back issues of *Hot Copy* and *Chika Chika* with centerfolds of aspiring actors in wet thongs, et cetera.

And, finally, weather-beaten, sweat-soaked, but not fashionably defeated Vince, wearing a light-blue linen shirt, khaki trousers, Panama hat, and on the verge of going ballistic because the line he's been standing in—though it looks more like a cornucopia—hasn't moved for the past half hour or so. Thanks to the family in front of him that began as a mother and son, and has since exploded into tribal proportion. The Americano—or "Kano"—in him is ready to explode, call it quits.

But I can't.

Why?

Because there's a part of me . . .

Which? Filipino or American?

. . . that feels sorry.

For?

Them.

Them?

The ones the government has to teach through its sponsored TV ads the basic how-tos in life. How to file in a single line. How to board a bus or jeepney without killing each other. How to cough in public.

Things they already learned in Good Guidance & Manners in elementary school. I took this class in second grade.

Then why do they insist on turning a straight line into a ball of tangled thread?

Look at their role models, for crying out loud.

Maybe the ways of the West don't work here.

Maybe the ways of the West is just a switch that they can turn on and off whenever they like.

To achieve what?

I don't know. Maybe to remind me of where I come from.

Is this what it always boils down to: me versus them?

Sila versus Ako.

Them, Filipinos, against me, American.
Stop being paranoid and pay attention to what they're telling me.
Which is?
That I, too, can switch it on and off if I like.
My Americanness, my Filipinoness.
Me versus the Other me.

Just then, another tribe member cuts in. Vince lets him. After all, he's already allowed over two-thirds of the village through. What else can he do except jump on their bandwagon? Why not? That's how he was able to get to the other side of the street. Following them, standing beside them on the curb, then, once the polluted coast looked semi-polluted, using them as his guides and shields and dance instructors, squeezing himself into their rhythm, even if it meant stopping unexpectedly at mid-point to let a truck racing with a bus pass by. A laborious task; who knew crossing a Manila street could be choreography: a combination of cha cha, waltz, jitterbug. And of course sweat and a lot of luck.

At the ticket booth, Vince agrees to buy the rider's insurance for an additional four pesos. The pregnant cashier tells him he's made the right decision. "Since head-on collisions happen frequently along General Douglas MacArthur Highway, on which you'll be traveling." She pauses to yawn, then explains that should he need urgent medical care the insurance will cover up to twenty thousand pesos. "If you lose an arm or a leg," she says, reading from the ticket voucher, "you will automatically receive thirty-five thousand pesos." Then she hands him the piece of paper that also states: "Should a bomb explode under your seat or a terrorist behead you, your beneficiary will receive forty thousand pesos." Great, Vince tells himself, my mother will be sixteen hundred dollars richer if I get blown up on the bus.

At the magazine stand Vince bides time, scanning the dailies that are basically screaming the same headlines. From *National Inquirer:* BINO BOCA KILLED IN CAR CRASH; KRIS FILES LAWSUIT AGAINST FILM ACADEMY PHILS; MT PINATUBO ROCKS MANILA. From the *Daily Star:* PINOY CINEMA DIES AT 53; PRO-U.S. BASE GAINS POPULAR SUPPORT DESPITE 5.0 QUAKE. From *Philippine Bulletin:* PRES. AQUINO ASKS SENATORS TO PROBE INTO POSSIBLE FILM AWARDS SCAM; IMELDA COMES HOME TO RUN FOR PRESIDENT; MANILA WAKES UP SHAKING; FILIPINO MALE, 23, PREGNANT BY SUGAR DADDY, 65.

TOKYO BOUND

The air-conditioned bus—one of the many contributors of second-hand pollution making the rounds in and outside Manila—was originally from Japan, purchased at a giveaway price. This explains why, upon sitting, the first things Vince notices, aside from the yellowing crocheted drape across the windshield with GOD BLESS OUR TRIP embroidered on it, and the two sticker signs below it that read DO NOT TALK TO DRIVER WHEN ROAD IS BUSY and FULL STRINGS ATTACHED WHEN REQUESTING STOP, are advertisement placards inserted into the panels above the passengers' seat windows, promoting Suntory whiskey, Sony, maps of Tokyo bus lines in kanji and katagana characters, and a pink bunny pimping the English language for Nova Institute.

One good thing about riding a bus bound for the province is that it's usually equipped with a color television with a built-in VHS machine. One bad thing is that often the movies shown are B-rated, straight to the bargain bin, or so violent you want to kill the stars and directors for making them.

Once the baggage compartments below have been loaded with balikbayan boxes and sacks of rice, and the roof piled up with more sacks of rice, wicker baskets containing vegetables, and chickens and ducks in crates, Vince's bus, like Noah's Ark on wheels, is ready to make its exodus to the greener pastures of the province. As it pulls out of the terminal and joins the gridlock traffic of EDSA, the bus driver, who wears a permanent Elvis Presley snarl, hastily makes the sign of the cross.

The ticket conductor, who sports Tom Jones sideburns with a matching gold medallion, turns on the TV. The monitor is installed right above the heads of two elderly women seated in the front row. A blue dot blossoms into a teary-eyed anchorman reporting that "devoted fans continue to pour into Studio 7 of ABS-CBN, where the body of world-renowned director Bino Boca lies."

Images flash across the screen: a caterpillar line of mourners outside the TV station; smiling vendors shouldering Styrofoam coolers; heavily armed guards body-searching mourners; vice-presidential candidates and senators surrendering firearms; close-up of Kris Aquino weeping over the body of Bino Boca; close-up of President Aquino in her signature outfit (a yellow sunflower-print housedress); more smiling vendors selling flowers and pirated Beta and VHS copies of early Boca films, like *P.S. U.S.A.: My Brother is Not a Pig,* his directorial debut based on the true story of an American soldier who accidentally shoots a Filipino boy after mistaking him for a wild pig.

Close-ups of Bino Boca inside a magenta casket, his favorite color; a fan holding a movie poster of Boca's international blockbuster hit, *Machete Dancers,* which chronicles the lives of three teenage boys from the province who, jobless in Manila, are forced to go into the underground world of drugs and teen prostitution, disguising themselves as cultural dancers a là headhunters in G-strings and brandishing machetes (hence the title).

"Why Tito Bino, why?" Kris weeps in the arms of her mother.

"Bino is now with God, hija," the country's president says.

Camera returns to the anchorman: "Mr. Boca was rushed early this morning to San Juan De Dios Hospital in Pasay City after the car he was riding in crashed into an electrical post near the city hall."

People crowding around a car smashed against a bent post; close-up of the driver's bloody face; of Tita G and Yermaphrodite hysterically crying as paramedics attempt to pull Bino Boca's head out from under the steering wheel.

"Mr. Boca suffered internal and brain hemorrhaging and was pronounced dead on arrival at 2:48 a.m."

Close-up of Bino Boca's face, his right eye gouged.

"The driver is identified as J. R. O'Neal, his protégé, who was set to star in *Machete Dancers II*. O'Neal remains in guarded condition."

Close-up of the young actor's portrait. Vince gasps. O'Neal is the postcard thief.

"The director, who made twenty-plus films, received his first directorial trophy at last night's Film Academy of the Philippines ceremony," the anchorman continues.

"Sayang," the ticket conductor says as he unravels a long cord looped around a microphone.

Sayang. Too bad. Too bad because Bino Boca was one of the first filmmakers to bring komiks to the screen. Too bad because he was the only one who knew how to turn a melodrama riddled with clichés, bad sound, predictable storylines, poor lighting, corny dialogue, bad dubbing, and too much make-up into a Cannes film festival favorite. Too bad because he was the country's best hope of winning a Palme D'Or, of garnering an Oscar nomination for Best Foreign Film.

Too bad for Vince too, who just lost his opportunity to appear in Boca's film.

Too damn bad. A sentiment shared by all the passengers transfixed by the mass of devoted fans outside the ABS-CBN studio. According to the anchorman, the line is now past the eight-mile mark and stretches as far as the Welcome Rotonda arch, where Manila meets Quezon City, the capital until 1976. The deluge of mourners brings back memories of Senator Aquino's wake in 1983, when the whole country flocked to Manila to pay their final respects to Marcos's archenemy.

"Please bring your umbrellas," the anchorman advises, as fans and paramedics are fainting under the blazing heat.

The conductor switches the channel to a blank screen, then turns up the volume to blast the sound of snow. "And now, da inn is near," he croons to the lyrics of "My Way."

By the time the bus reaches Balintawak, the northernmost part of the city known for its wet market spilling onto the highway, the passengers, because of traffic, have already sung all of Frank Sinatra's greatest hits and are now halfway through the best of Anne Murray.

I CRIED THE TEARS, YOU WIPED THEM DRY

Two hours later, at an intersection in the commercial district of Angeles City, Pampanga, a traffic director—fashionably attired in a cowboy hat and boots—motions for the bus to stop and switch off the engine.

"What now?!"

"Why aren't we moving?"

And the answer is right outside their windows: a convoy of u.s. military vehicles that, according to this morning's edition of the *National Inquirer,* is expected to be three kilometers long and carrying over 14,500 servicemen and their dependents. From Clark Air Force Base in Pampanga, the convoy will proceed to Subic Naval Base in Olongapo City, where the servicemen and their dependents will be flown to Guam.

All week the news has focused on the fate of Clark Air Force and Subic Naval bases, the last two u.s. military installations in the Philippines. They were part of the Military Bases Agreement (MBA) of

1947, which granted the United States a ninety-nine-year lease to more than twenty military facilities in thirteen provinces. Since then, the MBA had gone through several amendments, including reduction in the number of bases and changing the expiration date to September of 1991.

"It's about time," remarks the man seated in front of Vince. "They should've left a long time ago."

His wife nudges him. "Tama na. Baka ma-a-alta pressyon ka na naman." she says, which roughly translates to: "Quit that shit before your blood pressure kills you."

"I'm only speaking my mind," he tells her.

A woman wearing doorknocker earrings and sitting across from the couple turns to him. "I disagree with you," she says, then addresses him, in Ilocano, as "manong," to show him that, despite their conflicting views, she still respects her elders. "The Americans may have overstayed their welcome, but keep in mind, the bases are the bread and butter of our brothers and sisters."

She's right, Vince tells himself. If the bases shut down, what will happen to the forty-two thousand Filipinos employed at Clark and Subic?

"Our country doesn't have jobs for them," she says. "Are we going to export more labor to the Middle East and Japan and Singapore and Canada and Australia?"

A young man stands up and turns to face her. He is wearing a T-shirt with the word "Imperialismo" inside a buster logo. "The problem with us Filipinos is that we've become so dependent on our former colonizers that we're even willing to give up our human rights and be second-class citizens in our own country."

"Where are you from?" the man asks.

"Baguio, Manong," the young man says. "But I study at UP Diliman."

"What about our enemies? Who will protect us from them?" the woman argues. "Who will fight the Communists in the mountains, the

Muslims in the south, the terrorists bombing our megamalls and trains? And the coups—"

"What Communists are you talking about?" the student asks. "What coups? Gringo Honasan attempted a coup against Aquino last year, and now he's running for the Senate."

He's right, Vince thinks.

"Without the United States, our armed forces won't be strong," the woman argues.

"That's true," the old man interrupts her. Then, with a tinge of sarcasm, adds, "The American bases strengthened our national defense and kept Marcos in power for two decades."

"And made him and Imelda the richest thieves in the world," the ticket conductor adds.

"Let's not forget that when the U.S. goes to war, we go too. Their enemies become ours," the old man continues, referring to a stipulation in the Mutual Defense Treaty of 1951. "And let's not also forget that when an American serviceman commits a crime against a Filipino, he cannot be tried under the Philippine judicial system. He must be brought back to the United States."

Refusing to be defeated, the woman reiterates her pro-base sentiment. "What will happen to our brothers and sisters who rely on the bases for their survival?"

"They'll survive," the old man answers.

"What about the increasing number of stateless Amerasian children abandoned by their G.I. fathers?" the student retorts.

The woman answers by changing the topic to the dwindling value of the Philippine peso. "Can you believe that a year ago, the exchange rate was only fifteen pesos to a dollar? Now it's up to twenty-five. By 2003, I foresee it will be sixty."

"What about the sixteen thousand so-called 'hospitality girls' in Olongapo and Angeles?" the student says, pointing out the window at a truckload of women in skimpy clothes, laughing and dancing as soldiers serenade them about monkeys in Zamboanga that have no tails.

"Watching them is like watching the Filipino cast of *Miss Saigon*," remarks one of the old women seated at the very front row.

"Ay, I hope it comes out on pirated video soon," her seatmate says.

The mention of the Broadway musical hit, in which the majority of the cast, except for Jonathan Pryce, are Filipinas portraying Vietnamese prostitutes, restores harmony in the minds of the other not-so-politically-aware-or-interested passengers (two-thirds of the bus), bringing the showdown between pro- and anti-U.S. base supporters to an unexpected, anticlimactic conclusion.

"Pare, Lea Salonga won the Tony, di ba?" the driver says to the ticket conductor.

"Old news na, Pare. She also won the Drama Desk Award and the Laurence Olivier Award in London," the conductor says. "President Cory even went on TV to congratulate her."

"Mommy, why are the American soldiers leaving us?" Vince hears a boy asks his mother.

"Because . . ." the boy's mother pauses to think. "They're running away from the volcano."

Exclamations of "Dios kos" and "Lord, have mercy" accompanied by passengers making the sign of the cross reverberate around the bus.

"First, we lose our great director and now, a volcano is waking up after six hundred years to bury us all."

"Only in the Philippines."

"Napaka malas naman natin," the pro-base woman says, to mean: Jesus, such bad luck we have. "Earthquake, typhoon, craft, and corruption," she adds.

"Ay, naku, bahala na," the guy behind her says. "If it's the end of the world, let it end na, so I can finally be born again."

We Won't Go Back to Subic Anymore

Chorus:

Oh, we won't go back to Subic anymore.

Oh, we won't go back to Subic anymore.

Oh, we won't go back to Subic,

Where they mix our wine with water,

Oh, we won't go back to Subic anymore.

1.

Oh, the monkeys have no tails in Zamboanga.

Oh, the monkeys have no tails in Zamboanga.

Oh, the monkeys have no tails,

They were bitten off by whales,

Oh, the monkeys have no tails in Zamboanga.

Chorus

2.

Oh, the carabaos have no hair in Mindanao.

Oh, the carabaos have no hair in Mindanao.

Oh, the carabaos have no hair,

And they run around quite bare,

For the carabaos have no hair in Mindanao.

Chorus

3.

Oh, the fishes wear no skirts in Iloilo.

Oh, the fishes wear no skirts in Iloilo.

Oh, the fishes wear no skirts,

But they all have undershirts,

Yes, they all have undershirts in Iloilo.

Chorus

4.

Oh, they grow potatoes small in Iloilo.

Oh, they grow potatoes small in Iloilo.

Oh, they grow potatoes small,

And they eat them skins and all,

Oh, they grow potatoes small in Iloilo.

Chorus

5.

Oh, the birdies have no feet in Mariveles.

Oh, the birdies have no feet in Mariveles.

Oh, the birdies have no feet,

They were burnt off by the heat,

Oh, the birdies have no feet in Mariveles.

Chorus

6.

Oh, we'll all go up to China in the springtime.

Oh, we'll all go up to China in the sprin-n-ng.

Oh, we'll hop aboard a liner,

I can think of nothing finer,

And we'll all go up to China in the spring.

Chorus

7.

Oh, we'll all go down to Shanghai in the fall.

Oh, we'll all go down to Shanghai in the fall.

When we all get down to Shanghai,

Those champagne corks will bang high,

Oh, we'll all go down to Shanghai in the fall.

Chorus

8.

Oh, we lived ten thousand years in old Chefoo.

Oh, we lived ten thousand years in old Chefoo.

And it didn't smell like roses,

So we had to hold our noses,

When we lived ten thousand years in old Chefoo.

Chorus

The Eleventh Commandment

The driver, after repeated attempts to get the traffic director to allow them to pass through, returns to the bus and announces that if the passengers want to stretch out, grab a bite at Jollibee, piss in McDonald's, chain-smoke, or continue witnessing the United States quickly exiting their country, they are more than welcome to do so because it seems that the bus isn't going anywhere, not until the last of the servicemen and their dependents have safely crossed the dusty intersection and moved on to Subic.

In a matter of minutes everyone, except for the two old women in the front row, who say they'd rather die from carbon monoxide poisoning than heat stroke, has stepped off the bus to breathe in dust and diesel fumes and exhale clouds of cigarette smoke.

"That's how long that son of a gun has been sleeping," a bystander who has been watching the exodus since eight this morning says to no one in particular. "It has nothing to spit out, except the dust and ash it's buried in," he adds, shaking his head in disbelief as a truckload of dust-flaked soldiers waves at the crowd shouting, "Don't leave, Joe, don't leave." "We're not," a soldier shouts. "We're only going to Subic. We'll be back." "Not if Mount Pinatubo erupts," shouts the UP student, "and it will." Vince, who is standing right beside him, listens while a movie plays in his head.

WHO KNOWS WHAT TOMORROW BRINGS?

In the opening of Taylor Hackford's film, *An Officer and a Gentleman*, young Zach spends his youth at Subic Naval Base, where he gets an eagle tattoo to cover his right shoulder, and picks up karate from the

Filipino hoodlums who repeatedly kick his ass and steal all his money. Years later, in a bar outside the naval training grounds in Washington, Zach brags to his buddy about losing his virginity for only ten dollars to a whore who pronounced his name "Suck." "Only ten dollars, Suck." But he edits out the part where he repeatedly got beaten up while his father, stationed at Subic Naval Base, led the life of a sailor's wet dream —snoring naked beside a different Filipino whore every night and waking up to gulp San Miguel beer for breakfast.

It's all flashbacks in the beginning of the film, no opening music or credits; the credits come later, when an older Zach, played by Richard Gere, has already patched up his eagle tattoo and told his father he wants to be an officer. His father laughs in his face, tells him, "It's like you saying you're gonna run for president."

Vince practically memorized the movie, scene by scene. He owned a video of it, fast-forwarding and rewinding to certain parts, like Richard Gere getting out of bed, naked, the camera showing just enough pubic hair to titillate him and make him wish his mother had bought a video recorder with picture-perfect freeze mode. The movie is loaded with pubic-hair shots—one of the reasons why he'd seen it countless times on the big screen. First time was with Jing, Alvin, and their mother, though Alvin had wanted to see *Chariots of Fire*.

"Go by yourself, if you want," Jing had told Alvin. "Vince and I ain't numbing our butts for two hours just so we can watch a bunch of skinny-assed faggots run slow-motion on a beach. Why spend two hours in war-time England when we can be in boot-camp heaven staring at Gere's fuzz and the birthmark on his back? Besides, you'd need English subtitles just to understand what the heck they're saying. Right, Vince?" Vince nodded to close the case.

And though he had seen *An Officer and a Gentleman* a number of times, there had been a lot of scenes that Vince couldn't, didn't relate to.

One, he'd never had sex with a woman, let alone a prostitute. Two, he'd never, thank God, had to see his father naked and in the arms of another woman. And three, unlike Zach's, his mother wasn't dead, though there were countless moments throughout her married life when her husband's silence and disappearing acts made her feel worthless, if not invisible.

What hit home for Vince were the first ten minutes of the film. Young Zach, wearing a suit and a tie, arrives in a foreign country, lugging nothing with him but the first years of his life in Virginia. On the tarmac, a Filipino stewardess escorts him to a sea of greeters pressed against a chain-link fence. Zach stands where she tells him to and waits to be claimed, like a lost suitcase, by a father he's never seen before. Inside the half-empty jeepney bound for Olongapo City, Zach's father frankly tells him that he isn't cut out to be a dad, that he can't understand why the state of Virginia would do such an idiotic thing as sending his estranged son to him.

Would it have made a difference if, from the very start, my own father had been frank with me, the way Zach's father had been to him? Vince wonders. Would it have made a difference if, from the very start, my father had pointedly said: "Look, Vince, I don't have time for this daddy crap because that's not who I am"? Would his brutal honesty have made me respect him more and lessened my unhappiness and my craving to return to San Vicente?

Certainly. It would've explained, if not excused, Vince's father's distance at the dinner table; his moodiness that, at times, exploded into a screaming match with slamming doors; his repeated attempts, brief but sincere, at parenting; his periodic disappearances, reappearing days, sometimes a week later to kill more unwanted hours with his wife, more reenactment of scenes of her tossing dishes and him ducking and shouting for Alvin, Vince, and Jing to get back to bed as they watched him run toward their mother and shake fury and sadness and madness into her.

It would've explained, if not excused, his mother's long nights of waiting up with a plate of cold supper, of wondering who would give up the charade first, of wrestling with her emotions until she could no longer tell the difference between frustration, guilt, blame, remorse, rage, despair.

Why can't I be like Jonas the tour guide, who resented his father without ever making forgiveness an issue? Vince asks himself, knowing full well the answer—Jonas didn't have to forgive his father because he could not, did not, remember him, whereas Vince flew to his father, who had petitioned for his three children to come and live with him and their mother. To forge a new life, a new memory called family.

How magnificent and mutual was Ronaldo's and Carmen's unhappiness, Vince thinks.

It wasn't their fault. Carmen was young; Ronaldo was younger; love and recklessness ruled in their favor. They were restless youths who were so in love with the moment that the future wasn't part of their agenda. Right before Ronaldo turned eighteen, he was supposed to leave the Philippines to go and live with a great aunt in Florida for at least a year so he could maintain his U.S. nationality, as required by law at the time. But he was in love, and to prove it, he got her pregnant, stayed in the Philippines, and married her.

THOU SHALT NOT FORGET

"I feel like I was adopted twice," Vince told Jing and Alvin at their last get-together, the night before he flew to Manila. They were sitting on the lanai of Vince's and Alvin's condo, drinking red wine and chain-smoking. Earlier that evening, they'd had dinner with their mother, who had kept them waiting in front of the Spaghetti Factory for two hours.

"Are you gonna torture us with more stories of how much more pathetic your childhood was than ours?" Alvin asked as he reached for the bottle of Merlot.

"Why do you always have to complicate things, Vince?" Jing said. "You're so Filipino." She held up her palm to Alvin. "Stop. I'm working a double-shift tomorrow."

"Again?"

"It pays the bills and gets me to Vegas four times a year."

"It bugs me that I still feel like this," Vince said. "First by Lolo Al and then by them."

Ignoring Vince, Alvin lifted his glass to the Honolulu skyline and toasted.

Vince narrowed his eyes at Jing and Alvin. "Didn't you hear what I just said?"

"Of course we did," Jing answered, sarcastically, "you've only been saying it since polyester was the craze. Don't you ever get tired obsessing over it?"

"No. And I think you guys shouldn't either," Vince said.

"They got divorced," Alvin said, "big deal."

"It was the eighties thing to do," Jing added.

"What the fuck are you two talking about? They treated us as if we were somebody else's leftovers."

"Maybe you," Jing said. "Why do you give them so much importance?"

"Neither of them wanted us," Vince argued.

"Neither of them wanted each other," Alvin cut in. "We were living with two strangers trying to figure out what a home was."

"Home?" Vince said. "They stole us from our only home."

"If you mean that hot, humid, burning trash–smelling piece of dust called the Philippines, then you can have it," Jing said.

"I second the motion," Alvin said.

"How can you even say that, Jing?" Vince said. "You're the one who's always inviting us over to watch Tagalog melodramas."

"Well, it is hot, humid, and smells like burning trash," Jing said.

"But it doesn't mean she hates it," Alvin jumped in.

"That's right," Jing said. "Melodrama is one thing, pollution another."

Alvin laughed.

"Vince, you don't even care if you ever see the Philippines again," Jing said. "You're only going there because you joined that sad-assed pageant, which, hands down, you should've won but didn't because you refused to sell your share of the tickets."

Jing was right. Vince not only didn't sell a single ticket, he donated his two complimentary ones to Goodwill.

"Seriously though, Brother, you would've won," Jing continued. "Even the judges were all rooting for you."

"Until the Q&A," Alvin said.

"Don't remind me," Vince said, a little too late, for Alvin was already pursuing the topic.

"If you'd just told them the truth, that you'd want to spend your last day on earth in Jersey or Daly or Carson City, you would've gone home as Mister Pogi," Alvin said, straight-faced as possible.

"But no." Jing cut in, to drag the topic to the finish line. "You had to give them all that beauty pageant bullshit about going back to the motherland to croak. The damage wouldn't have been that bad if you hadn't ended it with that quote by Jose Rizal," referring to the famous saying by the revolutionary hero, that "A Filipino who does not know where he came from will never know where he is going."

"See, Vince?" Alvin said. "Lie and it will come true."

"Why drag the pageant into it?" Vince said. "I was talking about them—Carmen and Ronaldo."

"I know," Jing said. "Them and their hopeless marriage."

"'Hopeless' is the operative word," Vince said. "They weren't even at the airport to pick us up. They had to be paged, remember?"

"Big fucking deal, Vince," Jing said. "That happened like thirteen centuries ago. Let it go. Let them be."

"It's a big deal," Vince insisted.

"No, it isn't. Listen, brother, we're not the only ones with divorced parents. We're not the only ones who suffered. They suffered too. Imagine two people who no longer had anything in common trying to be civil to each other."

"They sucked at parenting," Vince remarked.

"I agree," Alvin said. "They fucked up. Royally. But give them a break. They tried. It might not seem so, but they did. You have to accept that. You have no choice."

"Mom tried," Vince said. "Not Dad."

"He did too," Jing said.

"He disappeared more often than Houdini," Vince said sarcastically.

"True. He wasn't there twenty-four seven, but he still had priorities," Jing said. "It wasn't like he just up and left us homeless and starving."

"Quit defending him," Vince said.

"I'm not," Jing said. "But he sacrificd his U.S. citizenship to be a father to me."

"Some sacrifice!"

"It is to me," Jing said. "He didn't have to marry Mom. He could've just left. He had the perfect reason for it. But he didn't. He stayed back. He had you. Then Alvin. He gave up being an American citizen and started all over again."

"Which he used against Mom in the end," Vince said.

"You don't know that," Jing said.

Vince remained quiet.

"Unless that's what Mom told you," Jing said. "Did she?"

Vince shook his head.

"Then for your sanity's sake and ours, quit thinking we're some bonus-point question in a Psychology 101 pop quiz," Jing said.

"If their marriage hadn't been heading for the rocks, we would never have left the Philippines," Vince insisted.

"Hello?" Alvin said. "Isn't that why we came here in the first place? To salvage their vows?"

"Why wait that long?" Vince asked.

"I don't know," Alvin said. "Maybe they needed more time to settle down."

"But six years?" Vince said.

"I wouldn't talk, Vince," Jing cut in. "You're twenty-three and you're still serial dating. And Alvin, we left because Lolo Al was getting sick," Jing said.

"He wasn't that sick," Vince argued. "And even if he were, he never showed it."

"He had emphysema, Vince," Jing said.

"Emphysema?" Vince asked. "The man never coughed. He had lungs of steel. I don't ever remember him sick."

"He was sick, Vince," Jing said. "Yaya Let even said so. But do you think he's going to show you or Alvin or me that he's dying? The man had pride, for crying out loud."

"Yeah, too much," Vince said.

"Brother, stop acting as if you didn't know him," Jing said. "You knew Lolo Al more than any of us. He spent more time with you than he ever did with me or Alvin."

"Yeah, Vince," Alvin said. "You were the one whose birthday parties were held in the plaza, while Jing and I had to make do with cake and ice cream in the kitchen, with the maids," an exaggeration that wasn't far from the truth.

"Hey, you two preferred hanging out with the maids," Vince said. "Emphysema. The man managed to live for another—what?—four, five years?"

"Vince." Jing's abrupt change in tone catches him off guard. "This is what it boils down to, isn't it?"

"What?" Vince asked.

"You're so unforgiving, brother," Jing said, lighting a cigarette then leaning back, her eyes on her brother. "You've never forgiven him, have you? That's why you didn't go back for his funeral."

"I missed his funeral because of Select Band rehearsals."

"You missed his funeral because of two words, Vince, and don't deny it either." Jing paused. "Carl. Yamagita."

THE BOYS IN THE BAND

Carl. Yamagita.

First Saxophone. First Chair.

Vince's best friend and his suffocatingly huge junior-high crush, ever since he'd heard Carl blow out *The Girl from Ipanema* from his saxophone. Carl was Vince's idea of the perfect romantic friendship. Lanky, goofy, with a post-braces smile, a jaw-dropping mole on his right temple, and a Fred Perry preppy-conscious closet. He wore Sperry Topsiders sockless, took pride in being the only Japanese boy in his very Japafied neighborhood whose family wasn't Buddhist, and loved sixth-period band with the same fervor and intensity as a Bible-quoting Born-Again. He carried around his saxophone like a second shadow and polished it daily because it was his Porsche.

In Vince, Carl found a confidant, an eager audience for his passion for jazz and his dreams of becoming Hawaii's own Stan Getz. Vince didn't mind, because when their friendship was formed, it was formed with equal certainty, mutual expectation, and shared intuition that, sooner or later, they would reveal to each other that they were both hiding in identical closets of desire that, in no time, would eventually break down. And they did. On the night Carl's parents left him and his never-at-home elder brother for one of their frequent trips to Vegas.

Carl, knowing his older brother would most likely be with his Mustang-driving friends, revving their engines across Ala Moana Beach Park, invited Vince over to practice for the upcoming Select Band concert. Vince, who was the first-chair clarinet, agreed, praying that the heart-pumping moment that Plato could only imagine had finally come. The moment came, and it measured exactly two minutes and forty-six seconds. But it weighed heavier than eternity.

As Vince later confessed to Edgar, "It all happened so fast. Faster than a dream." One minute, he and Carl were asleep. Or so it seemed. And then the next, Carl was on top of Vince, pushing his body forcibly against his, anointing his eyebrows, forehead, nose, with spotted kisses, sliding his tongue into his ears, sucking out his breath, then letting his tongue lodge in Vince's mouth, surrendering it completely for him to taste and remember the gravity of Carl's hunger. And then: nothing. Just more sleep, followed by bowls of cereal for breakfast, where neither made mention of their midnight and too-brief communion.

Vince went home, set aside his days and nights for Carl and speculations, such as their next snap-communion. Highly likely, he hoped, since it was Carl who had initiated Vince's headrush, his crave, his world-can-disappear-for-all-I-care attitude. And since Carl had made the first move, Vince felt it should be Carl who resurrected the moment, picked up where they had left off: in each other's hunger, in between their sleep.

So Vince had waited patiently, willingly, suffocatingly. Exhausted himself daydreaming of the what-ifs, banging his head against thick, imaginary walls over the pluses and minuses of phoning Carl, of showing up at the Yamagitas' front door, unannounced, embarrassed, with no special reason other than to ask, "Where to now, Carl? Please tell me."

And no matter what Vince did to try and tip the scale in his favor, the minuses always outweighed the pluses, the rational, the impulse. Fear beat out fearlessness: fear of consequences, fear of false moves, of tampering with what Carl had begun. Fear of losing Carl, his mind, their now.

After waiting almost an entire week for Carl to bring up the subject, make a move, reciprocate, Vince's anxieties were disrupted by his mother, appearing at the rehearsal to tell him his grandfather had just died, and the family was flying back to the Philippines to bury him. It was imperative that he went. He knew it. It was his grandfather. It was customary, especially in the Philippines, where the dead are feared perhaps more than they are revered.

Vince's thoughts were too crowded to be bothered. It wasn't as though his grandfather was dying; he was already dead. What did it matter if he were present or not at the burial? Besides, he didn't want his last memory of the man who had cared for him since birth to be tainted with a coffin-side vigil and tossed flowers over his grave. What was happening in his life was more urgent, more crucial: Carl was alive and could, at any minute, be his, whereas his grandfather's funeral would just be a bunch of relatives and little else. Hawaii's ninth-grade Select Band concert gave him a valid reason to stay home. The rehearsals were mandatory. It didn't leave room for more than one absence, excused or not. Besides, his grandfather wouldn't have wanted him to give up what he'd worked so hard to achieve; such an opportunity could not—and should not—be sacrificed. This was what he told his mother when she tried to persuade him. "Lolo Al would be very disappointed if you dragged me back there," he said. "He'd understand if I didn't go. I know."

"It's so you, Vince, to have used the concert as an alibi for your pursuit of false happiness," Jing broke in, disrupting Vince from his recollection of his crush, which in the end had amounted to nothing except indifference from Carl, which he'd combated by snubbing him back until the gulf between them had become wide enough to return the island back to the sea.

Humiliated, disillusioned, and demeaned, Vince dropped out of band the following school year and took up French instead. As Alvin aptly put it, "You fell hard and good for Carl, Vince. And love broke your heart."

"What happened between you and Carl, anyway?" Jing asked.

"Nothing."

"Nothing?"

"Nothing worth remembering."

"But you wished something had," Alvin said.

"Of course I wanted something to happen," Vince admitted. "But in retrospect, no."

"You did the right thing, brother," Jing said. Vince looked at her, not sure how to take what she'd said.

"Otherwise you'd be in deeper shit right now," Jing continued. "It's a good thing Alvin took you on as his roommate. This is the best place you've ever lived. If it weren't for our baby brother, you'd still be moving from one apartment to the next."

"Vince will never be content," Alvin said. "No matter which part of the world home is. He joined the pageant to get out of Hawaii, remember?"

Scavenged

It's already late in the afternoon by the time Vince reaches his stop along MacArthur Highway. He gets off the bus and is immediately ambushed by drivers offering to take him to San Vicente in their tricycles—motorcycles with a covered sidecar that's good for two passengers, though the driver usually crams it with ten. Vince turns them all down, fearing he'll be charged—or lose—an arm and a leg. Stuttering in Tagalog, he approaches a hot dog vendor and asks which jeepney is bound for San Vicente. She points to the one named KILLER POGI (devilishly handsome), where people are clambering into the cave-like opening at the back. Fortunately for Vince, there's room for one more passenger on the left side, right behind the driver. Crouching his way in, he feels the other passengers' eyes graze him.

Inside the jeepney, we're all the same. We all board KILLER POGI smelling of heat and dust.

It's been said over and over again that Filipinos, who thrive on talk, cannot live in silence. Only 0.5% of the population in the Philippines is Buddhist, and none of them are Filipinos. "The country is built of, and runs on, words," Bonifacio Dumpit writes in *Decolonization for Beginners*. "So call them chat-hoppers, walkie-talkies, storytellers; the more tongues, the juicier the stories." And in a communal place like a jeepney, Vince quickly learns that talk is free and everyone's a guest speaker.

Inside KILLER POGI several conversations are exploding all at once. A talk-stew of morning-old news peppered with tsismis, theories, and queries. Mount Pinatubo is rising from the dead because President Aquino refuses to grant Ferdinand Marcos a burial at the Cemetery for National Heroes. Imelda is coming home with Ferdinand's body. Kris Aquino lost the Best Actress award because, in the ten-minute sex scene, she only bared one nipple and not two. As for Bino Boca: did he really die while giving his protégé the blowjob of his life?

Inside KILLER POGI, Vince is practicing the art of self-restraint as passengers continue to fix their eyes on him.

"Are you Don Alfonso's grandson?" a stiff-haired matriarch sitting beside him asks. She's Doña Teresing, one of the richest people in San Vicente, whose towering coif has enough hair spray on it to survive a tornado.

Vince, shocked, looks up into her blink-free gaze.

Conversations go into pause mode as passengers wait for his response.

"You're right, Nina," Doña Teresing addresses the woman across from her. "It is Vicente."

"How'd you know my name?" Vince asks, wondering if they'd seen him on Kris's talk show yesterday.

"You and your grandfather used to spend your afternoons in my bakery," Doña Teresing says. "You and he were there practically every-day, reading."

"I told you that's Vicente," Nina breaks in, her face thickly covered with foundation to camouflage a lifelong battle with acne. "He's the carbon copy of Don Alfonso. Look at his broad forehead and his jaw-line, it's so—what's the word?—square!"

"Don't forget the dead giveaway: the widow's peak," Doña Teresing adds.

"We were wondering when you were coming back, Vicente," Nina says.

"You're like MacArthur," jokes the man sitting beside Nina. "Late, but you still returned." Pause. "You probably don't remember me now, hijo, because you were still young when you left, but you and your grandfather used to buy your magazines and books at my father's newsstand."

Without waiting for Vince to respond, Doña Teresing says, "Time flies by so fast I don't know if the future is coming or going."

A nostalgic sigh floods the jeepney, prompting many to resurrect scenes, events, and snapshots of a young Vicente, his grandfather Don Alfonso, Yaya Let, and the rest of Vicente's clan, alive and dead. They surrender their tongues to the past, interrupting each other now and then to insert an aside or correct each other's memories.

"Not stomach cancer. Don Alfonso died of emphysema."

"Remember the time Vicente fell off the guava tree?"

"Of course I do. Don Alfonso didn't sleep for a week."

"Yaya Let was the one who died of stomach cancer."

"My daughter was Don Alfonso's nurse right before he died."

"No, Yaya Let died from cancer of the liver."

"Iron lungs that old man had."

"Yes, poor child fell from the tree a day before his birthday."

"The man smoked two packs of Marlboros a day."

"I know so. I was the one who baked his birthday cake."

"Imagine, he was given one year to live, but he stretched it to five."

"If it weren't for the Japanese, he would've perished in the jungle."

"I wish I'd had his blue eyes."

"Correction: if it weren't for the Japanese, he wouldn't have fled to the mountains."

"How come Don Alfonso and Yaya Let never got married?"

"Vicente's guardian angel was watching over him on that day, or he would've gotten impaled by the fence."

"Because Don Alfonso never got over the death of his wife."

"Why shouldn't his guardian angel save him? The boy went to mass every day."

"Don Alfonso adopted his wife's name when she died. If that's not love, then I don't know what is."

"Altar boy na, choirboy pa."

"Lewis. His last name was Lewis before he added De Los Reyes."

"Soulmates on earth and in heaven."

"Don Alfonso—he was Vicente's guardian angel."

Inside KILLER POGI, chronology does not exist, time is derailed, the past becomes present, tsismis is truth, and who is speaking is secondary to what is being said.

A cloud of silence hangs over them. Nina pops it with a question that has been on everyone's mind. "Vicente, are you married?"

"No," Vince answers curtly.

"What about children? You have any sons, daughters?"

"Are you kidding me?" is what he wants to say, but knows that such a remark will only sharpen the sting of these scorpion-tongued folks. For in this Latin-machismo society, marriage and parenthood continue to be proof of a man's heterosexual drive. So Vince, still single at twenty-three, can only be a same-sex suspect or an Opus Dei member. Or both.

"At least he doesn't have to experience widowhood like his grandfather," Doña Teresing says.

"Or worse: Doña Martinez," Nina says. "That woman will die if she doesn't visit the cemetery at least once a day."

Another fast-moving cloud of silence, then: "Vicente, what happened to your complexion? You used to be so mestizo before," Nina says. Rolling up her sleeves, she adds, "Even I am whiter than you now."

"And what happened to the light-brown curls on your head?" Doña Teresing asks. "It must be the Hawaii sun," she guesses.

"It must be the Hawaii sun," the others echo.

"By the way, how are your parents?" Nina asks. "Your father used to call me honey pie, you know. Back in the high-school days."

"And how's Margarita?" Doña Teresing asks of Vince's stepmother. "Are they still together?"

"No," Vince says.

"That's good," Doña Teresing says. "That woman only wanted him for his money anyway."

"And left him after she spent it all," Nina says. "Typical Visayan. He had to file for bankruptcy in the end, remember?"

"What happened to your parents is so tragic," Doña Teresing cuts in. Then, as if announcing it for the world to hear, adds, "That's what America does to Filipino families: brings them together, then tears them apart."

Murmurs of "so true, so true" echo inside KILLER POGI.

"At least here in the Philippines," Doña Teresing continues, "we may not have much money, but our families stay and pray together, even if the mister is with a mistress."

"Is there any possibility of your parents reuniting?" Nina asks.

"No," Vince says.

"Was your stepmother the reason why you didn't come back for your grandfather's funeral?" Doña Teresing asks. "I'm sure it was."

"Don Alfonso named you after our town, you know," Nina says. "Your father Ronaldo wanted to name you after Don Alfonso, but your grandfather objected."

"That's how much he loved this small town of ours," the man next to Nina remarks.

"You were like a son to him," Doña Teresing says, "more than a son."

A row of transformer towers looming like giant headless robots means the jeepney will soon be approaching National Power, responsible for connecting and disconnecting San Vicente to the rest of the world. It was confiscated by the Marcos regime during martial law, then reclaimed by the Aquino administration in 1986, only to be sold to a Marcos crony in 1990.

A tricycle carrying at least ten bodies in the sidecar and four more behind the driver grinds its motor as it attempts to overtake KILLER POGI. Vince keeps his eyes on the overcrowded tricycle, waiting to see if it will collide with a truck or crash into a water buffalo as it crosses the highway.

"Does this jeepney stop in front of the plaza?" Vince asks.

"Yes," Nina answers.

"Are Felisa and Martin expecting you?" Doña Teresing asks, referring to Yaya Let's niece and nephew, who were hired by Vince's father as caretakers after Yaya Let passed away.

"How long are you going to stay in San Vicente?" Nina asks.

"Is there a night bus back to Manila?" Vince asks.

"You'd have to take a tricycle to the highway and wait for a bus there," Doña Teresing. "But it's way too dangerous to travel at night."

"Plus the volcano might erupt," the son of the newsstand owner says. "And if it does, you'll be in the hands of God."

"And then we'll all have to answer to Don Alfonso," Doña Teresing says. "And I'm already too old and too weak to be arguing with the dead."

"How quick naman your stay," Nina says.

"Tell Felisa not to cook anymore," Doña Teresing says. "You can have your meals at the house. I'll have my maid come get you."

"That's not necessary," Vince says.

"In that case, she'll deliver your meals," she insists, hushing his "But—" with her hand. "Just say thank you, hijo."

A painted arch and the Campo Santo—the cemetery—means they are now entering the small town of San Vicente. Passengers begin handing over their fare, saying "bayad po" (here's my fare) and "pakisuyo" (kindly pass it down). Vince watches coins and bills travel from one hand to the next, until they reach him. Then he drops it into the waiting palm of the driver, who has extended one hand over his shoulder while continuing to steer with the other.

Inside KILLER POGI, everyone is a part of an assembly line. All participate in the passing of the fare.

Vince peers out, notices that the bowling alley across from the cemetery is now brown grass, like the front lawn of San Vicente Elementary School. The building, with its corrugated roof is still standing, unchanged as the stage where, one first-grade Christmas, he'd recited a poem about winter.

But where is the open-air cinema? Wasn't it right next to the cemetery?

Slowly, the jeepney passes a figure, all in black, her face concealed by a shawl. "It's Doña Martinez," a woman announces. All the passengers, including Vince, turn to the rear of the jeepney to get a better view of the widow Vince could never erase from his memory.

Is she still stuck in the seventies, with nothing to look forward to except the daily trips to the cemetery to place flowers on her husband's empty grave?

She disappears from his vision as the jeepney makes a jerky left turn onto the street named after Don Joaquin Sanchez, the father of Vince's great-grandmother, who was the first mayor of San Vicente. This was in 1912, when the United States, under Governor-General F. B. Harrison, passed a bill allowing Filipinos to hold offices in the municipal and provincial governments. Don Joaquin took turns governing the town with his son Rafael, until he died twenty years later. Rafael presided as San Vicente's mayor until he succumbed to consumption. His sister, Doña Aurora Lewis, Vince's great-grandmother, who was vice mayor at the time, took over. She won in the next election and served as the mayor throughout the Commonwealth era, when the United States government had, after debating the issue for thirty-plus years, finally decided to give in to the Filipinos' long-overdue demand to govern themselves. A trial that was disrupted six years later when the u.s. entered World War II with the bombing of Pearl Harbor. Shortly after the war, the u.s. had granted the Philippines its independence. By then, the islands had been reduced to rubble and mass graves of war casualties.

If Vince remembers correctly, the plaza, also named after his great-grandmother, has a cement garden and a dry fountain that spouted water only when somebody important came to visit. Facing the square are the homes of landed-wealth families: the Martinezes, Garcias, and Vince's family—the Lewises before Don Alfonso hyphenated it with De Los Reyes.

The driver stops in front of a gate. Vince unwedges himself and, stooping, clambers his way out of the hole, like a baby crawling out of a womb. Passengers bid him another welcome back, telling him it's a sin to be a stranger, that San Vicente, wherever he is, will always be his home, and next time, bring pasalubong—chocolates, macadamia nuts, perfume, paper towels—and maybe he'll have a wife and child or two by then. Standing on the sun-baked earth, he thanks them with a folded-lipped smile—it's the best gesture he can offer to these memories then, strangers now, who throughout the ride have made it clear to him that once a San Vicente local, always a San Vicente local. Because people in San Vicente hold on to each other's history, secrets, memories, and failures.

The wrought-iron gate is as he remembered it. It is attached to a steel-matting fence once used by American G.I.s during the war as portable landing strips and for increased traction, especially while traveling over mud and sand. After the war, the u.s. government sold them to Filipinos, who converted them into fences. The fences had holes in them, which made climbing over them possible if not for the sharp tips that poked out dangerously. They had almost impaled Vince when gravity had sent him hurling from the branch of a guava tree into the muddy canal beneath it.

Every eye in the crammed jeepney is on him. Waiting. Wondering what's going through his mind as he stands facing his first home, the only home he's ever considered home. And then the jeepney speeds off, leaving Vince to contend with the growing coolness and silence that the May dusk in San Vicente brings.

Through the fence's rusty bars, he stares at the house that, though bigger, still resembles the one he's kept in his memory all these years. Here is the alpha of your history, it seems to be saying to him.

Not much has changed, he thinks. Potted bougainvilleas still line the small pathway that leads to the front steps, making him wonder if the huge door made of molave wood is still locked the old-fashioned way, with a heavy bar rather than bolts and locks. And the seashells from Capiz still cover the latticed windows, which, except during the monsoon season, were kept open all year long.

But where is the guava tree? Did he have it cut down? Was I five, six? Day before my birthday? Did he scoop me up from the mud and shout at God?

Clad in her mourning attire, Doña Martinez enters his sightline, bringing with her an air of solemnity.

It's Death marching to greet me. To punish me for all these years of not returning. To guide me to a deeper hell, the way Virgil guided Dante to hell nine times over.

"Vicente?" she says, removing her shawl to reveal a face disfigured by grief. The strong pull of time and sorrow has tightened the skin around her mouth.

"Doña Martinez?" He offers her a broken smile.

"You've finally come home," she says. "We were wondering when, or if, you were ever coming back. We're glad."

Vince is at a loss for words. Who did she mean by "we"?

"You and your brother and sister, you three, but especially you, Vicente, you were his life," Doña Martinez says. "The way my husband was my life."

"Your husband is your life," Vince says, not sure if he should correct his tense. "He's the love you haven't let go. But my grandfather sent us away."

"He didn't want to, but it was for the best," Doña Martinez says. "When you children left for Hawaii, it was as if you three took everything in that house with you," she says. "Nothing remained for him. Nothing was worth living for. He shut himself in the house, as if he was reliving what had happened when he came back from the war. Withdrawn, tight-lipped, boxed in."

"You and my grandfather, you two were close, right?" Vince asks.

"Yes, but not as close as he and Leticia," she says, referring to Yaya Let.

"But you visited him, talked to him, right?"

"Only when he was in the mood for my company," she says. "He hardly accepted visitors. He didn't want to speak or see anyone."

She pauses to point a finger up to the windows that face the plaza. "Up there, in that room, was his world. He spent his remaining years cooped up in there, surrounded by ghosts. If he needed something, someone brought it to him—books, newspapers, magazines, the barber, doctors. Father Mendoza dropped by once a week to give him his Communion."

"What did you guys talk about?"

"Your grandfather wasn't much of a talker, Vicente."

"I know," he says, "but did he mention me at all?"

"I did most of the talking. He just listened."

"When he was dying, did he ask for me?"

Her lips tighten as she looks at him. "Vicente—" she starts.

"He didn't want me to come back, did he, Doña Martinez?" Vince says, accidentally biting his tongue so hard that he can taste blood.

"There's nothing in there for you anymore, Vicente," she says, gazing up at the house. Before walking away, she tells him, "Forgive him, hijo. That's all you can do. Forgive him, because he did it for your sake. You knew your grandfather better than any of us. He would never do anything to hurt you. You know that."

"Felisa! Martin!" he calls out. A gray-haired woman approaches the gate. Worry lines crease her forehead.

Vince introduces himself as Don Alfonso's grandson. "Are you Felisa?"

Felisa nods, tells him he's wearing his grandfather's face. She leads him along the path, up the steps, into the living room. Bare. Except for an unmade and unrecognizable cot in the corner, where the guard sleeps at night.

What happened to the furniture and the appliances? The television can be spared, but not the antique Spanish furniture with its rattan backing, and the coffeetable that his great-grandmother had brought with her all the way from Seville. Where is the banquet table he dreamt of last night, the one where his great-grandfather and great-great-aunt were seated as he tried to talk to them, the one that four generations of Lewises had eaten at whenever they entertained visitors?

It used to be over there, he wants to say, pointing his finger to a corner right beside the vacant niche carved into the wall, where a makeshift altar had once held the plaster statue of the town's patron saint, San

Vicente, in his iconographic stance: right forefinger pointing to heaven, left hand holding a book, a pair of wings on his back, and, at the base of the statue, a gold plate with the inscription, "SAN VICENTE DE FERRER, PATRON SAINT OF JUDGMENT DAY."

And the photographs? What happened to the wall-to-wall photographs that showed generation after generation of the Lewis clan? Where are the hand-painted photographs of turn-of-the-century relatives, one who came to the tropics as a soldier to fight the Filipinos and another to teach them? And the airport group shots of himself, Alvin, Jing, Yaya Let, and Don Alfonso in front of the fountain on the afternoon they were sent off to their parents. Whom do they belong to now?

He reassures himself that they're upstairs. Of course, they're upstairs, where the bedrooms are. He runs up the wooden staircase, heads straight for his room as if he's lived there all his life. It too is empty. As empty as the succession of closets and cabinet drawers he pulls open, hoping to get assaulted by memorabilia smelling of mothballs. But nothing. Not one dusty shelf of books or issue of komiks. Empty as the grave of his neighbor, Mr. Martinez.

Fighting off tears, and with a heart that doesn't know when to give up hope, he searches room after room, wall after wall, for holes punctured by nails upon which used to hang gilt-edged picture frames. He checks the inside of doors for shadows of the photographs that had once been tacked there.

He took everything with him to his grave, Vince tells himself. He didn't want me to return and reclaim what was mine—my family history, objects from my childhood. Why didn't Alvin and Jing tell me? Did they even know? They must've known. Why did Lolo Al do this— erase all the dust and dirt of my past? Why did he renounce everything? Nothing salvaged. Nothing. Except this house smelling of newly waxed floors.

Back in the living room, he goes and stands by the window, an unlit cigarette in his hand, looking out at the white sheets and towels hanging on the clothesline, at the church steeple, and beyond it, at the Sierra Madre that gave birth to the legend of four women who had turned their backs on San Vicente; looking, just looking at the coming darkness the way his grandfather, on the same spot, used to sit on his favorite cane-backed chair, listening to the radio and smoking Marlboro Reds in his pajamas with his legs crossed, his foot tapping against his slipper, watching dusk as it claimed San Vicente light by light.

ACKNOWLEDGMENTS

Lisa Asagi, Justin Chin, and Lori Takayesu, who keep the fuel of friend-ship and writing burning.

Faye Kicknosway, poet, friend, mentor.

Allan Isaac, for his critical eye and ear, and Jeff Rebudal, "manong" of the angels.

Marianne Villanueva, Amalia Bueno, Devi De Veyra, Jae Robillos, Joel Tan, and Robert Diaz, hawkeyed readers.

Lucy Burns and Robyn Rodriguez.

Jessica Hagedorn, Karen Tei Yamashita, Bill Maliglig and Gordon Wong, Paul and Hyon Chu-Yi Toguchi, Mark Berkowitz, David Blackmore, Mike Santos, Marissa Diccion-Ocreto, and my brother-in-law Greg Boorsma, who offered me homes away from homes.

Rene Guatlo, Christine Balance, and Paul Nadal for the images. Ed Cabagnot De Los Santos for the scoops on the Film Center, Metro Manila Film Festivals, and Experimental Cinema of the Philippines. Jonathan Best for the beautiful postcards taken from his coffee-table book, *A Philippine Album* (Bookmark Inc., 1998).

Kirby Kim, my agent, for introducing me to the wonderful Sarah Bowlin. Harold Schmidt, Ira Silverberg, and Don Weise for believing in the manuscript from the get-go. Allan Kornblum, Anitra Budd, Linda Koutsky, Jessica Deutsch, and Tricia O'Reilly at Coffee House Press for giving this book a beautiful home.

And to my brothers Gus and William, my sister Ghel, our mother Cecilia, and our grandmother Purificacion: the sum of my forty-two years.

COLOPHON

Leche was designed at Coffee House Press,
in the historic Grain Belt Brewery's Bottling House
near downtown Minneapolis.
The text is set in Garamond.

COFFEE HOUSE PRESS

The mission of Coffee House Press is to publish exciting, vital, and enduring authors of our time; to delight and inspire readers; to contribute to the cultural life of our community; and to enrich our literary heritage. By building on the best traditions of publishing and the book arts, we produce books that celebrate imagination, innovation in the craft of writing, and the many authentic voices of the American experience.

To learn more about our books and authors, and to find information on how to support our program, visit www.coffeehousepress.org.

FUNDER ACKNOWLEDGMENTS

Coffee House Press is an independent nonprofit literary publisher. Our books are made possible through the generous support of grants and gifts from many foundations, corporate giving programs, state and federal support, and through donations from individuals who believe in the transformational power of literature. Coffee House Press receives major operating support from the Bush Foundation, the McKnight Foundation, from Target, and from the Minnesota State Arts Board, through an appropriation from the Minnesota State Legislature and from the National Endowment for the Arts. We have received project support from the National Endowment for the Arts, a federal agency. Coffee House also receives support from: three anonymous donors; Elmer L. and Eleanor J. Andersen Foundation; Allan Appel; Around Town Literary Media Guides; Patricia Beithon; Bill Berkson; the James L. and Nancy J. Bildner Foundation; the Patrick and Aimee Butler Family Foundation; the Buuck Family Foundation; Dorsey & Whitney, LLP; Fredrikson & Byron, P.A.; Sally French; Jennifer Haugh; Anselm Hollo and Jane Dalrymple-Hollo; Jeffrey Hom; Stephen and Isabel Keating; the Kenneth Koch Literary Estate; the Lenfestey Family Foundation; Ethan J. Litman; Mary McDermid; Sjur Midness and Briar Andresen; the Rehael Fund of the Minneapolis Foundation; Deborah Reynolds; Schwegman, Lundberg, Woessner, P.A.; John Sjoberg; David Smith; Mary Strand and Tom Fraser; Jeffrey Sugerman; Patricia Tilton; the Archie D. & Bertha H. Walker Foundation; Stu Wilson and Mel Barker; the Woessner Freeman Family Foundation; and many other generous individual donors.

This activity is made possible in part by a grant from the Minnesota State Arts Board, through an appropriation by the Minnesota State Legislature and a grant from the National Endowment for the Arts.

NATIONAL ENDOWMENT FOR THE ARTS — MINNESOTA STATE ARTS BOARD — TARGET.

To you and our many readers across the country, we send our thanks for your continuing support.

R. Zamora Linmark is the author of the novel *Rolling the R's* (Kaya Press) and two poetry collections, *Prime Time Apparitions* and *The Evolution of a Sigh* (Hanging Loose Press). Linmark splits his time between Manila and Honolulu, Hawaii.

Good books are brewing at www.coffeehousepress.org